PRA

# ARENA

"A stunning debut . . .
who've never picke
haven't read anythin
        —Ilona A

"Blistering action r
brilliant characters that kept me logged in to *Arena*. A thrilling
debut!"    —Jason M. Hough, *New York Times* bestselling author

"Think *Hunger Games* meets *Ready Player One*. *Arena* is
serious nerdcore entertainment. Gamers, get ready to plug in!"
                —Chloe Neill, *New York Times* bestselling author

"Depicting the action and excitement of virtual gaming that
made Ernest Cline's *Ready Player One* such a hit . . . Readers
seeking more fast-paced SF about virtual reality will be pleased."
                                        —*Library Journal*

"A nuanced and complex novel with a strong, imperfect heroine
and a different approach to the 'rebel in a dystopian society'
trope . . . Jennings faces down dark issues unflinchingly."
                                        —*RT Book Reviews*

"With action-packed battle sequences and older computer-game
references, [*Arena*] will appeal to fans of science fiction like
Ernest Cline's *Armada*."                    —*Booklist*

# ARENA

## HOLLY JENNINGS

ACE
New York

ACE
Published by Berkley
An imprint of Penguin Random House LLC
375 Hudson Street, New York, New York 10014

Copyright © 2016 by Holly Jennings
Excerpt from *Gauntlet* copyright © 2016 by Holly Jennings

Ace trade paperback ISBN: 9780425282878

The Library of Congress has cataloged the Ace hardcover edition as follows:

Jennings, Holly, 1985–
Arena / Holly Jennings.
pages cm
ISBN 978-1-101-98876-3 (hardback)
1. Video games—Fiction.   2. Video gamers—Fiction.
3. Murder—Investigation—Fiction.   I. Title.
PR9199.4.J453A84 2016
813'.6—dc23
2015024143

Ace hardcover edition / April 2016
Ace trade paperback edition / November 2016

Printed in the United States of America
1   3   5   7   9   10   8   6   4   2

Cover illustration by Larry Rostant
Cover design by Adam Auerbach
Book design by Kelly Lipovich

To my grandmother,
for teaching me to be strong and to always believe

PRESS THE START BUTTON TO BEGIN . . .

# LEVEL 1:

## THE DEATH MATCH

# CHAPTER 1

This wouldn't be the first time I died. Sure as hell wouldn't be the last, either. But while most watched this virtual world from the safe haven of reality, there was nowhere else I'd rather spend my Saturday night.

Crouched high on the tower's parapet, I overlooked a sea of wheat fields. The scent of lavender and taste of wheatgrass wove together in the air, drifting with the breeze as it swept through my hair. I took a deep breath and smiled at the irony, as thick as the mountain air filling my lungs. Lavender. Wheat fields. Tranquility.

Peace, in a place anything but peaceful.

Movement in the fields caught my eye, down and right. A zigzag carved its way through the ten-foot-tall stalks, heading straight for the tower. My smile widened. Maybe this sucker had the balls to take on Kali Ling.

The warrior.

I stilled inside. Even breaths. No fear. At the field's edge, the stalks trembled violently. The air filled with the rainstick rustling of brush and dry grass. Yes. Someone would emerge. I gripped the sword sheathed across my back and waited, muscles tight, mouth watering. Come on. Give me something. A brute. Six—no—seven feet tall, wielding a mace. Or an axe.

Give me anything.

A rabbit scurried out from the field. Nothing followed. The grass fluttered in the breeze. Birds chirped, nestled in the nearby sycamore trees. It was the rabbit, and only the rabbit.

For now.

I punched the parapet's brick wall, but when my frustration subsided, I realized another irony. In 2054, most twenty-year-olds hid behind a barricade—of textbooks. Studying for hours, days, or even years on end, they'd hide away from the real world only to remerge bright and eager to end up in jobs they'd hate. Meanwhile, I strapped on battle gear, sword and all, and headed into these fields.

Fields I now frowned at, which had stilled just to spit on my excitement. Only streams of sunlight punctuated the stalks from above, like skylights from the heavens. Everything blended together in shades of beige as if the landscape had been white-washed through a sepia lens. In the distance, the enemy's tower loomed, wrapped in a corkscrew of mountains and rocky terrain. How many of them remained? How close were we to victory?

Shuffling footsteps turned my attention inside. I leapt from my perch and landed on the tower's stone floor with the impact of a fallen leaf. The wind whispered around me as it bowed to my movements.

The warrior. Pffft. I should be the ninja.

A pigtailed blonde stood in the center of the tower, dwarfed by more than the stories-high walls around her. Lily, fair-skinned with delicate features, like the flower she was named for. Dressed like a scantily clad Scandinavian warrior, she wore nothing but fur-lined armor and a wicked grin. Her hands rested on the pair of short axes sheathed at her hips. Not so much like a flower.

Lily shook her head as she approached.

"Your eyes," she said.

"What?"

"They can't see your eyes." She pushed up to her tiptoes and brushed strands of raven hair away from my face.

"Does it really matter?" I asked.

She frowned. Of course it mattered. Soft and black, my eyes were a distinguishing trait. How marketable.

How perfect.

"It's the Death Match," she said with a tsk. "Everything matters."

"Did Clarence teach you to say that?"

"Do you think I would have listened?" She grinned and nodded at my perch. "How's the view?"

"Boring."

A piercing scream ripped through the stillness, resounding off the tower's walls. My ears perked up, and I seized the dagger at my waist. Dust clung to the air in suspended animation, trapped like the breath inside my lungs. Then, chuckling at myself, I exhaled, released my grip on the weapon, and nudged Lily.

"Really? Did they tell Hannah to go down easy? God, they'll do anything to add tension."

My chuckles faded when I met Lily's taut expression. She shook her head, drew an axe from her belt, and crept toward the tower's entrance.

I scoffed.

"Lil, come on. There's no way someone took her out that fast."

"I'll check it out anyways."

"From the treetops?" I called out.

"Where else?"

Lily disappeared from view through the tower's entrance. Leaves crunched, and branches snapped as she climbed. Then all went still.

A breeze drifted through the tower and brushed against my bare midriff. I adjusted the armor padding on my shoulders and gripped the sword at my back, drawing it out slowly, purposefully, to catch the late-afternoon sun glinting on the blade. As if millions were watching me.

Absolute quiet blanketed the tower. The birds stopped chirping. The wind stopped rustling.

My breath hitched.

I planted my feet, sword out. Ready. Scuffling footsteps and soft grunts sounded out beyond the tower walls, followed by sharp chopping and wet splats, like cleavers hacking up meat. Or a person. Then, nothing.

I took a step forward.

"Lily?"

Silence.

Then footsteps, heavy and rough, beat up the dirt path to the tower. Two men appeared in the entranceway, both tall enough to brush the top of the tower's entrance. The metal armor covering their chests, wrists, and calves struggled to contain the muscle beneath, every buckle and clasp strained tight. Ribbons of blood snaked down the swords gripped in their hands. Not bad, boys, but certainly not enough.

Not for me.

"Is this it?" I asked with a grin. "I was hoping for a challenge."

On cue, two more men appeared behind them.

Oh shit.

Four? What kind of crazy-ass ploy was this? Pushing into a tower with four left only one to guard their own. Where was the rest of my team? Why hadn't they taken the enemy's fortress?

Of the foursome, one had a cut down his eye and cheek and wore no armor on his chest. He moved toward me first, and the others fell in step behind. At the sound of their pursuit, he held a hand up and gave a swift shake of his head. They halted.

Taking me alone, One-eye? Impressive.

And completely dumb-ass stupid.

He broke off from the pack, leaving them at the door. The trio paced and whimpered, like hyenas waiting for the lion to make the kill. But like good animals, they obeyed their master.

One-eye charged, weapon raised, footsteps pounding across the stone floor. I remained, feet planted, bringing him to me. Breaths filled my lungs, slow and steady. A smile pulled at my lips.

Let's dance.

He grunted as he swung for me, muscles straining. I parried his blows and swept him to the side. Like wind. Like water. Metal clanged against metal in a steady beat, his weapon slipping across mine every time.

We broke apart.

He grimaced, muscles clenched. Sweat dripped down his face. I grinned and rolled my shoulders, muscles like liquid. His knuckles turned white around the hilt of his sword. My weapon rotated with the flicks of my wrist, like an extension of my own limb.

He came at me again, making chopping motions in the air. The wind whined under the sharp slashes of steel. I stood tall as he reeled back and swung. As his sword whooshed through the air, I ducked. He stumbled past, revealing the canvas of his back. My sword ripped across it in so many rapid successions, I nearly wrote my name.

Zorro could kiss my ass.

One-eye went down to his knees, shaking. Breaths rasped through his lungs. Snorting like a bull, he pushed up to his feet and came at me again. Wielding his sword with both hands, he swung it like a bat, hard. The impact reverberated down my arms and knocked the sword from my grip. It went flying, smacked the far wall, and tumbled to the ground out of reach.

He grinned at me and brought his weapon down. I rolled, missing the blow. Drawing the dagger from my hip, I pushed up to my feet and slammed the blade into his shoulder. It disappeared down to the hilt. He groaned. I jerked it sideways. He cried out and dropped his sword. It clanked on the floor.

Blood poured out of the wound, gushing over my hand. I lost my grip on the dagger and tumbled to the ground.

Get up.

The instant my back hit the floor, I pushed up, but my heels slipped across the bloody floor. One-eye ripped the blade from his shoulder and advanced. I scrambled backwards.

Keep space. He can't hit you if he can't reach.

I backpedaled, trying to get my feet beneath me, heels not catching. Blood sprayed out from my kicking heels.

My back hit the wall.

Cornered. First rule of fighting: never get cornered. Damn it.

One-eye closed in.

My chest tightened until I gulped for air. No. I was fine. I'd died before. Simulations. Practices. They teach you how to die. Fighting with honor.

For the show.

He knelt and delivered a swift backhand across my face. My head snapped to the side, vision reeling. Pain blistered across my face with the sharp sting of a rubber band. One-eye straddled me and pushed his weight into my stomach. I gagged and wriggled beneath him, trying to free myself. No luck. His weight and legs formed a vise around my lower half.

In a sweeping arc, he swung the dagger toward my neck, like

a reaper wielding his scythe. Skin slapped skin as I caught his forearm with both hands and strained against him. He grimaced and leaned forward, adding weight behind his strength. My hands trembled, muscles screaming in protest.

The blade lowered.

Cold steel kissed my skin. I gasped and bowed my neck in. Come on, Kali. Fight.

Every nerve in my arms and chest ached. The trembling in my hands descended into violent shakes. One-eye grinned down at me like an animal driven mad with hunger. The dagger dug into my throat, sharp and burning. I squirmed and clamped my teeth shut on a squeal.

"Shhh," he hushed, condescending and overexaggerated. His crew of douche bags giggled in the background.

Blood trickled out of my neck. Fucking bastard. Didn't cut deep. I'd bleed out in minutes, not seconds. He was drawing this out, purposely, to make me suffer.

With one hand, he pinned my wrists above my head and with the other, held the knife over my face. I braced for the final blow, straining every muscle against a shudder. But instead of bringing the knife down, he let it dangle just above my lips. My own blood, sweet and metallic, dripped down and seeped into my mouth. I sputtered and coughed. Laughter rumbled in his chest. He was enjoying this, sick asshole. And he should. He'd won.

I closed my eyes. This was it. Defeat. Might as well accept it.

No. That wasn't part of my image. That wasn't Kali Ling.

The warrior.

I wrenched a hand free and punched One-eye hard across the face. His head jerked sideways, but his weight remained planted on my hips. Damn it. I reached for his shoulder wound, dug my fingers inside, and pulled. He threw back his head and howled, legs convulsing around me from the pain.

I grinned, then faltered.

My neck.

My breaths morphed into gasps for air as the blood continued to drain from my throat. Numbness captured my fingers, and they slid down his chest, trailing three rows of fading blood across his skin. He looked down at me. Our eyes locked.

Mine fluttered.

He laughed, revealing a row of perfect, bleached teeth. That sardonic laugh reverberated in his chest, flexing muscles I'm sure were already flexed. It was over. He had won.

My hand collapsed to the floor. Coldness crept up my limbs as my vision whirled and faded.

No. This wasn't happening. We don't lose.

We never lose.

The weight pressed against my stomach lessened as One-eye leaned toward my face. His breath came out in snorts, ghosting across my cheeks. Sweat dripped from his skin and mingled with mine. It swirled together with the blood in my mouth, salt and metal. I gagged from the taste, and from the blood bubbling up my throat.

My breaths shortened. He grew closer still, until the heat from him radiated against my skin. An inch. Maybe less.

I could just picture the cameras zooming in.

"Night, night, sweetheart," he whispered as my eyelids fluttered, and my head rolled to the side.

Despite the numbness, a flood of emotions rushed through me. Shock from losing the fight. Fear as the darkness closed in around me. Rage fueled by the adrenaline pumping through my veins. And beneath it all, I had to admit I was impressed.

He knew how to put on a damn good show.

# CHAPTER 2

I opened my eyes.

White. Everything was white. They say in death, you'll be surrounded by a white light. Now, lying in the pod's shimmering opal core, I realized yet another irony. Win or lose, coming back to life always felt a bit like dying.

I reached for my neck and felt clean, smooth skin. A slow breath passed through my lips. Of course. Why would I expect anything else?

The speakers beside my ears crackled, and a voice cut through the pod's silence.

"And Ling's the last one out. Team Defiance just got crushed. What a match."

I wrenched the speakers off and punched the pod's innards. Pain retaliated, shooting up my arm. Real pain.

The thread-thin wires stuck to my face, neck, and arms detached and crawled away, scuttling across my skin like insect legs. The egg-shaped pod cradling me hissed and opened, its double doors sliding back from the center. As the lids retracted, the bright lights of the pod room poured across my face and into my eyes. I sat in the pod, blinking away blue and purple stars.

Despite my eyesight, or maybe because of it, my other senses took over. The air, so chilled and sterile, stung the back of my throat. It mixed with the scent of industrial cleaner and cold nothingness. But my hearing trumped them all. The soft beeping of the computers, the hissing of the other machinery, and the yelling. Lots of yelling.

"What the fuck was that?" Nathan's voice. "You were supposed to have my back. We lost because of you."

"No." That was Derek. "You were supposed to have my back."

My teammates. Or so I'm told. Just like the arena, with its digital fields and towers, it seemed our cooperation only existed in the virtual world.

"Kali." Another voice right beside me, feminine and musical. Hannah. A halo of her strawberry blonde hair appeared between the lights. Long, slender fingers closed around my arm and shook, as if it would help my eyes somehow. "Kali, they're fighting again. Can you do something? I already tried."

I sighed and pulled myself out of the pod. My feet touched down on the metal floor, as smooth and clear as glass. Everything inside the cylinder-shaped room of the virtual pod center was either white or a shade of gray. White pods, monitoring stations, computers, and screens. Gray floors and walls and accents. Nothing but clean lines, metal, and glass. From the past to the future in a blink.

My vision phased between blurry and clear as I pushed myself to the center of the room, where Derek and Nathan stood toe to toe. Both were dressed in the jumpsuits we're required to wear when we plug in. Stark white, just like the inside of the pods, as if the connection to the virtual world had to be immaculate.

"You had one guy to take out. One," Derek said, holding up a finger for emphasis. "If you can't handle that, maybe Lily should fight with me."

The five-foot-nothing blonde slunk against the far wall. Other than her pod suit, Lily was a mirror image of her virtual avatar. She twirled a finger through her pigtails and narrowed her eyes at Derek but kept her back pinned against the wall.

Nathan scoffed. "Haven't you seen her stats lately? She has twice the kills you do."

Standing so close, the two of them were like the opposing halves of a yin-yang symbol. Derek's dark skin and features versus Nathan's pale complexion, blue eyes, and light brown hair. Opposites in coloring and exactly the same in everything else. Same height, same muscular build, same alpha-male personality. When Clarence had assembled the team, he certainly didn't make sure we all got along with each other.

Derek waved him off. "Whatever. It's Hannah's fault, anyways."

"My fault?" Hannah exclaimed, taking a step forward. "You two were long dead before they came after me."

The programmers, who sat at the workstations behind the pods, stood and peered around the monitoring screens at the scene. One simply stood, started packing up, and shook his head, as if the scene in the middle of the room was nothing more than the same show stuck on repeat.

"It was no one's fault," I said. "They left one to guard their tower and pushed in with four. No one fights like that. We were unprepared."

Nathan nodded at Derek. "No. It was his fault. He went down first."

Derek pointed a finger back at Nathan. "Like you had nothing to do with it."

"We were all unprepared," I said, raising my voice over theirs. "We lost one. Get over it."

What the hell was I saying?

The last few months played back in my head. Hours of training, grinding against weights until my muscles screamed.

Endless battles in the virtual world, ripping my sword through any foe the programmer could muster. Weeks of preseason gaming, where no team could touch us. All that training, all that effort, and we had lost. No. Big. Deal.

Pffft. Even I didn't buy that.

Derek took a step closer, as if to challenge Nathan. The muscles in Nathan's jaw flexed.

"Get out of my face," Nathan warned.

"What are you going to do about it, Nancy?"

Nathan shoved him. Derek gripped his collar. They both pulled back to punch. I wedged myself between them and fisted a hand in each of their suits.

"Walk away."

They glared at each other, but neither threw a strike with me in the middle.

"Hey."

I tugged on their suits to get their attention. They dropped their arms, but neither looked down.

"Come on. We have a press conference."

I released my grip and walked toward the exit. Only two sets of footsteps followed. I turned back. Lily and Hannah halted on my heels, while Nathan and Derek remained in the center of the room, still locked in a staring contest a pace apart.

I tossed my arms up. "You need a room, ladies? Let's go."

Derek left first, head high, like he'd won. Nathan lingered, burning holes in the back of Derek's head. After releasing a shaky breath, he followed us to the exit.

Navigating the steel tunnels of the facility, I led the team to the double doors marked PRESSROOM. A guard manned either side. With bulging necks, tattooed arms, and ex-convict vibes, they were intimidating enough to make a group of Marines piss themselves.

"They're chomping at the bit," one of them said. "You ready?"

He looked right at me, as if I spoke for the entire team. I glanced back at my four teammates. Guess I was the one in front. I nodded at the guard.

"Go for it."

They opened the doors, and reporters poured out, like water from an open floodgate, jamming their microphones in our faces. Christ, were they trying to stick them up my nose?

"What happened tonight?"

"Has Team Defiance finally met its match?"

"What does it feel like to lose?"

Security wrestled them back enough for us to squeeze past single file to the stage, which was backdropped by an oversized banner reading:

### VIRTUAL GAMING LEAGUE
### 2054 RAGE TOURNAMENTS

We sat overlooking the sea of journalists and cameras. First Lily, then Derek, followed by Hannah, Nathan, and me. The way we're told to sit. The men between the women, short framing the tall, dark features mixed with light. Balance. Cohesion. Like this, we looked like a team.

Image is everything.

Cameras clicked and flashed, throwing lights across the stage. A middle-aged man walked up to the podium beside us, his shoulders nearly as slender as mine. Definitely not security. He tapped the microphone and waved a hand, appealing to the crowd of reporters to hush. A new emcee. Great. Another face, another name.

The roar of the crowd dulled down to murmurs and whispers.

"It'll be an open floor tonight," the emcee said. "I'll call on you one at a time. And I mean, one at a time. Now . . ."

The reporters threw their arms in the air as they waved, shouted, and teetered on the edges of their chairs. The emcee pointed to a man in the front row. He stood.

"Jeffrey Stout, *L.A. Times*. As a heavy favorite team in the competition, do you feel that the pressure to excel got to you tonight?"

"I don't speak for everyone," Hannah said into her microphone, pursing her lips, "but it's the pressure that makes me excel."

She winked at the reporter. He faltered, mouth hanging open, then managed to sit down and make a few notes on his tablet. The commotion started back up until the emcee pointed to a woman in the center. She stood, straightening her skirt.

"Kelly Martin, *Sports Illustrated*. Your opponent beat you in record time. How does that make you feel?"

"The Death Match is only the end of the preseason," Nathan said. "It just gives *us* a new record to beat in the tournament."

More shouting. The emcee picked another.

"Steve Trainor, ESPN. Now that your loss in the Death Match landed you in the losers' bracket, how can you guarantee to your fans and sponsors you won't suffer another like this one?"

"We train," I said, pressing my lips tight against the microphone so I'm heard above anyone else. "We work harder than we did before. We challenge each other and ourselves. Next time, we'll be ready."

More questions. More yelling and shoving. We took turns answering, making sure to stay in character. I sat in my chair, but there might as well have been a robot Kali in my place. There but not really there as the people shouted and the cameras flashed, all a distant echo. Maybe someone would ask what designer I was wearing while still dressed in my pod suit. Or better yet, how *tough* it was to be a woman in a male-dominated sport.

This was my reality.

I eyed the exit doors as images of the pod room trickled into my thoughts. Maybe I could sneak in a few hours of virtual time once this was all done.

"Okay, that's it for tonight," the emcee called. The reporters jeered and protested.

"No, no. Over here."

"Just one more question."

The emcee shook his head, refusing to give in. I tapped my microphone, but it didn't echo back. Already shut off. Couldn't answer if we wanted to.

Always leave them wanting more.

With security's help, we shouldered our way through the crowd to the double doors. The reporters chased after us, ignoring the sign marked FACILITY EMPLOYEES ONLY PAST THIS POINT. Security shoved them back and slammed the doors shut, cutting off the noise and commotion, as if sealing off a gateway to another world. I clustered with my teammates in the hallway, listening to the protests of the reporters in the other room, muffled by the metal doors, like being underwater.

"This is bad," Hannah said. "We should go out and be seen around the city, so people think we're not bothered by the loss."

"Fine," Nathan agreed. "We'll meet in an hour and hit a few clubs."

Derek stepped forward. "Who made you boss?"

Here we go again.

"Speaking of the boss, what's Clarence going to say about tonight?" Lily asked. Everyone looked at the tiny blonde, then exchanged glances with each other. My stomach swirled, and I had the feeling mine wasn't the only one.

"Just forget about that for now," I said. "Hannah's right. We should go out. Together. Show people we're still a team. And if we leave, we can avoid Clarence, too. For a while. Right?

Everyone exchanged glances again and, eventually, nodded in agreement.

"Good. Meet here in an hour."


An hour and some-odd minutes later, I stood between Derek and Nathan, posing for the cameras outside the club. Beyond the towering buildings of the city, the sun was slowly setting, and the heat from the mid-August day still curled through the air. Around us, the paparazzi plastered themselves against the guardrails, elbowing each other and clawing at us, out of reach. The boys wore casual suits, no ties, with several buttons left undone as if they'd started doing them up and forgot about the rest. Yeah. Forgot, on purpose. Every turn flashed another angle of the muscle beneath.

"Kali."

My name intermingled with the others. I pulled at the chain around my neck, so the yin-yang pendant showed above my shirt.

We all played our parts.

I struck a pose the way I'd been taught. Leg forward, weight shifted to one hip, the same one my hand gripped. Then I tilted my head and let a coy smile complement my slick dress pants and silk top. Conservative. Demure. Movie star.

Nathan leaned close and lowered his voice to a whisper. "Is your face going to crack, warrior?"

I spoke back through my teeth. "No, but yours will under my fist."

He chuckled, and murmured something that sounded like *saucy*. Hot rage flashed inside my chest. I snapped a quick blow against his ribs. He grabbed my wrist and twisted. A devilish grin filled his face.

The cameras exploded as the paparazzi pushed toward us. The guardrails whined in protest. They whispered among each other, but all were thinking the same thing. *Maybe they'll fight right here.*

Nathan turned to the crowd and held up his hands. "My fault. I should know better."

They laughed, and a voice from the back called out, "She'd pin you in a second."

Nathan laughed along with them, but leaned toward me and lowered his voice again. "And I wouldn't stop her."

Heat flashed through me again, but this time, it wasn't in my chest. Opposite the view of the cameras, his fingertips lingered on my lower back and grazed down. My breath hitched before I smacked him off. He winked in response.

I shook my head and glanced at Hannah and Lily on the carpet behind me, also posing for the crowd. Cleavage spilled out of the dress that barely covered Hannah's body, while Lily's pigtails, plaid skirt, and knotted blouse belonged to a schoolgirl about to be expelled. They laughed and waved, and kissed. The camera flashes turned to lightning strikes.

It's what they want.

The club's bouncer came forward and ushered us toward the club. Like the reporters in the pressroom, the cameramen shouted their protests. The bouncer shoved a few of them off the rails and started leading us toward the club.

"Fuck you, man," one of the reporters shouted as he landed on his ass. "I'm suing."

The bouncer whirled around and marched up to him. The man backpedaled away, eyes wide, as he clutched his camera.

"Kidding, kidding."

The bouncer scowled and led us into the club without further protest from the crowd. Inside the lobby, he turned to us.

"IDs?" he asked. We all laughed, and he joined in. "What? Afraid I don't know who you are?"

"It's the date of birth you'd have a problem with," Nathan said, nodding back at me, Lily, and Hannah. Derek and Nathan were both twenty-one, old enough to be in any club. The girls and I were all a year short.

The bouncer held up his hands. "Hear no evil, see no evil."

"Good man." Nathan patted his shoulder as he passed, but the bouncer grabbed his arm and pulled back.

"What the hell?" Nathan shook him off.

"You'd better let me take you straight to the VIP area," the bouncer said. He paused, and his gaze flicked toward the club's interior. "The crowd's a little pissed."

Of course they were. We were a heavily favored team because of how well we'd done so far in the preseason. Thousands, if not millions, had expected us to win tonight. After such a brutal slaughter, no one would be impressed.

Nathan's sharp expression softened into one of neutrality. "Yeah, fine."

The bouncer led us down a hall and through a set of doors into the club. When I crossed through the threshold into the warehouse-sized room, the pulsing bass blasted my eardrums into my brain. Vibrations shook the floor and traveled up my legs. Bodies crammed wall-to-wall, all writhing and rolling against each other, moving like seaweed in an ocean of darkness and strobe lights. Maybe no one would even notice us here.

We weaved our way through, led by the bouncer, and neared a table of men dressed in matching outfits, as if they were some lame techno band. The one closest to us was particularly sleazy, in leather pants and way too many gold rings. When Nathan passed, his eyes went wide, and he slammed his drink down on the table. "Hey, Defiance. I had money on that match. Suck my dick."

Nathan shot him the finger. "Suck mine first."

So much for not being noticed.

The bouncer stepped between them, facing the men. "Maybe you should just enjoy your drink, sir."

He sneered at the bouncer. One of his friends nudged him. "It's your fault. That's what you get for betting on girls."

"Yeah," another chimed in. "Who let them into this sport anyways?"

They laughed.

Suddenly, my middle finger wanted its moment in the spotlight, too.

Nathan nodded toward me and my female teammates. "You wanna go against them? Be my guest."

They laughed again until I moved forward. The bouncer glanced back at me and sidestepped out of my path. Sweat beaded on his forehead, though I doubted it was only from the heat in the club.

Most of the men peered up at me with smug grins, but a twitchy one at the back swiped the silverware off the table and hid it in his lap. I smiled and narrowed my eyes at him.

"The first man I ever took down in the virtual world looked a lot like you." I splayed a hand on the table and leaned toward him. "And I certainly didn't need a knife like the ones tucked under your balls to make him cry." His eyes darted about, and he shrunk down in his seat. My smile widened. "Did you want a demonstration? Why don't you stand up? In fact, why don't you all stand up?"

No one moved.

Silence settled around us, despite the pounding beat pulsing off the club's walls. Most of them swallowed and looked away. Finally, their leader found his voice and cleared his throat.

"Whatever. Enjoy your evening."

All eyes lowered to the table and never met mine again. Egos aside, I left the boys intact and followed my teammates through the club.

We emerged from the depths of the dance floor, climbing a single staircase to the VIP lounge that overlooked the rest of the club. From the view on high, I spotted the bar lining the back wall. Four bartenders raced to fill drinks as customers shouted and flailed, pressing themselves against the bar. One tender loaded glasses onto a minidrone and whisked it down the bar to a group of rowdy students. They blitz-attacked the machine and poured the alcohol into their mouths faster than they could swallow.

Above their heads, a sign flashed in green neon.

### GO VIRTUAL OR GO HOME.

A cluster of tables and a few couches punctuated the lounge. The five of us slipped into a U-shaped couch. The lounge was empty, save for a trio of men I didn't recognize, until the one with his back to us turned around.

"Oh shit."

The words slipped past my lips as I watched Mr. Gibson storm toward us. Nathan nudged me.

"What?"

I nodded to the distance. Nathan glanced behind him to see the potbellied man stalking across the floor. He turned back and lowered his voice.

"What the hell is the CEO of a sports-apparel company doing at a club like this?"

"Looking for us," I said between my teeth. "What else?"

The bouncer caught Mr. Gibson just as he descended on us, fisting his hands in his suit jacket.

"Hey, hey. Back off."

Gibson wrestled with him. "I sponsor these jerks. You back off."

The bouncer peered down at us, his cocked eyebrow seeking confirmation. Nathan sighed and nodded. The bouncer released his grip.

Nathan cleared his throat and turned toward the CEO. "Hey, Mr. Gibson. How's it—"

"You think I support a team of losers?" Gibson spat, looming over Nathan. "This is fucking ridiculous. The athletes wearing my brand of training gear can't even make it through the Death Match without losing. How do you think that looks for me?"

Nathan's fists clenched. He drew a shaky breath and swallowed. "We're not out of the tournament. We still have a shot at the championship."

"Maybe not, but now you're on the losing side of the elimination bracket."

"Which will make it an easy ride to the top." Nathan stared directly into his eyes, not backing down. The knuckles of his fists turned white.

Gibson folded his arms over his chest. "You went weeks undefeated in the preseason. And now, in the most important matchup, you lose. This is not what I wanted my brand associated with. There are dozens of other teams I could sponsor."

"Okay," Nathan said with a shrug, trying to be casual. "You could drop us. But how's *that* gonna look when we take the tournament?"

Gibson's jaw muscles moved beneath his skin as if he were chewing on his tongue. "Fine." He pointed a finger an inch away from Nathan's nose. "But you'd better hope you win."

With a huff, he left. When he rejoined his party on the other side of the lounge, the bouncer turned to us.

"You okay, then?"

We all nodded, and he descended the stairs to the club. A waiter took his place at our sides.

"Rough match, huh?" he asked as he lowered a tray to the table filled with several dozen shot glasses brimming with liquor.

Nathan chuckled. "No drone to serve our drinks?"

"No, no. You deserve the human touch."

In the center of the liquor tray was a yellow-tinted cut-glass bowl in the shape of a Pac-Man. It faced up, so its mouth was the bowl's opening. Inside the bowl was brimming with HP, the latest designer drug.

A few years ago, some biochemistry student—who spent a little too much time in his basement lab—ended up developing a designer drug that instantly found a market in the gamer community. It had a thousand street names, all based on gamer terminology. Power-up, 1-up, mana potion, auto-aim, cooldown, critical hit. Most people called it HP, which in gamer speak stood for health points. Its effects were . . . familiar. It turned colors more vibrant, tastes more pleasurable. All senses were enhanced. It didn't just make you feel good. One hit, and you were invincible. With every minute of our lives under strict control, HP was the only way to escape back into the one place we ever cared to be.

The virtual world.

"It's like I never left the pod," Nathan had said to me once, as we lay on his bed together. It was the first time we'd ever tried a hit. He turned to me and trailed his fingers along my forearm. "You feel like warm cashmere."

I hadn't moisturized in days. Cashmere. Yeah, right. I knew it wasn't true, but I didn't care. His fingertips were feathers grazing the inside of my arm, soft and ticklish. I giggled, and laughter rippled all the way down to my toes. When his tongue brushed mine, it tasted like honeydew. Every sensation was ripe, pleasurable, and perfect.

Only the virtual world felt like that.

HP came in capsules of mismatched halves consisting of three different color combinations. Yellow-blue, yellow-red, and red-blue. They were dead ringers for the pills from the old Dr. Mario game. The game might have been more than half a century old, but every gamer knew it, even those born forty years after its debut. We were all suckers for the classics.

"Well," the waiter began, "if there's anything else you need—"

"We'll let you know," Nathan finished. The waiter faltered but took the hint and left.

Nathan reached for a shot glass.

"Are you sure you can handle that?" Derek asked.

"Fuck you." Nathan held up the glass. We mirrored him. "A toast. To all things virtual. Where would we be without it?"

"Well," Hannah said, grinning, "we could always go to college."

We all laughed and slammed the shots back. The bitter taste of the liquor burned down my throat, forging the same path it did after every match. A shot for the team.

Nathan reached for the bowl of HP. I grabbed his arm. "Take it slow."

He shook me off and reached away. He split one of the capsules in half, cut the powder inside into a line, and snorted it right off the table. Hannah popped one in her mouth and downed it with another shot.

"You're not having anything, Kali?" Hannah asked. "Seriously?"

I shook my head. While my teammates dove into the tray

like frat boys at a buffet, the night's matchup replayed in my mind. The four men bursting through the tower's door. Their leader taking me down on his own with that wicked grin on his face. The feel of my own dagger ripping through my neck. I flinched and shook my head again.

"Anyone know where that team came from tonight?"

"No," Derek answered. "They must have held back until now. Kept themselves midlevel. Otherwise, everyone would have known about them. Interesting strategy."

Cunning, yes. Interesting? Shit, no. Especially if we'd have to face them again in the tournament.

"Well, we might have our answer," Hannah said, nodding at the far wall of the club. "Highlights. Check it out."

Above the bar, a gigantic screen spread the length of the entire wall. Along the bottom edge, the tournament's acronym was spelled out in faint lettering against the black background: REALITY-ALTERNATE GLADIATORIAL EVENTS.

Two fighters filled the screen, one wielding a battle-axe and the other a machete. The sound of metal clashing against metal mixed with the techno beat of the club as the pair parried and punched their way through the fight. The machete-wielding warrior slammed his weapon down, slicing his opponent's hand off. He screamed.

Nathan turned away from the screen, wincing. "Christ, that's gotta hurt."

Derek grinned. "Can't handle it, Nancy?"

Nathan slammed a fist on the table. "Call me that again, and I'll cut off your hand right here."

I held my breath and moved to the edge of my seat, primed to wedge myself between them again. But Derek shook his head and pulled back, and Nathan unflexed his hand. With everyone else relaxed, I released my breath. For now.

"It'll be awhile before they get to our matchup," Hannah said, waving a hand at the screen. She turned back to the table. "Let's party."

While my teammates tried to figure out which combinations between the shots and pills would make them forget their own names, I kept my eyes on the screen as the matches slid by.

An hour later, when the crowd had begun to dwindle, I ventured into the lower level of the club and pressed a hip against the bar. Between fights, the screen above the bar phased in and out of candid shots of the gamers from the RAGE tournaments. Fierce-looking warriors wielded battle-axes, longswords, and other blades. Pick your favorite. Root for them. Bet on them. Don't worry if they die. They'll be back next week.

The bartender appeared in front of me, splayed his hands on the bar, and leaned toward me. "What can I get you?"

"Do you have anything with coffee in it?" I asked, raising my voice over the music and pulsing bass around us.

He laughed. "Are you trying to sober up, or do you just really like coffee?"

I smiled. "Well, I don't like being sober."

He laughed again and scanned behind the bar. "Sorry. Nothing with coffee. Can I get you something else? How about . . ." He ran a finger across the bottles. "We have some Kubota Sake. That's Japanese, isn't it?"

With his back turned, I rolled my eyes and muttered under my breath. "Yeah, except I'm half-Chinese and was born here."

"What?"

"That sounds great."

He snatched the bottle off the wall and poured a glass. When he handed it to me, I smiled. Practiced. Perfect.

"Thanks."

"Of course." He leaned in close and lowered his voice. "You

need anything else?" He nodded inside the bar. I leaned forward, following his gaze, and spotted three more Pac-Man bowls filled with HP. Had they replaced peanuts and pretzels with these things or what?

I gave him another practiced smile. "I'm fine for now."

He blinked. "Really? You sure?"

I raised my glass to him. "The night's young."

"Okay." He rapped his knuckles against the bar as he left. "Just let me know when you're ready for a fix."

I nodded as I brought the glass to my lips. The liquor went down smooth, unlike most American alcohols, and left behind a clean, refreshing taste, sort of like sushi. Not half-bad, but not coffee, either.

Music blared from the wallscreen, even louder than the club's techno beat. The Virtual Gaming League's theme song. My gaze flicked up as the screen went black. White lettering appeared along the bottom edge.

THIS IS A REPEAT OF TONIGHT'S EARLIER BROADCAST.

The screen faded in to a pair of young men sitting behind a news anchor's booth with the VGL green-and-white symbol pasted to the front of it. Neither looked a day over twenty-five. The announcers, I mean.

"Good evening. I'm Marcus Ryan."

"And I'm Howie Fulton. And this is *Saturday Night Gaming*."

Radio voices. Perfect teeth. Tanned skin. Both wore small headsets with microphones, meant as a tribute to the original sets gamers wore decades ago.

"We're coming to you live from Los Angeles, home of the VGL national championships." Howie turned to his counterpart. "Well, Marcus, you know what month it is."

"Yes, I do. It's August, and that means the RAGE tournaments." He rubbed his hands together. "I'm excited. Are you excited?"

"You bet I'm excited."

Tweedledee and Tweedledum on TV.

Howie beamed. "Tonight's Death Match round certainly lived up to its name. Let's start off big and check out highlights from the most anticipated match of the night: InvictUS vs. Defiance."

The Death Match was the final round of the preseason, and had earned its nickname for a reason. Mostly, the preseason was just there for warm-up, so the teams could get to know each other, and the players to know themselves. But the Death Match was where most teams found their groove, and the gameplay found the true depth of its brutality, which we'd learned firsthand ourselves. It also divided the teams into two brackets, the winners' and the losers', and set the rest of the tournament in motion.

The screen cut to the match. Four of InvictUS's players crouched at the outer edge of the fields.

"They're fighting with four forwards? I've never seen anything like this."

"That's pretty bold. If anyone from Defiance gets through, they'll only need to defeat one at the tower to win the game."

"I'm not so sure anyone from Defiance is going to get through. Look at this."

Nathan and Derek moved through the fields, unaware, running straight for the trap. Just as they exited the stalks, the enemy lashed out, slicing through their calf muscles as they ran past. They both cried out and fell to the ground. InvictUS jumped on them, holding them down as they sliced them to bits. Looked like neither of them had died first. It was both their faults.

InvictUS took off through the fields.

"Wow." The announcer's voice overlaid the footage. "These guys are fast."

The screen flashed to Hannah, playing the middle man halfway between the two towers. InvictUS crouched low, moving through the fields like snakes weaving through the stalks. They flanked her and attacked from behind. Two stood back and watched, grins on their faces, while the remaining two baited her, swiping their blades through the air. Hannah held them back with jabs of her massive two-handed battle-axe.

One of the watchers circled the fight, and once at her back, he sliced across it, ripping her skin open. Hannah screamed, and the memory of it resounded in my mind. She fell to her knees, and another sword skewered her neck. Her scream cut off into a gurgle, then into nothing, as she collapsed to the ground.

"Three down already. This is unbelievable. Defiance doesn't have much hope now."

"I wouldn't say that just yet, Howie."

The footage cut to Lily, perched high in the sycamore tree. She watched the fields below, waiting for the enemy to appear.

One of the men emerged, followed quickly by another. They ran past her, under the branches. When no more emerged, Lily descended the tree. Looping between branches, she hit the ground with a soft thud.

Once she landed, two more men sprang out from the fields. They'd been waiting for her, knew her exact position and techniques.

"Oh, no. I hope they know what they're doing here."

They bolted for her. Lily turned, darted up the tree three steps and pushed off. As she rotated in air, she brought down her axe, slicing their leader from eyebrow to jawline. A tear of blood dribbled down his neck.

"She's a little tiger, isn't she?"

"I'm not sure about that, but I'd love to know what makes her purr."

She landed smoothly on the ground just as the original two runners circled around.

Surrounded. They closed in. With an axe gripped tight in each hand, Lily's arms moved like a cyclone through the air, keeping the enemies' weapons at bay.

It didn't last.

A sword impaled Lily's shoulder. She grunted, refusing to scream. Another blade ripped through her right hamstring. She fell to her knees. In unison, the foursome pulled back and plunged their swords into her abdomen. Lily seized as her body went rigid. Then, she crumpled. The men pulled back, still in unison. Perfect. These guys had practiced their fighting techniques as much as the rest of us did our smiles.

"These guys really know their opponent."

"InvictUS is just destroying Defiance. They never saw this coming."

The screen cut to me, crouching on the stone floor as the foursome appeared at the tower's entrance. My eyes went wide.

"Now, this is gonna be a hell of a show."

Their leader stepped forward and signaled for the others to wait behind.

"Nice. Very bold."

"Ling's one of the top-rated fighters in the tournament. They really should have used all of them to take her out. But—"

"They're giving us a treat."

"That's right."

Metal clanged together as our swords met, again and again. The footage transformed into slice-and-diced images of the fight. Flash. He knocked the weapon from my hand and me to the floor. Flash. In a sweeping arc, he brought the dagger down to my throat. Flash. I caught his arm with both hands and strained against him until my arms shook. Teeth gritting together, I grimaced. Sweat beaded along my forehead.

"Look at the way her hands are trembling. Ling's fighting like it really is for her life."

I grunted and squirmed against him as the blade dug into my skin. My eyes went wide as the fear seeped in. Blood oozed from my neck. I clawed the wound and gasped for air. Christ, it looked real. No wonder people were more addicted to this than porn.

"Hey. You okay?"

Nathan nudged me, his pale blue eyes narrowed in concern. He motioned at my neck, where my hand clenched the spot I'd been virtually cut. I dropped my hand, and a heavy breath passed through my lips. Just how long had I been holding it in?

On the screen, the footage cut back to the announcers.

"This was by far the biggest upset of the night, possibly of the entire preseason."

"Defiance is really going to have to work if they have any hope of getting back into this game."

"Okay, next up . . ."

The footage cut to another fight of the evening. Keep feeding the masses.

I smiled at Nathan, hoping the expression reached my eyes. "I'm fine."

"You, uh"—he brushed a hand over my hip—"wanna get out of here?"

His finger looped through my belt, and he tugged me against him. Heat flashed inside, where our bodies met. Over his shoulder, I scanned the club. Lily stood in the far corner, playing a

VR-arcade machine. At the end of the bar, Derek chatted up two sets of fake double D's. Which would he take home? Probably both. Hannah danced in the middle of the floor with some guy grinding against her, as if he actually had a chance. Did they all think she kissed Lily for fun? The flirt. It was her image.

I turned back to Nathan.

"Yeah. Let's go."

# CHAPTER 3

Back at the facility, my back hit the metal wall. Rough hands grappled my thighs as Nathan's breath panted in my ear. The edge of his jaw, sharp with stubble, rubbed like razor burn against my cheek. Same as any night. I raked my hands up his back. Every muscle from shoulder to hip was taut, clenched with tension. Saturday was supposed to be the best night of the week, even for those who lived in reality. But tonight couldn't get any worse. In either world.

I curled my fingers through his hair and my legs around his waist, forming my body to his. His breath caught. The rocking hitched, a momentary pause, before he slammed into me. He needed to work off the loss. The frustration.

So did I.

I drove my fingers through his hair, and his tongue assaulted mine. I tasted everything he'd done that night, a bittersweet mix of soda, vodka, and traces of HP.

HP. Nathan wasn't the only one wishing he was still in the virtual.

I closed my eyes and envisioned the tower, surrounded by stone and grass. The metal against my back turned to earth. Warmth spread through my body as the sunlight caressed my skin. The sweetest scent, like a thousand wildflowers, wafted against my nose, carried by the thick mountain air. It filled my lungs and breezed across my face. Reality was the game. Plastic. Metal. People. All fake. The game was real—tangible, sweet, and warm—and the only place I was alive and free.

Nathan released inside me, and the tension in his muscles melted. I moaned softly and murmured in his ear as pulsating shocks coursed through me, and my vision danced with black spots. The cold nothingness of the facility's walls and sterile air pressed against my skin, pulling me back to the present. Nathan held me, panting, shaking, then carried me to the bed, where we collapsed across it.

I sank into the foam mattress as it morphed around my body. Staring up at the ceiling, I surveyed the green-gray metal, same as the walls, floors, and everything else in the room. Only the bed and its sheets provided any color or softness. Every drawer and shelf was built into the walls, so they were perfectly smooth, broken only by the occasional seam or handle where a compartment opened. Save for the bed, only our scattered clothes took up any floor space.

Nathan's ragged breaths beside me slowed as he recovered, and grew even slower, descending into soft snores. I pressed my side into his, and the heat from his skin radiated against mine. I smiled and shut my eyes. Done. This sorry excuse of a night was finally over.

The taste of sake lingered at the back of my mouth, while sweet tremors still rippled through my nerves. If sake and sex could make a buzz together, then I was nestled comfortably on the clouds of oblivion. But no amount of sex or alcohol could ever compare to hours of REM.

Sleep. The sweetest escape outside the virtual world. A middle finger at reality.

Tomorrow would be back to training. During the preseason, the RAGE matchups had taken place every Saturday night. On the days between, we trained and promoted our sponsors, the latter taking up more time than the former. But now, we'd be grinding our asses into the mats, and hopefully, the tournament's matchups would go better than tonight's.

No, it had to go better than tonight's. One loss in tournament play, and we'd be eliminated.

I shifted to my side, listening to Nathan's deep breaths. Air filled his lungs, expanding his chest, and left on an exhale. The calming rhythm brought forth my own drowsiness, and I drifted toward sleep.

A soft ping dragged me back from the edge of slumber. Grumbling, I ground my fist into the mattress. Peeking out from beneath the scattered clothes on the floor, my tablet blinked. New message. It pinged again.

With a heavy sigh, I pulled myself out of bed, dug my tablet out from the pile of clothes, and tapped the screen. The message opened.

Kali,

Meet in my office at 01:15.

Clarence

My gut twisted. What did he want? If it was about our loss tonight, wouldn't he message the entire team? I glanced at the current time above the message—01:07. Shit. I scrambled for my clothes. A zip of my pants and a clasp of my bra, and I was halfway dressed. Then I located my shirt and one shoe. Great. I knelt next to the bed and lifted the overhanging blanket to peer beneath. The bed shifted as Nathan leaned over the edge toward me.

"What are you doing?"

I groped around the shadows beneath the bed until I landed on the soft, velveteen lining of my missing high heel.

"I gotta go," I said, pulling my shoes on.

"Why?"

"Clarence wants to meet with me."

I looked up and met Nathan's cold expression.

"Why's he asking for you and not all of us?"

I slid my arms through the sleeves of my shirt. "I don't know."

"What does he want?"

"I don't know." I glanced down as I fumbled with the last few buttons. There. Decent.

"Why—"

"I don't know," I snapped. "He wants to meet. That's all it says. Read it yourself." I motioned at my tablet on the bed, where the message still blinked across the screen. Nathan glanced between it and me a few times, then waved me off.

As I headed for the door, the bed shifted as Nathan stood. Was he following me? Then I heard a drawer pulled open and the sound plastic makes when it crunches between fingers. When I looked back, Nathan was cutting lines of white powder on a shelf he'd pulled out from the wall.

"Are you stupid?" I spat. "How much did you already do at the club?"

He sent me an incredulous look. "How else am I supposed to get to sleep?"

If he needed it to get to sleep, that meant only one thing: heroin.

HP was a stimulant and could keep you up all night if you did enough hits. Most gamers did enough to enjoy themselves at the club but not so much that they couldn't relax after. Nathan lacked such control.

"We have testing tomorrow," I reminded him.

He shrugged. "Bought and paid for."

Bought and paid for. That was one of the first things we learned about the life of a pro gamer, when Clarence had assembled the five of us in his office for the first time.

"You'll be expected to be in the public eye at all times," he'd said, after basic introductions and some other drivel I'd tuned out. "There are clubs in L.A. that cater exclusively to the gamer scene. Be there every night. If you drink or do anything else there, the cost will be covered. Just make sure you're seen by the cameras, and you're sober enough for training in the morning."

"What?" Hannah had asked. "Don't we have to be clean for testing?"

Clarence chuckled to himself, one of the only times I'd heard him laugh. Even then, a smile hadn't touched his face.

"They're cute when they're new," he'd said, speaking to no one in particular. He shook his head and looked back at us. "Like I said, *anything* you do at the clubs will be covered."

It didn't take an expert in reading between the lines to know what he meant. The technicians had been bought off, and no matter what we did, our drug tests would always read clean.

I glanced between Nathan and the shelf a few times but couldn't think of anything else to discourage him.

"Whatever. Just, for God's sake, take it easy."

I exited the room and turned back to the door to enter the lock code on the keypad. The door slid shut as Nathan sniffed the first line up his nose.


"I hope I didn't interrupt anything."

Clarence stood with his back to me, in front of the floor-to-ceiling windows of his office. The team's facility lay sprawled beneath, mimicking the outline of a steel-and-glass sand castle. Or a prison. Half-sunken tunnels ran between several central hubs. An outdoor workout yard and running track took up the north end. Cinder-block walls surrounded it all. No barbwire, though, or manned guards. At least, that I knew of. Beyond it lay the city of Los Angeles. If I squinted, I could make out the U.S. Bank Tower and the Aon Center among the collage of glowing skyscrapers. Darkness bled through the rest of the city, between the thousands of twinkling lights, as if a galaxy had nestled itself into the ground.

Clarence gazed out the window, overlooking the facility as a god does its own creation. He owned the entire compound. The training rooms. The virtual pod center. The bunks. Even us.

I sat in the chair across from his empty desk, tapping my foot against the floor. The carpet was so wiry and dense, it scratched at my shoe with every tap. The office was one of the few rooms with drywall instead of steel, and it was painted to match the sullen green shade of the carpet. Only the white border of the baseboard separated them. High in the ceiling overhead, dim lighting shone down but failed to reach the floor, as if trying to hide the imperfections of the room. There weren't any. Clean lines. Perfect spacing. All as rigid and unyielding as Clarence himself. Why is it when people decorate they splatter more of themselves over the walls than paint?

"No," I said, shifting in the chair. I stopped tapping my foot and watched his back. "You didn't interrupt."

"There was a problem tonight."

Though the dim lighting in the room left our proprietor masked in shadows, it failed to hide the subtle heaviness in his tone. Did he expect us to win every match?

I shrugged. "Yeah. We lost one. They were prepared. We weren't."

"And why do you think that was?"

"Maybe because we spent the last three weeks promoting our sponsors more than practicing."

Clarence cleared his throat, the same way my teachers used to whenever I'd shoot my mouth off. How some of them didn't end up with throat cancer is beyond me.

"Promoting the sponsors is essential to electronic sports," he said. "They're the ones who pay for the tournaments and prizes. Without them, the gaming league would fall apart." He paused, still gazing out the window. "I know my team. The problem is with your leader. You don't have one."

I suppressed my scoff. "Actually, we have two. Unless you missed the after-arena fight."

He nodded. "I was in the observation lounge. It was hard to ignore."

Located above the pod center, Clarence always watched us through the tinted glass—before, during, and after the fights. Though I never saw his image on the other side, I had always felt him there, like the monster that hides under kids' beds.

"Could you smell the testosterone up there, too?" I asked.

He clucked his tongue at my comment. Guess that was his version of laughter.

Around the office, posters hung at regular intervals, three feet above the floor and one foot between. The flexible LED screens shimmered with life-size images of the team. First of Nathan and Derek, both shirtless, their chiseled abs glistening with sweat.

WE DRINK PROTEIN ENERGY BOOSTERS®.

One of Hannah. Perfect, tanned skin. Model height. Posed with her hands on her hips while a wind machine whipped her waist-length, strawberry blonde locks around her hourglass figure. She wore training gloves and a sports bra that jacked her breasts up to her chin.

I WEAR GIBSON® TRAINING GEAR.

Clarence left his post at the window and strolled toward his desk, finally revealing himself from the shadows. He wore a suit so crisp and stark green, he blended into the walls behind him, only to reappear when he crossed in front of a poster. His blond hair was just long enough to pull into a low ponytail. With tight skin and hard features, he was one of those people born looking plastic, even without the surgery. A Ken doll, and not in a good way—if there was one.

"Two leaders?" He nodded. "Yes, but neither will back down from the other. So, how do I choose?"

He sat at his desk, steepled his hands against his lips, and stared at me. Silence fell over the room, leaving the hum of air-conditioning as the only resonance. On the wall behind him, our logo shimmered on another screen, though this one was much wider than the individual posters of my teammates.

I took a breath through my lips, as if it would break the tension. The taste of antibacterial soap invaded my mouth and nearly bleached my tongue. I coughed, clearing my throat. "Are you asking my opinion? I'm not exactly an impartial judge."

"Why? Because you're fucking Nathan?" he quipped, raising an eyebrow in my direction. A shudder quivered up my spine. How did he find that out? God, was he watching the bunks like he watched over the facility?

"Like I said," he continued, "I know my team."

He narrowed his eyes and stared so intensely, I had to look away. My gaze landed on a poster of Lily dressed in her battle gear, pigtails curling over her shoulders. Lily. The tiny one. The blond one. Delicate and sweet until she cut you into a dozen pieces before you could blink. People really do love irony.

"Normally, the owner chooses the leader of the group," I said, managing to meet his eyes again.

"I was waiting to see if one naturally rose out of the ranks before the start of the tournament."

"Look, if you're asking me to choose—"

"I'm not asking you to choose," he said. "I know who I want."

"Who?"

"You."

Laughter gripped me, and I doubled over in the chair. Since when was Clarence funny? When I recovered, I met the tight lines of his mouth. My smile faltered.

"You're serious?"

He nodded, one swift jerk of his head. I should have known he was. Clarence never cracked a joke. He was a businessman to the core.

A businessman . . .

Wait. This was a ploy. A way to force a truce between Nathan and Derek. Of course, he couldn't choose either of them to be the team's leader. They'd rip each other's throats out. I was just the pawn he'd decided to stick between the warring knights.

"I'm not getting in the middle of this," I said. "Someone else can do it."

"I'm not picking someone else."

"Why? Are you afraid Hannah or Lily will spit in your face?"

"Lily and Hannah do what I tell them."

I scoffed. "Did you tell them to be a couple, too?"

"No. That was a serendipitous outcome. People love it." He waved a hand at the window, as if the city represented the masses.

I crossed my arms over my chest. "Well, you can forget it."

"This isn't open to debate."

"You're right, because I'm not doing it."

"Let me put it this way." He leaned forward and rested his arms on his desk. "Do it, or you're off the team."

My mouth fell open. "You can't do that."

"Actually, I can."

"The team is so popular because of all of us," I said. "You can't just kick me out. I have fans. They'll hate you."

"Don't overestimate your value. You are replaceable. Two weeks, and you'd be forgotten."

I opened my mouth to argue, but nothing came out. How could he do this? I wasn't replaceable. I was loved. By everyone. I gave the people what they wanted. I put on a good show and acted my part. How could he think I was expendable?

"I thought you'd be more excited at the opportunity," Clarence said, letting out a weighted sigh. "No woman has ever led a team in the VGL before. If you won the tournament, it could mean worldwide recognition. Maybe even the eSports Hall of Fame."

Holy S-H-I-T.

Worldwide recognition? The Hall of Fame?

I went numb all over—except for my heart, which fluttered. I'd be set for life. I wouldn't even need to compete for money or sponsorships. They'd be handed to me. Not that I'd ever quit competing. Well, maybe when I got old.

You know, like thirty.

"I take your silence to mean you're reconsidering?" Clarence asked, a smug tone laced in his voice.

I nodded, still spinning from the glory and flashing lights in my head. "I'll do it. I'll lead the team."

"Good." He pushed himself away from the desk and stood.

"You're dismissed for now. I don't need you looking tired. Get back to your bunk." He cleared his throat again. "Or Nathan's, since you seem to prefer it."

My jaw clenched. I glared up at him, digging my nails into the arms of the chair. "Are you going to make that public, too?"

He shrugged. "If it becomes profitable."

I drew deep, shaky breaths to calm my nerves, but heat still coursed through my veins. He knew what I was capable of. Why wasn't he afraid I'd cut off his head in his sleep? If this was the arena, if I had my sword . . .

Clarence stared down at me, unwavering, like he was looking through me. Like he could see my thoughts and knew they were wrong. Whatever. I swallowed the smart-ass remark creeping up my throat and pushed myself out of the chair. As I turned, the wall behind me buzzed and faded into a screen. A wall that wasn't really a wall, just mimicked the green walls and white border when it wasn't on. Artificial intelligence in all its glory.

A reporter popped up on the screen in front of a background of gray rubble and ash.

". . . as you see behind me the devastation still left behind as thousands of drones and other robotic resources continue to be part of the cleanup effort . . ."

The caption at the bottom of the screen read:

DISASTER AT DIABLO 2053: ONE YEAR LATER

I don't know what genius decided to put a nuclear reactor near a fault line, but we'd learned the full stupidity of it last year. Apparently, power plants don't like earthquakes. Who knew? But since when did Clarence watch anything other than the VGL's home channel, let alone updates on the disaster cleanup efforts?

The channel changed abruptly.

The screen went black at first. Then the RAGE standings faded into view, featuring the double-elimination bracket used in standard championship play in any Virtual Gaming League event. Every team in the tournament was now divided into the winners' bracket or the losers' bracket. The layout reminded me of a lineage tree, except this one only expanded sideways. Our team, Defiance, sat in the losers' bracket.

The screen clicked off. I turned to find Clarence standing only inches away. A chill crawled up my spine, and my feet itched to take a step back. What a creep.

He leaned over me, head high as he looked down his nose. "Don't disappoint me."

I stared into his eyes, black holes of endless depth. Like hopelessness, or death. Swallowing, I lowered my gaze to his chest and nodded.

"Good," he said, tone surprisingly light. "I look forward to seeing what you're capable of. You're dismissed."

I left, feet carrying me swiftly to the exit. When the beast says you can go, you run.

At the doorway, I paused. Next to it was a poster of me. An iridescent shimmer rolled through the LED display as the air-conditioning sent tremors through the paper-thin screen. Unlike my teammates, I was posed fully clothed, my half-American, half-Chinese heritage emphasized through the outfit I wore. A traditional Chinese cheongsam dress in style—high collar, tight waist, and a long slit over one leg. But also Americanized— shimmering white and no pattern like the pods' cores. It cut several inches too low down the chest, only a pin's width wide, to reveal a hint of cleavage. A symbol of demure, deadly beauty. Tasteful. Acceptable. Desirable, even.

It's what they wanted.

I always gave the people what they wanted. Once I led the team to victory and became the first female captain to take a championship, Clarence would see I wasn't so expendable. None of us were.

Back at the bunks, I crawled into bed next to Nathan. He lay facedown in the center between two pillows. I glanced at him a few times, expecting him to stir or shift over from my movements. He didn't budge, so I snaked my body against his and toyed with my pendant as I debated with myself. I could tell him what was said in the meeting. Tell him I'd been ap- pointed leader of the group. He'd have to listen to me, to my command. Did I want another fight right now? Another scream- ing match? Or a good night's sleep?

Tomorrow. I'd tell him tomorrow.

I nestled into my sliver of the mattress. The heat from Nathan's back kissed my skin, and I had to smile. Maybe things weren't really so bad. We'd lost once. Once. We were still in the tourna- ment, and as Nathan had pointed out, ending up in the losers' bracket meant facing off against the weaker teams, making an easy ride to the top. To the championship. Where we'd win, and I'd be the first female captain in history to capture the title.

I wasn't just at the top of my career. I was on top of the world. No, both worlds: the real and the virtual.

Funny thing about being on top: It's a long way down when you crash.

# CHAPTER 4

The alarm blared, short, annoying spats like a mechanical bird on steroids.

*Beep. Beep. Beep.*

I groaned and waited for the slap of Nathan's hand against the snooze, same as every morning. Five seconds passed. Then ten.

I nudged him. "Nathan. The alarm."

He didn't move. I nudged him again. Nothing.

"For Christ's sake."

I smacked a hand against the bed, reached over him, and hit the digital clock built into the wall. Nathan slacked against me. I shook him.

"Come on. We have to get up."

Nothing.

"Get up," I shouted, pulling the covers back. He still didn't move. Lazy, fucking moron.

Then the deafening silence of the room closed around me. No alarm. No sound. No breaths but my own.

My pulse quickened. I grabbed his arm.

"Nathan?"

No response. I shook him again.

"Nathan. This isn't funny."

I groped his neck for a pulse, and instead, met the cold clamminess of his skin.

I screamed.

I scrambled off the bed, hit the floor with a thud, and back-pedaled until I bumped the wall. With a trembling hand, I reached up and felt along the wall until I hit the panic button next to the door controls. An alarm sounded, like an amplified version of the clock. The lights brightened, highlighting the horror in the room. My stomach sank through the floor, and my breaths came out in pants as I stared at Nathan's body. Lifeless. In the bed where I'd just slept.

Oh my God. This isn't happening. No, no, no.

A computerized female voice filled the room.

*We are sending medical personnel to your location now. If this alarm was triggered in error, please deactivate it immediately.*

No. Come.

Come now.

I hugged my legs to my chest and buried my face in my knees. I counted. One-two-three. Isn't this what children do when they're scared?

I forced my chin up. Nathan lay on his side, back to me, slumped, relaxed. He looked like he was sleeping. Something inside nudged me toward the bed. Go to him.

No. He was dead. He'd been so cold. I plastered myself against the wall and buried my face against my knees again.

Footsteps pounded down the hall, followed by rapid knocks on the door. A male voice came through the door. "EMS. Are you in need of medical assistance?"

I opened my mouth, but only rapid breaths passed through my lips. A heavy fist beat against the door again. "We will enter under medical authority unless you decline."

There was another pause. Several soft beeps rang out, muffled by metal, as a code was entered into the keypad.

The female computerized voice spoke again.

*Security override.*

The door slid open. Two men entered, their footsteps clunking on the floor. One went to the bed. The other rushed to my side and knelt.

"Are you okay, ma'am?"

Ma'am? Why did he call me ma'am? These medical personnel were here to service us. Didn't they know my name? Didn't they know who I was?

Didn't they watch the tournaments?

I buried my head farther in the tent of my limbs and nodded feverishly against my knees. "I'm fine."

"This one doesn't have a pulse. He's not breathing," the one from the bed called out. The paramedic at my side hurried to him. Footsteps circled the bed. The men exchanged a few sharp whispers. Then it went quiet. Too quiet for too long.

The footsteps returned to me.

"Hey." A hand gripped my shoulder and shook hard. "There's residue powder in his nostrils. What did he take?"

I pointed to the back corner of the room, keeping my head down.

"Top drawer."

He left again, and I heard the drawer pull open, followed by a few sharp curse words and the sound of plastic crunching between fingers.

"Jesus," one of them murmured. "Something that size would've held five grams." Then louder, to me. "Was this full? Did he take it all?"

I pressed my face harder against my knees. One-two-three.

"Hey. Look. Up."

The words rifled through the air, echoing off the bunk's walls. I lifted my head. Two men in blue medical uniforms stood in the far corner. They looked blurry, as if standing behind a panel of wet glass. Was I crying?

One held up an empty plastic baggie and shook it at me. "How much did he take?"

"All of it." My voice came out in squeaks. The warrior, squeaking like a little mouse.

"Was it full?"

"Yes."

I buried my head again as another barrage of swearwords spilled out of their mouths.

They started compressions. The bed shifted again as they worked around Nathan. Their breaths came out in pants. Just like me, they counted. At least theirs had a purpose.

Then the compressions and heavy breaths faded into silence. The bed stopped shifting.

"Forget it. There's nothing to bring back. He's cold."

"Are we calling it then?"

Shuffling footsteps were the only answer to the question. At least, from what I heard. Then, new footsteps entered the room. Lighter. Hesitant.

"Kali?" A female voice, soft and sweet. Hannah's voice. "Oh my God. Are you okay?"

My stomach churned.

"I think I'm going to throw up."

"Come on."

Her long fingers wrapped around my arm. Strong hands gripped the other but felt too small to be a man's. Lily. Together, they carry-dragged me to the bathroom and set me down in front of the toilet just as the contents of the previous night came rushing back up. Lily held my hair back with one hand and rubbed circles against my back with the other. In the background, the faucet squeaked as Hannah turned the water on and doused a cloth beneath the stream.

Once my stomach retired, I rested my cheek against the side of the toilet, the coolness of it burning into my skin. Lily leaned over me and hit the button to flush. The whirlpool whisked the contents away. Too bad I couldn't do the same with the memory.

When had Nathan died? Was he still breathing when I got back to the room? I thought back, forcing my brain to sort through images and memories. Snippets flashed across my mind, blurring together. I entered the room. Then I crawled into bed. God, was he already dead? Did I sleep next to him all night like that?

My stomach lurched. I gagged, but nothing came up. Lily drew bigger circles on my back.

"I don't know which is worse," I said. "Wondering if he was still alive before I fell asleep, and I could have saved him, or that I slept next to a dead body all night."

"Then don't think about it," Hannah said as she patted my forehead with the damp cloth. The coolness of the fabric burned against my flushed skin. "It wouldn't have mattered. The paramedics said there's no way he could have survived. Not with the amount he took."

Did they? I hadn't heard.

Someone pulled a brush through my hair. Lily, still at my back. The bristles massaged my scalp from forehead to neck and around my ears. I shut my eyes, focusing on that soothing sensation. Something silky brushed my shoulders and wrapped around my back. A robe. Hannah guided my arms through the holes and tied it shut around my waist. A tank top and underwear was all I'd been wearing when the paramedics arrived. Guess I'd been too shocked to even realize it.

Hannah continued to pat the cloth against my face, then

lowered it to my neck. Lily brushed my hair. I'd never had many female friends. It never bothered me much before, but now I realized how much I'd missed out.

The cold edge of a cup pressed against my bottom lip.

"Drink," Hannah said.

I gripped the cup while Hannah held it steady. Water poured past my lips and down my aching throat. I coughed, and my stomach gurgled, but the liquid stayed down. Pulling myself away from the toilet, I slumped against the closest wall, eyes still closed. I breathed. Wisps of air whispered through the slit in my mouth. Funny how you how become aware of your breaths in moments like these.

Hannah knelt close, and I caught the coconut scent of her shampoo.

"So. You two were, um . . ."

"Sleeping together?" I finished. "Yes."

"Mmm-hmm."

Her tone sounded as if she wasn't surprised.

"You knew?" I asked.

"Well, with the way you two were always sneaking off, we kinda figured."

Oh, great. So much for keeping it a secret.

I kept my head resting against the wall, gaze focused on the corner of the bathroom as I counted my breaths again. Hannah placed a hand on my arm. "Did you love him?"

"What? No. Not even close."

What was she thinking? Warriors don't fall in love. Still, it didn't lessen the sickening sensation rolling over me. My stomach was a rock-lined cavern, that empty yet weighted feeling you get at the top of the roller coaster, just before the big drop. Now imagine never really coming down. Suspended animation. That was me. Right now. On the worst ride of my life.

I shook my head. Shock. I was just in shock. How could I care about someone I'd barely known outside of the team? No strings attached. That was the deal. No. I didn't feel this way because I cared. A warrior can't love. It wasn't part of my image. I felt this way because I woke up next to a dead body. Traumatized. That's all it was.

"Kali?"

Hannah shook my arm, snapping me back to reality. Why? Why did she have to? It was peaceful in the little black hole that was my mind. But the way she'd drawn my name out held a certain tone that only comes before someone makes an accusation. My stomach clenched, despite the boulder inside it.

"What?"

"How come you didn't stop Nathan from taking so much?"

"I didn't know."

"Were you high, too?"

"No." I shook my head against the wall and the movement reverberated in the metal. "I wasn't there. Clarence called me to his office for a meeting."

"About what?"

"He appointed me team captain."

Silence. A drop fell from the sink's faucet and splashed on the metal rim below. I opened my eyes. Hannah's expression was taut and her gaze flicked around the room as she processed my words. Lily's bow lips were pressed together in a tight line. Seconds passed. More silence. Another drop in the sink.

"Good choice," Lily finally said.

I waved her off. "He just did it to make a truce between Nathan and Derek. He couldn't choose one or the other, so he picked me instead."

My breath hitched. With Nathan gone, would I still lead the team? Derek was the obvious leader among those of us left. I'd be passed over for the position now. Hell, was there even a team to lead anymore? Holy shit. Did my career just die in that room along with Nathan? These games were my life, my everything. This wasn't happening.

This couldn't be happening.

My chest tightened and my breaths came in gasps. The walls closed in around me. My gasps turned to heaves. I had to get out of there. Had to get some air.

I pushed myself up against the wall. My knees wobbled but held. The girls hovered over me, Hannah in front and Lily behind. Both had their arms out as if to catch me from falling.

"You don't look so good. You should rest," Hannah said, gripping my elbow. "We'll get you back to bed."

I recoiled. "Where Nathan died?"

Hannah frowned at herself as she realized what she had offered. "Yeah, sorry. We'll get you back to your own bunk. Or you can stay with us."

Lily nodded.

"No." I pushed myself off the wall. Hannah and Lily mirrored my movements, arms still extended. "I need to get out of here. I need to get this out of my head."

"Fine." Hannah sighed. "You want a fix?"

"What? Nathan just died from an overdose. How could I, after that?"

"I know," she said in a soothing tone. "It just seems like you need to escape for a little while. No one should have to deal with what you just went through."

Escape. That was exactly what I needed. An escape.

"We have more than one way for that," I said. "And it's better than anything you could get at the nightclubs."

Sex, drugs, and alcohol. The staples of any rock star or

celebrity. But gamers had something more. Something no one else would ever understand. The greatest high. The biggest thrill.

The arena.

Hannah studied me through the slits of her eyes as she processed my words. Then her eyes went wide, and she gasped.

"You're gonna plug in? You can't go virtual now. Not in your state of mind. It's not safe."

Watch me.

I stumbled out of the bathroom and started dressing, despite their protests. The EMS workers were gone, and had taken Nathan with them. What would happen to his body? Guess they'd transport it home to his parents. Did he have any family? We'd never talked about much besides the tournaments.

"I really don't think this is a good idea," Hannah said again as she watched me pull my clothes on.

"I appreciate what you did for me just now, but I need this. Leave me alone."

I staggered out the door and down the hall without looking back. They didn't object or follow as I headed for the virtual pod center.

So what if it wasn't healthy to plug in when I was so emotionally and physically drained? I needed this. To get away from everything. The night. The loss. My death in the digital world. Nathan's in this one. It all swirled together in my mind, virtual blending with reality, until I was certain about only one thing.

This was way too real.

# CHAPTER 5

With a pathetic grunt, my opponent collapsed to the ground, sending sheets of sand billowing out around him. Blood bubbled out of his mouth as he coughed and gurgled. With one arm, he clawed at the ground, pulling himself toward where the other lay several feet away. Red streams squirted from the stump of his shoulder. He gasped for air as he dragged himself along, breaths growing shallower with each pant.

Three feet from his severed arm, his body slumped against the sand, and his head slunk to the side. Blood pooled out of the holes in face and body, some natural and some I'd added myself. He seized, a final breath rattling through him. Then he stilled.

The crowd roared.

Bloodied sword in hand, I stretched my arms out toward the surrounding stands, closed my eyes, and smiled, basking in their praise like it was sunlight. The cheers of a thousand spectators blended together into a thunderous applause. The pulsing beat of their hands and feet rippled through the air and pounded against my skin. So what if none of it was real? Adrenaline pumped through my veins. Pride practically glowed from my skin. There were no cameras here. No feuding teammates.

Just glory.

My toes dug into the field of sand as I stood surrounded by stands on all sides. This was the original gladiatorial stadium before they developed more complex arenas to entertain the masses. Capture the tower, my ass. I loved going back to the original. You know, to de-stress. Some people watched TV. Others went for a run.

I had this.

The sound of clinking chains pulled my eyes open. A black-masked undertaker dragged the hacked-up remnants of my opponent away, kiting streaks of blood across the sand. A breeze brushed against my skin, clean and untouched. Not one cut. Not one ache. Invincible. Here, no one could touch me.

Beneath the stands, a gate crawled open from the bottom up. Grinding steel squealed as the bars lifted, revealing my next opponent. Male. Six feet. Well built. Wearing full armor, including a helmet and shield. He wielded a longsword and swung it about, cutting through the air with such precision it whistled sharp little whimpers with each swing. A pro. A real gladiator.

Goody. A challenge.

As he walked forward and into the sunlight, the crowd booed. Standard programming.

I loved standard programming.

He stopped five feet away and took his position. An open stance, with too much space between his back and front feet. Powerful, yes. But that delicate spot between his legs? Not so guarded. I smiled. No, that was too easy. I'd take this one the old-fashioned way.

With a solid ass kicking.

The crowd quieted to a rumble.

I squared my feet, one slightly forward, sword pointed down, chin pointed high. The wind swirled through my hair. Here, it was my only teammate, and my greatest ally.

The gong clanged.

He charged, sword raised. Our weapons met with a sharp

clang. I deflected him, sweeping him to the side. He circled back for me, attacking in short, choppy blows. I moved through the air like I was a part of it, like it flowed both within and around me.

The end of my sword nicked his arm, slicing a two-inch gash into his skin. He flinched and grunted as his hand instinctively went for the wound. Momentary weakness. A fleeting distraction. I used it.

I spun my sword around his, tangling his arms together, and knocked him back. He stumbled and nearly fell.

Oh. Come. On.

He regained his footing and came at me again. We danced. Through his puffs of breath and the clangs of sword meeting sword, I could smell his sweat and traces of blood. It smelled like fear.

I grinned.

I dropped to the ground, spinning, foot out, and caught both of his. He hit the ground, back first. I pounced on him before he could recover, reeling my sword back to deliver the final blow.

Our eyes widened. His from fear. Mine from hunger.

The crowd screamed. Their feet pounded the stands, beating like a hailstorm. They chanted: Kill, kill, kill. Despite it all, a bubble of silence enveloped me as the wind murmured in my ear.

Night, night, sweetheart.

I stabbed my sword down, aiming for the break in his armor at his neck. An inch away, I halted.

Grinding steel echoed throughout the arena again as the stadium's gates opened. Two more gladiators emerged, ducking below the rising bars.

What the hell was this? The fight wasn't over. Standard programming was one-on-one, or sometimes two-on-one just for show. But no one was watching me now. What was my programmer doing? Why had she changed the code?

I stood tall, leaving my opponent cowering on the ground. As the newcomers grew close, my mouth went dry, and a knot formed in my stomach. They weren't men. They were giants, towering well over ten feet tall, with limbs as thick as my waist. The closest one bolted for me. His feet pounded the sand as the ground trembled beneath him. The sound echoed through the arena like the beat of a bass drum. But it dulled in comparison to the thunderous pounding of my own rapid heartbeat.

I turned and took two steps when he grabbed the back of my armor and slammed me into the ground. A deafening crack ripped through the arena. I cried out. My back. Was it broken?

Get up. Now.

My legs wouldn't move. I flailed my arms, trying to hit anything I could with my sword. The giants closed in, weapons raised. Bile burned at the back of my throat. No.

No.

They plunged their swords into my stomach, stabbing and skewering me like meat. Blinding pain ripped through my entire body so hard, the back I was sure was broken bowed to the onslaught. A bloodcurdling scream ripped from my mouth.

Oh, God. Just let me die.

Let.

Me.

Die.

With a gasp, I slammed back into reality, like jerking awake from a falling dream. Sweat beaded across my forehead as breaths panted through my lips. I ripped the wires from my skin and clawed at the pod's inner lid. Let me out. Now.

Now.

The pod hissed and opened. I collapsed to the floor on my hands and knees, gasping, trembling. My vision faded in and out of reality. Or focus. Whatever.

Clacking footsteps approached, and a pair of shoes came into view. I narrowed my sights on them, trying to ground myself in this world. Perfect designer shoes. Not a mark on them, as if right out of the box.

Clarence.

"What the hell do you think you're doing?"

God, he sounded like my mom whenever she'd catch me sneaking out the back door for the arcade.

I stared at the floor, still trembling. "I needed—"

"Do you know what I had to do to pull you out of there?"

It was dangerous to pull anyone out before they died, or before the simulation ended. Sometimes it seemed like there was a trap between reality and the virtual world. Yank someone out, and they might not make it all the way back.

Images of giants flashed through my head, and my teeth ground together.

"Did you change the programming?" I asked, finally looking up at him. He stared down, fierce and unyielding, and nodded once. My trembling hands morphed into clenched fists. How could he do that to me?

I glanced back at the workstation behind my pod. No one sat at the chair behind the screen. "Where's my programmer?"

What was her name again?

"I fired her."

"You fired her? She was *my* programmer."

"On *my* payroll. She was irresponsible, letting you plug in like that off schedule and in this state." He motioned at me with a flick of his hand.

I frowned at the floor, unable to find an argument.

"You need to go see the doctor," he told me.

I scoffed. "I just had a complete physical three weeks ago. He said I was an Olympian."

"Not that doctor. The therapist."

Pffft. I erupted with laughter before I could slap a hand over my mouth. Clarence frowned.

"I'm not kidding, Kali. I can't have you leading the team with this kind of mind-set."

"Oh, what does it matter?" I pushed myself off my knees to sit on my butt. "With Nathan gone, you'll make Derek the leader."

"No. You will lead this team."

What? That didn't make any sense. "But you put me in command so Nathan and Derek wouldn't rip each other's throats out."

"No. I didn't."

Then why had he? There was no reason to assign me as the team's leader other than to create a wedge between my feuding teammates. A wedge that was no longer necessary.

Then the realization hit me so hard, I nearly smacked myself in the forehead. I was marketable. A female gamer. The first in history to lead a pro gaming team. I brought men to their knees. I was a powerhouse for the sponsors. They'd eat this up.

Maybe they'd make little Kali action figures.

Sarcasm aside, the thought tightened my chest. This was the chance of a lifetime. A career-defining moment. And it was still within my grasp.

"So, I still have a chance to do this?" I asked. "To be the first female captain in history?"

"Only if you go see the therapist." He knelt close to me, as if he was actually trying to generate a bond between us. "I understand that Nathan's untimely demise is disappointing." Untimely? Disappointing? Looks like the Ken doll was made of plastic on the inside as well. He continued, "But that doesn't mean the world stops because of it."

The world keeps going, sure. But some people's lives would grind to a halt. What about Nathan's family? What about his fans? Not everyone was as phony as the man in front of me. And now he expected me to go see some dumb-ass therapist just so I could lead the team. This was stupid. I was twenty now. An adult. I'd kissed my mom and dad good-bye two years ago for a life in L.A., the West Coast equivalent of New York. I could do whatever I wanted.

"You know what?" I said, raising my voice. "I'll lead the team, but I'm sure as hell not going to any therapist."

"Yes. You will."

"I don't have to do what you say."

Clarence stood and folded his arms. "I have a contract that says you do."

Replaceable. It echoed in my mind on an endless loop. Was there really nothing I could do to lead the team other than go into therapy?

"Go take a shower. You're a mess," Clarence said. "Then report to the medical wing. I'll tell the therapist to be ready for you."

He left me on the floor as he walked toward the exit. I watched him leave.

"Where are you going?"

"I have things to arrange."

My stomach twisted. "You mean Nathan's funeral?"

Clarence paused at the door before walking out. "No," he said. "His replacement."

# CHAPTER 6

The shower helped. Therapy didn't.

I tilted and balanced my chair on one leg as I glanced around the office. The walls and carpet were a familiar stark green, with white edging throughout. The stench of anti-bacterial cleaner lingered in the air. Either Clarence had puked all over this room, too, or the therapist was just like him.

Dr. Renner sat across from me, with her weight resting on one hip. Chocolate-brown hair, perfectly styled, fell in extravagant waves to her shoulders. Her face was an artist's rendering of symmetry and balance. Big eyes and full lips with a small nose and chin. A former model turned medical professional? Did Clarence hire everyone based on their appearance?

She shifted her glasses where they rested on her nose as she looked over the tablet in her hand. Why do shrinks always wear glasses? No one needed them anymore. One quick trip to the optometrist, a zap in each eye, and bam: perfect vision. Fashion, I guess. Glasses conveyed a sense of intelligence and professionalism. Looks like it wasn't just the gamers who played their parts.

"Kali Ling," she finally said, drawing out my name as if it stuck to her lips. Must be injections. "You have quite the reputation."

She didn't sound impressed as she flicked through her tablet with a few swipes of her finger. I smiled anyway.

"Quite the reputation," I repeated. "Do you mean in or out of the arena?"

"Pick one."

She looked up and stared straight into my eyes, as if trying to bore through to the back of my skull. Then she shifted her head, trying to appear innocent. She didn't.

"You look uncomfortable."

I shifted in my chair. "That's because I feel uncomfortable."

"There's no need. Most gamers are in therapy. They're prone to an unusually high likelihood for psychological instability." The woman spoke like a computer: matter-of-fact and little variation to her tone of voice.

"Psychological instability," I repeated. "What does that mean?"

"They lose their grip on reality."

My stomach twisted as thoughts drifted through my mind, a juxtaposition of both worlds: the swaying wheat fields and mountain air of the virtual against the plastic and metal of this one. One of warmth and light against one sterile and barren. And fake. No wonder gamers got lost in what was real. But not me. I was in control. I practically owned the virtual world.

Whenever a gamer did lose it, an official statement was immediately released to the press to squash any rumors. Retired early to spend time with family. Left the tournaments to pursue other interests. Hospitalized for exhaustion. Really, who ever buys that one? That old saying *There's no such thing as bad press* is bullshit.

The doctor toyed with her glasses again.

"Tell me, what do you feel when you look at yourself in the mirror?"

"Like I'm looking at myself in the mirror." I forced my tone serious, but it wavered toward sarcasm by the end. This was so stupid.

"Did you know that the first wave of participants in the VGL were athletes turned gamers? It was—"

"A disaster," I finished for her. "Athletes don't understand the virtual world. How could they? A fish can't swim in honey just because it's liquid."

"That's"—she paused as she processed my words—"an interesting analogy."

"Most of them lost their minds. Or, excuse me, were subject to psychological instabilities." I forced my lips into a smile. Her eyes narrowed slightly. Guess she figured out my sarcasm. She wasn't wrong, though. When virtual gaming went fully immersive, they'd first pulled in athletes to play the games. In most video games, a character is assigned to you. On occasion, the game allows you to create one of your own, most commonly in RPGs and MMOs. But in pro gaming, you are your avatar, and what you were capable of in reality was parallel to the digital domain.

Gaming evolves quickly. Every few years, a new system comes out capable of ten times what it did before. In only a few decades, VR went from basic headsets to full immersion. But when it hit, almost no pro gamers were already in top physical condition. So, they pulled in athletes, who had already trained their entire lives to play a pro sport, and tried to teach them gaming.

But going virtual required something more. Something only gamers understood. As much as skill sets depended on physical ability in reality, they were only valuable if you knew what you were doing inside a game. All their lives, gamers had learned how to manipulate the virtual, how one action or choice could change the outcome of the entire game. We'd learned to read the lines of digital fate. We'd learned how to make the games do what we wanted.

We'd learned that death was nothing more than a do-over.

Athletes didn't. They couldn't. So once the attempts to turn them into gamers had failed, they started turning gamers into athletes. Required to train in everything from weight lifting to weapons, gamers had become the greatest competitors the world had ever seen.

"Gamers are the only ones who can handle fully immersive VR," I told the doc. "We grow up wrapped in a virtual world. We die every day on the screen in console and arcade games. It's no different when we plug in and go virtual."

"Is it?"

My gut twisted again. I shrugged it off. "Well, sure, the pro level is something else. With the safeguards off, we feel pain. Things seem real, sometimes realer than this place." I waved a hand at the office. "But it's just like a dream. You can feel pain or fear in a dream, but once you wake up, you realize it was no big deal."

The doctor scoffed. "People don't go crazy from dreaming." She looked down and mumbled the words, as if they weren't really for me to hear. Silence fell over the room while she made a note in her tablet. "Speaking of dreams, how are you sleeping?"

"Fine . . . until today."

"Clarence told me what happened with Nathan. Did you want to talk about that?"

"No."

She rested the tablet against the desk and leaned toward me. "I'm not going to force you on the topic. Not during our first meeting."

Our only meeting.

"But in time," she continued, "it might be good for you to open up about that. Keep it in mind."

I nodded. Yeah, right.

She stood and walked over to a cabinet on the far side of the room. "Just in case you have trouble sleeping," she said as she unlocked the door and reached inside, "I'm going to give you some pills to help. Don't be afraid to take them, but only if you have to. Use discretion."

She handed me a small, silver package, like the kind gum comes in. Sample pills. I took it in my hand.

"I won't give you any additional pills for a while," she said. "Not until those should be gone. I trust you can manage it." She motioned toward the exit. Guess it was time to leave. "My door is always open."

I offered a smile as fake as her lips and left. Open door, my ass. A degree in psychiatry hadn't taught her much. Like I'd ever come back here. Instead, I headed right for the one place I could really work out my issues.

The training room. My teammates were already there.

Hannah stood in the warm-up area. A trainer clamped his hands on her stomach, keeping her abdomen rigid, as she leaned into a stretching lunge. She grimaced and grasped her knee. Must have overdone it this morning. The trainer shook his head and dropped down to examine it.

Across the room, Lily ran on a treadmill. Another trainer tracked her time and heartbeat. Running wasn't just cardio for us. In the arena, speed could mean life or death, and a second faster in this world meant a second faster in the virtual.

The trainer barked something, and Lily's legs pumped faster.

Derek stood on the side of the floor mats, where we practiced fighting. He saw me and flashed a grin.

"Care to join," he called, holding up two wooden swords. "I need someone who'll give me a challenge."

Therapy. Pffft.

This was therapy.

He handed me a sword, and we took our stances on the mat. Derek squared his feet and raised the sword until it was parallel to his head and pointing right at me. My breath caught in my throat. It was the same pose Nathan had struck the last time we fought, just two days before. I shook my head and charged him. He swiped my thrust down and slammed his shoulder into mine, knocking me to the side. I grunted and circled the mat. Derek took the same pose. I cringed, charged again, and swung, missing him by a good six inches. He grabbed my wrist and pointed my sword down.

"You okay?"

"I'm fine."

"No, you're not. Most days, you're so smooth, you move like a freaking ballerina with a sword. Today, you're a mechanical wind-up toy."

I looked up at him, blinking. My jaw was clenched. Breaths wheezed through my lungs. Every muscle was taut and tense.

I sighed.

My shoulders dropped, and my sword tumbled to the mat with a dull thud. I plopped down and buried my face in my hands.

No, I was not okay.

The whole world was inside out and backwards. Nathan was gone. Our team was on the edge of forfeit and one loss away from defeat. This was not how things were supposed to go. Why couldn't I just jam my fingers inside the path of my life and make it go straight again? This was not the way I pictured my career as a pro gamer would go when I'd made it into the amateur league only the year before.

They say you'll always remember the firsts. First kiss. First car. First time away from home. None compare to the first time you go virtual.

The first time I'd climbed into the pod, eyes wide, and watched as the doors closed around me and the wires attached to my skin. Their soft, pulsing jolts flooded my skin with chills. I exhaled slowly, pushing out the giddy nervousness with my breath. Then I felt the pull, and disappeared into a world where the strength and speed of the body and the focus and discipline of the mind became one. I'd never gone virtual. Not like this. Where I closed my eyes on reality and opened them to something more.

Inside the tower, I closed my eyes and breathed deep. The scents of lilac and wheatgrass filled my lungs as the wind breezed across my face. I knelt and sieved my fingers through the sand. It was warm and grainy, and golden like the sunlight streaming in through the tower walls.

Footsteps pounded up the path to the tower. A simulated opponent appeared in the doorway and lunged for me. I scrambled for my sword and pushed to my feet just as he attacked.

When his sword sliced through my skin, I froze.

Pain ripped through my abdomen with a sharp, stinging heat, like I'd been lashed by a whip. Thick gobbets of blood oozed from my stomach. I touched it tentatively and came away with soaked fingers. Something pink and shiny prodded through the opening. I gagged.

He drove his sword through my chest and ripped it out again.

I dropped to my knees. My fingers went numb and ice-cold. Death was an animated thing, slithering up my arms and chest until it wrapped around my throat and crushed my last, gasping breath.

I woke with a jolt, slamming back to this world. Slick with sweat, trembling uncontrollably, I breathed through my hand and forced my stomach calm, thankful that the pod's solid doors kept my reaction concealed from everyone else. I coughed and sputtered until tears stung my eyes and dribbled down my face. As my body slowly recovered, I started to laugh, and kept laughing until there were new tears in my eyes. Nothing like seeing your own insides to make you feel mortal.

Nothing like coming back to life to make you feel like a god.

Something happened to me then. I'd passed enough milestones in life to recognize that paradoxical sensation: a dose of fulfillment that leaves you feeling just a little bit empty. High-school graduation. Loss of virginity. Right then, in that moment, I knew without a sliver of a doubt: Another piece of my innocence was gone.

When I exited the pod, my teammates scoffed at me.

"Nice going, Ling. My grandmother could fight better than that."

Even in the amateurs, expectations ran high. Everyone here was trying to make it to the pros. I scowled at myself. I could do better than that. I had to do better.

The next simulation, I dropped my sword on the stone floor and drew my dagger instead. They'd put two of us on defense this time, and my teammate surveyed my dropped weapon with a furrowed brow.

"What are you doing?"

Footsteps beat up the path to the tower. I bolted. Just when a simulated warrior appeared, I jumped up and pushed off the entrance's edge. I flew. My blade sliced through his throat in a single swipe. When he collapsed to the stone floor, I ran down the path from the tower. Behind me, my teammate's footsteps followed and stopped at the tower's entrance, knowing he couldn't leave and still hold the tower.

"Kali!"

I pumped my legs, ignoring the clawing fingers of virtual delicacies. The sights and smells, and overwhelming sensations.

I slipped through the fields, weaving like a serpent through bamboo. From tower to tower, I became an assassin, pouncing on backs and ripping my dagger through the throats of every virtual opponent—much to my teammates' openmouthed reactions. I slid into their in-progress fights and took out every enemy with nothing but a single blade. On the final opponent inside the enemy's team, I hooked a leg around his knee and followed him down, jamming my dagger through his heart. A last, heaving breath escaped his lungs, and his eyes glazed over.

Victory.

I closed my eyes, and gave myself to the virtual world. To the white-noise whispers of the wind through the stocks. To the wheatgrass and lilac, and the golden rays of light. I stood and raised my arms in the air. There were no cheers, no applause. But honor, greatness, and pride were all mine, filling my chest until I thought it would explode.

I was born to do this, and only this.

I woke without a gasp, as if I'd simply opened my eyes from sleep. But as I stared into darkness inside the pod, nothing but emptiness thrummed within me, as if the greatness I'd felt had been just another construct of the digital world. Of all the competitions I'd won, everything I'd accomplished in my life, nothing had compared. That was true glory, and it only ever manifested itself in one place.

The arena.

If I'd been granted one wish in my entire life, I would have cashed in right then.

Let me go back.

When I exited the pod, my teammates stared at me, stunned and blinking. I cringed, waiting for their retaliation. They surged forward and tackled me. In celebration. They whooped and hollered, and wrapped me in giant bear hugs, hoisting me off the ground, squeezing me against their chests until I couldn't breathe. I'd proven myself, and they gave me a name.

The warrior.

But now, sitting on the mats inside the facility, I felt like anything but my given namesake. I scrubbed my palms against my eyes. I should have told Derek everything. How sleep was a distant thing. How tight my chest got whenever I'd think about . . . anything, really.

How sure I was that my dream of making it as a pro gamer was about to be snuffed out.

"I can't focus," I told him.

Yup. That's all that came out.

The mat sank in front of me as Derek took a knee.

"It's because of Nathan, isn't it?"

That made up a good chunk of this mess, yes. I muttered something inaudible against my palms. Even I don't know what I said.

"Look, it's hard, and I understand that. And it's important to remember him. But you can't let it get to you like this. It's in your head and in your muscles. You're feeling it everywhere, and that's not good. If you keep it in your heart, it'll fuel you. If you keep it everywhere else, it'll weigh you down."

"It's easy for you. You didn't even like him."

"Don't say that. We're all feeling the loss. I miss him, too, you know."

Yeah, like a cat misses a dog. I looked up at him.

"You hated each other."

He shrugged. "Sure, we didn't get along too well, but we were teammates. Even when you hate each other, you gotta find a way to make it work. Yeah, there were days I wanted to just punch him in the head. But he was an awesome gamer and an incredible athlete, and I respected him for that. With everything we gotta do together, living together, working together, that makes us like family. And you love your family, no matter what, even when you hate them." He paused and glanced in the distance. "Which is kind of weird calling this family because I think that's hot."

He nodded behind me.

Hannah sat against the far wall as Lily wrapped a brace around her knee. She trailed her fingers across Hannah's skin as they traded heated, fleeting glances and soft giggles. Lily secured the brace and kissed Hannah's knee. Then they pressed their foreheads together, nuzzled noses, and smiled.

That was love. Real love. Not media-driven, photoshopped, airbrushed bullshit like so many of the relationships in this industry. All the rivalries, friendships, and twisted love stories in the VGL, more often than not, were purely constructed. For ratings. But whether or not Clarence had manufactured that particular relationship, what those two had was melt-together, crush-your-heart real.

I hadn't loved Nathan. Not like they loved each other. Hell, I didn't know what that even meant, to feel that kind of emotion for another human being.

"You know," Derek began, "the real gladiators would have honored Nathan by fighting for him, by earning him victories in the arena. Not by sitting on the mats."

I frowned but knew he was right. I wasn't achieving anything by moping.

He stood.

"Come on, warrior," he said, offering both his hand and a grin. I glanced between him and his open palm a few times. He sighed. "Don't make me haul your ass up."

Now, that lit the fire inside.

I smacked his hand away, grabbed my sword, and shot to my feet.

His grin widened. "There you are."

I grinned with him, but inside the fire waned a little. Derek was the natural leader here, not me. And yet, I was captain of the team. I should have told him right then. The girls already knew.

He took a stance opposite me and waggled his eyebrows. I chuckled and raised my sword. He advanced, moving swiftly across the mats. We met, wooden swords clacking together. Everything felt just a little bit lighter with an animated blade in my hands, real or not. It stirred within the qualities most familiar to me. Strength, determination, and an unstoppable, unquenchable drive—to kick ass.

Once the new recruit was here. Then, I'd tell Derek.

For now, we fought.

# CHAPTER 7

Thursday was the day.

At the crack of dawn, after nearly murdering my alarm clock with my bare hands, I rolled over in bed to see my tablet blinking with a new message from Clarence.

When the five of us had first arrived at the facility, we were required to turn in our phones and other devices and were issued tablets, with a catch—they had no access to social media. We could make and receive calls, review Web sites, or watch videos, but couldn't post anything online. Heaven forbid we said something the sponsors didn't like. Any comments or messages posted by "us" were the PR reps posing as the team.

Since Nathan's death, we hadn't been allowed out, either. No press conferences. No photo shoots. Only four on the team would make us look weak and incomplete, and that wasn't good for our image. Only when the new recruit arrived would we be free to make appearances again. In the meantime, it had been three grueling days of endless training. Single-leg jump rope. Handstand push-ups. One-arm pull-ups. Combinations that would have made army generals raise an eyebrow. The trainers were especially harsh since we'd lost the Death Match and couldn't afford to lose again.

Yesterday morning had been the third in a row of nonstop torture until I heard the sweetest three words of the entire week.

"Five-minute break," the trainers called.

The only thing better would have been *The coffee's ready.*

I collapsed on the mats, breathing hard. Sweat matted my hair to my forehead. One by one, my teammates slumped down beside me. We must have looked like scattered bowling pins.

"This blows," Hannah said between gasps. "We're already in top physical condition. Why are they drilling us like this?" She nodded back at the trainers, who were huddled together in the far corner, probably formulating a plan for how to finally kill us.

"Hey, we did lose one," Derek pointed out. "Obviously, we need it. This is what it takes to be a pro."

We all grimaced but nodded in agreement. He was right. My stomach sank as if it had gone right through the mats. Derek was so clearly the leader, and yet I had been crowned with the task. It was like choosing a peasant instead of King Arthur to rule over Albion. Not that I didn't believe in myself. But hey, King Arthur.

"Are we even a team anymore?" Hannah asked. "We don't have a fifth player."

Somehow, my stomach sank even more, down through the subfloor. I stared up at the ceiling, blinking. There were only a few days before the next match and if the new guy didn't get here soon, we'd have no time to make us into a team again.

*I'd* have no time to make us into a team again.

"InvictUS knows what it takes," Lily said. "To beat us, at least."

Hannah leaned closer to us and lowered her voice. "I don't know about you guys, but I'm still reeling. How come we did so well in the preseason, then got creamed by them? I thought we were unstoppable."

Because they'd practiced their brains out, played it smart by

holding back in the preseason, didn't waste so much time promoting their sponsors, and had a strong leader.

A strong leader. Time to start stepping up.

"Leave the past in the past," I said. "If you're always looking
behind you, you'll miss what's happening right now."

It seemed like the right thing to say, but my teammates all
stared at me, blinking, as if I'd just started speaking in tongues.
I frowned.

"I mean, what's done is done. The only way to be ready for
the next match is to focus on the here and now."

Hannah glanced back at the trainers as they broke from their
huddle and came toward us. "Well, what's here and now is
another five laps around the track."

My teammates groaned. We still had a good eight hours of
training left even though we had about eight minutes' worth of
energy between us. What would a leader do in this situation?

Bolster their spirits.

"Quick," I said. "Favorite classic video game. Go."

Derek started it off, and the rest of us followed suit.

"Street Fighter II."

"Zelda's Ocarina of Time."

"God of War."

"Bubble Bobble."

Derek sat up. "Which one of you just said Bubble Bobble?"

Hannah pointed at her girlfriend and giggled. "Lily!"

Derek tilted his head at her. "Seriously?"

She shrugged. "I like bubbles."

We all laughed.

"Thanks, Kali," Hannah said. "I needed that."

Well, that went exactly how I'd hoped. Leadership skill +2.

The trainers appeared over us, hands on their hips. They

looked like shadow figures against the harsh lighting overhead, like cowboys in an old Western at high noon.

"Get up," they barked.

These guys were lucky they weren't my alarm clock.

Every day went like this. At least the physical training was interlaced with more and more time in the virtual world. Without the barrage of public appearances, I could return to the only place I'd ever truly belonged without convincing my programmer to risk her job just so I could get a few extra minutes in the digital.

Every night, I'd pop a sleeping pill and face-plant into bed. The exercise put me under instantly, and the pills kept dreams of Nathan at bay. Guess the extra workout was good for more than just the arena.

Then, on Thursday morning, it happened. The new recruit was here, and this boot-camp nightmare that had become my life was about to end. Well, at least ease back a notch. Never thought I'd be looking forward to the media events, but now I was practically drooling for them.

I picked up the tablet and tapped the screen to open the message.

Team,

Meet in my office at 07:30.

Clarence

I didn't know how Clarence managed to make e-mails so circumspect, but he succeeded. With no details whatsoever, the message was agonizingly thought-provoking. Who was the new recruit?

I rushed through my morning shower and was mostly dressed when the buzzer at my door rang. I scrambled to answer it, rolling my shirt down as I went. When my bunk door slid open, Derek stood on the other side.

"Hey. Did you get the message from Clarence?"

I nodded. "I'm assuming it's about the new recruit?"

"Yeah. Hannah and Lily are already there. You ready? Wanna walk together?"

"Sure."

I punched the lock code into my keypad and fell in step beside Derek down the metal corridor.

"Any word on who this guy is?" I asked.

"No." He paused. "Wait, you know it's a guy?"

I shrugged. "Just an assumption. I mean, four girls wouldn't give a balanced look to the team. You know—"

"Image is everything."

We said it together, exchanged glances, and burst out laughing. Clarence had programmed us gamers almost as much as the game itself. To see female gamers in the VGL wasn't unusual. In fact, the ratio was nearly one in three. Ever since the VGL was founded, female gamers stood alongside men and competed in the same tournaments. Hell, the first year had a girl gamer as the third overall draft pick. She'd never been named captain, but she went on to win several championships in both the Special Ops and Racing events. Her name was Jessica Salt.

If I could, I'd kiss her feet.

But women in the RAGE tournaments were a bit of an oddity. In a game that relied so heavily on physical strength and size, the only women who made it through had elite fighting skills and a deep understanding of using their opponent's weight to their advantage. And to have a team that was majority female was unheard of. Until now.

"Not that I'd mind being with four ladies," Derek continued. "I'd prefer it, actually."

I punched him in the arm, and he laughed.

"Well," I began, "let's hope whoever he got isn't some bottom-of-the-barrel chum he recruited at the last minute."

"Are you kidding? I would have cut someone's legs off if it gave me the chance to go pro."

Competitive, much? We all were. It was part of the game.

"What did you do before you were here?" I asked him.

"I was in school for computer programming."

"School?" I repeated. "Computer programming?"

"What? Can't I have an interest outside of games?" he asked. "Okay, okay. I was on the school's eSports team, so I had to take something. Was pretty damn good, too."

"At programming or gaming?"

"Both."

He flashed me a grin. On most people, an ego that size would have been off-putting, but there was something about Derek's lack of modesty that came across as charming, not arrogant. He glanced at me a few times.

"I never got to ask before," he began, pausing for a beat. "Are you okay?"

"What do you mean?"

"You know, with Nathan."

"Well, to lose a teammate is—"

"Listen." He gave me a look. "I know you two were . . . umm . . ."

I threw my arms up. "Is there anybody who didn't know?"

"The press didn't. That's what matters."

Was it?

The mention of Nathan churned my heart. Not because of

me, really. Nathan and I hadn't been much more than friends with benefits. But for his family. His future. Gone at twenty-one. All the things people say when someone dies young crept into my thoughts. So much potential. So much talent. Wasted.

Could I have done something to save him? If I hadn't gone to Clarence's office . . . if I'd taken the drugs away . . . Oh hell, I didn't know.

Clanking footsteps echoed in my ears. I snapped back to reality and glanced at Derek. He stared at me with squinting eyes and a furrowed brow. I must have been quiet for a several minutes since he'd asked.

"I'm fine," I finally said.

"I heard you saw the shrink."

I waved a hand to dismiss it. "Clarence's orders. Not my choice."

"Still, considering what happened—"

"I said I'm fine," I snapped.

Derek recoiled and held up a hand. "Just checking."

I pulled back and glanced at my feet. "Yeah. Sorry."

"Whatever. It's fine."

But silence dominated the conversation between us as we reached the elevator and stepped inside. It started the slow climb to Clarence's office at the top of the tower. For once, I found myself wishing for some cheesy elevator music to ease the weight of the crushing quiet around us. I had a topic to break the silence. Hey, guess what? I've been named team captain, not you. Yeah, that would go well. I sighed. Better to tell him myself. He'd find out eventually.

Okay, here goes.

"I need to tell you something you're not going to like," I said, as if it would buffer the blow. I kept my eyes pinned on the elevator's doors. "Clarence appointed me team captain."

After more seconds of silence, I glanced at him out of the corner of my eye. His features were soft. No set jaw or grinding teeth. Well, at least he wasn't too pissed about it.

"Really?" he asked.

"Yeah. At first, I thought Clarence just did it to keep you and Nathan from killing each other. But now, even with Nathan gone, he's not changing his mind."

The elevator dinged. We walked down a hallway of floor tiles and drywall. Green and white. What else?

"Has there ever been a female captain at the pro level before?" he asked.

"No."

He looked up at me. "Then you need to take this opportunity and own it. You have to. That's a big deal, to be the first to do something."

I pressed my lips together. It was, but was I ready?

"Besides," he continued, "I'll be captain one day. Come on, look at this face."

He unleashed a million-dollar smile. I laughed.

Of course he'd be captain one day—IF I didn't screw it up for him. My stomach twisted sideways. The team's fate now rested on my shoulders. Their careers, their futures, their hopes and dreams, all depended on my ability to lead them to victory. I took a deep breath and swallowed, but my stomach kept swirling. Why had I been so eager for responsibility as a kid? Was this what it was all about? Seemed ulcer-inducing now.

We pushed through the double doors to Clarence's office. As Derek had mentioned earlier, Hannah and Lily were already inside.

Hannah hurried over to me.

"Something's wrong," she announced in a hushed voice.

I stopped dead. "What?"

"I was gay before I entered the office. And then, that happened."

She pointed to the guy standing with Clarence on the other side of the room. My mouth dropped open, and my swirling stomach became an inferno, spreading heat . . . everywhere else. His chiseled cheekbones and hard jaw looked as if the Romans themselves had carved him out of stone. But wait, hello, a statue didn't boast tanned skin or piercing, dark eyes. Along with his six-foot frame and perfect build, give him a couple of scars, and he'd be a gladiator in true form. And, who knew? Maybe he did have some scars, hidden somewhere beneath his clothes.

Clarence's gaze fell on the four of us, and he led the new recruit over, motioning with an outstretched hand like a used-car salesman leading his newest victim through the lot. He smiled, and I thought his face would crack.

"Good morning, everyone. Allow me to introduce your newest teammate: James Rooke."

So, the statue had a name.

Clarence motioned toward us again. "James, meet your team."

"Rooke," the recruit corrected. "I go by my last name."

Clarence studied him for a minute. "Good. I like that better."

Of course he did.

"This is your captain," Clarence told him, nodding at me. I stepped forward and started to extend my hand when Clarence turned back to him, and asked, "Is that going to be a problem?"

Rooke studied me through the slits of his eyes. Then, he scoffed and shook his head.

"No."

Wow. What the hell was that about?

Rooke stared at me and blinked once, emotionless. Then his gaze flicked back to Clarence and never left, as if the rest of us weren't even in the room. Jeez, he really was a statue, and had brought with him a front colder than anything that had ever passed through California. Was there any personality behind that stone façade? Hell, was there a person back there?

Or was it all just part of his image? A hard-ass. A stone-cold soldier. Sounded like something Clarence would come up with.

"We have only a few days before the start of the tournament," Clarence said to the group. Like he had to make the announcement. To gamers, these tournaments were religion. Except everyone in this room prayed to the gods of Xbox and PlayStation.

"I expect you to train a minimum of ten hours each day," he continued. "I also expect you to be out every night. You need to be seen by every camera in the city."

"Why?" Derek asked.

"Why?" Clarence spat. "First you lose, and now this little disaster." He flicked a hand toward a poster of Nathan. "We have to damage-control this situation before no sponsor will ever touch us again. Expect a barrage of interviews and photo shoots and whatever else I can land us. If you can still see after all the camera flashes, then we haven't done enough. Is that clear?"

None of us answered, or argued. We all knew what was expected of us.

"Now, if you'll excuse me," Clarence continued, "I have some announcements to make regarding our new recruit."

When he exited the room and shut the door behind him, he left behind the awkward silence that usually accompanied him on the way out. I stood with my teammates on one side while Rooke stood alone on the other, a good five feet between us. No one made a move to welcome him. Oh wait, I was the team's leader now. Guess that was my job.

I took a step forward. Rooke stared straight ahead, as if admiring some spot in the wall beyond me. Heat burned in my chest, though not the enjoyable kind like earlier. My fingers itched to clamp onto his jaw and force his head down, to meet my eye.

Just then, his gaze flicked to mine, dark eyes penetrating right through me.

The good kind of heat was back. I ignored it.

Mostly.

Rooke stared at me, unwavering, with the same stone-faced look as always. Did this guy have another expression? Or did he really think he could intimidate me with that glare?

It was time for him to meet the warrior.

I stepped up to Rooke, closing the gap between us, folded my arms as I stared up at him, and let a cunning grin curl through my lips.

"Okay, pretty boy. Let's see what you can do."

I worked with the new guy.

Well, *worked* was a generous word. It implied progress, like the kneading of clay. It starts out tough but gradually warms up until the sculptor and material become one. Rooke was nothing but a concrete block, refusing to mold at all. I felt like a toddler trying to smash the square peg into the round hole.

"Okay," I said, standing across from him on the mats. "I'll attack first. I want to get a feel for your defensive skills."

I took up my position and attacked.

So did he.

He swung, knocked my sword to the side, and rammed his shoulder into mine. I spun, lost balance, and hit the mat. Hard.

Okay, yeah. The guy had skill. But for everything he had in talent, he completely lacked in teamwork and personality. This guy belonged with InvictUS, not us.

I pushed up to my feet and retrieved my sword.

"You fight like InvictUS," I told him. "And I mean that as a compliment. They destroyed us in the Death Match."

"I saw it."

Three words. That was the most I'd gotten out of him so far. I was starting to wonder if this guy was really on the team, or if Clarence was just paying him to test my leadership skills. And my temper. What the hell was I supposed to do with him? I was Kali Ling the warrior, not the diplomat.

After three more rounds exactly like the last, I called a break before I went all Incredible Hulk on his ass.

Leadership skill -5.

I plopped down on the nearest bench, scooped up a water bottle, and chugged half, straining not to crush the bioplastic beneath my grip. Across the room, Rooke pressed himself into a corner and stared at the floor. His jaw was clenched so tightly, it looked like he'd bitten his own tongue off. Did this guy have some kind of injury he was hiding? He didn't move like it on the mats, but now, huddled in the corner, every muscle taut, he looked like he was trying not to vomit.

"How's training with the new guy?" Hannah asked, sidling up beside me.

"I think I'd rather chew scrap metal."

She chuckled and glanced at him in the corner. "Maybe he's just nervous or feels left out. He is coming into this late."

"Yeah. He's not exactly making it easy, either."

She shrugged. "Well, you're good at finding ways to make this fun. Why not show him that?" She looked across the training room and caught eyes with her trainer. He hooked his finger at her, a signal to return to the treadmill. Her shoulders sank. "Fun. Heaven forbid." She pushed up from the bench and started toward the trainer, looking back at me as she left. "I mean, isn't this supposed to be a game?"

As Hannah resumed her workout, I sat on the bench a minute longer, letting her words sink in. Make it fun. I took another swig of water before getting to my feet. As I walked toward the mats, I waved the recruit over. Rooke stood and met me halfway.

"Before we begin again," I said. "Favorite classic video game. Go."

He blinked. Come on, guy. Give me something. I crossed my arms and waited him out. Finally, he sighed.

"Final Fantasy VII."

I resisted the urge to take a step back. The man had taste.

"Not bad," I said, "if you like turn-based."

I grinned. He didn't.

Arrrgh.

Kali! Smash!

The rest of the morning played out the same. I did everything I could think of to make it fun, trying to draw Rooke out from his rock-hard shell. All I got in return was a combo of icy stares and grumbled half sentences.

We had forty-eight hours to prep for the next round. Since the Death Match loss had landed us in the losers' bracket, one more loss meant we'd be kicked out. Every Saturday, another round of the tournament would air. Those victorious in the winners' bracket advanced. Those who lost dropped down to the losers' bracket. Those who lost in the losers' bracket went home.

That afternoon, I gathered the team around and threw together a plan for the matchup on Saturday.

"Are you comfortable with going on offense?" I asked Hannah.

She nodded. "It's been awhile, but I've done it before."

"Good. We're going two on three. Hannah and Derek on offense. Lily, myself, and Rooke"—I glanced at him—"we'll go on defense."

Rooke stared back, expression cold, but didn't argue. Good. Given his unsportsmanlike attitude, I wanted to keep an eye on him.

"Three on defense?" Derek asked. "That's a little basic."

"It's standard, but we've just reformatted the team. We need to play it safe."

Derek considered it. "Yeah, you're right. Sounds good."

We had a plan. Everyone on the team had their place. Too bad the next forty-eight hours didn't follow suit.

Derek and Hannah worked together in the training room with practice swords. Derek attacked, holding nothing back. He pummeled Hannah's sword again and again until she tumbled off the mat.

"What is your problem?" she demanded, pushing herself up.

"You have to fight hard on offense. Step it up."

Hannah scowled and shook her head, but they paired off again. When Derek swung, he hit Hannah's weapon so hard it went flying to the side, where Lily sat watching. It smashed into her ankle. Lily's yelp echoed through the training room. The trainers had to carry her to the medical wing. A sprain. She'd be playing on a weak ankle. Even in the virtual world, the injury would carry over. The pain would be much less than here but would still affect her speed and mobility.

Fan-fucking-tastic.

Speaking of injured players, Rooke was definitely hiding something. During training, he'd grimace and grit his teeth when he thought I wasn't looking, had to take way too many breaks for someone in top physical condition, and was locked in his bunk any minute we weren't training together or doing media events. Even when we sat down for meals, he'd take his food and leave, head held high like he was better than the rest of us. I felt like gouging out his eyes with my spoon.

The virtual simulations weren't going any better. Long after I'd jolted back to reality, I sat in my pod, shaking my head. We'd already wiped three times that morning.

Derek shot out of his pod the second the doors opened.

"Hannah, how many times do I have to say it?" he demanded. "You can't fight cautiously on offense. You have to charge, no holding back."

She threw her arms up. "I haven't gone on offense since the amateurs! What do you expect? I need time to adjust."

"We don't have time."

"Guys," I began. "Let's reevaluate the gameplay—"

"What do you want to do?" Hannah continued, staring straight at Derek. "Change our format?"

"We can't change our format. It's less than twelve hours until the matchup."

"We're not changing our format," I tried again. "Listen—"

But my words were drowned out by Hannah and Derek's argument. Every attempt I made at neutralizing the situation failed. I sighed and looked around the room. Lily stood off to the side, well out of the fight, leaning against a wall to keep the weight off her swollen foot. Rooke watched for a minute, too, and left, disappearing through the exit without a word to anyone. Goddamn recruit. I considered going after him; but what was the point? With Hannah and Derek screaming at each other, Lily not caring to get involved, and Rooke only focused on himself, something inside me simply gave up. I shuffled over to my pod, climbed inside, and buried my head in my hands.

After a minute, I pressed my back against the seat, silently praying for the jolt out of reality, out of this situation, and out of my life. It wouldn't have mattered. There was no escaping the hopelessness of the situation.

We weren't a team, we weren't even close to being ready, and we were out of time.

# LEVEL 2:

## THE TOURNAMENT

# CHAPTER 8

For what seemed like the last time, I stood inside the tower. Now that the tournament had begun, and we were already sitting in the losers' bracket after the Death Match, one loss would send us home. After what I'd witnessed in the past two days, there was no way we'd make it through this round. Even if I'd had any inkling of hope of us working together and making it through the match alive, it had since been crushed by Rooke. As soon as we loaded into the game, he turned away from me and stared at the wall.

Teamwork. What was that again?

In standard play, the matches endured until the last man died or the tower was captured. For tonight's matchup, Hannah and Derek had run for the enemy's tower. Lily hid in the trees. Rooke and I guarded our tower. Two on offense and three on defense, as was the plan. For what it would be worth.

The match was thirty seconds in, and while InvictUS had shown how quickly a team could sweep through the fields, no one could make it to the opposing tower in under a minute. Which meant I had a bit of time to check Rooke out—for his injuries, of course.

I looked at him. Er, no—I dug holes into his bare back with nothing but my eyes. He wore plated armor, not much more than wrist bracers and shoulder armor, and enough leather to cover his feet and goody package. Sunlight streamed in through the tower's barred windows and glistened across his tanned skin and on the dual short swords he wielded. Yup, a gladiator. Traditional to the core. But it was what I didn't see that bothered me. No wounds. No burns, scars, or signs of broken bones. Either his injuries were internal, or something else was going on with him.

Maybe he just plain hated working with me. I had two guesses why.

"Hey."

No response.

Rooke kept his back to me. A quiet calm filled the tower, a direct contrast to my trembling fists and clenched teeth. I drew my sword from its sheath and smacked the flat side against his leg. He jumped and turned enough to glare at me over his shoulder.

"What?"

"I have a question for you."

"You wanna chitchat through the match?" he asked. "Is that why you lost the last one?"

I met his biting stare. When I held it for more than a minute, he rolled his eyes.

"Before you ask," he began, voice dull as if he'd repeated the words several times before, "I have hundreds of hours of experience in simulated battle situations—"

"Are you racist or sexist?"

He faltered, mouth hanging open for a second before he pushed more words out of it. "Excuse me?"

"When Clarence asked if you had a problem with me as team captain, you hesitated. Now, you've been a complete pain in the ass since we've met for no reason other than you've had to work with me. So I'm asking, is the reason because I'm a woman or because I'm part Chinese?"

He looked me up and down. "You're only part Chinese?"

Bingo.

I took a breath. Okay, everyone has their gripes. Best way to deal with it is to show how we're all the same, underneath. Still, something churned in my chest. Heartburn? No. Disgust. I swallowed it down and forced the next words out through my teeth.

"I'm half-American, if that helps anything."

He studied me for a minute and returned to his staring contest with the wall. "It doesn't matter."

"Because only completely American counts?"

"Because I don't care."

The trees rustled just outside the tower. Sharp, rough movements, not from any wind.

Lily's signal.

The enemy approached.

Rooke's grip tightened on his swords and moved toward the tower's entrance. I grabbed his arm and pulled back.

"We wait here. Draw them in."

He shook his head. "That's stupid."

"Forcing your enemy to fight on two fronts is not stupid. Lily's got the rear."

"By herself?"

"Trust me."

He stepped forward anyway, until I pressed my sword against his neck. He halted.

"One more step, and I'll take you out of the fight myself," I warned.

He stared me down, trying to call my bluff. But I don't bluff. When I held his glare again, he scowled and took a step back.

Footsteps echoed up the tower's path. Rooke's attention snapped to the entrance. My grip tightened around my sword. Two men and one woman appeared at the mouth of the tower.

Pushing in with three. Because of InvictUS's format during the Death Match, other teams were becoming bolder in their strategies as well.

They advanced toward us. We held, waiting for Lily to appear behind them.

They split into two as they approached, the larger male going for Rooke. He waved him forward, taunting him. Rooke went for it and met him in the middle. The clang of sword meeting sword echoed off the walls of the tower.

Damn it. Fucking amateur.

The remaining warriors bolted for me.

The guy reached me first, several feet ahead. I bent at the knee and propelled myself into the air, kicking out with both feet. I hit him squarely in the chest. He went flying back. The axe tumbled from his hand.

I landed on the ground in a crouching stance as the woman reached me. Swinging out with my sword, I sliced right through her kneecaps. She screamed as she collapsed to the ground, legless. I pounced on top of her and slit her throat. Her screams ceased, and her eyes glazed over. She went limp. Instant kill.

Her teammate recovered, now on his feet. Axe in hand, he raced toward me. Metal clanged against metal as his axe smashed against my sword in rapid succession. He spun, locking my arms around his. His axe neared my face. He pushed his weight into it and barreled down on me. My legs trembled and bent. I grimaced and strained against him.

My knee touched dirt. His axe inched closer.

And closer.

Steel grazed the skin of my cheek, piercing at the outermost layer. Cool. Smooth. It was nothing. A paper cut. I swallowed my gasp and pushed. My hands started to shake.

He grinned.

I'm dead. Game over.

Lily appeared behind him, an axe gripped with both hands. She brought it down and sliced through his neck in one swipe. His severed head landed on my feet and rolled away. Blood gushed out of his neck as he fell forward and onto me. I kicked the body away, but not before blood doused me from head to toe.

Lily helped me to my feet. I ran my hands down my body. Blood splattered on the stone floor in thick splats.

Rooke pulled his sword out of his fallen opponent and turned to us. He gave me the once-over, taking in my drenched appearance, and offered a cocky grin.

"Nice teamwork."

That asshole.

I charged for him. As I neared without slowing, his grin faded. I raised my sword. He took a defensive stance, sword held horizontally in front of him. A grin tugged at my lips. Another one that had underestimated me. This would be oh, so sweet.

Just as I reached him, an arm wrapped around my waist and lugged me back. Lily. Jesus, how strong was she? I struggled against the viselike grip around my waist, sword still pointed at Rooke.

"What the fuck is your problem?" he demanded. He had the nerve to look pissed.

Lily released me, and I marched up to him. "My problem? You disobeyed my orders."

"Lily didn't round out the rear fast enough, which means we'd have to attack fast to gain the advantage. As team captain, I figured you'd have a better understanding of that."

"How can I lead someone who isn't willing to be part of the team?"

"You call this a team?"

"Yes, and you're lucky to even be on it."

"Lucky? I earned my way here."

"And you should be proving it, not questioning my authority."

"That's enough."

The stark male voice cooled the heat of the argument and sent a chill up my spine. I turned to find exactly who I expected standing behind me. Clarence. In the pod room.

The pod room?

I blinked and looked around. I stood inside the concrete cylinder room, lined with metal and glass. The programmers peered around their screens at me. I glanced up at the screen above the doors. DEFIANCE: VICTORIOUS. Well, at least we'd won. But when had the match ended? When had I left the pod?

Why couldn't I remember the gap in time?

I glanced up at Rooke in front of me, dressed in his white pod suit. He stared down at me, unwavering. Nothing had fazed him. Was I the only one who'd felt it?

Around the pod room, my three other teammates and the programmers stared at us in the center of the room. Rooke and I must have looked just like Nathan and Derek when they used to fight.

Clarence pointed a finger at the screen showcasing our victory. "What the hell was that?"

"We won the match, didn't we?" I protested.

"You got lucky. And if it wasn't for Lily, you might have lost. I've come to expect better from you. All of you."

Clarence's gaze darted over the entire room, as if trying to pin each person to the wall. My teammates all looked at their feet, unable to meet his eyes. Even the programmers shifted away from the weight of his heavy stare. Finally, Hannah—either very brave or very stupid—made a move for the exit.

"Where are you going? You have training."

"More?" Hannah asked, eyes wide. "We just trained nonstop all week."

"And you'll do more tonight. This is completely unacceptable," he barked. He waved a hand at the programmers. "Get out."

The programmers left. Quick patters of feet swept out the door. Having nothing to do with our physical training in this world, they were free from Clarence's wrath. Lucky bastards.

Clarence turned back to us, trembling so hard the veins in his skintight, plasma-injected forehead were about to burst. He took a breath, rubbing his temples with index fingers, then waved us toward the exit. "Get to the training room. I'll have the coaches meet you there."

Gradually, my teammates made their way toward the door. I grabbed Lily's arm as she walked past.

"Lily, what the hell? Why did you wait so long?"

Her expression grew solemn. "Sorry. When I jumped down from the trees, I landed wrong and just . . ." She glanced down at her swollen foot.

I sighed. "Yeah. I understand."

"I thought I'd be able to handle the trees," she continued. "The pain isn't that bad once I plug in."

Nothing was that bad once you plugged in.

"That's okay," I said. "It's my fault as team captain. We'll work on a different format for next week if it's still bothering you."

She gave me a sympathetic smile and trudged after Hannah through the doors. I glanced at Rooke across the room and met his stone profile. He chatted with Derek as they headed for the exit. I scowled and marched after them, purposely keeping my distance from the rest of the team. Namely Rooke.

"Kali," Clarence called.

I turned back. He waited to speak until everyone else filtered out of the room. Once we were alone, Clarence loomed over me and eyed me with his head still held high. Condescending jackass.

"Get your team under control."

"My team? This is your team. When we go through a player change two days before a matchup, I think this is expected."

"For Christ's sake, Kali. You know these fights don't always go as planned. Look at last week's matchup. You should be more prepared and learn to adapt when things go wrong."

"Look, I'm dealing with injured players and—"

"Players?" he asked, emphasizing the letter *s* at the end. "Who else is hurt besides Lily?"

I opened my mouth, and nothing came out. Lily's ankle sprain was minor. If I exposed Rooke's injuries, which seemed much worse, he'd be off the team. And we'd be done.

"I just mean with Nathan gone and us having to reformat the team so quickly—"

Clarence crossed his arms. "You are one of the top fighters in this competition. Possibly in the entire league. This shouldn't even challenge you. Get it together."

I threw my arms up. "This is ridiculous. I didn't sign up for this."

"Yes, you did. Now get this team in order, or you'll be out the door."

I clenched my fists behind my back, so Clarence couldn't see, and turned my gaze to the floor. He took a step closer, and I caught a whiff of his cologne, evergreen mixed with something else that I couldn't quite put my finger on. Does money have a scent?

Clarence loomed over me, veins in his forehead throbbing. My fingers itched to push them back in, so I jammed them into my pockets to prohibit any misdemeanors caused on their behalf. Clarence took a deep breath, but his neck and ears still blazed red. God, I'd really pissed him off. I'd never seen anyone that mad. Not even when I told my parents I wasn't going to college so I could become a pro gamer.

"Get to the training room," Clarence barked. "Now."


After everyone had left the training room for the night, I remained behind, pounding a punching bag as I imagined it was Clarence's face.

Fucking.

*Bam.*

Pigheaded.

*Bam.*

Jerk.

*Bam.*

With every punch, something tapped the skin just below my neck. I glanced down. My pendant dangled above my shirt. I tucked it in and continued assaulting the punching bag.

Footsteps padded along the floor of the training room. I glanced back. Rooke walked through the room, along the far edge, the sweet stench of arrogance wafting right along with him. He looked past me at a spot on the wall. I must have been a blur to him, which means he'd never see my fist before I turned those pretty brown eyes black.

Swiveling back to the bag, I pummeled it instead and let the rhythmic beat reverberate in my hands. Musicians had drums. I had bags of sand. Each made music to our respective ears.

"You need someone to spot you," Rooke said as he passed by. "Look at your stance. You're off."

I gnashed my teeth together. *Actually, I need you to stand in place of the bag, please.* I stopped pummeling and glanced down at my feet. "The coaches are finished for the day."

"That's no excuse."

"Are you offering then?"

"No."

"You complain we don't work as a team," I said, raising my voice as he walked away, "and as soon as there's a chance to help, you go off by yourself. Why don't you shove—"

I swallowed the rest of my sentence when he abruptly turned back. He braced his right shoulder behind the bag, giving himself enough leeway to peer around the edge. Most of him behind the bag, and his face right next to it. Looks like my target would improve after all.

He nodded at me. "Go."

I pounded the bag, picturing him instead. *Bam*. Solid blow to the face. *Bam*. Swift hit to the ribs. Oh, don't cry now. Here, just let me . . . *Bam*.

"Your feet are still too close together," he said, interrupting the fantasy. "Square them with your shoulders."

I paused and squared my feet, then returned to punching, focusing solely on the bag. At every punch rumbling up my arm. At every crunch of my knuckles against the leather canvas and the sand within. At the piercing brown eyes watching my chest with every movement.

"What are you looking at?" I demanded. I really was going to punch him in the eye.

Rooke took a step toward me, still staring. "Is that a taijitu?"

"What?"

I glanced down myself. My necklace hung over my shirt again. Since when did an American know the traditional name for a yin yang?

I tucked the pendant inside my shirt and disregarded it with a wave of my hand. "Typical Asian symbol. They want me to play it up whenever I can. You know, for the cameras."

"And the cameras are here now?" he asked, raising an eyebrow.

I stared back, unwavering. Seconds passed before I answered. "You never know."

"Funny, because it's also a symbol of someone who appreciates Taoism and the teachings of Lao Tzu."

I clenched my jaw to stop it from dropping. Where had he learned that? So few people made the connection. So few Americans, at least. I kept a straight face.

"It's just a necklace," I said.

"Your hair is up, you've got no makeup on, and you're dressed head to toe in training gear. But you leave the necklace on for show?"

Rooke stared down at me, his eyes searching my face as if looking for my soul. He wouldn't find anything. I'd already sold it to Clarence.

"Look," I began, "whatever you think it means, it doesn't. Not anymore."

"Why wear it then?"

"I told you. It's part of my image, all right? I forgot I even had it on."

He scoffed. "I don't believe that."

"Well, then . . . it's a good thing I don't care what you believe."

Was this guy going to question everything I said? Bile burned at the back of my throat. God, he made me want to puke.

"You really think your image is that important?" he asked.

"Of course it is."

How could he even ask that?

He shook his head. "You won't catch me buying into that bullshit."

"You have to."

"Not a chance."

"You signed a contract, didn't you?"

He frowned.

"I guess it's bullshit only up to a certain point." I cleared my throat. "Or, should I say, a certain *price*." He shot me a look. "What? You gonna act like you didn't know this is what it's like being a pro? You're about to become Clarence's new poster boy. Speaking of, we have a photo shoot tomorrow. *Pro Gamer Weekly*, the cover."

With a circulation of over twenty million, *Pro Gamer Weekly* was the top gamer magazine in the world. Along with reviews of at-home games, its primary focus was the life and times of virtual pro gamers.

It was owned, in part, by the VGL.

Rooke blinked, unimpressed. I made a sweeping motion with my hand toward the door, as if to shoo him away. "You'd better go get your beauty sleep."

"How did you know?"

"What? That you need beauty sleep?"

His jaw set. Hard. "About the photo shoot?"

I opened my mouth, and—to my surprise—a nonsarcastic answer trickled out. "Did Clarence issue you a tablet when you first got here?"

"Yeah. I had to trade it for my cell."

Of course he did, along with his firstborn child.

"Your tablet will be updated every morning with the team's itinerary, usually a few days in advance. Expect this week to be a little chaotic, though."

Was I just helpful to him? I'd have to watch that.

He nodded. "Yeah, thanks." His expression softened a little then. "Look, for what it's worth, I'm sorry. I shouldn't have questioned your authority, not in front of the team."

Huh. An apology. Okay, not bad.

I kept a straight face.

"That's all right, as long as it doesn't happen again."

His gaze flicked down to the necklace again. Or at least to where the chain disappeared under my training top. "Is it honestly just a symbol?"

He met my eyes again, and for once, his own were brimming with curiosity instead of ice.

"Yes," I told him. "It's a symbol. That's it."

He looked a bit disappointed, but seemed to accept it. "Wanna go again?" He reached for the bag, then suddenly doubled over, as if he'd just been punched in the gut.

"You okay?" I asked.

After a minute, he shook himself and straightened up. "I'm fine."

"You don't look—"

He turned on his heel and walked away without another word. Okay, sure. I was done talking. That's it. I had no doubt now this guy had an injury. He was hiding it, because if anyone found out, he'd be kicked off the team. And I couldn't let that happen. We were already a wreck and couldn't afford to lose and replace another player.

I let it go.

As he walked away, I shifted my weight from foot to foot. Should I thank him? He'd helped me, too, after all. Oh, just make the effort. It won't be that bad.

"Hey. Thanks for the spot."

He didn't look back as he waved me off—which if I wasn't sure had included his whole hand, I would have thought he'd just flipped me off. The door slammed shut behind him. The bang from the door meeting its frame echoed through the room like a ripple in a pond, but brought with it a tidal wave of anger.

I stood there, blinking. Don't let it bother you.

Don't. Just don't.

I returned to the bag and pummeled the life out of it, so hard I was sure the innards would spill out on the training-room floor. What. An. Asshole.

Eventually, I tired and hit the showers. Back at my bunk, the hair dryer whirled in my ear as strands of my hair danced like black streamers in the bathroom mirror. This was the only place in my bunk where everything wasn't built into the walls. Toilet, shower, and counter with a sink. Still all metal and glass, just like the rest of the living quarters.

As I set the dryer down on the counter, something crinkled beneath it. A small, silver package. The pills the shrink had given me. It had been almost a week since I saw the doc, and several of the package's tiny, metallic bubbles were crushed. How many more nights would I need them to sleep? I shrugged. Couldn't hurt. She'd prescribed them, after all. The package scrunched under my thumbs as another pill popped out. I took it and crawled into bed.

"Lights off."

The room went black. A smile curled through my lips as the darkness enveloped me in its comforting quiet. I sighed, drifting away toward sleep until a weight shifted in the bed beside me and ice-cold fingers wrapped around my elbow.

I screamed.

I catapulted out of bed, slapping my arm as if a spider had just run across it. Shudders shook my spine so hard, I became a hunchback. Nathan wasn't there. I knew that. Still, my gaze fixed on a spot on the floor and wouldn't even nudge toward the bed, as if stuck against an invisible wall.

Good time for a walk, yeah?

I paced around the hallways of the facility in an endless

circle until the blinking red light of a surveillance camera caught my eye. Clarence's voice echoed in my head. What are you doing up? I can't have you looking tired. Not for the press. What if they got a picture of you with those baggy eyes?

I returned to my bunk and stood looking at myself in the mirror. God, I looked terrible. Pale complexion, sunken cheeks, dark eyes. I fiddled with the package of pills and popped out another. Small, white, and round, it was just like a mint. Or a piece of gum. I brought my hand to my mouth and halted. Was it smart to take two in one night?

Whatever. It was just for tonight. For the sake of the team. For the show.

I swallowed the pill and went back to bed. As I nestled against the pillow and chills started jolting through me again, I squashed them with thoughts of sand, blood, and glory. We'd made it to the second round and now had five on the team to carry us through the tournament. Scratch that. Four on the team and one giant asshole, but it was enough to play the game. For as long as we would last.

I shook my head. I shouldn't think like that. Their futures were on the line. My future was on the line. If we could learn to work as a team, or at least get along, we had a chance. I could still be the first female captain in history to win a championship. I rolled over in bed, closed my eyes, and sank into a vision of my team, working together, winning the tournament. Hell, maybe even having a little fun along the way. I couldn't help but smile.

Soon, sleep's prying fingers pulled me down to slumber. But instead of the tournaments, I dreamt about my new least favorite person in the world.

# CHAPTER 9

O kay, the shrink never said anything about side effects.

I ran my thumb over the fine print. *Drowsiness. Dizziness. Unusual dreams.* Whatever. I tossed the package down on the bathroom counter and rubbed my eyes, sore and heavy. Maybe it wasn't from the pills. Maybe it was because I'd spent most of the night dreaming about Rooke, hacking off his limbs and listening to him scream. Wait, wasn't *unusual dreams* on the list? And they prescribe this stuff to people they were concerned about losing a grip on reality. Ah, there was my old friend again. Irony.

In the mirror, my baggy eyes and pale face phased between blurry and clear. God, I really was tired.

I took a shower, hoping the drowsiness would pour down the drain with the water. It did. Somewhat. Of all the technology in the world, why hadn't they figured out how to insert caffeine directly into my veins? As I rubbed dry with the towel, the heaviness lifted. Ah, better. But my optimism was quickly dashed when dressing became a new form of acrobatics.

"Damn it," I muttered at the tag sticking out the front of my training shirt. After flipping the shirt around in enough directions, I managed to dress myself above the skill of a third grader and left my bunk.

As my bunk door slid open, a tablet-sized object fell in and clunked against my foot. I knelt to examine my inanimate foe, and my jaw dropped to the floor. Seriously. You could have sunk billiard balls in my mouth.

The object in question was a hardcover with a jacket, and weighed heavy in my hand, unlike the typical featherweight of a tablet. Holy shit. It was a book. A real book made of paper, and not that synthetic crap either. It was cut-down-a-tree, piss-off-the-nature-lovers real paper.

I lifted the cover, thumbing the hard surface between my fingers, and ran a hand over the first sheet. It felt smooth and a little cool. Glancing around the hall to make sure no one was watching, I brought the book to my nose, closed my eyes, and inhaled deeply. Wood. I should have figured that's what it would smell like.

A note was stuck to the cover.

*Thought you'd benefit from this.*

No name. Nothing else. Still, I knew who it was from. Only Rooke had the arrogance to assume he'd know what I'd benefit from. But where on Earth did he get a book? Forget that, where did he get this note? I peeled it off and pressed my finger against the back edge. Sticky. A sticky note. A book. What decade was this guy from?

I glanced over the cover though I recognized the title before I even finished reading it. *Tao Te Ching.* The Taoist bible, or as close as it got to one. In the bathroom, I fished an eyeliner pencil out of my makeup bag and scribbled a reply on a tissue. Really, who keeps paper on hand?

I leaned the book against Rooke's door with the tissue tucked in the cover.

*Read it when I was twelve. I'm sure it's the same.*

Even though I wasn't hungry, my legs directed me to the cafeteria. Routine. In the kitchen, I grabbed a mug emblazoned with our team logo, filled it to the brim with coffee, and proceeded to the eating area. Hannah and Lily sat beside each other in the middle of a long table. Hannah's mouth moved nonstop, and she motioned with her hands while Lily nodded and doodled on her tablet-turned-digital-sketchpad. Derek and Rooke sat at the far end of the table, deep in conversation. Wow, the almighty had joined us for a meal. Well, joined Derek at least.

I sat across from the girls.

"Morning," Hannah chimed, her chirpy tone jabbing needles into my skull. Lily nodded, her signal for *good morning*. I grumbled a response over my coffee mug and hooked my thumb toward the end of the table where Derek and Rooke sat alone.

"Is it boys versus girls now?"

Hannah glanced at them. "Must be. I'm glad they're getting along."

"Speak for yourself."

Her eyes widened and her face lit up like a fourteen-year-old girl's about to hear the latest gossip. "Ooooh. Problem with the new guy?"

I glanced down the table at him, then leaned toward her and lowered my voice. "He's injured."

"What?" Hannah asked, mirroring my pose. Even Lily dropped her tablet and leaned in.

"After you guys left the training room last night, he and I talked for a bit. Out of nowhere, he doubled over like he was in pain, then he practically ran out of the room."

Hannah waved me off. "He probably had a muscle spasm or something. You're overreacting."

"I'm telling you," I insisted. "It's not the first time I've noticed. He's trying to hide it, but there's definitely something going on with him."

"Okay, so what are you going to do about it?"

I shrugged. "Nothing. I don't think I should do anything about it. If I bring it to anyone's attention, Clarence might kick him off the team, and we can't afford to replace another player now. We're barely holding it together as it is."

"True. Hey, where's your breakfast?" Hannah nodded at her own tray. Dry cereal, yogurt, and an apple. Lily's tray mirrored hers.

I shook my head. "Nah. I'm not hungry."

"You're not supposed to stray from this diet." Hannah flicked a finger against the tray's edge so it clanked on the table for emphasis.

"You sound like Clarence."

She frowned. "It's not a bad thing to eat right."

"If coffee is a bad thing"—I took a long sip—"then call me evil."

The liquid poured down my throat, warm and soothing. Around me, the lights brightened, and the needles in my brain dulled. Unlike those damn pills, coffee had amazing side effects.

"I thought Chinese people only drank tea," Hannah teased with a grin.

"I was raised in America. I inherited all of your bad habits."

She laughed and looked down the table at Rooke. "You can see why Clarence chose him."

"Sure, the guy has skill, but he's got a lot to learn about being on a team."

"Skill?" Hannah leaned toward me again and lowered her voice. "You understand how Clarence chooses his team, right? And why we're the only one in the tournament with more women than men? It's not just about talent. We're beautiful."

I studied her solemn expression, waiting for it to crack back into a smile. I waved her off.

"Pffft."

"I'm serious," she continued, taking a sip from her cup. "We look good, so sponsors want us to represent their products. Women want to be us. Men want to watch. We get paid the most, the best trainers, the best equipment. So we win. It's all about marketing."

"It's all about *money*," Lily corrected.

Hannah speared her spoon toward Rooke. "You're seriously going to tell me he's not cute."

I glanced at him, trying to be casual, and shrugged. Hannah scoffed and shook her head.

"You. Are. Hopeless," she said, emphasizing each word. She reached for her tablet on the table and started scrolling through it as she stuffed a spoonful of flakes into her mouth.

"What are you doing?" I asked, nodding at the screen.

"Shopping. New weapons came out today." She tapped a finger against the tablet. It projected out a six-foot-long war axe. Hannah stood, grasped the projected image, and rotated it in her hands.

"What do you think?" she asked. "Too butch?"

I studied her. "At your height, I think you could pull it off."

She tapped the projection off, sat back at the table, and continued flipping through the images on her tablet. "There's some you might like if you'd ever put that Dao sword down."

"No Dao sword? I don't think that would go over well."

She nodded. "Right. Your image. God, what would people expect if you were completely Chinese?"

"A hand fan that shoots poison darts?"

We laughed, even Lily, as she hunched over her own tablet, lightly scrolling her fingertip across it in a looped pattern.

I nodded toward her. "Whatcha drawing?"

Hannah snatched it and held it up for her. An outline of soft petals and a long stem graced the screen. While the flower wasn't quite finished, if I hadn't known better, I'd think it was a half-erased professional work of art.

"Wow, Lil," I said. "I didn't know you had that kind of talent."

Lily shrugged and snagged the tablet back from Hannah. Modesty turned her cheeks a dusty shade of pink.

Hannah waved it off. "She can draw all kinds of things. Give her an image-editing program, and she can do anything."

"Then what are you doing in the RAGE tournaments?" I asked her.

Lily glanced up at me and shrugged again. "Better exercise."

We all laughed again, though we all knew the real reason. Most graphic designers didn't make seven-figure salaries. Most pro gamers did. And those that won a championship could bring in eight figures easy.

We chitchatted through the rest of breakfast, the girls with their cereal and fruit, me with my coffee, and the boys at the end of the table. After weights, workouts, and laps around the track, we were piled into a black SUV and shipped off to the photo shoot.

Minutes into the ride, I slunk against the window, watching L.A. slide past, a supercity that stretched over 750 square miles. Metal skyscrapers pierced the sky while digital billboards and ads filled every free inch of space. Buy this. Upgrade that. You need it now.

Street level was an endless line of glass windows and minus-zero-size mannequins wearing the latest trends. Like a looping video, or a glitch stuck on repeat. Glass. Plastic. People. Plastic. All perfect in every way. If cities were clothing, then Los Angeles was that spandex shapewear women squeeze themselves into. You know, body hose that gives the illusion of no fat and an ideal figure.

The fashion director at the photo shoot was the very embodiment of L.A., with airbrushed makeup, a too-thin nose, and a shiny sheen to her skin, like she was wearing one of those clear, plastic face masks, or she'd just had enough surgery to give the illusion of one.

"You have a half-decent chest for someone of your descent," she said as she buttoned up my blouse. "Too bad you're not taller."

I gritted my teeth together. I also have a killer right hook. Wanna see?

Hands in pockets. Put your hands in your pockets.

I jammed my fingertips into the pockets of my jeans. At least, as deep as I could wedge them into the skintight fabric.

The fashion director took a step back, tapping a finger against her lips as her gaze weaved its way up my form. When she reached my eyes, she looked at them without really looking at me. More like she was outlining the shape with her own gaze. She smiled. "No wonder you're good at video games."

I went cold. Despite the numbness in my fingers from being wedged in my pants, they still twitched with the desire to punch her in the face for real. Sure, I was part Asian. I was also good at video games. Why couldn't those two things ever be separate? Why couldn't I be good because of dedication, hard work, and talent? But nooo. Somehow, the shape of my eyes alone made me better at pushing buttons on a controller.

With a flick of her wrist, the fashion director undid the top two buttons so the edges of my bra peeked over the sheer, cream-colored fabric, as if it wasn't see-through already. Then she waved me off, walked over to Hannah, and peered up at her.

"Now, *you* I can work with," she said, pushing her breasts up until they practically fell out of her dress. Hannah glanced at me with a curled lip and an eyebrow to match. I left her to fend for herself.

On the white backdrop of the photo area, I found the male counterparts of my team. Derek leaned against a piece of equipment, shirt open, chatting up some girl with a clipboard. He smiled, and not-so-absentmindedly twisted his torso so his abs flexed. The girl blushed and looked down at her feet.

Rooke stood alone against the white canvas, like a model ready to be painted with his piercing gaze and jaw set hard enough to complement his equally hard body. Forget chiseled from stone. The gods had carved this one in their own likeness. Sure, skill mattered more when battling foes, digital or otherwise. Looks mattered more when . . . well, anything. Digital or otherwise.

They'd dressed him the same as Derek, open dress shirt and pants hanging low enough to reveal that V men get around their hips. Oh-so-defined, and oh-so-lickable.

Lickable?

"Did they forget half your clothes?" I asked him. Rooke looked me up and down.

"Speak for yourself."

My teeth ground together. Hands. Pockets. Now.

Why were these pants so damn tight?

Hannah stumbled out of the dressing room and made her way over to me in four-inch heels, waddling like a newborn deer. At nearly five-foot-nine, I doubted she'd ever worn heels that high. She was all legs and breasts in a dress that barely covered the space between. How something indecent didn't spill out was beyond me.

"I don't know what just happened," she said to me, running a hand over her midsection.

"Just be thankful you're not a model."

She glanced around at the white backdrop, cameras, and our nearly naked teammates. "How would that be different?"

I grasped her hand. "It's all right. When we get out of here, we'll go clubbing, okay?"

She nodded and let out a slow breath.

Lily joined us last in pigtails, oversized fur-lined boots, and a mini pleated skirt, mimicking the style of her battle gear. The guys with schoolgirl fetishes would jizz themselves.

The photographer took several photos of the whole group in different poses. I could see the headlines now. Meet the team. No, it's really them. Never mind the makeup, perfect lighting, and endless editing. They're real. We swear.

The camera flashed until I went blind. We could have been there for hours. Maybe days. How did models do it?

"Break," the photographer called, waving his hand around like he was signaling a helicopter. Everyone scattered in slow motion, like they'd been stuck in the same position for too long.

I rolled my neck and made my feet move forward. Finally free. But at the edge of the canvas, the photographer blocked my path.

"Clarence tells me you've taken the role of team leader."

"Yes, that's right," I confirmed.

"Then I'd like to get some shots of just you and the new recruit."

My stomach dropped. What? Just me and him? I forced a smile across my face as my mouth went dry.

"Sounds great," I said through gritted teeth.

They posed us facing each other, but heads turned toward the camera. I purposely kept a six-inch gap between us. The photographer waved at us.

"No, closer."

Of course closer. What's that old adage? Sex sells.

I took a breath to settle my churning stomach. Why was this bothering me so much anyway? It was only for show, and I was strong. Hell, I was the warrior.

Closer. Okay.

I closed the gap entirely and pressed my body against his. Hadn't I done this exact pose with Nathan once? No big deal.

I looked at the photographer. "How's this?"

He grinned. "Perfect."

I rested my head against the skin of his chest, and the warmth from him kissed my cheek. Rooke went so still under my touch, I couldn't tell if he was only holding his breath or had stopped breathing altogether.

The camera started up and flashed dozens of times until the room morphed into a psychedelic blur. I let my vision fade, and my other senses kicked in. The scent of wood brushed against my nose. What was that? Pine, or maybe cedar? I shifted my head against his chest, and his heart beat against my ear. Images flashed across my mind, like flicks of the camera. Snapshot thoughts of running my tongue over his skin just to feel his pulse thread against it.

Whoa.

I jerked away from him, shaking my head. The photographer appeared over the lens.

"Problem, doll?"

I stared at him, blinking. Then I looked up and met Rooke's eyes. They'd narrowed, and I could see the question dwelling within them. *What the hell is her problem?*

I smiled at the photographer. "It's nothing. Sorry."

After several dozen more photos, maybe hundreds, the photographer finally called it quits. I relaxed and pulled away from Rooke. My knees ached and my back felt stiff. Apparently, I'd held myself so rigidly against him, I'd given myself premature arthritis.

Rooke left abruptly. So abruptly, in fact, he would have knocked me over if I hadn't sidestepped out of his path.

"What's wrong?" I called out. He glanced back at me. "You don't like to cuddle?"

He scowled and stomped away. Wow. Did this guy ever smile?

Hannah came up to me.

"You looked comfy in his arms," she said. "The photographer loved it. He took more pictures of you two than the whole group combined."

I waved her off. "He could probably tell I was fake smiling. Had to take plenty to catch one that looked natural."

"It looked pretty natural—"

I shot her a look that would have made any warrior bow down.

"Or not," she finished. "Yeah, or not."

The rest of the day went without incident, until that evening, when we went clubbing.

Rooke didn't join us.

"Where's the new guy? Already left the team?"

The same question from a dozen different people. The reporters, the press. Hell, even the bartenders. Didn't Rooke understand how important our image was? Five on the team, and only four go out. I'd have to deal with him at some point. Maybe if I waited, Clarence would chew him out first.

The next morning, after shaking off a mild hangover (whether from the shots or the sleeping pills, I wasn't sure), I turned to leave my room. As soon as the door to my bunk slid open, a hardback copy of *I Ching: The Book of Changes* clunked against my foot with a new sticky note on its cover. Who the hell was this guy, a twentieth-century librarian?

*Nice note. I used it to blow my nose.*

Jackass.

I scooped the book into my arms, marched down the hall to

Hannah's room, and pressed the buzzer on her keypad. Footsteps approached the door.

"Sticky notes," I said, as the door slid open.

Hannah's brow furrowed as she pushed strawberry blonde tangles away from her face. Looks like even she wasn't perfect in the morning.

"What?" she asked.

"Do you have any sticky notes?"

"Sure," she said slowly. "They're with my typewriter. Help yourself."

I frowned. "I'm serious."

Her gaze lowered from my face and landed on the book in my arms. "What is that?" She leaned toward me, and her eyes went wide.

"Is that a book?" she gasped. She reached forward—tentatively—as if her touch would both make it real and make it shatter. When I pulled back, she snapped out of her trance and met my eyes again. "Why do you have a book?"

"Never mind. Do you have sticky notes, or paper? Anything?"

She shrugged. "No."

I sighed, letting my shoulders fall in defeat, and headed down the hall.

"Is everything okay?" Hannah called out from her doorway.

I glanced back at her as I stormed away. "I'm going to war."

I followed the hallway to the admin/IT department of the facility, found the closest security guard, and half begged, half charmed him into opening the supply-room door. After rummaging through the entire closet, I found a dust-covered box near the back. Inside, among some writing utensils, was a pad of pink sticky notes.

Victory.

I snatched up the notes and two pens and returned to my bunk. A few minutes later, the book was at Rooke's door.

*Thanks for noticing my incredible improv skills on my last note.*
*BTW—I hope you got eyeliner up your nostrils.*

A different book was back at my door the next day and every morning after, with a new, snappy comeback stuck to the cover. Within minutes, it was returned to his door with my own brand of equally sarcastic reply.

This quickly became my new morning routine. On my way to the cafeteria, I'd drop the latest hardcover off at the library of Rooke. In the lunchroom, I'd sit across from Lily and Hannah with a brimming cup of hot java in my hands while the boys chitchatted at the end of the table. The usual, now. Standard programming in a way. Except today, either the boys were late or I was early because the end of the table was empty, and as I sat across from my female teammates, they had abandoned their breakfasts for the tablet gripped in Hannah's hands. Their faces were so close to the screen, they could have kissed it.

"What are you guys looking at?" I asked.

They both jumped, as if they just realized my presence at the table. Hannah hid the tablet behind her back.

"Nothing."

I frowned at her. "You'll have to be less obvious than that."

"I swear. It's nothing."

I grinned. "Are you peeking at naked ladies?"

"Uh, yeah. That's it." She relaxed a little. The tablet now rested near her side.

"Oh, okay. In that case . . ." I reached across the table and snatched it from her.

"Kali!"

"Come on. What's the big deal?" I brought the tablet up to my face.

"Please don't be mad."

"Why would I be mad?" I tapped the black screen out of sleep mode. Our issue of *Pro Gamer Weekly* magazine flashed across it. "Hey, it's out already . . ."

My voice faded as I realized the picture they'd chosen as the cover. My head resting on Rooke's chest. His hands fingering through my hair. Not the team. No. Not all of us.

Just me.

And *him*.

The caption read:

In the wake of tragedy, RAGE warrior Kali Ling finds
comfort in the arms of her team's newest recruit.

I gripped the tablet so hard, my knuckles turned white. Hannah's breathing went rapid. "Oh, God. She's trembling. It's like watching a volcano as it explodes."

Lily shrugged and stabbed at her cereal with a spoon. "I told you she'd hate it."

"What—the hell—is this?" I screamed.

Hannah tried to pry the tablet from my hands. "Kali, please. A flexible LED screen is not indestructible."

I ripped it from her grip and marched toward the cafeteria's exit just as Derek and Rooke walked in carrying trays. As I passed by Rooke, I tore the tray from his gasp and tossed it on the nearest table. He shot me a look halfway between confused and pissed.

"What's your problem?"

"Come with me."

I grabbed his arm and dragged him along by the sleeve. He shook my hand off but followed me down the hall.

"Where are we going?" he asked.

I shoved Hannah's tablet into his hands. "You know anything about this?"

Rooke went quiet as he studied the screen. "No." He scrolled through the magazine. "There's an interview here. And quotes. But they didn't even ask us any questions. Can they do that?"

I flashed him a sarcastic grin. "Welcome to Hollywood."

Several swear words, a few sharp retorts, and one elevator ride later, we entered the green-and-white walls and antibacterial stench that was Clarence's office. Lo and behold, guess what was plastered across the wallscreen.

That. Fucking. Picture.

Stretching across the length of the room and nearly two stories high, it was spectacularly more annoying at ten by twenty than it ever was on Hannah's tablet. Hell, add some spotlights overhead, and it would be a billboard for *fuck Kali's life*.

With a cell phone pressed to his ear, Clarence waved us into the office. Everyone thought all phones would be videos one day. Pffft. Sure, video conferences were common enough, but no one wants to look perfect all the time. Smeared makeup. Baggy eyes. Even in Los Angeles—the land of the perfect—some people shuffled around in their pajamas at five in the afternoon.

Finished with the call, Clarence pulled the phone away from his face and snapped it against his wrist. It curled around his skin like a wristwatch, but as thin as cardboard. Or plastic. Just like everything else in this world.

"Ah, perfect," he said as he approached, sounding way too chipper for the crack of dawn. Or seven thirty. "I was about to go looking for you two."

"No kidding." I marched across the office, pointing at the wallscreen. "We have to talk about this."

Clarence nodded. "Yes, apparently the issue is selling faster than any other in history."

I stopped dead.

"What?"

"Did you really expect any different?" Clarence asked. "The RAGE tournaments are one of the most popular divisions in the VGL, and our team was the highest-rated in the preseason. Intertwine a love story, and it's liquid gold." He turned to the screen and studied our picture for a moment. "I'm glad I came up with it."

My jaw clenched. "You *what*? This is because of you?"

"Everyone saw you two fighting inside the last match. Do you have any idea how bad that looks? Painting you two as a couple turns your little screaming contest into a heated lover's quarrel. People love it. They're eating it up."

A knot grew in my stomach, folding over itself again and again. I forced the next question through my lips, worrying I already knew the answer. "And what are we supposed to do about it?"

"You'll do what's expected of you," Clarence said. "You'll play the part."

Yup, knew that. I folded my arms and shook my head. "Absolutely not."

"We've already gone public with this. It's part of your image now."

"Then publicize our breakup."

Clarence mirrored my stance, folding his arms. "I thought you always gave the people what they wanted."

"Not this."

"Yes, Kali. You will." He loomed over me, doing that thing

where he looked down his nose into my eyes. "I'm getting sick of your little attitude. I don't care if the relationship between the two of you is real or not, just as long as the cameras think so. You'll act as if you're together, and you'll do it with a fucking smile on your face."

He glared down at me, and his eyes became endless black pools. Like death. Or a game-over screen. I faltered and looked away, my gaze trailing across the office. The posters of Nathan were already gone, replaced with various shots of the group and a few solos of Rooke. Clarence's words echoed in my mind. Two weeks, and you'll be forgotten. Would it even take two weeks for everyone to forget about Nathan?

With renewed strength, or anger, I returned my gaze to Clarence's face. "I'm not about to pretend to be with some guy because Nathan died. 'In the wake of tragedy.' That's bullshit. I'm not about to spit on his memory."

Clarence sighed. "Kali, he died of an overdose. It's not like he sacrificed himself saving a baby from a fire. Get over it."

"But he—"

"Leave it," he snapped. "I'm not going to let your conscience ruin this team or our chance at the championship. Every sponsor we have is two seconds away from dropping us. This"—he pointed at the picture on the screen—"is the best thing to come out of the whole Nathan incident. We can't risk any bad publicity right now. If I ever hear that name again, you'll be the same as him. Forgotten. Is that clear?"

I looked down at my feet, unable to meet Clarence's eyes again. Nathan shouldn't be swept aside. Maybe it was a drug overdose, but he still died. He died because of the games and this lifestyle. But still, this was my career on the line. The rest of my life. If Nathan were the one still here, wouldn't I want him to keep going in the tournament?

I sighed. "Fine."

Before I said anything I shouldn't, I marched toward the door, the burning anger within growing with every step.

Three feet from the exit, Clarence called out.

"By the way, certain tabloids are offering seven figures for the first shots of you two kissing, so expect the paparazzi to be more aggressive than usual."

Oh, fantastic.

"Make sure you hold off on getting too physical in front of the cameras," he continued. "We'll decide when the world is ready for that."

No problem on the first point, and my ass you will on the second.

I gripped the door and pulled. Six inches open, it stopped dead. I looked up to see what it had caught on and found Rooke's hand bracing the door a foot above my own.

"Shouldn't I get that for you?"

Cute.

Rooke stared down at me as he held the door. My gaze flicked to the wall behind him, where the *Pro Gamer Weekly* cover still shimmered on the screen, and for the first time, I really looked at it. My head rested against his chest, in the crook of his unbuttoned shirt. A coy smirk curved through my lips, the one I'd been taught to portray. A cunning warrior's grin. Still, I couldn't remember smiling like that during the shoot. And Hannah was right. Nestled against the recesses of his muscular build, I did look comfortable.

Rooke leaned toward me and kept his voice low, so our team's owner wouldn't hear. Didn't he know gods were omnipotent?

"We should talk about this."

"There's nothing to discuss. Clarence made the decision. It's not our choice."

"But—"

"No. No 'buts.' That's it. End of discussion."

I needed time, and space, to process all of this. Time alone. So before he could say anything more, I squeezed through the small gap in the door and jerked the handle as hard as I could, slamming the door shut in his face.


Of all the places in the facility, this was the one where I felt most like myself.

I sat on the roof of the central hub above Clarence's office, overlooking the facility. Below me, people moved through the tunnels and hubs, little blips in the windows. An ant farm, and I was the rebel, the five-year-old boy on top of it all. Too bad I didn't have a magnifying glass and a target on Clarence.

I closed my eyes and took a breath, feeling the warm, late-August breeze caress my face. Fresh air. An endless morning sky. This was rebellion, freedom, and countless possibilities.

"Hey."

So much for freedom.

My shoulders tightened at the sound of someone else on the roof. I glanced behind me to find Rooke strolling across the metal canopy.

"I'm not even going to ask how you knew I was up here, but you can leave," I said, returning my gaze to the sky. "There aren't any cameras around now."

"You never know."

My jaw clenched as he threw my own words back at me. Rooke reached my side and sat.

"You okay?" he asked.

"This is fucking ridiculous." I exhaled, letting out the steam still coming out of my pores. "Why doesn't he just whip his dick out and piss directly on Nathan's grave."

"We don't have to go along with it, you know. Image isn't everything."

I threw my head back as laugher spilled out from deep in my stomach. "You are in the wrong sport. Maybe you should try golf, where they wear plaid pants."

His face lit up. "Hey, you ever try virtual golf?"

"Oh God, you play virtual golf?" I held up my hands so they blocked his face. "I can't even talk to you now."

"Everyone needs something to relax. I'm sure you've meditated before."

My jaw clenched. "If this is about the Taoist thing, just leave it alone."

He turned to me then, sitting cross-legged, so he faced my profile. "Look, I only mention it because I'm interested."

"You mean because you're nosy."

"No. Because I'm interested," he stressed.

I glanced at him. He stared back, expressionless, like a blank slate. Like he really was just interested in what I'd say.

"I just don't practice it anymore."

"Why?"

"It doesn't have a place in my life now. I'm in the sport of the future, and I believe in the philosophies of the past?"

He blinked. "Isn't that what a yin yang represents?"

Smart-ass.

"My father taught it to me as a child, okay? I really admired my dad as a kid. I tried to do everything like him. But living in America and practicing Taoism, it's just . . ."

My words trailed off as a knot formed in my throat. As if growing up half-and-half wasn't hard enough at times. But then, add in anything that made me non-American? Forget about it. Maybe as a kid I didn't care, but as a teen—no way was I keeping Taoism in my life. Try being different in high school. Noticeably, physically different. To everyone. My friends just didn't understand even when they tried, let alone the bullies who seized every opportunity to point out the color of my skin or shape of my eyes—until I'd punch them in the mouth.

Is that American enough for you?

"You know what most people think of meditation?" I began, my voice higher and shakier than intended. "That it's New Age mysticism. That it's magical bullshit. They don't realize it's as old and sacred as prayer."

I met his eyes then, and we just stared at each other for a while. His expression went hard until he was all jaw and cheekbones. But his eyes looked distant, foreign, as if he'd just peeked at the world through mine, and it was a place brimming with shadows and hate.

"People are stupid," he finally said. "But not being yourself because of their ignorance is worse."

My lips split apart, and my insides went cold. He was wrong. So very wrong. In this life, no one was themselves. We were whoever the media and the masses decided we were. In this world, so plastic and fake, what did it matter, anyway?

"If your beliefs came from your father," Rooke began, eyeing my pendant again, "is the necklace from him, too?"

I glanced down it. The golden pendant shimmered in sunlight, reflecting the brilliance of the sky above us. There were no engravings marking the necklace, front or back. He wouldn't know.

I tucked it in my shirt.

Rooke looked me over, but didn't push it further. Hmm. Arrogant but intelligent. Point for him.

One point.

Rooke turned his attention back to the sky. "I'll admit I have an ulterior motive—"

"Here we go."

"I got into Asian philosophy when I started studying martial arts, but I've never had someone to talk to about it." He glanced at me. "I was kinda hoping you were it."

Given the recent deluge of books at my door, I wasn't that surprised by this little admission. But reading Asian philosophy and playing virtual golf for fun? This guy was as interesting as my grandfather.

"Not all Chinese people care about philosophy," I told him.

"They're not all Taoists, either. I know."

I drew a deep breath, one that came from my belly.

"I'd be open for discussions," I began, "if you're really that desperate."

He opened his mouth, and I held up a hand.

"Not now. This is about as much coolness as I can handle for one night."

"Can I ask something else instead?"

"No."

"You said you're only half-Chinese."

I blinked. "That's not a question."

"You said no."

A scoff stifled the laughter rumbling in my chest. This guy was a pro at getting to me, in a good way.

A good way?

Finally, I sighed.

"My mother's American," I told him. "My father immigrated here as a teenager and enrolled in the same high school as Mom. Mom said she just couldn't resist helping the cute, foreign boy with his English."

"And did she?"

"No. Dad spoke English better than she did. But," I stressed, "that didn't stop him from *pretending* he didn't speak English just to keep her attention." I winked at him.

Rooke made a sound at the back of his throat, like he was trying to stifle laughter—if he was even capable. "So, what do they do?"

"They're both in engineering. They own a firm back home in San Diego."

"Do they watch the tournaments?"

"Not really. They're not much for violence, even if it is all virtual. Do yours?"

He nodded. "Yeah. They watch, back home."

"Which is where?"

"Never mind."

He grinned one of those grins that stretches from ear to ear. An honest-to-God, wholesome grin. I think it was the first time I'd genuinely seen him smile. Oh, now I had to get it out of him. I nudged his shoulder, hoping to coax out this suddenly playful side of him. "Tell me."

"No."

"Why?"

"You'll laugh."

I gave him an incredulous look. "Oh, no. It's one of the square states, isn't it? Which one? Wyoming? Nebraska?" I cringed. "Utah?"

"Canada."

CANADA? I pressed my lips together, as if it would restrain my giggles. It didn't. I snickered through my nose and had to slap a hand over my mouth to contain the rest.

He frowned. "I told you."

I giggled more, wiping my eyes. "So, are you from the whole country, or . . ."

He frowned some more. "I'm from Vancouver, okay?"

"Aren't there pro tournaments in Canada?"

"Yeah, but not like here."

"What do you mean? What's different?"

"It just is," he snapped, and looked away.

The shimmering mirage of a friendly Rooke faded in an instant. Like the illusion in the desert, apparently I'd gotten too close.

So, leaving home was a sore spot for him. I tucked it away for future consideration. Maybe I'd be able to use it at some point. To my advantage.

If Rooke hadn't snapped, I wouldn't have thought twice about his reason for coming here. Most gamers came to Los Angeles to play. This was the home of the championships. Sure, people played in their own states and countries. They could plug in and join from anywhere in the world. But this was L.A. This was Hollywood. If you wanted to be noticed, you had to be here.

I turned away and gave him space. Usually, I might have enjoyed pissing him off, but he'd given me an ounce of respect regarding my necklace. If I paid it back now, I wouldn't owe him anything more.

I looked back over the facility again, counting the insects scurrying through the tunnels. In the background, the sun glistened in the sky just over the horizon, highlighting the thousands of vehicles driving themselves through the streets. The warm, morning breeze picked up, pricking at my skin, but stopped suddenly, as if even it couldn't cut through the tension in the air between us.

"I suppose L.A. is the best place to be if you want to go as far as you can," I tried, "especially in the RAGE tournaments."

Nothing.

No response. Not even a nod. Okay. I tried. This was over. I threw one last glance out at the city and started to push myself up when he spoke.

"Sorry about your friend."

His tone was hard and unemotional, and he kept his gaze fixed on the sky, but at least he was talking and trying to keep things civil.

I lowered my butt to the roof. "What?"

"Your teammate. The one who died."

Nathan. My stomach sank, and I let a slow breath pass between my lips, hoping Rooke wouldn't notice.

"Were you close?" he asked.

What was I supposed to say to that? Tell this guy I was screwing Nathan when we weren't even dating? No. That didn't match my image.

I clicked my fingernails against the roof as I searched for an answer and eventually settled on a neutral one.

"Close enough."

"Will there be a memorial for him?"

I scoffed. "Didn't you just hear what Clarence said about the whole thing? The sponsors will never go for that. Can't do anything that might upset the perfect world of gaming. People might realize it's as fake as the worlds we fight in."

Rooke stared at me for a minute. Maybe it was the first he'd known of it. Sure, there were whispers in the amateur tournaments. Gamers still lost their marbles at that level, too. Not as often, given they didn't put in the same number of hours or deal with the same level of stress. Looked like Rooke was unaware of the dark side of virtual gaming.

Finally, he blinked and shook his head.

"You know, the original gladiators fought for honor." He waved a hand out at the facility. "Is this honor?"

I smiled at the error in his words. "The original gladiators were slaves and forced to fight. We're not slaves."

"You signed a contract, didn't you?" He met my eyes, and

that dark stare pierced through mine. My stomach turned, though I wasn't sure if it was because of the weight of his words or the weight of his stare.

"Were you surprised when Clarence named you captain?" he asked.

My stomach turned again. Definitely the weight of his words.

"A little, yeah. Knowing him, it's just some marketing scheme."

"So you don't really care?"

I gnashed my teeth together and pushed down the burning sensation in my stomach.

"Yes," I strained. "I do care."

He didn't say anything more. It was silent again for several more minutes before I decided I was done.

"Well, I'm heading in. You?"

"No. Think I'll sit out for a while."

"All right. See you in the training room."

He nodded, though he kept his attention on the cityscape. I walked away. A foot from the door, he called out to me.

"Aren't you going to kiss me good-bye?"

I missed a step and stumbled into the door. After steadying myself, I glanced back at him. "Not even if I got that million dollars myself."

"Some guy could put his kids through college, you know."

"Yeah, and not much else."

"Still, you could give someone a chance at a better life," he continued. "Seven figures is a lot of money to some people. You don't know what kind of impact it could have on another person—"

I left the roof and closed the door on his words. There was no point to returning to the cafeteria now, and I still had half an hour before I had to meet the team in the training room. With all the bullshit of the morning, I was left craving one thing, and it wasn't coffee.

I followed the hallway to the pod room. My new programmer sat at her workstation, typing on the screen. She smiled as I walked up to her.

"Hey, Kali."

What was her name? Elise. It was Elise.

"Hey. Do you think you could plug me in?"

"Really? It's early."

I faltered for a second.

"Uh, I know. I just . . . I need some extra practice."

She shrugged. "Okay. Sure."

She tapped a few buttons on the screen. The pod doors opened, and I climbed in as they closed around me. In the darkness, alone, I smiled to myself. In here, there were no flashing cameras. No tabloids. No fake relationship. The virtual world was becoming even more real than this place.

The wires crawled across my skin, sending little jolts of anticipation running through me. I took a breath, pressed back against the pod, and disappeared into the place where there were no magazines, or sponsors, or bullshit. The place where anything was possible.

The place where I was a god.

# CHAPTER 10

"Team Defiance really took a beating last night. It's a wonder they survived."

I sat on my bed watching the VGL's *Sunday Morning Highlights* on my tablet. During our latest Saturday night matchup, Lily and Hannah had bit the virtual death. By some miracle, Rooke and I managed to hold on to our tower, and Derek had taken the enemy's by himself.

"What was once the heavy favorite to win the tournament is now just barely scraping by in the losers' bracket."

"Looks like Kali Ling should be focusing more on her team than her love life."

I pulled the covers over my head and groaned. The week had been a disaster.

I wasn't sleeping. The team was still fighting. If it wasn't Hannah and Derek in the training room, then it was me and Rooke in the pod room. Despite our talk on the roof and daily exchange of books, we still hadn't broken through the differences between us—namely his arrogance and my stubbornness. Luckily, there hadn't been any new injuries, but Lily still limped around on her ankle, and Rooke gripped his stomach and grimaced when he thought no one was watching.

I looked over my tablet again, reading the names of the teams still left in the tournament. In the winners' bracket sat InvictUS, their name glowing in red as if the computer itself was trying to make them even more ominous. They'd crushed every opponent the tournament could throw at them. They kept winning. If, somehow, we kept winning, eventually our paths would cross.

And explode.

Every week was another step up, a harder fight, as the weaker teams got knocked out of the tournament. If I couldn't get the team working together soon, InvictUS would be the least of my worries. So when the third round of the tournament was announced on Monday morning, and I had our opponents for the week, something solidified within me. I hadn't fought my way into the pros just to be out in a few rounds. We had the skills to be one of the best teams in the league. It was my fault that we weren't. Having to switch in a new player right before the start of the tournament hadn't helped, but I was the one who was supposed to make us into a team again.

Inside my bathroom, I propped my tablet up on a few towels and watched our opponent, QuickZero, in their preseason fights as I dried my hair and brushed my teeth. We had five days to cream them in the arena.

When I turned to leave my bunk, and the door slid open, I halted at a sight I never expected to see.

Nothing.

No book sat waiting for me outside my door. My heart sank. If there was one thing Rooke and I had in common outside the game, it was those books. Maybe we'd had one fight too many, or something I said had really pissed him off. Whatever the reason, the sticky-note battle was over, and possibly our only chance at rapprochement. I chewed my bottom lip and sighed. For the first time in my entire life, winning a game didn't taste so sweet.

Whatever. I'd have to find another way to make things work with him. With the entire team, really. And I'd have to coordinate a plan for our opponents this week. Something that didn't result in our fighting each other or nearly wiping out.

Nose pressed to my tablet, I walked into the cafeteria and groped around the counter for the coffeepot, and landed on a hard, thick cover instead.

You have got to be kidding me.

In front of the coffeepot sat *The Inner Chapters* waiting for me. Sticky note? Of course.

*In his teachings, Chuang Tzu often refers to wandering in a world beyond life or death. Could the virtual world constitute such a place?*

Shut. The. Front. Door.

Rooke was comparing Taoist philosophy to the virtual world? Wow, what a hell of a way to get my attention. In all my years of reading Taoist texts and playing video games, I'd never thought of one in comparison to the other. Interesting. Even better, it looked like he hadn't given up on figuring out our differences. But he'd tapped my competitive side now. Did he really think he could beat me at video games or Taoist references, let alone both together?

I tucked the book under my arm and filled a mug until it was brimming with the good stuff. In the lunchroom, Rooke sat alone at the end of the table. He glanced up from his breakfast, noticed the book in my arms, and grinned.

"How's your coffee?" he asked.

I narrowed my eyes at him.

Oh, it's on, recruit.

It's on like Donkey Kong.

Before morning practice, I snuck back into my room and scribbled a reply on a sticky note.

*The virtual world is not beyond life and death.*
*You always wake up, eventually.*
*It goes hand in hand with reality.*
*Isn't THAT what a yin yang represents?*

I walked briskly through the halls to the pod room. Elise glanced at me when I entered.

"Plugging in *again*?" she asked.

I waved her off. I didn't plug in *that* much. I scurried over to Rooke's pod, entered a command on the screen to open the doors, and left the book inside before they shut again. I winked at Elise as I headed back out of the room.

"I wasn't here."

She watched me go with a furrowed brow but didn't protest.

In the training room, I continued to watch my tablet on breaks, trying to learn everything I could about our opponents. QuickZero had four decent players plus one seven-foot ogre who made the members of InvictUS look like gnomes. He wielded an axe the size of me, sending people flying into the walls with sickening smacks. His swings, while powerful, were slow, almost labored.

I looked up and scanned the training room until I spotted Lily climbing off the treadmill. No one seemed to pick a fight with her, and she was too laid-back and quiet to go looking for one herself. Maybe centering this week's matchup around her would work. I waved her over.

"How's your ankle?" I asked.

She glanced down at it, shifting her weight side to side. "Still tender, but it's getting a lot better."

"Do you think you'll be recovered by this weekend?"

She shrugged. "Maybe. Why?"

"Check this out." I held out the tablet for her to watch as

Zero's ogre crashed through the tower's door and started slaughtering his opponents. Lily's eyes went a touch wide.

"He's a freaking beast."

"I think you could take him out easy."

Her eyes went wider. "Really?"

"He's huge, but he moves slowly. You're faster than anyone I've ever seen in the arena. You could get the drop on him before he can take anyone else out. Think you could handle it?"

She considered it. "Yeah. Might be good if I could practice against someone that size."

No one here was even close to seven feet tall. I spotted Rooke across the room and waved him over. He'd have to do.

"You're the tallest one here," I told him, as he stopped in front of us. "Do you mind sparring with Lily for the week? She needs to work with a larger opponent."

He nodded. "Sure."

They paired off on the mats. Lily's gift was her speed, and against Rooke, she was a Tasmanian devil with a pair of short axes. Even with the practice weapons, Lily moved like a hurricane, spinning and whipping faster than Rooke could keep up. Looked like my plan might work.

After lunch, I laid out a potential strategy for the coming matchup.

"I think three on defense and two on offense would work best against QuickZero," I said with my teammates huddled around me. "Hannah and Derek will go for their tower while Rooke, Lily, and I guard our own. Lily will be the one to take out the ogre. If something goes wrong, Rooke and I will be there to back her up."

Derek stepped forward. "Still going two on three? Kali, let's be serious. No pro team keeps three on defense. It makes us look weak."

"Lily's still recovering from her sprain. Plus, Zero always goes three on offense and two on defense. It's their style. If we mirror them, it'll be one-on-one. Since we've replaced a player, and we're still not used to each other yet, I think it's best if we play it safe for now. At this point, we're not here to show off. We're here to survive."

"And what if they try a different formulation to screw us up?"

Good question.

"I'll think about that," I said. "We'll go with this setup for now."

Everyone agreed, but Derek had a good point. What if they changed up their format? How could we prepare for that?

The next morning, a hardback copy of *The Art of War* sat waiting outside my door with a new sticky note on its cover. Guess he wanted me to find it right away today.

*Which of the thirteen chapters do you think best applies to the virtual battlefield?*

Is that all you got, recruit? I was going to own his ass. The thirteen chapters in *The Art of War* each dealt with a different aspect of warfare. It wasn't a Taoist text in the strictest sense, but employed many of its concepts and ideals. Tapping a pen against my bottom lip, I flipped through the pages a few times to refresh myself on the material.

A few minutes later, the book somehow ended up in the men's changing room of the training area, tucked in Rooke's locker.

*Chapter Seven speaks about adapting to the fluidity of the battlefield.*
*The virtual world is programmed. Therefore, it is more fluid than any.*

As I walked toward the cafeteria for a cup of my personal poison, I thought about *The Art of War*. I'd never considered the virtual battlefield as fluid before, but the programmers could reformat standard programming to do almost anything they wanted.

I stopped dead.

That was it. The answer to the question Derek had posed the day before. We could run various scenarios of QuickZero's possible attacks in the virtual world and master any format they threw at us. As fate would have it, Elise turned a corner and started coming toward me. I jogged up to her.

"Hey. I'm going to need you to plug us in later."

Her face fell, and she sighed. "Look, Kali, I'm going to lose my job."

"What?"

"The other programmers said you got the girl before me fired for letting you plug in off-hours."

I shook my head. "No, no. This is practice for the whole team." I smiled as I lied through my teeth. "Clarence already approved it. You won't get in trouble."

She brightened. "Oh. Okay then."

In the cafeteria, I hurried over to the team as they sat eating their breakfasts.

"We're going to spend more time in the virtual world," I told them. "I'll get the programmers to create simulations with opponents similar to QuickZero's size and skill. Then, they'll run the different ways they might attack. Three on defense, three on offense, four on offense. If at any point we wipe out, we can rerun the same scenario until we figure out how to beat it. That way, we're prepared no matter what they do."

Everyone exchanged glances and nodded in approval.

"That sounds . . . perfect," Derek said. "Good idea."

"Well"—I glanced at Rooke at the end of the table—"someone reminded me how fluid the arena is and how fast we need to adapt."

Rooke smiled but said nothing.

The rest of the week, we fell into a pattern. Mornings in the training room, afternoons in the virtual, and nights at the clubs, intermixed with media events and my ongoing sticky-note war with Rooke. Sometimes I'd find a book outside my door, waiting for me in the mornings. On other days, I'd stumble across one in my pod, on the roof of the facility, or on top of the gaming consoles in the facility's rec room.

The gaming consoles. Now that gave me an idea.

Like Hannah had said, I was good at finding ways to make this fun. So, on Friday night, after an entire week of nonstop action, I decided I needed a break. We all did. After returning from the clubs, I led the team through the hallways of the facility.

"Where are we going?" Hannah asked too loudly, obviously still feeling the effects of the shots she'd done earlier.

"Shhh, you guys," I warned. "Quiet."

"Where are you taking us?" Derek asked in a hushed voice.

I smiled. "To fight."

"Oh, God," Hannah whined. "We're going to practice, aren't we?"

I ignored her and led them past the training room and into the rec room. When the door slid shut behind us, I quickly entered a lock code on the keypad and turned back to my teammates.

"With the amount of training we go through, I think sometimes we forget that this is a game." I grinned. "I have a surprise for you."

I walked over to the television. The rec room consisted of a wall-sized television screen, all the modern gaming systems, and an oversized couch, long enough to seat a dozen people. I grabbed one of the systems, booted it up, and started searching through the menus. When I located the spot where I'd down-loaded a few classic video games, I clicked on one. A remake of Super Smash Brothers popped up on the screen. It wasn't the original game, but a tribute with updated effects and graphics. The original only ran on old systems, and almost no one had those anymore. At least, not ones that worked.

"Yes!" Hannah screeched, practically diving for a controller. "I'm Peach!"

Derek scooped up the second controller. "Who in their right mind picks Peach? What is wrong with you?"

She giggled as she tapped a few buttons. "You're about to have your ass kicked by a princess."

"Just to be clear: Are we talking about the character or you?"

The trash-talking had already begun. I couldn't stop a smile from spreading across my face. Lily snatched the third controller, and I motioned for Rooke to take the last. He hesitated for a second before joining the others in front of the wallscreen.

I sat on the couch behind them all and watched. As they chose their characters and set up the fight, the trash-talking continued between Derek, Hannah, and Lily. Rooke sat at the end, some-what excluded from the conversation. After joining the team late, he was still on the outside looking in. Now, that just wasn't right.

"Hey, guys. Take it easy on the recruit," I said. They all glanced back at me with confused looks on their faces, espe-cially Rooke. I grinned. "He likes virtual golf."

My teammates exploded.

"Virtual golf?"

"Oh, no. Now we'll lose tomorrow night for sure."

"Should we trade your sword for a five iron?"

They all laughed, and soon, Rooke was laughing with them.

Nothing like a good razzing from your teammates to feel like you're a part of the group. I felt sort of proud in that moment. We were becoming a team again, and, more importantly, we were having fun.

The game started up, and the room filled with sounds of cartoon attacks, explosions, and karate chops.

"What are we going to do next?" Hannah asked, eyes glued on the screen. "Ancient video games?"

Yes, games now had eras. Ancient was anything from the first computer-based games in the 1950s and '60s through to the video game crash of 1983. Classic games were from the release of the original Nintendo Entertainment System in the mid-1980s through to the first at-home VR headsets in the mid twenty-teens. Modern was anything from VR forward, including non-VR games.

On the screen, I watched as four characters battled each other, until Peach went out, then Samus, then Fox. Pikachu was left dancing on the platform, claiming victory.

Lily raised her arms triumphantly.

"Not bad," Derek said, "for someone who likes Bubble Bobble."

She punched him in the arm.

"Ow." Derek turned back to the screen. "That's it. Rematch."

The next round started up.

I sat back against the couch and let my vision go fuzzy. Besides the media bullshit and torture-based training, life was pretty good. I was on my way to becoming a permanent pro gamer, and the team was gelling over classic video games. This was heaven, almost as much as the virtual world. Almost. But only with a sword in my hand was I truly invincible.

I pushed deeper into the couch and pictured the virtual tower. A soft rustling, like trees in the wind, filled the air around me.

I took a breath, breathing in the deep, lavender scent. Stone, wheat stalks, and sand. I was home.

"It's your turn."

I glanced around the tower, looking for the owner of the voice. Who else was here?

"Kali?"

I blinked and looked up at Hannah standing over me. I was on the couch of the rec room, not inside the tower. My other teammates sat on the floor in front of the TV. I blinked again and rubbed my eyes.

What the hell just happened?

"It's your turn," Hannah repeated, holding her controller out to me. Her brow furrowed, and she tilted her head. "Where were you just now?"

I sat up straight and cleared my throat. "I must have been dreaming."

"Your eyes were open."

Huh.

"Daydreaming," I sputtered. "I meant daydreaming." I glanced between her and the controller, and pushed it back toward her. "You go ahead. I'll watch another round."

She grinned. "Well, I'm not going to say no to that."

She scurried back to the group. I followed the line of my teammates' backs until I met Rooke's eyes. He was the only one still facing me, and he stared like he was trying to look through me.

Derek nudged him. "Hey, choose a character."

Finally, Rooke turned back to the screen and tapped his controller.

With his back turned, I released a breath. I lifted my hands off the couch and studied them. They were shaking. My stomach swirled. What was wrong with me?

Nothing. I was tired. That was all.

My teammates battled each other until they were too exhausted to hold the controllers. We filtered out of the rec room and down the hall to our bunks. Everyone said their good nights and wished good luck for tomorrow. Inside in my bunk, I stared down at the empty bed though a phantom ghost memory of Nathan filled in the other side, like every night. Forget it. I'd never sleep. Maybe I could go for a run around the track. Never mind. Clarence would be watching. What are you doing, running this late at night? It'll throw off your entire schedule.

In the bathroom, I poked a few pills through the package, popping out them out like pieces of gum. Two. Three. What do they call that? A cocktail? Nah, that's only when you mix. I must have a natural resistance to these things.

I tossed the pills in my mouth and groped around the counter for a glass. Bottles clanged together in my search, which turned up nothing but liquor minis, lotion, and makeup bottles. Whatever. I downed the pills and emptied one of the liquor minis in one swipe. It slid down smooth, barely even burned anymore. Looks like it wasn't just video games I'd become professional at doing.

I wrapped myself in a towel and sat on the bathroom floor, waiting for the drowsiness to grip me before returning to bed. Maybe if I waited until I was tired enough, I'd fall asleep as soon as I hit the pillow and wouldn't even think about a dead Nathan beside me. But before I ever got back up, everything went black.

# CHAPTER 11

White light streamed in through the tower's barred windows, splaying sunlight across the stone floor. I stood in the center of the tower, basking in it. The trees outside rustled in the wind. Through the tower's entrance, Lily's feet disappeared up branches to her hiding spot. Rooke paced in front of me, in minimal armor, muscles gleaming in the light. Not that I was looking, or anything.

"You think we're ready?" he asked in a low voice, so the audio wouldn't pick up his words. Last thing we needed was for the world to see another argument between us, or for the press to take something that was said and spin it out of proportion.

I spoke back through my teeth. "We practiced hard and played hard. We had fun. There's nothing more we could do. We're ready."

He stopped in front of me. "You really believe in having fun, don't you?"

I shrugged. "It's a game, isn't it?"

Footsteps beat up the path to the tower. I gripped my sword and drew it out from its sheath. Rooke mirrored my pose. Two of QuickZero's players burst through the tower's entrance. The ogre clambered in behind them. The formation we were most expecting. Perfect.

Lily jumped down from the trees outside the tower and dove

for the seven-foot brute, slicing through his calves with the speed of light. He clomped around, trying to find her as she weaved through his legs. They looked like a cartoon of an elephant stomping around a mouse as it scurried beneath its feet.

A warrior closed in on me.

His footsteps pounded as he bolted, sword out. I waited, drawing him in, grinning my warrior's grin. His feet pounded faster. That's it. Fuel your rage, my dear. It will do you no good.

He swung as he reached me. I dipped under his arm and elbowed his ribs. He stumbled back, coughing, gripping his side.

He charged again.

Sword met sword as he swung. I followed his blow, flinging his arm to the side, leaving his chest wide open. Big mistake, pal. With two quick spins, I sliced an X across his rib cage. Blood sprayed out, slicking his lower half with red. He cried out and went rigid. Then he collapsed to his knees and fell forward, practically kissing my toes.

I looked to my teammates. Both still battled their opponents less than a foot apart, nearly back-to-back.

I retrieved my opponent's sword from the stone floor and bolted. Just as I reached the brawl, I dropped down, slid between the remaining enemies, and slammed both swords in either's back. They gasped and went rigid. I ripped my weapons out, and they collapsed to the ground.

Rooke and Lily glanced down at the floor and back at me, their mouths slightly agape. That's right. There's a reason why they call me the warrior.

I closed my eyes and smiled, waiting for the jolt back to reality. We'd done it. We were working as a team again. There were kinks, sure, but we were on our way.

"Should two of us move up to the enemy's tower in case Derek and Hannah need help?" Rooke asked.

Sure, whatever.

I took a deep breath, inhaling the lavender and the wheat-grass, and the mountain air in all its perfection.

"Kali?"

An elbow nudged me. Hard.

"What?" I snapped.

Rooke stared back, eyes wide, dressed in his pod suit. He sat beside me in the conference room, in front of a sea of reporters. I blinked and looked out at the crowd. Shit. How much time had I lost now? Forget that. When had I left the real world for this place?

Okay, press conference. Right. Someone must have asked me something. I pressed my lips to the microphone. "Could you repeat the question please?"

The reporter stared at me for a second and cleared his throat. "For the last few weeks you've been struggling in your match-ups, and now tonight, you didn't lose a single player. What do you attribute to your improvements as a team?"

What was I supposed to say? I couldn't mention anything about the books or that we'd been sneaking moments of fun between training.

"We practiced fighting each other in various scenarios," I said. "It helped us to better know each other's styles, strengths, and weaknesses. Then, we worked together to become stronger. We're really starting to gel as a team." I grinned. "Which I think you all saw tonight."

The crowd laughed, and I laughed with them. Good. I'd recovered. As my teammates answered the reporters' questions, I looked down at myself dressed in my pod suit and forced my brain to trudge backwards, sorting through my memories. I was in the tower, then I was here. Nothing between. No. There must have been. I must have left the pod and walked here. Was

I on autopilot? I got to the destination but couldn't remember the journey.

When the conference ended, we hit the clubs. The cameras clicked and flashed as I posed with my teammates on the carpet. Saturday was our busiest night. The match had long ended, but the real game had just begun. Look good for the pictures. Promote the sponsors. On display for all to see.

Which world was the true arena?

Rooke stood at my side, lingering so close that accidental touches were as frequent as the camera flashes. All nothing more than featherlight strokes. Still, every one made me tense behind my smile. Sure, he wasn't being a *complete* asshole every spare second anymore. Somewhere between training and classic video games, he'd started to come out of his shell and become part of the team. But being told to like him was another thing altogether. Heaven forbid I was my own person, with a brain and feelings of my own, being free to like whoever I wanted. But to the camera's eyes, Rooke and I were a hot-blooded, hot-tempered mismatched pair of desire and disaster. Would our fights rip apart the whole team? Or would our love bring out the strengths in each other? Everyone just had to know.

I felt like banging my head on a wall.

"How about a kiss?" someone called out from the crowd.

Head. Wall.

The crowd laughed.

Rooke leaned toward me and lowered his voice. "Wanna head inside?"

I spoke back through my teeth. "Yes, please."

As we turned to enter the club, a grade-school round of AWWWW came from the crowd, followed by several individual protests.

"No, no. One more shot."

"Marry me, Lily."

Rooke led me toward the entrance doors. I walked under his arm, straining against my faltering smile until we disappeared into the club's darkness. Once inside, he dropped his arm and led the way through the club's darkness. I followed close behind and disappeared into the pounding beat, shouldering my way through the throngs of clammy bodies on the dance floor. Green spotlights swirled through the darkness, pouring down from the ceiling like lines of code. Like I was still in the virtual world.

I closed my eyes and basked in the sensations. Bodies writhed against mine, bumping me like a pinball through the crowd. The smell of sweat and alcohol filled the dense, heavy air. No mountain breeze. No lavender or wheatgrass. This would never be the virtual world. No sensation, none of it would ever be real enough.

In the VIP lounge, we sat in our usual spot. Derek waved to the waiter to bring us some drinks. When I glanced to the side, Rooke was gone.

"Where did he go?" I asked, nodding at the empty seat beside me.

"Bathroom," Derek answered.

I sighed and glanced at the hallway leading to the washrooms. I'd long figured that he wasn't much for partying, but anytime the alcohol appeared, he did the opposite. Maybe if I broke into the men's room, he'd realize he couldn't hide. Stick-figure signs and pee-pees don't stop Kali Ling.

The waiter came over to our table.

"Loved the fight tonight, guys," he said as he set the tray down. As usual, a bowl of HP sat in the center. "So did the crowd."

"Thanks," I said.

"That new guy is working out well." His eyes slid over to mine, and he nudged me, like we were best friends. "But I guess you'd know that better than the rest of us."

My fists tightened under the table. Had everyone seen that damn magazine? I shot him a tight-lipped smile. "Yeah. Sure."

"Too bad about your other teammate. What was his name?"

"Nathan," I told him.

"Nathan," he repeated, and shrugged. "Not sure I even knew his name. Shame how he died. What did I read? A heart defect? Anyways, at least you found a replacement so quickly. You're not out of the tournament, and that's what matters, right?"

My mouth soured, and I hadn't even downed the shot yet. A heart defect? Nathan died of an overdose from drugs he got at this very club. I tapped my foot on the floor, trying to contain my growing anger, and failing. But just behind the waiter, an ad next to the bar caught my eye. Protein Energy Boosters. One of our sponsors. Can't piss off the sponsors. Can't let the media know the truth. Can't ruin the magic façade that is being a virtual warrior.

I stopped tapping my foot and swallowed thick.

"Right," I said. "That's what matters."

The waiter left, and Rooke reappeared. He pressed himself into the couch next to me, staring straight ahead. There was a faint tremble in his hands, and his lips were nearly the same color as his skin. He looked like he'd just puked his guts out.

I leaned toward him and lowered my voice, enough that my teammates wouldn't hear, but he still would.

"Are you sick?"

He met my eyes for half a second and looked away.

"I'm fine," he muttered.

He was not fine. I was team captain, and it was my job to look after my teammates. But for the first time, Rooke and I weren't at each other's throats, and the rest of the team was starting to fall into place. If he could handle whatever was going on with him, maybe it was best if I just left it alone.

Across the club, music from the wallscreen blared, the VGL theme song. Highlights of our fight flashed across it.

"Good evening, ladies and gentlemen. I'm Marcus Ryan."

"And I'm Howie Fulton. And this is *Saturday Night Gaming*."

More theme music. The camera angle panned, then zoomed in on Howie.

"Let's take a look at the highlights from tonight's RAGE matchups. First up, FoRCE vs. InvictUS."

InvictUS. The five brutes who'd ripped us a new one two weeks ago.

The screen cut to the opposite team, the new prey for InvictUS. While four remained behind to guard their tower, a lone warrior disappeared into the fields. My stomach sank. You know that sickening sensation you get watching the gazelle run straight for the lion you know is hiding in the grass? But you can't just look away? Yeah, just like it. Guess that's why people watched this so much.

The lone warrior burst through the fields on the other side in front of the enemy's tower. He hesitated and glanced around. Where was InvictUS? From their hiding spots high in the sycamore trees, the foursome jumped down and surrounded him on all sides. His eyes went wide for half a second before his expression transformed into gritty determination. It wouldn't last.

Seconds into the fight, a sword slid through his abdomen, another into his thigh. He screamed. The tip of a blade swiped across his throat. His scream cut to a gurgle as he collapsed to the ground. Dead.

InvictUS raced for the tower.

In front was their leader, old One-Eye, who'd sliced my throat in the Death Match. According to his stats at the bottom of the screen, he had a name. Trent Amos. Didn't sound so much like an archnemesis, but alas, he was mine.

When he'd led his team through the fields and burst through the entrance, the scene inside the tower became a massacre. Wet slurps and screams filled the audio. Limbs dropped to the floor. Swords plunged into flesh until ribbons of blood snaked through the grooves of the tower's stone floor. Within a minute, all four remaining members of the other team were dead. InvictUS walked away from the match untouched. Not a scratch.

Invincible. In the world of gaming, these guys were redefining the word.

The footage cut back to the announcers. Howie shook his head. "Wow. These guys destroyed heavy favorites Defiance in the Death Match, and they just haven't let up since. Where did they come from, Marcus?"

"I don't know about that, but they certainly are the team to watch in this tournament."

So, guarding the tower with four wouldn't work, and neither did standard format: two defense, two offense, and a lone middleman. Maybe nothing could stand against the powerhouse that was InvictUS.

Warmth blossomed against my leg, where Rooke had let his hand come to rest on my knee. Though he wasn't looking at me. Did he even realize he was touching me, or were we just getting that used to posing with each other for the cameras? I leaned toward him and nodded at the screen.

"They're strong," I said.

He shook his head. "They're *organized*."

I considered it. "Yeah. That. *And* they're strong."

Rooke studied me. A slight grin pulled at his lips. Most men were intimidated by my domineering attitude. Others bowed down and got the hell out of my way. At least this one could handle it. In fact, when his grin broke into a full-out smile, I knew right away. Oh God, he thought I was cute. Warriors aren't cute.

"Hey, Kali."

I turned and followed the voice to Hannah. She was holding out a hit of HP to me. Sure, I'd dabbled with HP before, but hadn't done it since I'd been named captain. I scooted closer to her and reached for it. Why not?

I snatched the pill from her hand and popped it my mouth. Together, we did a shot and slammed the glasses down, laughing.

I nestled into the couch and watched the dancers on the floor below. Gradually, the pounding techno beat radiating off the walls slowed and pulsed beneath my skin with minivibrations. Beams of laser light streaming from the ceiling doubled in width and began undulating, like light reflecting off bodies of fish as they swam in and out of sight. I nuzzled farther into the couch, its leather upholstery as soft as seal's fur. The purest air, rich and mountainous, filled my nose and lungs with a single breath. The couch was a cloud, and I was floating in a ball of warmth. I smiled, closed my eyes, and sighed. Everything was soft, and calm, and perfect.

Nathan was right.

It was like I'd never left the game.

The next morning, I woke with my head on a pillow and sheets tucked in around me. Despite the dull ache pulsing through my body, I smiled to myself and nestled into the memory-foam mattress. Finally. I'd slept in a bed instead of the bathroom floor. About damn time.

Then, a warm body stirred against my back.

Shit. Shit. Shit.

How drunk did I get last night to end up in bed with Rooke? I took a deep breath, glimpsed over my shoulder, and found a mess of blond pigtails behind me. Lily, not Rooke. Thank God.

Hannah lay on the other side of her, asleep. I sighed, closed my eyes, and nestled back against the pillow.

Good. I hadn't slept with Rooke. I'd slept with the girls.

Wait.

*What?*

My eyes flew open and I bolted up in bed.

I instinctively felt around my body, starting at my torso and working my way down. Minus my shoes, I was still dressed in my clothing from the previous night. So were Lily and Hannah. Good. That's good.

I slipped out of the bed and into the natural-disaster zone that was the bunk's floor. Debris consisted of bits of clothing, empty liquor minis, and uniquely shaped paraphernalia that I really hoped had to do with drugs. After performing search-and-rescue for my shoes, I carried them by the straps and tip-toed to the door. I'd nearly escaped when something crunched underfoot. I froze and cast a glance at the girls still in bed. Hannah stirred but remained under sleep's mesmerizing spell. Lily never budged. I breathed a sigh of relief and knelt to retrieve the noisy culprit. The crumbled silver package opened like a blossoming flower in my hand. My sleeping pills. The package was empty. Every pill was popped out.

I shook my head, blinking. Gone? Every one of them? The girls must have had some. No way had I taken that many.

Not a chance.

I tapped the door-control button. When it slid open, I peeked around the hallway. Deserted. Good. God, what would Clarence think of my coming out of Hannah and Lily's bunk? Maybe he'd market that next.

Back in my bunk, I showered and changed into my training gear. At breakfast, I plunked down across from Hannah and

Lily. They regarded me with their usual nonchalant morning attitude. I, however, was anything but nonchalant and must have worn it on my face like a horror-inspired Halloween mask.

"You okay?" Hannah asked when she looked over my expression.

"Do you remember what happened last night?"

She shrugged. "We went out. Hit a few clubs."

"And then?"

"We came back here and hung out."

I raised an eyebrow. "That's it?"

"Yeah. Why?"

"I woke up in your bed."

The girls laughed.

"Oh, relax," Hannah said. "You just crashed with us. Why are you so worried about it? You weren't naked, were you?" She glanced over my frame in a way I wasn't so sure was neutral.

"Um, no."

"Then what's the problem?"

"I can't remember anything. It's like I blacked out."

Hannah's expression grew a little serious then. "You really weren't drunk enough not to remember. Maybe you did some extra shots when we weren't looking."

Lily nodded. "Yeah, off Rooke's stomach."

My own twisted at the thought. The girls burst out laughing again. At least someone thought this was funny.

"Hey." Hannah sat up straight, as if she'd just realized something. "Maybe it was that hit of HP you did."

I went numb.

"What?"

"You did a hit with me last night. Don't you remember?"

No. I didn't. Sure, I'd done HP before. Every gamer had. But

I'd never blacked out. Was the pill laced with something else, or had the combo of alcohol and sleeping pills done it? I couldn't remember anything at all. How many did I even take?

The blood drained from my face, and my gaze searched around the table for nothing at all. Hannah grasped my wrist.

"Hey. You look upset. I really wouldn't worry about it."

I'd blacked out and couldn't remember a thing. It was something to worry about.

I shook her off and took a long sip of my coffee. Just like every morning, the thick, rich blend coated my tongue and washed down my throat, warming me on the inside. But the comfort it usually brought was absent.

I sat at the table in silence for the rest of the meal, nodding whenever someone spoke to me, until the girls' trays were empty, save for the apple cores and a few rogue flakes of cereal.

"We're hitting the track now," Hannah announced as she grabbed her tray and stood. "You coming?"

"No. I have something to do this morning."

She tilted her head. "Like what?"

"Just things," I mumbled as I left, heading in the opposite direction of the track and workout area. After wandering aimlessly around the hallways of the facility for several minutes, I eventually found myself in a familiar, stark green room. It wasn't Clarence's office.

"I bet you're surprised to see me," I said. "Do gamers ever come back unless they have to?"

The shrink nodded, and I half expected her lips to start bouncing.

"Sometimes," she said. "But sometimes it's just for more pills. Is that why you're here? Because if you need more already, that's a concern—"

"No. I'm fine."

You could get sleeping pills on the street, right? Well, we had people for that. Nathan had gotten an endless supply of whatever he wanted from one of the security guards. Now I'd ask him for sleeping pills. I'm sure that would be a request he'd never heard before. But I needed those pills. Sleep was the one comfort I had left, and I had no chance of getting there on my own with the thought of Nathan's dead body beside me.

"What brought you into my office today?" the doc asked, peering through her glasses at me.

Despite the churning sensation in my stomach, I pushed the words out of my mouth. "I think I have a problem."

"Is it the game?"

I looked down at my lap and shook my head. She sighed. She didn't buy it. Guess that degree in psychiatry had taught her something.

"Let me guess," she said, making notes on her tablet, "you're beginning to experience gaps in time."

I looked up. "What do you mean?"

"You're in one place, then you're suddenly somewhere else without memory of how you got there."

I stared at her, trying to blink away the dread in my eyes. My Halloween mask was back.

"I'll take that as a 'yes.'" She made another note on her tablet. "How often?"

I fumbled with nothing in my lap. "Twice. Maybe."

She nodded and wrote more.

"What does that mean?" I asked, lifting my head, trying to peer at her tablet. She tilted it toward herself, away from my view.

"We'll come back to that." She looked me square in the eyes. "I'd like to talk about Nathan. Are you ready?"

No.

I shifted in my seat, drawing deep breaths that did nothing to help my churning stomach. It was time, but the words wouldn't leave my mouth. Come on, Doc. Tell me I *have* to talk about it.

She didn't. She sat there behind her desk, studying me with a look that was both patient and sympathetic. The idea of holding my breath until she made me spill seemed childish, though it did cross my mind. No. I could do this. I could face it.

I nodded. "Okay."

"How did you feel when he died?" she asked.

I shook my head. Way to go, Kali. You lasted two seconds.

"You're not sure how you felt, or . . ." Her voice trailed off, leaving me to fill in the blank. I pressed my lips together and offered no reply.

She studied me for a minute and sat back in her chair. "I'll wait, then. You just take your time."

I mashed my lips together and felt childish again. Though I secretly hoped the motion would relax the tightness in my chest. Warriors weren't supposed to feel. I eyed the door. I could get up and just walk out. Nothing was keeping me here since I'd come on my own terms. Clarence wasn't forcing me. No one was. But warriors don't run either.

"Fine." I let out an exasperated sigh. Maybe I had been holding my breath. "I felt responsible. And selfish."

"These are normal emotions, Kali," she assured me in an even tone, one I'm sure was supposed to keep me calm. "Everyone feels responsible when someone dies. Now, why did you feel selfish?"

"Because I just sat there. I did nothing. I didn't stop him from doing the drugs. I didn't check on him before I went to sleep. And when I woke up the next morning and found him dead, I hid in the corner like a child."

"Most people would have reacted the way you did, especially those without medical training. Most people would have been afraid."

"Yeah, well, they aren't warriors on television."

She smiled. "Most people on television are actors."

I recoiled, pressing myself into the chair. "So, that's it. You think I'm acting all the time. You think on the inside, I'm actually a weak, little girl."

"No, no. I think you're very strong."

I blinked. "Why?"

"You came back here." She waved a hand at the office around her. "You took charge of the team. You're pushing through the situation the best you can."

"The best I can." I scoffed. "I don't even know what I'm doing. I'm supposed to know. I'm an adult now. I should be able to handle all of this, and I can't."

"Being an adult doesn't mean you know everything. Sometimes it means you know enough to admit when you need help, and you're not afraid to ask for it." She took off her glasses and leaned toward me. "Look, I pulled the M.E.'s report on Nathan's death. As far as they can tell, he died in his sleep in the early morning. All he would know was that he went to bed next to someone he cared about. He didn't suffer."

Good. That's good. He hadn't suffered. Though my stomach still churned at the thought, it buffered the blow to know his passing had been peaceful. I swallowed.

"Thank you."

My voice squeaked. I pressed my lips together, hoping the doc hadn't noticed. She replaced her glasses and made more notes on her tablet.

"You know," she began, "gamers in the RAGE tournaments

are the most prone to psychological issues. You could participate in another branch of the VGL. Maybe something a little less violent?"

I laughed. "What would you have me do? Special Ops? Dungeon raids? When you get down to the nitty-gritty, they're all violent in their own ways. First-person shooters, RPGs, it doesn't matter. The endgame is always the same. Kill the enemy."

Dr. Renner clicked her tongue as she looked over her tablet. "I'll be honest, Kali. I'm concerned for your health. Experiencing gaps in time is a common symptom for those beginning to lose their grip on reality. I don't know if you should go much further with this, and I have medical authority to pull you out."

My stomach dropped to my toes. "Are you saying I can't stay in the tournament? I have to stay in. My teammates are counting on me. If they had to replace another player now, they'd never make it. This could ruin their careers."

Dr. Renner studied me for a minute, then smiled like she was proud. "What about your career?"

Yeah, what about mine? Suddenly, it didn't seem so important anymore. In fact, it hadn't even crossed my thoughts. Did I just put the team before myself? Maybe I really was becoming a leader.

A leader. Four other people were counting on me now. Counting on me to lead them through the tournament to victory. Their careers, hell, the rest of their lives rested with me. I could be strong. I could do this for the team.

"I have to stay in the game," I said. "Tell me what I need to do to fix this, and I'll do it."

The doc leaned toward me again. "If you meet with me on a regular basis, so I can monitor you, then you can stay in for now. You need to come to me the minute you don't feel right, understand?"

I nodded. "I will."

I left the doc's office feeling stronger than I had in a long time. Each step that pounded into the hallway's metal floor sent another shock wave of perseverance through my body. This wasn't just about me or my career. The team was counting on me to lead them to the championship. That's what mattered.

But the problem with living in a reality so plastic and fake and a virtual world so full of life was that the lines between what matters and what doesn't get blurry.

Fast.

# CHAPTER 12

The next round of the tournament was announced on Sunday afternoon. As teams were eliminated, and there were fewer to match up, we were getting our opponents sooner than the previous week. Which was a godsend. Every step up through the tournament was a bigger challenge, and the more time we had to prepare, the better. This Saturday we'd be facing Celestial Elite.

The week was a carbon copy of the former. Mostly. We worked out briefly in the morning and ran virtual simulations the rest of the day, whenever we didn't have a media event.

The evenings were something else.

Since the *Pro Gamer Weekly* cover, publicity had become a nightmare. Actually, having a nightmare would imply that I'd slept sometime in the last several days. Despite new issues of the magazine being released every week, ours was still the top seller. On the carpets, in front of the cameras, Rooke had to lock his fingers through mine more than once to stop me from clocking someone. Yeah, okay, I was extra grumpy, but at least the paparazzi had a field day over us holding hands—which made me want to punch them even more. The shots in the club and hits of HP made reality bearable. Maybe if I could get a decent night of sleep, I'd be able to deal with everything even better.

Luckily, I found my salvation on my way back to my bunk after an especially grueling morning training session.

"Hey, Kali. Got what you asked for."

Reynolds, one of the security guards, waved at me as he approached. He slipped a package of sleeping pills into my hand. "That's the first time any of you asked for that. Sure you don't want something harder? I got a few things that'll—"

I held up a hand. "I'm fine. I just need to rest."

He laughed. "Yeah. The game can mess with your sleep. I get it."

"It's not the game. It's because of Nathan."

"Yeah, sure. Lemme know if you need more, or something else."

As he walked away, I studied the package. A feeling washed over me, like relief from finding a lost tablet or purse. Somewhere inside, I sighed. Finally, I'd sleep.

Inside my bunk, I left the pills on my bathroom counter and changed into my pod suit. Just like the week before, we were running afternoon simulations against digital versions of our new opponents. But by the time the third simulation had ended, I sat inside the pod, shaking, begging my stomach not to revisit lunch. When the pod doors opened, I pulled myself out and wavered on my feet and shook my head. Dizziness spanned out around me, like rippling waves in an invisible pond.

What was wrong with me?

A hand landed on my elbow. I followed it up until I met Hannah's face.

"You okay?"

I shook my head. "I'm going back to my room for a while. You'll have to practice without me."

She looked me up and down. "Are you getting sick? The doctor's always on call—"

"No, no. I just need to go lie down. Do me a favor. Tell the others I was feeling a little weak and needed to rest. I'll try to join you for supper."

She studied me through the narrow slits of her eyes and eventually nodded. "Okay. Let me know if you need anything else."

"Thanks."

I managed to slip out of the room, avoiding everyone else until I arrived at my bunk. The room swirled around me as I sat down on my bed, holding my head in my hands.

It'll pass. Just wait it out.

The room stopped spinning, but somehow, my body went numb and tingled at the same time. I pulled my hands away from my face and studied them. They trembled violently, as if I hadn't eaten in days. Sweat beaded across my forehead. Hot chills washed over me in waves. What was happening to me? The flu. It must be the flu. I just needed to rest. That's all. And now I had my pills again. I'd be fine.

My tablet chimed on the bed beside me. I groaned. What now?

Incoming call from San Diego.

Shit. Only one person would call from San Diego. I gathered my strength, scooped up the screen, and tapped it. The face of a middle-aged woman with dark hair and fine lines tracing her eyes and lips appeared.

She smiled. "Hi, Sweetie."

"Hi, Mom."

Her eyes narrowed. "Are you okay? You look pale."

From warm to hostile in a nanosecond. Nothing like a sick child to bring out the army general in any mother.

"I'm fine. It's just the screen."

Great. Now I was lying to my mom. Thumbs-up, Kali.

"Oh, good. So, anything new? Any *boys*?" She drew out the last word and gave a suggestive tweak of her eyebrow. She'd seen the article. Or the billboards. Or the pictures scrolling across every digital bookstore and magazine stand.

I rolled my eyes. "Mom, I told you not to believe what you read in those magazines. Most of it is crap, okay?"

"I know, I know. And it's a good thing, too. I don't know what I'd do if my baby was actually out every night partying in those clubs."

My stomach twisted. I smiled, the fake one. "Right."

"Especially considering this opportunity you've been given. Not everyone who wants to become a pro gamer actually makes it there. I expect someone as smart as you to realize that."

How were mothers such experts at laying on the guilt trips even when they didn't realize it?

"Your father and I are very proud of you," she added.

I suppressed my scoff. "Really?"

"Is this because we don't watch the tournaments? You can't expect us to. Imagine watching someone you knew getting a sword stuck in them."

It made sense when she put it like that.

"I understand."

"Then why wouldn't you think we're proud of you?"

"You didn't seem too happy when I left."

She frowned. "Of course we weren't. We just didn't want to see you go. For you, it's off on this big adventure. For us, it's . . . what do they call that? Empty nest." There was a pause. "But," she stressed, "your dad pointed out that if you got drafted into the MLB or NHL, we'd be excited. How many people's kids get to do that? What you're doing is no different. It's just . . . video games? It takes some time to get used to the idea."

Dad. The wise one. Sometimes I missed his talks and the

sensibility of his thought process. But really, my parents had plenty of time to get used to the idea. I'd played games since I could hold a controller.

"Mom, national gaming competitions have been around for over fifty years now."

"But fully immersive virtual reality didn't exist when your father and I were kids. It's still new to us. We don't really understand all of this."

Most people didn't, other than gamers and the fans, whose number was growing by the day. Not since poker at the turn of the century had the world seen such a fast-rising sport.

"You know," she continued, "the article in *Pro Gamer Weekly* said you've been named the team's captain. Is that crap, too?"

My eyebrows went up. "You actually read the magazine?"

"Of course," she scoffed. "You were on the cover."

Sure, but I never thought she'd look further than that.

"Uh, yeah. I'm captain."

"So, what does that mean?"

"I lead the team and instruct them on strategy. Things like that."

She beamed. "That sounds like a lot of responsibility. Are you sure you can handle it?"

I gritted my teeth. "Yes, Mom."

She narrowed her eyes again at my strained expression. "Are you sure you're okay?"

"Yes," I stressed. "We just ran through some simulations, and I'm a little tired. I know it's not going to make much sense to you, but it drains you physically. I just need to relax."

"Oh, okay. I'll let you go then."

"Thanks."

She paused. "I love you."

I smiled, not the fake one. "Me too, Mom."

The screen went black. I stared at it, blinking for a moment, trying to process exactly how the call had made me feel. Then, my hands trembled, and my stomach churned again. Sleep. I had to get some sleep.

With Mom gone, I dropped the façade and gave in to the weakness, hand-crawling along the wall to the bathroom. Inside at the sink, my fingers fumbled as I struggled against the package of sleeping pills. One popped out, skipped along the counter, and landed in the sink. I chased it, but grabbed nothing but air. It looped around the metal basin like a marble in a funnel until it disappeared down the drain.

Damn it.

Damn it. Damn it. Damn it.

A buzz came from my door. Hannah. Probably called the doctor despite my protest. Screw it. I picked up the package and pressed my fingers against another metallic bubble.

The buzz came again. I sighed.

"Hannah, fuck off and go away."

"Do you always talk to your friends like that?"

Rooke. Shit. What did he want?

I marched out of the bathroom and tapped the door control.

"What?" I asked as the door slid open.

Rooke stood on the other side, arms crossed, brow furrowed, looking remarkably cute for someone so concerned.

"You okay?" he asked.

I shook my head. "I'm not feeling so hot. I'm just going to lie down for a while."

"Do you need the doctor?"

I spoke through gritted teeth. "No. I just need to rest."

*Which doesn't involve your being here.*

"I can go get someone for you," he offered. "Or walk you down to the medical wing."

My teeth gnashed together so hard, they should have cracked. "I said I'm fine."

Why didn't anyone believe me?

Rooke studied me for a second, then shrugged. "Okay." He started to turn away when his gaze locked on the package in my hand. "What's that?"

The pills. I'd never put them down. I couldn't hide, so I defaulted to my own standard programming—sarcasm.

"Hang on," I said, bringing the fine print of the package up to eye level. "It says it's fifty milligrams of *None of Your Business*. Take one or two before bed." I dropped my arm, and the act. "They're sleeping pills. The shrink prescribed them, okay?"

There. No lies. A doctor told me to . . . even though the name on the package wasn't mine.

He sputtered. "But . . . I've seen you drinking at the clubs." His jaw flexed. "Along with other things."

"So?"

His eyes went wide. "Kali, didn't you read the package? You can't mix sleeping pills with alcohol and street drugs."

"Oh, like you don't use," I said, crossing my arms in defense. "Everyone who goes virtual does something."

"I don't."

I thought back. He'd disappeared when we drank shots at the club, and I never once saw him inhale anything other than air, even while the rest of us were cutting lines and popping pills. Maybe he really was clean. That made him the only gamer in the history of the VGL not to dabble. God, was he really such a choirboy?

I shrugged it off. "So I drink sometimes at the clubs. Get over it."

"Don't you know how dangerous that is?" He took a step toward me. "What are you doing to yourself?"

"Whatever I want with my life."

He looked directly into my eyes. His blank, stone-cold façade from when we first met was back.

"You're going to kill yourself," he said. "You need to wake up and realize what you're doing."

I stepped up to him. "You have no idea what happened to me. You know Nathan, the guy you replaced? He died next to me in bed. I woke up to a dead body. Can you blame me for having trouble sleeping?"

"That's no excuse for abusing yourself. You're hiding from it, not facing it. You're going to end up just like him. You're not invincible, Kali."

Who the fuck did this guy think he was? He couldn't tell me what to do. No one could. I wasn't just an adult. I was a gamer. We ruled both worlds, the real and the virtual. No one could touch us.

"Do you think this makes you a good leader?" he asked.

I reeled. "And not sleeping makes me a better one? I'm doing this *for* the team, not despite them."

"And when you do a hit of HP at the clubs, is that for the team, too?"

I ground my teeth together. Whatever I chose to do at the clubs was none of his fucking business.

"You can't keep going like this," he stressed. The muscles in his neck went tight. "You could die, Kali. Don't you see that?"

Pffft. I waved him off. "We don't die, you idiot. We never die. We just wake up. You know why the rest of us do this? Why we drink and party and get so high we can't remember our own names? It's just to pass the time until we can go back to what's real."

He took a step back, and the color drained from his face. "What did you just say?"

"Nothing. I don't know."

He took my head in his hands and forced my eyes up. "Look at me. What do you see?"

"An asshole." I slapped his hands, but his grip only tightened on my jaw.

"How many times have you died?"

"What?"

"How many times?"

"Thirty, maybe. Forty. I don't know."

"Dying here isn't like the games," he said. "This is reality."

And a hell of a place it was. After all my time inside a fully immersive, no-holds-barred video game, I'd learned one thing: reality was more programmed than the virtual world. Why couldn't Rooke see that? Better yet, why couldn't he just shut up and leave me alone?

"Kali, look at me."

No. Go away.

But there was a certain roughness to his voice I'd never heard before. Curiosity pulled my gaze up to his. His jaw was clenched tight, and the veins in his forehead throbbed. Yup, definitely not impressed.

"If you die here, that's it. It's game over."

Oh, shut up. Just shut up.

He took another step toward me, and his voice rose with it. "There aren't any one-ups or chances to continue. It's actual death. Do you understand?"

His voice practically vibrated down the walls as he towered over me. I swallowed thick. Wow, I'd really pissed him off.

He shook me.

"Do. You. Understand?"

For the love of God, shut up.

I kissed him.

There. That shut him up.

But, wait—hello there, soft lips. Wow, he tasted sweet, too, like he'd just sipped a sports drink. I sank into him, the kiss, everything. His arms slid around my waist, and the sudden warmth from his closeness was a bucket of cold water.

What was I doing?

I broke the kiss, but remained close, so his breaths tickled my nose. He stared down at my mouth, blinking, as if trying to process what had just happened. Was the kiss that unexpected, or had he felt something? He tilted his head and closed in, tentatively. My heart thrummed in my ears as his lips lingered over mine, featherlight touches, like he was debating whether to taste something that was both incredibly pleasurable and potentially toxic. Oh, he'd definitely felt something.

He pulled back, closed his eyes, and sighed.

Damn.

"Are you really that desperate to hide?" he asked. "You can't face it, can you? You have a problem."

I did not have a problem. I couldn't sleep. That was all.

"You think it's such a problem? Here." I chucked the pills out the door. The package landed ten feet away and skipped a few steps down the hall. "They're yours. Now I'll never sleep. Happy?"

"Why would I be happy to see you like this?"

"I don't give two shits what you feel about me," I said, pushing the words through my teeth. Once they'd left my mouth, my chest went hollow, as if I'd just given up my heart to go with the soul I'd long kissed good-bye. "My life is my business. Get out of my bunk."

He didn't move.

"Get out."

I shoved him.

He reeled back, eyes wide. His fingers lingered over where I'd hit. Then he scowled, left the room, scooped up the package of pills in the hall, and disappeared. The door whooshed shut behind him.

I sank to the floor, pulled my legs to my chest, and pressed my face against my knees. Why was Rooke being such an asshole? Nathan wouldn't have done that to me. He would have popped the pills and gone for the ride. My eyes burned, and my heart ached like an open, bloody wound. Shit, I missed him.

Now, Nathan was nothing more than a statistic. A statistic no one knew about except the gamers themselves. A victim of the minefield that was the life of a virtual gamer. Drugs. Alcohol. Obsession. Mental illness. All shrouded in darkness by a world faker than the arena itself.

Time passed as I sat on the floor. Maybe minutes, maybe hours. I sobbed against my knees until my crying fit descended into nothing more than dry heaves.

I pushed up to my feet, dragged myself to the bed, and collapsed across it. As the foam mattress morphed around my form, it was the only comfort of the moment. My face felt swollen and sore. My eyes burned from the dryness, completely drained of tears. For the rest of the afternoon, I lay there alone, drifting between reality and a sleepless sleep.

At dinner, I plunked down at the table with a mug of coffee in my hand and eyed the food on Hannah's plate with a curled lip. Salmon, brown rice, and an apple. Fuck food. Fuck it all.

"Are you okay?" Hannah gasped. "You look exhausted."

With her eyes wide and eyebrows raised, I knew she was saying it out of concern, and I knew exactly what she was looking at. My reflection in the mirror left no doubt. Baggy, swollen eyes and a droopy face. I really did look awful.

I narrowed my gaze at Rooke, sitting at the other end of the table, in his usual spot across from Derek. He didn't notice or feel the weight of my glare, no matter how much I lasered my eyes into him.

"I'm fine," I grumbled. "Just didn't sleep."

"Maybe you should eat," she suggested. "It might give you some energy."

I scowled at first, then snatched the apple off her tray. Hannah opened her mouth to protest but snapped it shut when she saw the look in my eyes. The bittersweet taste swirled in my mouth as I chewed. Apple skin. Blah.

I stared straight ahead at the wall behind Hannah. She chewed her dinner, softly, as if even the crunching of her teeth would piss me off. Probably not so wrong. At some point, Lily appeared, saw my face, and sat in silence with us.

That evening we had a television interview, to be aired around midnight. One of those late-night talk shows. I avoided Clarence until we left for the studio. Last thing I needed was a speech about how tired I looked. How could you possibly appear on TV like that? On the ride over, I kept my head down as much as I could, or rested it in my hands and feigned a headache. It wasn't much of a stretch.

"Didn't get enough sleep?" the makeup artist chimed as she layered concealer under my eyes.

I sat slumped in the chair, not even bothering to straighten up for her as she worked. "I had a rough day."

She smirked. "Oh, you kids. Partying. Drinking 'til the morning hours. Life's tough, huh?"

I ground my teeth together. What did she know? People saw

what my life was in the magazines and thought they knew me inside and out.

Honey, here's your wake-up call.

I nodded at her, simulating a sympathetic tone. "Yeah. I guess you're right. My life's not that tough. Waking up at the crack of dawn to train, lift weights, and run for hours every day. Then I spend my weekends surrounded by death. Blood and guts smeared everywhere. Do you know what it smells like when you cut open someone's stomach, and their digestive juices spill out all over your feet?"

She blanched, and her cheeks puffed out as if she was about to vomit.

I smiled and nodded at her makeup brush. "You wanna trade?"

She left. Someone else finished my makeup. In silence.

After hair and makeup, the stage director lined us up backstage while the host introduced the night's topic to the cameras and the crowd.

"Video games. Once a child's plaything. Once blamed in part for the obesity epidemic that plagued our country decades ago. Now, eSports are the fastest rising trend in history. Thanks to advancements in virtual reality, participants have to be in top physical and mental condition as the games place extreme demands on both body and mind. Tonight, you'll be meeting one of the hottest teams in the country. But first, we'll look into the history of gaming, how the Virtual Gaming League formed, and why these games have become so popular. Let's just say, we've come a long way from Pong."

Behind stage, Hannah nudged me. "You ever play Pong?" she murmured.

I glanced back at her. "A remake of it, yeah. Not on the original system."

"Of course not," she scoffed. "Who has an original system anymore?"

"I'd give my right foot to play on one, though."

"I know. Wait, right foot? Isn't the saying, you'd give up your right *hand*?"

"If I gave up my hand, there'd be no way to play." I thumbed an invisible controller in my hands to demonstrate. She laughed.

After the introduction and history of the VGL played in a comical animation for both the audience and the people at home, the host raised his voice. "And now let's meet one of the top teams of the RAGE tournaments: Defiance."

The stage director shoved me forward.

I led the way onto the stage. The blazing studio lights stabbed ice picks through my brain. I waved to the audience and smiled through gritted teeth. Practiced. Perfect. Between it and the mountain of makeup on my face, no one would know.

I sat closest to the host's desk. Hannah sat beside me, followed by everyone else. Rooke sat at the complete opposite end, but somehow, it wasn't far enough. Hell, it wouldn't be far enough if they put his chair in the parking lot. Yeah, I was still just a teensy bit mad at him over the sleeping-pills incident hours earlier.

The host greeted us from behind his desk. "Hello. Welcome."

"Thanks for having us," I said as I sat in my chair and crossed my legs.

"Of course." He smiled and focused his attention on me. "I'm sure most people know by now, but congratulations on being named the team's captain, the first female one in history."

Applause came from the audience, along with a whistle and a few catcalls. I smiled and waved to them again.

"Thank you."

"That has to be quite the honor. There are probably hundreds, maybe even thousands of young female gamers watching this at home." He motioned toward the camera. "Now you're their role model."

My expression fell, and my stomach went right along with it. I glanced at the camera. Were there little-girl gamers looking up to me now? Oh, hello swirling stomach. So glad you could make another cameo appearance.

I clicked my fingernails on the arm of the chair and shifted my weight as I thought to myself. I offered a meek smile, letting the audience see something real. "You know, I never thought about that."

The host laughed. "Look at her, so modest."

"Give her a sword," his cohost chimed in from across the stage, next to the band. "Maybe she'll be more comfortable."

The host nodded at him. "Yeah, but then I'd be the uncomfortable one."

The audience laughed along with the host. I joined them, façade back in place despite my churning stomach.

The host motioned toward the camera again. "So explain to our viewers at home who might be unfamiliar with the RAGE tournaments how a team that lost can still be in the competition?"

I perked up. Gaming history was about the only history I enjoyed. "Double-elimination tournaments are standard format for most divisions in the VGL. When video game tournaments first began, this style of tournament eventually became the norm so that teams who traveled hundreds, or even thousands, of miles to compete could lose more than once before they were sent home."

"I see."

I continued. "In the VGL, the Death Match divides the tournament field into two halves: those who lose and those who don't. The undefeated teams play each other until only one remains. The same goes for those in the losing bracket. Then, the champion of the defeated teams and the champion of the undefeated play each other for the title."

The host nodded as he thought that over. "Then, you still have a chance to come back."

I grinned, sly and cunning. The warrior. "We will come back."

The audience clapped wildly. At least the fans were still with us. Some wavered between the most popular teams, but the diehards would always be with us. Probably. Unlike the sponsors.

"So," the host began, tapping his knuckles on his desk as a grin filled his face, "apparently, there's a little romance on the team?"

Kill me now. It was going so well. The audience erupted in a jumble of applause and cheers. I laughed and feigned innocence.

"Oh, you mean these two," I said, motioning to Lily and Hannah.

The host waved his hand. "No, no. I'm talking about this."

He swiveled in his chair to the screen behind him. The *Pro Gamer Weekly* cover flashed across it. At the sight of my head resting against Rooke's chest, my stomach twisted so hard, my lips and toes nearly followed suit.

The crowd exploded into ooohs, jeers, and whistles. Even a *whoop* called out from the back corner.

Whoop? Really?

On stage, Hannah pressed her lips together to hide her smile. Derek playfully punched Rooke in the shoulder. I wasn't sure either of them was acting.

I looked down the row to Rooke, passing the buck to him. The host leaned forward in his desk and raised his voice. "Do you have anything to say for yourself?"

Rooke paused for a second, then said, "I'll let the lady answer."

The host laughed. "Smart man." He turned back to me. "Well, Kali?"

I blinked and sighed inwardly. With the endless hours I'd spent training in the virtual world to become pro, I never realized how much I'd have to fake in reality. Was it worth it? Of course it was. If it meant I got to play the sport I loved, I was willing to do anything. Even this.

I turned to the audience and offered my best smile. "My feelings for him are as real as in any world."

The audience applauded feverishly. Good. They bought it.

Hannah leaned toward me, and murmured, "Nice."

"Mmm-hmm," I replied through my teeth.

The host turned to the cameras. "Well, that's all we have time for tonight. I'd like to thank my guests, team Defiance, for joining us. I'm going to close with the VGL motto: Go virtual or go home. Good night, everybody."

After the stage lights clicked off, and I shook hands with the host, I trudged toward backstage, tracing lines in the floor with my gaze. Were young gamers really looking up to me now? What kind of role model was I? One in the tabloids every week. Drinking. Partying. Popping pills.

"Kali." Hannah grabbed my arm and yanked me back. I looked up at her, blinking. "You're walking in a trance."

"I just have a lot on my mind."

That was the understatement of my life. I couldn't get a decent night's sleep. My teammate had died, and nobody cared. My love life had become grade-A gossip for everyone else's amusement. On top of it all, I was suddenly a role model for young gamers? Me. A role model. Like a bathtub and a toaster, those two things should never be put together.

Hannah sighed as she looked over my face. "I feel like I'm

asking all the time now if you're okay. I'm worried about you. What do you need?"

"Space," I told her, walking away. "I need space."

I knew what I needed even more than that. I needed an escape. But no drug or amount of alcohol would calm me. I had only one thing. The only place that had ever brought me peace.

The arena.

# CHAPTER 13

The stadium smelled of death, and of victory.

The crowd roared as the undertaker dragged my latest victim—I mean, opponent—away. The metallic scent of blood filled the air. Sand swirled between my toes as I stood alongside my favorite ally: the wind. It whipped black strands of hair around my face and in my eyes. I let it. In moments of bliss, you just don't care.

I closed my eyes and basked in the sounds around me. The clanking chains of the undertaker. The chanting mob. *Kali, Kali, Kali.* Then, above it all, I heard something else. Four simple words that clenched my rib cage around my heart.

"You come here often?"

I froze at the sound of the familiar male voice that twisted my lips into a scowl. Then I forced the grimace off my face and turned to him. Rooke stood behind me in his battle gear, short sword in each hand, ready to join in a fight. What the hell was this guy thinking? Only hours ago, he'd practically spit in my face over the sleeping pills, and now he was ready to fight along-side me.

The wind whispered in my ear. *Cut his fucking head off.*

Or maybe that was just my subconscious.

Still, a grin touched the corner of my lips. The sword in my hand. His bare neck. Maybe it was time for an introduction.

"This is *my* simulation," I said. "You can leave."

Rooke took a few steps toward me. The exit was the other way. "Give me a chance. I had my programmer cook up a little something for you."

The gates opened around, and six gladiators stepped out, surrounding us on all sides. At least they were average-size men and not giants.

"Oh, look," I said, speaking in a computerized voice. "Now we will have to fight as a team."

Rooke frowned and shook his head at my sarcasm.

Guess this was his way of making amends over the sleeping-pills incident. And honestly, a unique battle simulation wasn't a bad effort. Well, for a girl like me. Most boyfriends bought their girls flowers or jewelry to apologize. Mine had given me an arena full of virtual opponents. A chance to test my fighting skills. Of course, most girls had real boyfriends. Or, a real relationship, at least.

We went back-to-back, his skin pressing against mine. Heat emanated from him, baked in the glowing sun. His muscles moved across mine as he rotated his swords with his wrists. I smiled at the sensation.

Wait, wasn't I still mad at him?

The horde closed in from all sides, weapons drawn, death in every eye. Rooke spoke over his shoulder to me.

"You nervous?"

"No." I smiled at the approaching men. "I'm hungry."

Rooke made a sound in the back of his throat. A sort of grunt I could only describe as stunned approval.

"With this many," he began, when he found his voice again, "we'll need to take some out fast to contain the fight."

"We'd do even better if we ran ahead and met these ones first," I told him, pointing at the three men in front of me.

"We?"

I glanced back as I started to run. "If you can keep up."

He did.

He caught up to my side in seconds, just as we reached the trio of attackers.

As I ran, I dropped to my knees and slid, like I was surfing, spraying up waves of sand. Skidding past the first opponent, I lashed out with my sword, slicing through his calf. He cried out and stumbled face-first into the ground. I pounced on his back and slammed my blade through his spine. He grunted and went limp.

I turned around to find Rooke fighting the other two at once. One had his back to me. Oh, this was just too easy. I jumped up on his back, rocked his head back, and ripped through his neck with my sword. He crumpled to the ground.

Two down, one to go.

I circled around Rooke and the remaining attacker as sword clanged against sword. Rooke deflected every move with ease. Damn, he had skill. The muscles in his arms rippled with each strike. Yup, could definitely watch that all day long.

Rooke went down on one knee and smashed the side of his opponent's leg with the hilt of his sword. The fighter screamed as his bone broke through the skin. He landed hard on his back, arms flailing as he wailed with pain. Rooke pulled back and motioned for me to take the kill.

"Ladies first."

He had the audacity to give me a cocky grin.

I grinned back.

Pressing a foot into the enemy's chest, I gripped my sword with both hands and slammed it through his heart. A puff of air wheezed out of his lungs, and his eyes glazed over.

Around us, the crowd screamed with delight, pounding their

feet into the stands until the stadium itself came alive with its own pulsing heartbeat.

I yanked my sword out of the latest victim and looked for Rooke, who had started toward the remaining three warriors. He glanced back and nodded, signaling me to join him in the fight. I judged the distance between me and him, and the warriors closing in. Thirty feet. Then twenty. I shook my head.

"Kneel down."

Rooke's brow furrowed, like he didn't understand the command. I bolted for him, full speed.

"Kneel."

The word ripped from my mouth like a battle cry. He knelt, back toward me, shielding his head with one arm. I ran up his back and pushed off his shoulder. I flew, right over the three men. On my descent, I spun in the air, sword out. I became a whipping blade, cutting through my enemies' backs like putty. I landed behind them in a crouching stance, one hand on the ground, one gripping my sword out and to the side.

Perfect ten? Thank you, judges.

I remained crouched as I listened to the wet, slopping sound of my opponents' body parts raining down behind me until the last hit the ground.

Silence.

The world froze in that moment. Sand sprinkled the air around me. The wind looped through my hair and swirled around my figure. I took a breath. Cool, clean air pumped through my lungs. I smiled.

Perfection.

Nowhere was better than the arena.

The crowd roared as they leapt to their feet. Glory rushed through my veins. I pushed up to my feet and presented myself to the mob, soaking in their applause. Applause that was mine.

Over the pile of dead bodies, Rooke stood eyeing me with a cocky grin and his eyebrows raised, the look a man gets when he's turned on. Given our recent fight, I thought I'd be disgusted. But I couldn't ignore the ego boost I felt instead.

I placed a hand on my hip, remaining casual. "You impressed?"

He rubbed the shoulder I'd pushed off from and shrugged. "No. More surprised than anything. I didn't think you'd weigh that much."

My mouth fell open as a flash of anger exploded inside. Rooke grinned and walked away, arrogance swirling around him like a genie's puff of smoke. As I watched him leave, his unguarded back taunted me. The sword itched in my hand. My eyes narrowed on target.

I went for it.

Moving across the sand like the wind, Rooke didn't hear my approach until I was inches away. He spun around and brought his sword up just in time to block my swing.

The crowd erupted around us.

We stood there, locked in the moment. Our eyes pinned on one another, his glinting with curiosity. His shoulders moved with heavy breaths as he watched me, waiting for my next move. And I had one. Plenty of them.

I snapped forward, knocking an unsuspecting Rooke back half a step. His guard dropped and I punched him hard across the jaw. His head turned sideways from the blow and took longer than it should have to turn back. When he looked at me, wiping a dribble of blood away from his lip, I thought I'd see anger on his face. I didn't. Fire erupted in his eyes. I'd fueled him. Unleashed the beast.

He grinned wickedly and came for me.

Sword met sword again and again in an endless battle. We mirrored each other. Move-for-move, foot-for-foot. A dance, in which neither led nor followed. Balanced. Even.

Then the blazing sun seared my eyes just as he swung. I caught the blade with my own but stumbled and fell. The second I hit the ground, he was on top of me, pinning me down with his weight. I struggled beneath him.

He glanced between us. "Now, here's something I haven't tried digitally before."

He grinned as he pressed down harder, and our lower halves melded together. I grunted in protest and wriggled again, discovering more of his weight rested on his right side. Victory. I hooked my leg around his left knee and rolled. He went easy and landed on his back with a grunt. This time, I grinned as I peered down at him.

"A virtual virgin, huh?" I said. "I wouldn't waste your time in here, but they have programs for that in the back rooms of strip clubs, *if* you can afford it."

He grinned. "I prefer most things the traditional way." He glanced between us and back up at my eyes. "This isn't bad, though. Can't say I'm surprised you like being in control."

I laughed. "You couldn't handle me."

"Couldn't handle who? A role model for young women?"

My grin fell, and I felt like punching him in the face for real. A sickening sensation slid through my stomach as I slammed back to reality while still in the virtual space. Damn it. I was here to elude the pressures of the real world. Was there nowhere to find peace? Nowhere left to escape?

"Fuck you."

He reached for me. "Being a role model is a good thing. I didn't mean—"

I scowled, pulled off him, and marched toward the arena's exit. The crowd booed. Standard programming. Suddenly, I hated standard programming.

A computerized voice echoed overhead as I walked out of the arena.

*Simulation complete.*

I opened my eyes to the pod's shimmering opal core. I took a deep breath and let it out slowly, as if the air were draining from every finger and toe. It didn't help. As much as I tried to push my emotions away, the darkest ones kept resurfacing. Guilt. Anger. Betrayal. Virtual or real, Rooke's words had struck home.

When my pod opened, Rooke was already gone. I sat on the edge for a while, between the gateways of the real and the digital. This was a game. It was supposed to be fun. I'd tried so hard to make it that way for the team, but I no longer felt it myself.


I spent the rest of the week studying our opponents, prepping the team, and trying to sleep in between. While my teammates were living it up in the clubs and sneaking in bouts of classic video games in the rec room, I was straining to keep my meals in my stomach and my eyelids open, which conveniently only happened when I lay down to sleep. By that Saturday, the team was more than ready to kick ass and take this tournament home.

I was a train wreck.

For tonight's matchup, Hannah and Derek had run ahead to the enemy's tower while Rooke and Lily guarded our own. I was the middleman. The middleman did exactly that. Stood guard in the middle, taking out attackers as they advanced. Available to run forward or back depending on how the game fared. Offense or defense, on demand.

The field ahead of me crunched, northwest of where I stood. Still crouching, I skirted through the stalks until I was parallel with the sound. I hunched down, drawing my dagger from its sheath. A single opponent appeared as fractured glitches of armor between the stalks.

He never saw me.

As he passed, I lashed out and sliced through his calf tendon. He yelped as he went down on one knee. I jumped up, wrapped a hand over his mouth, and slit his throat. He crumpled to the ground instantly.

Easy kill. I should be a freaking spy. Maybe next year, they'd introduce an assassin game into the VGL tournaments.

Something crunched behind me, hard and rough. Another opponent. I ducked just as an axe whooshed over my head. I came back up and met his blade with my own. Metal met metal as we danced through the fields. Stalks whipped around us, slashing at my ankles and calves. A few hit my face. I ignored the sharp stings, trying to focus on the fight. My opponent phased between blurry and clear, the beige tones of his skin blending in with the sepia fields around him. I blinked and shook my head. My vision went hazier. Damn it.

His sword caught my thigh, slicing a deep gash between my hip and knee. I cried out, unable to stifle the pain. Using the injury, I feigned a fall, hooked my good leg around his ankle, pushed. He fell.

I pounced on him the second his back hit the ground and sunk my sword into his chest. Steel sliced through tanned skin to the deep red beneath, like cutting open a cherry pie. Air rushed out of his lungs. Limbs collapsed at his sides. Eyes glazed over.

Dead.

He didn't suffer.

I collapsed to my knees and rested my forehead against the

hilt of the sword, panting. My chest tightened. Breaths went in and out but provided no oxygen. Since when was I so tired after a basic fight? I closed my eyes and focused on breathing. It's okay. You're okay.

Everything is fine.

A computerized voice echoed overhead.

*Match complete.*

I gripped the edge of my pod with shaking hands and pulled myself to my feet. My stomach lurched, and my head swam, but I managed to stay standing. On the screen above the pod doors, Howie and Marcus beamed.

"What a match. Defiance advances and Celestial Elite goes home. While there are still several more rounds to go in the losers' bracket, the winners' bracket is quickly coming to an end . . ."

Several more rounds before the championship. I could make it.

I had to make it.

Hannah appeared beside me, bouncing as if she had a pogo stick crammed up her ass.

"Hey. Great match," she said, brimming with energy. Must have been adrenaline from the fight. "Which club are we hitting tonight?" But as she gave me the once-over, her expression fell, and she stopped bouncing. "Are you all right?"

I smiled. "Yeah. I just need something to drink."

She laughed. "After the conference, we'll party. Hard."

Good. I needed it.

Once again, I made it through the conference on autopilot, thankful that for once I'd had the answers programmed into me. As soon as we were in our seats at the club and the waiter set down the tray of liquor and HP, I slammed back two shots in a row. Hannah laughed at me.

"Not taking it easy tonight, huh?"

"Shut up."

She laughed again, and I joined her.

Across the club, the wallscreen blared with the VGL theme music. The scene cut in to Howie and Marcus, the VGL announcers.

"Okay, ladies and gentlemen. We're set to tune in to the final matchup from the winners' bracket of the RAGE tournament. Whoever wins tonight secures their spot in the championship."

The winners' bracket finals. Was that tonight already? Of course it was. The winners' bracket always played out faster than the losing side.

I sat back for the fight.

The scene cut to the sepia fields of the digital arena. The VGL stamp appeared at the top of the screen, superimposed over the view inside the game. The tournament matchup stats flashed across the screen.

WINNERS' BRACKET FINALS

PARADOX

VS.

INVICTUS

The matchup's stats faded into the rustling wheat stalks, like white noise on a dead channel. The camera angle rotated between several different views of the fields between the towers. No lines carved through the stalks. No warriors screamed out battle cries. The grass waved in the breeze. A bird fluttered past the screen, chirping softly. Just peace.

The announcers' voices overlay the footage.

"I love this setting. No matter how many times I see it, it always gives me chills."

"I hear you, Marcus. The engineering here is just brilliant.

Golf would be a lot more interesting if you knew people were about to beat each other to death with their clubs."

"Maybe that'll be next season."

They shared a laugh.

The camera angle changed as four members of InvictUS disappeared into the fields, the wheat stalks whipping around them as they ran.

"Here's the usual formation InvictUS has become known for."

"I'm surprised they've never changed it up, but so far no team has been able to crack them. Don't mess with what works, right?"

The camera flashed to the other team, mirroring the same formation. One in the tower. Four pushed in as they flew through the fields. The gap between the two teams began to close.

"Looks like Team Paradox is trying to meet the brute force that is InvictUS head-on. We're about to see an all-out brawl in the center of the fields."

The crunching of the wheat stalks rose to a crescendo as the teams raced toward each other. Thirty feet. Then twenty. Weapons came unsheathed, gripped tight in hands. Blades glinted in the soft, golden sunlight. Someone shouted, and soon, they were all shouting as they plowed toward each other.

The camera flashed between the teams, back and forth, as they neared. My stomach curled tighter with each step they took. This would be a bloodbath, and I had a feeling I knew who'd end up the victims.

The groups collided.

One from Paradox went down instantly, an axe slicing through his throat. Already three on four. Not good.

"Oooh, one from Paradox goes down hard. I keep telling you, Marcus, nothing can touch these guys."

"Hey, the fight's not over yet," Marcus protested.

"It's about to be. Check this out."

The rest went down in a matter of seconds as InvictUS ganged up on the remaining members of Paradox. Swords swiped through the air. Blood splattered the beige stalks of the fields. Screams of pain filled the audio. Not one from InvictUS took a hit. Not one scratch. These guys were an impenetrable wall of blades and death. When the last of Paradox had fallen with an axe to the back, InvictUS gathered up their weapons and charged for the tower.

My heart sunk. Four on four was not the solution, and no one could push in with five and leave their tower unclaimed. If that didn't take out InvictUS, what would?

The scene cut to the single remaining member of Paradox inside the tower. His armor clanked as he shifted his weight, sword gripped in hand. His breaths were even. His eyes looked about, attentive but calm.

Then footsteps echoed up the path. I flashed back to when I first heard those same footsteps when we'd faced off against InvictUS. I'd been naïve then, unexposed to the ruthlessness that was my opponent. But unlike me, this guy knew exactly what was coming for him. His calmness evaporated. Sweat beaded on his lip, and his knuckles turned white around his sword. His breaths weren't so even now.

InvictUS burst through the entrance and surrounded him on all sides. His eyes went wide, and he swallowed thick. He brought his sword up in defense, for whatever it was worth.

I squirmed in my seat, struggling to keep my eyes on the screen. My heart thudded in my chest. This is why people watched. The tension. The violence. And above it all, they could tell themselves it wasn't real. Gamers, on the other hand, knew. We knew the pain that seared through our bodies with every slash of a sword or stab from a dagger. We knew the anxiety and the dread when the darkness crept in, and coldness captured our souls.

Ignorance is bliss.

InvictUS circled their prey, a wolf pack taunting the poor, baby sheep. They mocked him with false swipes of their swords. He tensed at each jab, too anxious to deflect moves that were nothing more than feints. Sweat poured down his face.

InvictUS stepped closer.

My stomach tightened.

Their swipes morphed into more than just teases. One blade sliced through his calf. Another nicked his shoulder. He cried out and fought to stay on his feet. The audio filled with the sound of steel slicing through skin, again and again, until their target looked like he'd just run a mile through brush and thorns.

Finally, one of the InvictUS fighters dove forward and jammed a blade through his neck from behind. The camera caught the perfect angle as the tip protruded through his Adam's apple, blood spraying out like a busted faucet. My own throat gagged in response.

Eyes wide, he clawed at his own neck until his eyes rolled back in his head, and he collapsed.

InvictUS celebrated over his dead body with sword clangs and chest bumps, like jocks on the football field, and the corpse beneath them was nothing more than pigskin.

The match's stats appeared on the screen.

INVICTUS VICTORIOUS.

I knew it. I knew they'd win. Still, a rock settled in my stomach.

The footage cut out to Howie and Marcus at their desk.

"And InvictUS takes it in another knockdown fight," Marcus exclaimed, reeling with adrenaline. "What a night."

"There you have it. InvictUS is your winners' bracket finalist. The team that survives the losers' bracket will be facing off against them for the championship." Howie laughed. "Whoever it is, I hope they're prepared."

The rock in my stomach started rolling. Even if somehow we managed to make it through the losers' bracket and into the championship, we'd have to face off against InvictUS—the team that no one could touch. The team that gave new meaning to the term invincibility.

"That's it," I said, reaching for the bowl of HP on the table. "I need a hit. Now."

Hannah laughed at me again.

"It hits faster if you take it out of the capsule," she said.

Good point.

I broke the capsule open, and drew out a line on the tray. Hannah handed me a straw and I dropped down to my knees.

I froze.

Here I was, on my knees, in the middle of a club, about to sniff some drug up my nose. As a role model. Had my own role model, Jessica Salt, ever done this? I couldn't remember her in the tabloids, cutting lines and downing shots. What I did remember in that moment was Nathan. Pulling lines up his nose. Like he needed it just to get through the day. Just to deal with life. Right before his ended. Permanently.

What the fuck was I doing?

I scrambled to my feet.

"Kali, where are you going?" Hannah asked.

I didn't answer. Hell, I didn't even know where I was going myself. I just had to get out of there.

I stumbled away and down the stairs into the dance floor, and began shoving my way through the crowd. I got halfway to the door when my elbow snagged on something. Rooke's hand. He dropped his grip on my arm and moved close, so I could hear him over the music.

"What's wrong?"

"I have to leave. Now."

He glanced between me and the lobby. "I'll go with you. For the cameras. You shouldn't have to explain to Clarence why the tabloids are printing pictures of you leaving a club obviously upset and without me."

Inwardly, I groaned. I just wanted to be alone. But I didn't want to deal with the paparazzi or Clarence either.

I sighed, and nodded. "Fine."

"Just smile and act like we're together. For thirty seconds."

He took my arm and led the way, threading a path through the crowd. Outside, the flashing started as soon as the cameramen picked up on us. I smiled that fake smile, for the cameras of the fake magazines, eager to photograph this fake relationship. We reached the SUV, and Rooke held the door and ushered me inside. When the door shut behind us, people swarmed the car and pounded on the windows like undead mobs. Cameras flashed at the same speed as hummingbird wings.

Was this my life now?

I covered my face with my hands, though it did no good against the onslaught of the press. Inside, I felt like I was drowning. Like I was completely detaching from it all. From reality, my life, and myself.

What the hell had I become?

# CHAPTER 14

"What happened back there?"

Once we'd cleared the mobs, and the car had begun guiding itself through the streets of L.A., Rooke turned toward me. I didn't answer him.

"Kali?"

I glanced at him and looked away again. "Nothing."

"Nothing? One second you were sitting beside me, and the next you were gone. I barely caught up with you."

I fiddled with nothing in my lap. "I almost did a hit of HP."

"And?"

"And? AND? Didn't you see me? I was on my knees about to snort it off the table like a freaking anteater."

"Technically, I don't think an anteater snorts—"

"THAT'S NOT THE POINT." I covered my face with my hands. "What's wrong with me?"

"You're an addict."

I reeled. "An addict? Are you mental? I do a few hits of HP, and suddenly I'm an addict?"

"I'm not talking about the drugs. You're addicted to the virtual world. HP is just a means to an end."

I scoffed. "I'm not addicted to the virtual world."

"You sneak into the game off-hours."

"That's just—"

"You can't sleep at night.

"Because Nathan—"

"You make constant excuses."

"But—"

"You're missing gaps in time. You phase out even when you're not plugged in. Are you gonna argue with that, too?"

I didn't. I pressed my lips together and listened to him.

"I know the signs," he continued. "It's the game, Kali. It's always the game."

I scowled. "How would you know?"

"I know."

"What?"

"I. Know."

I met his eyes. He stared back, completely solemn. It was the kind of look you'd expect to see only inside a confessional. Coincidentally enough, one was coming.

"It starts with sneaking into the game," he explained, looking out the window. "You convince your programmer to let you in off-hours. For extra practice. For the sake of the team. Only soon it's not enough, so you start hitting HP. And when that's not enough, you'll go for something harder." He turned back and locked eyes with me. "Before I got here, I was so strung out, I couldn't tell you what was real."

I scoffed. Yeah, right. Straight-and-narrow Rooke was a former druggie. Then, as his words solidified in my mind and the dots connected, I gasped.

"That's why you were so miserable when you first got here, isn't it? And why you seem like you're in pain sometimes. You're detoxing."

He nodded so slightly, I might have missed it if I hadn't been looking at him dead-on. I turned to the window, letting the situation sink in for a moment. No wonder he'd been so pissed when he caught me with the sleeping pills.

"Do I have to quit the games?" I began. "I can't quit. The team won't make it replacing someone this late into the tournament. No, I'm the captain. I have to pull through this. You're getting through it, and you still plug in. What did you do? What do I do?"

He laughed, and not just a soft chuckle. I'm talking head thrown back, chest rumbling laughter. I frowned.

"Thanks, asshole. I'm kinda having a crisis here."

"I'm laughing because if it were anyone else, I wouldn't know what to say. But you've studied Taoism, Kali. Look, if you don't believe in it anymore, then that's fine. We'll find another way. But if you do, then you have what you need. The core concepts of nature, balance, harmony."

He took a breath and looked out the window again. "There's a well-known Native American story about how we all have two wolves inside us fighting for dominance. One is full of hate, anger, and everything evil. The other is full of peace, clarity, and everything good. The one that wins is the one we feed. I'm not saying the virtual world is evil, but you've filled yourself with so much of it, you can't see anything other than what's fake. You just have to balance it out and focus on what's real."

"What's real?" I scoffed, and motioned at the city around us. At the plastic, the airbrushing, and the bubble lips. "What's real in this place?"

"Find it. A city can't exist without nature inside it. We can't breathe without air or drink without water, right?"

I stared at him, blinking. Then I looked out the window again. At first, the city was all concrete, glass, and traffic patterns. Slowly, the realness emerged. The wind whistled through the alleyways and whipped through flags. On the sidewalk, a man's cell phone unclamped and tumbled from his wrist as he walked along, unaware. A teenager with neck tattoos and body mods rushed to scoop it up.

"Hey, I think you dropped this."

Even inside the car, the air-conditioning tickled my skin. The slow, drawn-out beat of the techno jazz streaming from the radio enveloped me like a warm bath and calmed my heartbeat. For a second, just a second, Rooke squeezed my hand. Not for the cameras. There were none here. They say even the smallest gestures can speak volumes, but this one said one thing.

I'm here for you.

Once we'd arrived back at the facility, we walked down the hallway toward our bunks. I stopped in front of mine, glancing between him and the door.

"Now what?"

"You need to take a shower."

I frowned. "Hey."

He smiled. "It'll make you feel better. Trust me. It's like a metaphorical cleansing. Just stay in there until the water turns cold. When you come out, you'll feel better, almost like you're on the other side of something."

"And then?"

He shrugged. "I don't know. You have to figure that out on your own. But I do know that this isn't going to work if you're not honest with yourself. Do what feels right, not necessarily what seems right."

"You mean listen to my heart more than my head?" I asked. He smiled again and nodded. "Yeah, okay. Thanks. For every-thing."

He turned and started down the hall, glancing back as he walked away. "If you need to talk, I'll be in my bunk."

I watched him leave, then disappeared into my own. When

the door whooshed shut behind me, I leaned back against it and closed my eyes. My nerves jittered, and my stomach swirled. I was on the edge, teetering. How long had I been doing exactly that? On the edge. Teetering. Time to pull myself back.

I stripped down, stepped in the shower, scrubbed my skin, rough, like I was trying to clean all the negativity out of it. My father believes that water has a natural calming property. My mother believes it's good "to wash all the shit away." Funny how, when I put those two together, it became "washing all the shit away to reveal the calmness beneath."

After scrubbing, I sat on the shower floor. Droplets cascaded down my skin. Steam spiraled up from the stall's cool tiles to kiss the glass walls, turning them opaque. I did nothing but sit alone in the box of water and steam. Not thinking. Not moving. Just breathing.

A weight lifted, like my soul had pushed it out through my head and shoulders.

My soul. Hadn't I sold that to Clarence?

I didn't cry. I didn't scream. I just let go of all the frustration, and anger, and sadness I felt over everything. The tournaments. Clarence. The media. The sponsors. Even Nathan.

The water turned lukewarm, then cool, sending a chill across my skin. I wrenched the tap off. After toweling off, I dried my hair. In the mirror, my reflection didn't phase. Bags still circled my eyes, but my skin had a soft, subtle glow to it now. I smiled, just a hint curling up the corners of my mouth.

As I studied my reflection in the mirror, my gaze drifted down to my stomach. I touched just below my navel, where my chi should have been. Chi is a sort of life force, and my father always emphasized its importance. It didn't hold much weight in America other than in martial arts. How long had I gone without thinking about it?

After I finished drying my hair, I lingered in front of the counter as my gaze trailed across the banquet of liquor minis and pills. The pendant around my neck gained ten pounds. Alcohol itself was not a bad thing. It was just a drink, just an object. So were pills. Like sugar or salt, how much of it we ingested was what made it good or bad.

It was a matter of balance.

I ripped the lids off the liquor minis and turned them upside down in the sink. Every pill I could find chased the liquid down. After I'd cleared the counter, I crawled into bed. Even as the memory foam morphed around my body and cradled my head, I stared up at the ceiling and sighed. Would I sleep? I glanced beside me, where Nathan had once been before he died, and where I'd seen him several times after. But now, that side of the bed remained empty. I patted it with an open palm. I'd finally begun to let him go and accept what had happened. Mostly. Clarence and the sponsors were still wrong to bulldoze over his death—whether it was a drug overdose or not—but at least he'd left my nightmares now.

I scooped up my tablet and tapped it out of sleep mode. The default app for reading eBooks was blinking. Update needed. Well, wasn't that ironic? I okayed the update and browsed the online store for the *Tao Te Ching*. How long had it been since I'd read it? I downloaded it and started flicking through the pages. When I was younger, reading a few pages of the book brought with it a sense of calm and peace. But that was before. Before life as a pro gamer. Before the virtual world. Before all the bullshit. After a few minutes, I sighed and dropped my tablet. This wasn't working. But it wasn't the book itself that was the problem.

I left my bunk, walked down to Rooke's door, and pushed the buzzer on his keypad. After some rustling inside, it slid open.

He was naked.

Fine, not completely. But I wasn't the only one who had just showered. A towel sat around his shoulders. Water dripped from his hair and slid down his neck to his bare chest, following the recesses of his muscular build. His pants hung so low around his waist that one little tug would have sent them sliding to the floor.

"Uhh . . ."

What was I here for? Oh, yes.

"Can I borrow your copy of the *Tao Te Ching*?"

He nodded and disappeared into his bunk. "That's practically the Taoist bible," he called out. "Don't you have one?"

He returned to the door, book in hand.

"On my tablet, yes. But . . ." I took the book from him and ran my fingertips over the cover. "I needed something real."

He grinned. "You'll have to tell me your favorite quote."

"What's yours?"

"A man with outer courage dares to die. A man with inner courage dares to live."

I considered it. "Not bad."

"Do you want it on a sticky note?"

I almost punched him then. Or caressed his skin. Whichever.

"Pffft. My quote is going to own your quote's ass."

He laughed, and his abs tightened. Oh my. Maybe I should have outlined every ridge and groove with my fingers. I mean, he was real. That counted, right?

"You gonna be okay?" he asked.

"I think, yeah. Thanks," I said, and managed to push myself down the hall and away from his slick skin. As I walked back to my room, I let a slow breath pass between my lips. I couldn't deny it. We could have been a real couple. There was a natural attraction there, and more than enough chemistry. Maybe the photographer at the magazine had picked up on it, too. Is that why they'd made us into a couple?

Was it time to make that real?

Okay, whoa. One thing at a time, captain.

Back in my own bunk, I climbed into bed and curled up with the book. It weighed heavy in my hands as my fingers glided across the pages. Smooth. Cool. Just like the air around me. In that moment, everything felt just a little closer to the genuine. Not so plastic. Not so fake.

I took a breath, a deep breath. My insides steadied. Energy pulsed through me in soft, soothing waves. No dizziness. No jittering nerves. No churning stomach.

Just calm.

I had a long way to go, but I was finally ready to start living again.

The next morning, I woke with the book making a tent across my stomach. I blinked a few times and turned my gaze to the ceiling. I'd slept through the night. Rubbing my eyes, I groaned. A dull headache roamed from temple to temple. Not the best night on record, but I'd slept—in my own bed and without any pills.

Before I'd fallen asleep, the book had reminded me of my life before now. I chuckled, remembering how much I protested the first time Dad unplugged my gaming console.

"What the hell?" I demanded, flailing my ten-year-old arms. "I finished my homework."

Dad frowned, and not just at the cussword.

"You need more balance than that, Kali," he said. "Go outside."

I pointed at the now-black screen. "I was outside. My character just reached the Forest of Enchanted Truths."

Dad shook his head. "You need some exercise. You know? Get your lungs and heart pumping."

I grabbed the controller and flicked it with my thumbs. "If you bought me an immersive VR system, I'd get lots of exercise."

I didn't get a VR system. I got martial arts classes.

"She's a stubborn little thing, but she has what it takes," the instructor told my father. "She pinned one of the boys today. He cried."

Dad glanced down at me out of the corner of his eye. I beamed as brightly as my crisp, white uniform.

"I think it would do her good to participate in some tournaments," the instructor continued. He leaned in close to Dad, where he thought I wouldn't hear. "It might help with her discipline."

Dad agreed.

They had no idea what they were creating. Dr. Frankenstein built less of a monster.

When I won my first tournament, my love of competitions exploded. One tournament became years of competing. Winning meant prize money—funds my parents thought I'd put toward an education. I bought a top-of-the-line VR system instead. The living room became my battlefield, where I'd tuck and roll with a visor strapped over my eyes and bands wrapped around my wrists and knees.

Several broken lamps later, I was relocated to the basement.

"Aren't you mad?" I asked Dad one day, as we sat on the basement floor together.

"No. Why would I be?"

"Mom's mad."

He chuckled. "As soon as she goes shopping, she'll feel better."

"I'm not talking about the lamps." I sighed, and Dad's face grew solemn. "She says I live down here, in my little hole."

Dad frowned, glancing up at the ceiling where the living

room would have been. He reached into his pocket and produced a small box.

"I was waiting for your birthday, but I think you need this now."

He flipped the box open. Inside, cradled by silk, was a gold taijitu pendant on a chain. Dad placed it around my neck.

"You've learned to appreciate how important balance is, Kali, and I'm proud. You're one of the top students at the martial arts studio, and you're doing very well in school. Keep it up, and you'll be able to go to whatever college you want."

I bit my lip at the mention of school and turned my gaze away from his eyes. As a distraction, I studied the necklace. Upside down or right-side up, a yin yang was always the same. Two halves of a whole. Feeling a little closer to Dad in that moment, I asked him, "Can you do something for me?"

"Yes? What is it?"

I held the visor out to him. "Try it."

Dad looked between my face and the visor a few times and recoiled. I sighed. He wasn't going for it. Then, like he was reaching for a grenade, he took it in his hands.

"Don't tell your mother."

Dad never played again after that night, but he never scowled at the system anymore, either.

Life became a loop stuck on repeat after that. Mornings at school. Afternoons in the studio. Nights in the basement. Until I graduated high school and left. For this place.

This place.

Oh shit. My alarm. It hadn't gone off.

I bolted up in bed and my gaze snapped to the wall clock— 06:43 blinked across the screen. Since when had I woken up before the alarm?

In the kitchen, I grabbed a breakfast tray. Yes, real breakfast. Yes, coffee included. In the cafeteria, I sat alone at the table.

I was halfway through my apple when Hannah sat down across from me and surveyed my tray. I thought she'd be pissed at me for running out of the club the previous night, but instead, she smiled like a proud mama.

"Look at you, eating breakfast."

She eyed my mug.

"Don't get too excited," I said, picking it up. "It's still coffee, not water."

"If it wasn't coffee, I'd be more worried than impressed."

I laughed.

Eventually, Lily joined us, and I ate the rest of my meal while chatting and laughing with the girls. No one asked about what happened to me in the club the previous night. Regardless, I knew I couldn't hide anymore.

Before starting morning training, I walked down the hall and stood in front of a familiar door for a few minutes before swinging it open.

Dr. Renner looked up from her desk and smiled.

"Hi, Kali."

I sat down in the chair across from her and said nothing. Silence settled between us.

"Is something wrong?" she finally asked.

"Last time I was here, I told you I thought I had a problem."

She nodded. "Yes. I remember."

"Well, now I know I have a problem, and it's gotten much worse."

She considered that for a moment. "Okay. Why don't you tell me more?"

"It's the virtual world. I feel like I want it too much. Like the second life gets hard, I'm looking to escape instead of owning up to it. I'm using the game to get away from reality, not to have fun. And that's what games are supposed to be. Fun." I paused for a long time before letting the next sentence through. "I think I'm addicted."

"I understand what you're saying, and I'm glad you came to me to talk. Based on what you've told me, I'm reluctant to call you an addict—"

Because she didn't know half the truth.

"—But if you feel like you need to change, the most important factor is your motivation to make that change."

"Oh, I'm motivated," I said. "And not just for me, but for the team. I thought I was ready before, the last time we talked. But I wasn't really there yet. I am now."

"That's normal. Sometimes, even when you think you should change, you have to pass a tipping point before you realize just how important it is. In your case, it would be where what's bad about the virtual world outweighs what's good about it."

I nodded profusely. "I'm past the tipping point."

"Regardless of the reason, if you want to change, the best thing you can do for yourself is come up with a plan, then share it with people who will support you. It's important to talk to someone about how you feel, too. It doesn't have to be me, but make sure it's someone who will understand without judging. There's a reason why alcoholics meet with each other in support groups. Staying committed is easier when you have someone else in your life who is going through the same thing. Do you know any other gamers who have struggled like you?"

Nope.

Ugh. Yes, there was. Of course, there was. I bit my lip. Whether the doc knew it or not, there was someone in my life going through the same thing.

I let a slow breath pass through my lips.

"Yes," I finally admitted. "I do."

After my meeting with the doc, I stood in the training room, watching my teammates on the treadmills and weight machines. Rooke stood on the other side of the room, working out with Derek. I wasn't going to talk to him. Not yet. Not until I'd had a bit of time to process everything myself. But I wasn't about to go running miles or pumping iron, either. Not while my stomach was still realizing it had more than coffee in it and might rebel.

I caught my reflection in the mirrors lining the wall beside me. In my early teens, I'd practiced Tai Chi in front of a mirror wall just like this one to monitor my movements and perfect the method. I hadn't done it in ages.

I lifted one leg and guided it to the side until I was in a squatted stance. Then I slowly lifted my arms. In the mirror, I searched for my teammates' reflections. No one had noticed me. Rooke spotted Derek on the bench press. Hannah and Lily jogged beside each other's treadmill, chatting. None of the trainers approached me, either. Poor guys probably drew straws every morning on who had to work with me. The one with the shortest must have run and hid.

I closed my eyes and focused on the sensations around me. My bare feet sinking into the cool padding of the mats. The sounds of my teammates in training, the huffs of their breaths and their feet clacking against the equipment. The voices of the trainers guiding them through with basic commands. With a deep breath, I blocked everything out and zeroed in on my chi, the core of my energy. A swirling-yet-calm vortex orbited my navel, as if the rest of me revolved around it. Stillness settled inside me, a sort of peace I hadn't felt in years, maybe ever.

Then I felt something else. That tugging sensation you get when someone's watching. I opened my eyes to find Rooke standing a foot away, arms crossed.

"Am I interrupting?" he asked.

I smiled and continued through the movements. "Not at all."

"How did you sleep?"

"Not horribly, but not well."

He nodded. "It'll get better." He moved closer and lowered his voice, so the others wouldn't hear. "You aren't in that deep, so the withdrawals shouldn't be too bad. It would probably help if you could avoid plugging in for today. Maybe we could convince the team just to practice in here."

"Yeah. Sounds good."

He glanced down at his feet and shifted his weight a few times. "So, uh . . . I was wondering . . ." His voice trailed off, and he rubbed the back of his neck. What was with him?

"What are you planning on doing tonight?" he finally asked.

Clubbing had been my answer for so long, it was like my mouth didn't know how to form other words. Finally, I shrugged. "Don't know. Why?"

"Because I'll be here"—he nodded down at the mats—"if you'd like to join me."

He turned and walked away, and returned to working out with Derek. He never made eye contact again or said anything further.

Tai Chi was all about fluid, flowing movements. But I stood there, frozen in pose, as I tried to comprehend what had just happened. A strange mix of emotions swelled within. Curiosity. Anticipation. Subtle fear. I pushed through the rest of my routine to the close and held it, concentrating, breathing, trying to ignore the thought screaming through my mind.

Holy shit.

Kali Ling, you have a date.

# CHAPTER 15

"Dr. Renner says I should stay in for the night."

Every teenager masters the art of lying about where they'll be for the night by the age of sixteen. Early on, I'd learned that adding an adult's name to the mix beefs up the authenticity of the excuse. Still, I never thought I'd be doing it myself as an adult, or as an excuse *not* to go out for the night.

"There are some exercises she wants me to try before bed," I continued. "She says it will help in the virtual world. I figure it's best for the team."

It was a flat-out lie, but I doubted Clarence would actually check with Dr. Renner to verify. Besides, if he did, I also doubted the good doctor would think it was a bad idea for me to stay in once in a while and focus on my sanity.

Clarence flicked through the tablet on his desk, failing to look up at me. "Fine. Whatever. As long as it's just for tonight."

"I thought that Rooke should stay in, too. If he goes out without me, it could give the wrong impression."

He paused as he considered it. "Yes, you're right. I trust you can tell him yourself."

Since Clarence's attention was solely on his desk, I let a smile creep across my face. "I'm sure I'll see him."

Clarence said nothing else as he flipped through his tablet.

After standing in awkward silence for more than a minute, wondering if the conversation was over, I gave up and left.

Inside the training room, my feet padded along the cool canvas of the training mats and stopped in front of a pair of bo staffs. Rooke stood on the other side of the staffs, dressed in training gear. I considered telling him some guys train without a shirt, but it looked like it wasn't going to be that kind of a date.

"We're covered for the night," I told him.

"Good." He nodded at my feet, where the bo staffs lay on the mats. "Pick one up."

Good evening to you, too.

I knelt to retrieve a staff. The wood felt smooth against my skin and weighed heavy in my hand.

"You got me a stick? I was hoping for flowers."

He smiled slightly. "You don't seem the type for flowers."

I spun the staff around in my hands a few times, getting a feel for its movements.

"So, you've trained with a bo before," he concluded.

"I've studied martial arts for years." He nodded, like it was nothing new. I narrowed my eyes at him. "You already knew, didn't you?"

"It's in your stats."

"Checking out my stats, huh? I'm flattered."

"Don't be. I study everyone's."

I glowered at him until I gave myself heartburn. Cocky bastard.

"You took a little of everything," he continued. "Why the variation?"

"Every martial art has something different to teach," I explained. "I wanted to learn them all."

"Any favorites?"

"Tae kwon do. I know it's Korean, and I'm half-Chinese, but I liked the combination of strength, speed, flexibility, and balance." I paused. "Tai Chi, too. But I think that reason is obvious."

He nodded. "The Taoist martial art. Yeah, I got that."

He stepped forward on the mat, going for the remaining staff. But instead of picking it up, he rolled it under his toes, catapulted it horizontally four feet in the air, and caught it with one hand.

So not impressed.

If he'd been shirtless, maybe.

I took a defensive stance opposite him. He mirrored me. For a fleeting moment, his eyes looked soft and warm as they weaved their way up my form. Then they turned to hardened steel as he met my stare. Statue mood. Posed with the staff, the muscles in his arms flexed, and his jaw set hard. Only the shallow breaths expanding and contracting his chest revealed he hadn't actually turned to stone. But replace the staff with a blade, and he was a gladiator. A real gladiator. Christ, this guy even looked like a warrior in the real world, even without a sword or armor to match.

So it would be that much sweeter when I made him cry.

I took a breath and waited for his attack. The gap between us was no-man's-land, where no soul ventured. With a breath, I sprinted and swung the staff, aiming for his midsection. He blocked, knocked me sideways, and smacked the back of my hand. Pain shot up my arm. I dropped the staff and ground my teeth together to stifle a hiss.

"You okay?" he asked.

"Fine," I grunted, and knelt to retrieve my weapon.

Still kneeling, I spun and lashed out with the staff. Rooke parried my surprise attack and clipped my shin, wood snapping against bone. Holy Mother. I hopped around on one leg until the sting of the impact lessened.

"What martial art did you study?" I asked. "Karate?"

He nodded.

"I'm going to assume you're a black belt," I said, and he didn't argue. "At least second degree."

"Third, but close enough."

A grin touched his lips. Super cocky bastard. I was starting to like that look. Hoping he was off guard, I lunged. He deflected.

Rooke took a step back and shook his head. "Stop trying to hit me so hard. Even just a tap with these things will hurt enough." He held up his staff for emphasis.

"You have to understand," I began, "my target is you."

He blinked but didn't frown. Looks like he was becoming immune to my sarcasm. "Aren't you noticing a pattern here?"

"Yes. You're continuously pissing me off."

"I'm not attacking. You are." He closed the gap between us. "I've watched your fights, Kali. You never attack first. Not unless you have the perfect opportunity. So why are you being so aggressive now?"

I opened my mouth to let loose another smart-ass remark, but he moved even closer, and the words caught in my throat.

"We're not here to see who wins." He gripped my hand where it wrapped around the staff. "We're here to focus on the real."

I glanced down at his hand resting over mine. Heat emanated from him and brushed against my skin. He'd long made his point and still held on.

Finally, he released my hand and backed up several feet.

I took a breath, absorbed his advice, and focused on my surroundings, inside and out. Steady breaths expanded my lungs. The scent of canvas and leather filled the room, wafting off the mats and training gear. The breeze of the air-conditioning brushed my skin again, refreshing and cool. I smiled. Kneeling low, I held the staff along my arm, so it was a part of me. A new limb.

I met Rooke's eyes and swear I saw him grin, but he pressed his lips together to hide the evidence. He spread his feet shoulder width apart, balanced. Silence settled between us again. I closed my eyes and focused, waiting for the sound of his attack. Seconds passed. Then, his footsteps padded along the mat toward me. Eyes closed, I moved. Without thinking, without trying, I just moved.

I deflected Rooke to the side and, as he passed, snapped the staff down and caught the back of his thigh. He jumped but recovered quickly.

"That's better," he said, though I noticed a slight limp in his walk as he circled back to me.

We continued the pattern, attacking and breaking, occasionally getting a solid hit in. After a while, I actually felt a grin tugging at my lips when a wave of sickness washed over me. I pulled back from the fight and doubled over, gripping my stomach. Rooke paused and waited as I leaned on my staff for support.

"That's the start of the withdrawals," he finally said.

"You think?" I spat.

He said nothing else, giving me some space. I tried standing up straight, but my knees instantly gave out, and I slumped down on the mat. The staff landed with a *thunk* beside me.

"Damn it."

"Kali, why don't you take a second? There aren't any cameras here."

"You never know." Grunting, I used the staff to push myself up. My stomach roiled, and I slid back down the staff to my knees. "Just so you know, I'm taking a second."

I stared down at the mat, breathing through my mouth,

trying to convince my stomach not to revisit any previous meals of the day. Rooke crossed the mat and knelt beside me.

"It gets better," he said. I glanced up and met his face, only inches from mine. His expression was soft, understanding. "It really does. I swear."

Heat blossomed against the small of my back as he rubbed his palm in small circles. Then he halted suddenly and pulled back, as if he'd just realized what he was doing. We locked eyes. My stomach curled in on itself, and not just because of the nausea. Despite the sounds of the facility humming around us, silence settled between us as thick and heavy as humidity in the Amazon.

"Can you talk about something?" I looked down and gripped my stomach, swallowing thick. "To get my mind off the nausea."

He thought for a second. "You never told me your favorite passage."

"What?"

"From the *Tao Te Ching*."

The *Tao Te Ching*. Right. Words and passages flowed through my mind, but I didn't need to reread the book to know which spoke the most to me.

"Mastering others is strength. Mastering self is true power."

Rooke considered it, then smiled and nodded.

"Nice choice."

"Are you two planning on eating dinner tonight, or just beating each other up?"

In the doorway, Hannah stood, hand on her hip, in a barely there dress and heels that could have doubled as stilts. Weeks ago, I'd never seen her in heels. Guess that was part of her image now. I glanced at the clock above the doors. It was 21:32. Party time.

She waved me over.

Rooke leaned toward me and lowered his voice. "Can you stand?"

I took a deep breath and nodded. "It's not so bad now."

I pushed myself up slowly, and when my body didn't protest, crossed the training room to Hannah's side.

"If we would have known you two were still training," she said quietly, "we would have joined you."

"Would you want to?"

She shrugged.

"We worked our asses off all day," I said. "This should be your time to do what you want. If you want to train, train. If you want to go out, go. But the nights should be ours to do whatever."

She laughed. "Yeah, right. That'll be the day."

"I think it's reasonable. Sometimes we need time apart. Sometimes we need time alone."

Hannah glanced at Rooke in the background. "Oh. Time alone. I see." She winked. "Have fun."

"It's not like that."

"Yeah, right." She leaned toward me. "I might not know much about men, but make sure he wears a rubber and holds you afterwards."

I chuckled. "Fuck you. Get out of here."

She left with a smile. I listened to her heels clicking along the hallway. Once she was out of earshot, I turned back to Rooke and grinned.

"One more round."

It was actually three more rounds and several fresh bruises later when we finally called it quits. My stomach held off for the rest of the night, and my love of competing and drive to make Rooke cry pushed me on until I couldn't hold the staff anymore. In the women's locker room, I showered and planned on bed. Another early night wouldn't have been a bad thing. So how I ended up alone with Rooke in a darkened hallway was another story.

I huddled near the exit door, hugging myself.

"I can't believe I let you talk me into this," I told him. I squinted at his outline in the shadows. "I'm leaving."

He grabbed my arm. "It'll be great. I promise." He spoke in soft, soothing tones, the type men use to coax women into trouble. "You won't regret it."

I glanced at the hallway corners, looking for the red light of a camera. "What if we get caught?"

"We won't."

"I don't think you realize how much Clarence watches us."

He stepped up to me and his face appeared in the darkness. "I don't think you realize how much I want this."

He looked down at me with pleading eyes, and when I saw the hunger within them, I believed it.

I sighed. "All right. Fine. How much longer?"

On cue, several loud knocks pounded on the door beside us, followed by a gruff voice.

"Pizza delivery!"

Rooke grinned and yanked the door open. The sweet smell of dough and mozzarella wafted in, curling through the sterile air of the facility. My stomach rumbled. Maybe this was a good idea.

I poked my head out the door as Rooke took the pizza box in his hands. The delivery guy's mouth fell open.

"Holy shit, you're Kali Ling."

That's me, baby. Loud and proud. I signed for the pizza and started entering a tip. He waved me off. "Hey. No tip required."

"Why not?"

"Geez, you know how much your autograph is worth? You never sign things for the fans."

A chill ran through me. I glanced between him and my signature on the digital receipt. And I thought my mother was good at inadvertent guilt trips. I nodded, though my head didn't feel quite attached to my body.

"Yeah. Right."

He beamed. "Wait until I tell my friends. They're never going to believe this."

He walked away, shaking his head. As I watched him leave, my conscience did a tap dance at my heart. I sighed, and pursued him.

"Hey, wait."

He turned around.

"What's your name?" I asked.

"Mike."

I nodded at his tablet. "You got a camera on that thing, Mike?"

"Uh . . . yeah."

I looped an arm around his waist. "Well, take a pic already. My food is getting cold."

He froze for a second, then fumbled with the tablet. I kissed his cheek just as the camera clicked, and could have sworn I felt his knees buckle. He stuttered out a word that sounded like "thanks" and stumbled back to his car, grinning in a way I'd only seen on Cheshire cats.

Rooke's eyes narrowed as he watched the delivery guy float away.

I folded my arms. "Jealous?"

"Of course," he said, ducking back inside. "He gets to eat pizza all day."

I glowered at the spot where Rooke had just been, gritting my teeth together. My heartburn was back. Since when did I have competition as the leader of the smart-ass-retorts domain? I caught the door just before it closed and followed Rooke down the hall.

"Up to thirty-five years ago," he protested, as we entered the rec room, "that's the way everything was delivered."

I sat on the floor. "I'm just saying it's still weird to see a person instead of a drone."

He sat next to me and placed the pizza between us. "After the government commandeered so many for the Diablo cleanup, I think it'll be a while before everything gets back to normal."

"Probably just in time for the next disaster."

Rooke shrugged. "I don't know. I kind of prefer the human element. It's nice to have a person tell you to have a nice day instead of a machine."

"Really?" I gasped, placing a hand over my heart. "You prefer things the old-fashioned way? You don't say. Remind me to get you a loom for Christmas."

He frowned. I laughed.

I grabbed the first slice from the box, watching the cheese pull into foot-long strings. When I took a bite, my eyes fluttered shut. The gooey mozzarella melted in my mouth. I smiled at Rooke as he picked a slice for himself.

"How is it?" he asked.

I sighed. "Almost as good as coffee."

He chuckled, shook his head, and devoured his slice in three bites.

Boys.

"How's your stomach?" he asked as he reached for another piece.

"Good. I'm taking it slow."

As I chewed my own slice, the incident with the delivery guy came back to mind. I'd never signed anything. For anybody. None of us had.

"You okay?" Rooke asked, looking over my expression.

"No. That pizza guy was right. We never do things for the fans. We should. They're the reason for all of this."

"You really think Clarence would go for that?" He scoffed.

"He's trying to give us a godlike status. I don't think interacting with the fans would help our image."

I shook my head and frowned. Image. How important.

I turned to the wallscreen and raised my voice. "On," I commanded. "Station: VGL."

The screen flicked on and jumped to the VGL's home channel.

The entire wall filled with a scene on a mountain cliff, where two cars raced side by side up a narrow path. As they entered a tight corner, the inside car swung wide, driving his opponent out. He skidded along the corner, his back wheel cutting off the edge. I stopped chewing and leaned toward the screen.

The scene slowed, purposely entering slow-motion mode as the car teetered. The camera panned up, revealing the stories-high drop into the rocky shards below. My breath caught in my throat. Inside the car, the driver slammed the clutch into gear, and the car rocketed down the road. Safely. For now.

I sighed. "Ugh. I forgot it was Sunday. Virtual car racing." I made a face and glanced at Rooke. His grin matched the delivery guy's from earlier. My jaw dropped open.

"You like this stuff?"

He nodded eagerly.

"Oh God, you're one of those men who thinks it's an art form, aren't you?"

His grin faded as he grew defensive. "Of course it's an art form. Who drives their own car anymore?"

I rolled my eyes. Rooke nodded at the screen.

"You ever play anything other than the RAGE tournaments?" he asked, between swallowing pizza slices. "I mean, at this level. Full immersion with no safeguards."

"Not really. You?"

He nodded. "A little of everything. I doubled up in the amateur league, RAGE and Special Ops."

"Really?"

"Yeah. Better chance of getting picked up as a pro if you do more than one."

"Is there much difference between them?"

He half nodded. "Yes and no. They're both about tactics and eliminating the enemy, but you tend to die faster in the Ops. It's all about shooting, so without limbs flying off everywhere, it's not nearly as brutal. At least, when you're on the inside. Some viewers think it's just as bad. And by bad, I mean good."

We shared a grin.

"Does getting shot hurt?" I asked.

Okay, yes, I'd played enough first-person shooters to be an army commander. But never had I played one at the pro level, where I'd actually feel the bullet puncturing my body.

"Usually, swords hurt more, but it really depends where you get hit," he explained. "You have to take out your opponent as fast as possible in the Ops games. Even when they're down, they can still shoot you or throw a grenade. It's not like in the RAGE tournaments where you'd only have to stay at arm's length to avoid getting hit. Plus, in any type of army setting, you tend to wear armor, so when you get hit, either it doesn't go through or you get killed instantly."

"Hey, we wear armor, too."

"Yeah, but there's a lot more skin exposed."

His eyes landed on my stomach when he said it, and for a second, he seemed to forget about the pizza in his hand. His gaze slid up my form, slowly, and met my eyes. Warmth curled through me, and my breath shortened under the intensity of his stare. I swallowed the bits of pizza in my mouth in a gulp. Finally, he seemed to remember he was in the middle of speaking and cleared his throat.

"So, it's easier to find vulnerable spots and kill your opponent in a multitude of ways."

Multitude. Pffft. Who uses that kind of word in everyday speech? Though judging by the look in his eyes, it wasn't killing me he was thinking about doing in a multitude of ways. I was pulled out of the thought when Rooke folded two slices together and stuffed them into his mouth at once.

I motioned at the synthetic box the pizza came in. "You gonna go for that next?"

He shrugged. "What? Haven't you seen a guy eat before?"

I scoffed and turned back to the wallscreen. A giant boulder tumbled down the mountain's side and crushed a car on the road. The vehicle flattened and burst instantly, like a balloon popping glass shards and metal bits instead of pink rubber.

Rooke winced. "Yeah. That's not fun."

"You've done car racing, too?" I asked. He answered with the same cat-inspired grin. I shook my head and glanced at the open doorway to the facility. "Clarence would kill us if he walked in right now."

"Sure, he's a dick, but you have to feel for the guy a little. His brother was killed in the Diablo disaster."

I nearly choked on my food. "What? Are you serious?"

Rooke nodded. "Yeah."

"So, his brother worked at the plant?"

"Are you kidding? They owned the plant. That's how his family made all their money. Nuclear energy."

"Wait, how do you even know that?"

"Like I said, I read *everyone's* stats."

I chewed a little slower then as my body went numb. I didn't know Clarence even had a brother, let alone that he'd died. Is that really why he was such a dick all the time? Guess everyone in this industry had a story to hide and a part to play.

"I still find it surprising," I said, "that people love to watch virtual gaming so much. You'd think with all the violence and war threatening to break out all the time, they'd be looking for entertainment that's a little more . . . mellow."

"War is always threatening to break out. It's nothing new. Bottom line: People know this is fake. I think it helps them to deal with violence. Makes it not so real, you know?"

I nodded. "Yeah. Maybe."

"You have a point, though. Maybe that's why the Special Ops and other games aren't as popular."

"You mean they're too real? Like, something in the past or future is unfamiliar, so people enjoy it more. But something present-day just reminds them of the negative aspects of their lives."

"Exactly. The RAGE tournaments are based off ancient Rome, so no one nowadays ever experienced that before. It lets them escape."

On-screen, the racing cut out to a special promo. Five familiar warriors appeared in their battle armor, each a gigantic brute with a menacing grin, gripping a blade covered in blood. YOUR 2054 RAGE TOURNAMENT WINNERS' BRACKET FINALISTS. I swallowed thick and dropped my slice of pizza back in the box. "I think I just lost my appetite."

Rooke looked over the screen and shrugged. "They're just human guys. Painting them as invincible is part of their image."

"Then they're damn good at playing the part," I said, just as the contents of my stomach roiled, and a bitter taste filled my mouth. I gripped my midsection and doubled over, breathing sharply through my mouth.

Rooke surveyed me for a second before his gaze stopped on my stomach. "That's not because of InvictUS, is it?"

I shook my head. "Why do I feel so nauseous? Is it the pizza?"

"You didn't plug in all day. Plus, isn't this the time you'd usually be doing a hit at the club?"

Yeah, it was. Guess this was the withdrawals he talked about earlier.

"What other symptoms should I expect?" I asked.

"Maybe some headaches. But it will be more psychological than anything."

"You mean I'll crave it?"

"That, and when you don't let yourself have it, you'll get . . . irritable."

"You mean I'll be a bitch."

He laughed. "Sure, if that helps."

The waves in my stomach gradually subsided, like when the ripples of a pond smooth out again. I took a deep breath and slowly pushed myself up straight.

"I talked to Dr. Renner about what's going on," I told him, staring at the wallscreen. "She says I need to come up with a plan to change and share it with someone who will understand." I glanced at him. "So, I guess I'm asking for your opinion on what to do. I can't cut out of the virtual world entirely. I still have to plug in for the team."

"You don't have to cut it out completely. The sleeping pills, and the HP, and whatever else—that should go. We could sneak out of the clubs early. That will get you away from the drugs and give you some time at night to focus on yourself. I think as long as we leave together, it'll be fine."

"And then?"

He shrugged. "Whatever you need. We could come back here. Train. Sit out on the roof. Meditate."

I hadn't meditated in years. But it had always been a way of quieting the mind and connecting to the body—two things I needed desperately.

"And you're not wrong with thinking that games are supposed to be fun more than anything else," he continued. "You just need to retrain your mind to think that way. The virtual world is just for fun, and reality is the place worth living."

"How do I do that?"

"You focus on the real. You have to learn to appreciate everything that's here."

My hand instinctively went for my necklace. I thumbed the pendant, outlining the shape of the yin yang, especially the S curve down the middle that separated the whole into two halves. Virtual and real. They went hand in hand. Together, they symbolized my life as a gamer. But one had completely overtaken the other. Looks like it was time to brush up on the importance of balance. I think I had more than enough books to refer to.

"When it comes to games," he continued, "stick to consoles more than virtual. The classic ones seem to help." He grinned. "We could play a few rounds."

I dusted off my hands and stood. "Not tonight."

Rooke peered up at me. "Where are you going?"

"To bed, and part of you is coming with me."

He choked even though there wasn't any food in his mouth. "What?"

"Yes," I said, smiling. I leaned toward him. He retreated, eyes darting about, like he didn't know how to react to my closeness. My smile grew even wider.

"I have reading to do."

# CHAPTER 16

This became our new standard programming.

Every night, Rooke and I would meet on the mats. Darkness and moonlight no longer signaled parties and drinking, but instead meant the weight of a staff in my hands and the sounds of feet padding the mat and wood hitting wood echoing through the room. The night always ended in the rec room, studying matches and various VGL tournaments over whatever food we snuck into the facility for the evening.

After devouring my fill and getting a few jabs in with Rooke—physical and otherwise—I'd return to my bunk to reread the *Tao Te Ching* and other books. Just before sleep, I'd sit on the edge of my bed and meditate, focusing on my body. Focusing on the real. We couldn't come up with an excuse to stay in all the time, so we developed a routine. For show. We'd go to the clubs with the team, scoop a couple of hits of HP from the tray, and disappear onto the dance floor, crushing the pills beneath our feet.

No one was the wiser.

On the dance floor, I pressed my back against his front. His hands immediately gripped my hips and pulled me even tighter against him. I sighed and melted into him, pressing myself into every valley and crevice. Together, our hips rolled in harmony with the pulsing beat of the club. Within seconds, my heartbeat matched. I was completely aware of my body. And his.

Hey, I was supposed to be focusing, after all.

Everyone in the club stared. The bartenders, the patrons. Even the other gamers. Some straight-out gawked while others flitted glances with as much heat in their eyes as there was between us. I smiled my practiced warrior smile and gave them what they were silently begging for. I reached up and wrapped my arms around Rooke's neck, threading my fingers through his hair. Then I jerked his head down, pressing his lips against my neck. He chuckled, and his hot breaths flashed across my skin. I let my eyes roll back, let everyone watch, as his hands devoured my form, as he wrapped himself around me until his body practically swallowed mine.

He pressed his lips to my ear.

"Wanna leave?"

For what?

I shook my head, and my brain cleared.

Training. Yes, training.

I led the way back to the VIP lounge, where our teammates sat watching whatever VGL event was on that night.

"See you guys later," I said, grabbing my purse from the booth.

"Where are they going?" Derek asked, as we walked away.

"To 'practice,'" Hannah told him, making quotation marks with her fingers.

Derek watched us leave through thin slits of his eyes. But Lily—stone-faced Lily—winked at me.

Even the girls were buying it.

The second we stepped outside, the cameras flashed. All the paparazzi were still there, as some of the other gamer celebrities were just arriving to the club. We stole the spotlight every time as we left, fondling each other, acting like no one else could see us until we'd disappear into the car.

As soon as we arrived back at the facility, we'd rush to change into our training gear and meet on the mats. At some point in the night, I'd slump against the mat, trembling with nausea and weakness. Tonight was no different. Down on my knees, I braced my hands against the mat, waiting for the dizziness to pass. Rooke sat beside me.

"You wanna call it quits for tonight?"

"No," I said, just as a gagging fit seized me. Rooke steadied me, bracing his hands on either side of my abdomen. When my coughing fit subsided, I slumped against him, breathing careful, deliberate breaths through my mouth to calm my raging stomach. He paused for a second before wrapping his arms around me completely. I didn't protest. His closeness, his arms around me, knowing he'd been through this, too, all gave a sense of comfort. So I stayed against him and listened to his heart beating soundly in his chest.

"You said it gets better."

"It does. You're doing well," he insisted. "You're not as nauseous as often, or for as long. And you never did anything harder than HP. You're recovering quicker than I did."

"You didn't have help."

It hit me then. He went through this alone. I'd be a miserable asshole, too, if I had to deal with all this by myself.

"Look," I began. "Sorry if I was rude to you when you first joined the team. I didn't realize what was going on with you, but that shouldn't have mattered anyway."

He shook his head. "I should have told you. As team captain, you should have known what was wrong. But I was worried I'd get kicked off the team, and I needed this."

I looked up to his face, and he tilted his down at the same time. For a minute, we just sat there, looking at each other. This wasn't like in the clubs, where it was all for show. Something passed between us, like a moment of understanding. His jaw slacked, and his features went soft. I could have kissed him then—IF my stomach hadn't been a looping roller coaster. When I met his eyes, they were staring at my lips, as if he was thinking the same thing.

He cleared his throat and looked down at the floor. "Are you going to be okay for Saturday?"

Saturday. Another matchup. Another time where I'd have to go virtual.

"I have to be. For the team." I looked up at him again. "Do you think they know?"

"No. Training has been going well all week. As far as I can tell, they don't know you're sick."

"Because you've been helping cover it up."

"You could tell them. I think they'd understand."

"Maybe, but I'm not ready for them to know."

"That's fair. What do you want to do for the rest of the night?" he asked. "Classic video games? It's your turn to pick."

"Mortal Kombat."

He laughed. "Nice choice." He got to his feet and helped me up. My stomach behaved itself and even retreated a little.

In the rec room, we each snatched up a controller, and the room filled with the sounds of me kicking his ass. Digitally, of course.

"You better not be letting me win," I warned.

He glanced at me, scowling. "I'm not."

I laughed, and soon he was laughing with me.

The rest of the week went like this. Some nights after training and studying, we'd just talk. About everything. Video games. Taoist philosophy. Our lives before pro gaming. Others, I'd be too weak for even that, so he'd help me to bed or rub my back whenever my stomach wasn't behaving itself. On Saturday night, right before we stepped into our pods for the next match, our eyes met. Despite the busyness of the pod room, a sort of silence settled between us. We had a bond, now. We'd gone through battle together, and not just in the arena.

Inside the tower, I took a breath and tightened my grip on my sword. I felt strong. Stronger than I ever had.

When the other team burst through the entrance, Rooke and I fought side by side while Lily took the rear. Our blades swirled through the air, in and around each other, making figure eights and S shapes in our foes. Like our nightly matchups, we were becoming synchronous.

When we left the pods, our eyes met again. This time, we were both smiling. We weren't the only ones. Above the pod doors, Howie and Marcus beamed at the camera.

"Another amazing match. Defiance, welcome to the losing-bracket semifinals."

We had two teams left to beat. The last team left in the losers' bracket, and the team InvictUS had defeated in their finals.

Rooke and I kept up the same routine into the next week, sneaking out of the clubs early to return to the facility and practice together. My nausea became less, my sleep got deeper and more restful. I hadn't lost time or phased out in days, and I was lasting longer and longer during our nightly training. It was going smoothly until halfway through the week when my tablet pinged in the middle of practice. I dropped my staff, jogged over to the bench where I'd left it, and tapped the screen.

Kali,

Report to my office immediately.

Clarence

I frowned, and my shoulders fell.

"Oh shit."

"What's wrong?" Rooke asked.

I held up the tablet to him.

"We're caught."


I scrambled to change back into my clubbing clothes, and stumbled into Clarence's office like I'd had one too many.

"You wanted to see me?"

"You've been ducking out of the clubs early."

Great. He'd figured out our little ruse. I couldn't give up training and staying away from the clubs. Not with how much better I was feeling by the day. How was I going to salvage this?

"Uh, yeah," I began. "The scene has kind of sucked lately. You know, midtournament lag. It's bound to pick up again—"

"I don't care what your excuse is. It's brilliant."

I blinked. ". . . what?"

"By leaving early, you're catching maximum exposure to the paparazzi. You've made the cover of every tabloid so far this week. Good job."

Uhhh, was this actually going in my favor? I went with it.

"You mean I have to keep it up?" I whined. "This blows."

"Of course you have to keep it up."

"But—"

He slammed a hand on the desk. "Enough. You will continue to leave those clubs early every night. Is that clear?"

I sighed. "Fine. Whatever. Can I go?"

He nodded and waved like he was shooing me, and turned his attention to his desk. I pressed my lips together to hide my smile. I left, changed back into my training gear, and returned to the training room. Rooke met me with a serious expression. "What's the damage?"

I smiled.

"Absolutely none."

Before we returned to sparring, I sat on the mats and crossed my legs. Rooke looked down at me with narrowed eyes and a tilted head.

"What are you doing?"

"Centering myself." I tapped the ground in front of me. He reluctantly sat and mirrored my pose.

"Have you ever tried meditating?" I asked.

"Once in a while."

That didn't surprise me, given his appreciation of Chinese philosophy.

"How about before a fight?"

He considered it and shook his head. "Never."

"You know, in feudal Japan, samurais would meditate before battle. In certain martial art schools, they'll have you meditate in a position that's uncomfortable, sometimes even painful. You'll sit on your knees, or your knuckles, or even hang upside down. And you'll stay like that for minutes, maybe hours on end. The point is not to learn to ignore the pain or even find a way to alleviate it. The point is to accept it. Training your mind to be calm while the body is suffering makes you a stronger fighter. That way, when you're hurting or even dying, you won't panic. You'll focus on the battle, not yourself."

He smiled. "Sounds like the School of Kali Ling."

"Well, I'm not going to hurt you if you behave. Now, focus on connecting your mind to your body."

"How?"

"You find your chi." I pressed my hand against his stomach, just below his navel. He glanced down.

"I think mine is a few inches lower."

I punched his gut. He grunted, then grinned. "Hey, you said—"

"You're not behaving."

He nodded, but his grin didn't fade. "Fine."

"Rest your hands on your knees and straighten your spine," I told him. He did. "Your body should be aligned, but relaxed at the same time. Deep breaths help. Close your eyes."

He did that, too, and I closed my own.

"Now what?" he asked.

"Focus on your body. Feel your muscles relax. Sense your heartbeat, your pulse. Just be still and listen."

He went quiet then, and didn't ask any more questions. I took a breath, eyes still closed, and focused. Energy teemed inside me. Robust yet passive. Solid yet fluid. A perfectly balanced moment. Life was starting to fill more and more with these moments. I was at peace. I was myself. Even with the soft breaths caressing my face.

Soft breaths?

I opened my eyes. Rooke's face was an inch from mine.

"Bah!"

I recoiled as he exploded with laughter. I punched his shoulder. "This is serious."

"I know. Your concentration is good if you sensed me that close."

"Maybe I smelled you." I frowned at him. "The point was to focus."

"I did. Honestly." He smiled. "Thanks for sharing that with me."

He stood and offered a hand to pull me to my feet.

We took our positions on the mat, staffs in hand, and attacked. The staffs became a blur. The sharp chopping of wood echoed through the room in a pace so fast, woodpeckers would have fainted. Circling each other on the mats, we both feigned, swung, and snapped. Neither landed a shot. There were no weaknesses left between us.

We broke apart, panting, both leaning on our staffs. Adrenaline coursed through my veins, and the smile wouldn't leave my face. God, it was like a drug. No, better than a drug. This was bo-staff-training sex.

"Hey. Am I interrupting?"

I glanced to the side. Derek stood at the edge of the mats. I nodded at him.

"Not at all. What's up?"

He rubbed a hand against the back of his neck and shifted his weight. "Um, can I join?"

I glanced at Rooke, who nodded eagerly. I grinned.

"Here. Take my spot."

I passed him my staff and took a seat on the edge of the mats. Derek rotated the staff in his hand a few times, staring at it like it was a stripper pole. I could practically read his mind. *What the hell am I supposed to do with this?*

Rooke stood tall, staff in hand like it was part of his body. His chest barely moved with his breaths. There was my gladiator again.

My gladiator?

Rooke attacked slowly, letting Derek get a feel for the rhythm. Then he snapped the staff down and caught his shin. Derek hopped around on one leg, hissing.

"Holy shit, that stings."

I chuckled to myself, realizing this is what I must have looked like the first night.

"You had enough?" Rooke asked.

"Hell no."

The boys spun around each other, snapping staffs and breaking apart. Derek never got a hit in, but he never gave up either. At least, until he held up his hand and took a knee on the mats, panting. When he caught his breath, he looked between us.

"You guys ever try this virtually?"

Rooke looked at me. Since my little meltdown at the club, I hadn't plugged in at all except to run virtual simulations with the team, and even that was kept at a minimum. But if I was going to overcome the virtual world, I needed to start facing it head-on. I took a breath and nodded at him.

It was time.

It wasn't real. That's what I kept telling myself.

The three of us stood on the edge of a cliff that plummeted a hundred feet and ended in a desert garden of rocky shards and spikes. A purple-pink sky swirled overhead as the dying sun crested the horizon. It was stunning but engineered. The sky was too impeccable. The wind was too perfect. Imperfections were far more beautiful. A blemish on the skin. An extra five pounds. That was real life.

That was true beauty.

"Ready?" Derek asked, swirling the staff in his hand.

Rooke and I nodded.

Three warriors materialized on the sands and bolted for us. As my opponent reached me, I ducked and maneuvered around his sword as it chopped through the air. One too many steps back and my foot slipped half off the edge. I pushed forward and dove low, knocking my opponent off balance. He tumbled over me, and off the edge. His scream descended down the cliff and cut off abruptly when a spike punctured his stomach. A single warrior among a forest of miniature mountains and corkscrews of rock.

He wasn't alone for long. My teammates' opponents ended up impaled beside him.

Derek motioned at the sky, and shouted, "Too easy. Send us something different."

Oh, the programmers would love this.

Six new opponents phased into view. Rotting flesh peeled away from their faces, revealing gray muscle and stringy innards beneath. Zombies. Wonderful.

They came for us.

Two grabbed my staff and pushed in, snapping teeth in my face. My back bowed against the onslaught. Strong little fuckers. I shifted my weight to the side and they slid off the staff. One hard whack against their backs, and they joined the growing collection of opponents at the bottom of the mountain. I leaned over the edge and surveyed the potluck mix of gladiators and zombies on spikes. Hunters had antlers on their walls. Pffft. I had this. So. Much. Cooler.

Derek jousted his staff at the heavens.

"Come on," he baited. "I could program better than that."

I laughed at him. "Don't be too full of yourself or anything."

"I tell no lies," he said with a grin. "I can program anything."

Just then, three giants materialized on the sands and bolted for us. I nodded at them.

"Could you program a way to beat that?"

Derek closed his mouth and backed up to the edge.

The sands pounded as the titans closed in, one heading straight for me. He swung his sword. I danced, ducking and swirling around the blade. He cut through the air with such strength and precision, he could have sliced molecules in half.

The sword came down on top of me, aiming to split my cranium in two. I dropped to one knee, and a sickening crack echoed above me.

Shit.

I stilled, listening to my body. But there was no pain. No sudden jolt to reality. I glanced up. My staff had been split in two, not my head. Grinning, I drove one jagged end into the giant's throat and twisted in. He gasped. A pinwheel of blood gushed out around the staff.

Bull's-eye.

I ripped the staff out of his neck and stepped aside. The giant fell to his knees and tumbled over the edge. A hop, a skip, and a jump down the cliff, and he face-planted into the shards below. Sweet victory. Turning to Rooke, I held up my now dual short staffs, dripping with blood.

"How come we haven't trained like this?"

Rooke held a hand up toward the sky. "Cancel the opponents for a while."

The boys flanked me. I positioned myself evenly between them, back to the cliff.

They attacked.

Staff met staff and clacking wood echoed through the rocky basin. The same basin I grew closer and closer to with each hit. Smack. An inch. Smack. Another inch. The strength behind their blows left me teetering on the edge.

I closed my eyes, and focused. Yes, with the boys smacking me with sticks, on the edge of a cliff, I dropped into a meditative state. Every muscle relaxed. All the tension evaporated. With a deep breath, I moved with the wind.

I tucked, rolled, and sprang to my feet, spinning out with my staffs, snapping kneecaps and thighs. I was a flash. A bolt of lightning. Both men landed on their backs, groaning, gripping their legs. As he recovered and pushed himself up to sitting, Derek grinned and looked around my legs at Rooke. "That's why they call her the warrior."

I smiled down at the men at my feet. "I also answer to the Goddess of Gaming."

They laughed.

I turned to the cliff, letting my toes hang off the edge. I lifted my face to the sky, closed my eyes, and outstretched my arms, like I was ready to sacrifice myself to the gods of the virtual world. Except, I wasn't. I wasn't giving myself to anything.

Rooke grasped my arm.

"Hey."

I turned to him. A look of concern masked his face as his eyes searched my own. I smiled.

"I'm okay."

His concern didn't falter. I rested a hand on his arm.

"I'm not lost."

"Really?"

I drew a deep breath and slowly let it out. "No. Not anymore."

I wasn't naïve. I knew I had a ways to go before I'd kick my addiction. Maybe it was something I'd have to be wary of my entire life. But I wasn't a prisoner of the virtual world now. It didn't rule me.

I ruled it.

The next morning, Hannah slapped her breakfast tray down on the table across from mine. I jumped, dropped my spoon, and peered up at her.

"What?"

"Derek says last night you guys fought zombies and giants on a mountain with bo staffs."

Lily stood beside her, arms crossed. I glanced between them and grinned.

"What?" I asked, feigning innocence. "Did you wanna play?"

They answered in unison.

"Hell yes."

———

Fourteen hours a day. That was our minimum. Now, even the rest of the team was ducking out of the clubs. Outside of the media events, 110 percent went into training. Code practically bent around us. Whether in the cool starchiness of the training room or under the pink-purple sky and golden rays of the virtual battlefield, we fought with staffs in hand. We mastered our opponents. We mastered each other.

We mastered ourselves.

No one was drained. We were in the cafeteria earlier and earlier, scarfing down our breakfasts so we could rush to the training rooms. Eight to ten hours of physical training. The rest went to the digital world.

We took turns fighting each other, all of us. Both in the real world and the digital. We noted our strengths and weaknesses, both in ourselves and each other. We worked. We worked harder than we ever had in our entire lives.

And then we worked even harder.

When the staffs transformed to blades in the virtual arena, the blood spilled was never our own. One-on-three, two-on-four. Not a scratch. Nothing the programmers formulated could touch us. InvictUS was still the invincible team in the tournament, patiently waiting for the losing bracket to play out.

We were gaining.

That Saturday, we huddled together in the pod room, moments before the semifinal round.

"Are you sure we're ready?" Hannah asked.

I smiled. Not the fake one.

"We're more than ready."

I felt it. In every nerve, in every fiber, we were more prepared than ever. Not just because we'd practiced more or had fun while we were doing it. Because I'd begun to appreciate the virtual world in response to the real, and vice versa. Inside the facility, I noticed the grooves in the walls, the inconsistencies. The dust along the tabletops. Even the whooshing sound the doors made when they opened and closed around us. Reality and virtual were becoming one. They were two halves of a whole. Before, I'd only treasured the virtual side, and even then, I'd never really gotten everything I could out of it. Because I'd never gotten everything I could out of reality.

Now I was beginning to understand it all.

Inside the game, Hannah and Derek flew through the fields while the rest of us guarded the tower. Three men burst through the entrance door and charged.

I smiled.

They bolted for us, screaming, swords raised over their heads. We waited, bringing them to us. At the last second, just as they brought their weapons down, we ducked and stepped aside. One rolled over Rooke's shoulder and landed hard on the ground. The other two went soaring past. In unison, we whirled around, plunging swords into backs, throats, and chests.

The match was over in seconds.

"That was incredible," Marcus practically shouted, bouncing in his chair. "Wait a minute." He placed a finger against his headphones, as if listening to something. Howie glanced off-screen and made a waving motion with his hand, as if to say, *Come on, tell me.*

New record. It had to be. We gathered in front of the screen. My breath snagged in my throat as the announcers waited for the signal. Say something, damn it.

Say it.

"New record."

We screamed and tackled each other in the center of the pod room until we became a pig pile of gamers and pod suits.

"Defiance, welcome to the finals."

We were in the finals.

Was this real? It had to be. I'd never felt so alive.

The next week was an onslaught of interviews and television appearances. We quit going to the clubs, so we could train every spare moment. Bo staffs. Endless opponents. Real and virtual. In the moments in between, I'd thumb my necklace and reflect, a moment of quiet in a swirling vortex of chaos and action. Now, in the virtual world, I looked forward to the real one. To the mats and staffs, and training with my teammates.

The week soared past, moving as if time were stuck on fast forward. In a good way. Before, it felt like life was slipping me by. Now, I was living every minute, breathing every breath to its fullest.

On Friday, while the rest of our teammates had retired for the night, I slinked across the mats, attempting to bring Rooke to his knees with nothing but a bo. Maybe I really was a ninja. Tonight in particular, I was kicking his ass.

I swept the staff under his foot. Rooke went down on his back hard, catching my bo between his ankles. Both staffs scattered. I rolled on the mat, retrieved the closest one, and raised it high over my head, ready to slam it down on his head. His eyes went wide.

"Okay, okay," he said, holding up a hand.

"You forfeit?" I teased, grinning.

"It's nearly three a.m."

He motioned toward the clock, nestled high in the wall where it met the ceiling. The time flashed across it—02:49. Even when I'd partied this late, I never felt half this good.

I bounced on the edge of my toes. "I could go all night."

He grinned. "Really?"

Shock coursed through me as I realized the sexual connotation behind my words. As my eyes widened, so did Rooke's grin. I slammed the staff down. He rolled just in time, and the staff hit the mat with a thud. Rooke turned back and clamped down on the staff, keeping it pinned against the mat. Then he jerked it toward himself, pulling me with it. I tumbled forward and nearly landed in his lap. Catching myself on my hands and knees, I looked up at him, our faces now parallel and only inches apart.

"I think we should call it quits for tonight," he said. "With training, at least."

He inched the staff back, pulling me even closer. His gaze surveyed my lips, as if trying to memorize the color. Gradually, his eyes drifted up to mine. A chill shot through me under the intensity of his stare. Goose bumps peppered my skin despite the heat curling low in my belly. Memories flashed across my mind of the time we'd kissed, when I'd thrown myself at him in my bunk to distract him over the pills. That night had been a low point for me, filled with darkness and misery. But now, all I could think was how soft his lips had felt.

I looked down to the curves of his mouth, and the stubble along his jaw, grown since his early-morning shave. I closed in, wondering what he'd taste like. His hand grazed against my hip and I snapped back to reality. What was I doing? We weren't in the clubs now. No one was watching.

Since when wasn't this just for show?

I pulled away.

"Call it quits," I repeated with a shaky breath. "You're right."

Inside the women's locker room, I wrenched the shower tap on. After washing my hair, I stood directly under the cascade.

The steady stream pelted my back. Comforting, even when it hit a fresh bruise.

I pressed my hand against the cool, tiled wall of the shower. Was Rooke on the other side of this very wall, in the shower, water slipping down his skin. Maybe I could sneak into the men's locker room for a peek. You know, just one warrior admiring another, all those ripples and planes.

I took a breath and closed my eyes. Calm, Kali. Remember calm? Okay, I couldn't deny it any longer. The attraction I'd felt toward him had grown. Twofold. No, times ten. I'd gotten involved with a teammate once already, and it had ended in the worst way imaginable. While I doubted either Rooke or I would have any difficulties now with our grip on reality, mixing love with work wasn't always the best idea. What if it didn't work out? What if we broke up and were stuck on the team together, hating each other?

What if it was worth it?

When I left the changing room, Rooke was leaning outside the door.

"Were you waiting for me?" I asked.

"I was about to give up. What took you so long?"

*Picturing you naked took so long.*

"Nothing," I quipped, pushing past him.

We walked down the hallway together toward my bunk. Our feet tapped along the floor, emphasized by the echo down the empty corridor. There was something magical about this time of night. Like you're the only person in the world. As much as I looked forward to my nightly fights with Rooke, this part of the evening never quite felt normal to me, almost like we were in high school again, and he was walking me to class or back to my door after a date.

"You ready for tomorrow?" he asked.

The finals. My chest tightened, and I forced a breath through my lungs.

"I think so."

"You think so?" He laughed. "Three matches ago, it would have been an automatic 'yes.' I thought all this training would have bolstered your confidence, not lowered it."

"It has, but three matches ago we weren't in the finals." I paused, shuffling my feet against the floor. "It's not so much us as the other team that I'm worried about. I need to study them more. We're down to the top ones in the country."

"Kali, you've studied them all week. You know what you're doing."

We reached my bunk, and I tapped my lock code into the keypad. When the door opened and I stepped in, Rooke's footsteps followed. I whirled around, blocking his path in the doorframe.

"I think this is where you are a gentleman and say good night."

His gaze flicked down to my arm.

"Are you sure you don't need help tending to that?" His hand grazed my elbow, where a fresh bruise had begun to blossom. "It looks rough."

His fingers lingered, triggering goose bumps. I shook him off and folded my arms. "Then maybe you shouldn't hit me so hard."

His grin widened. "Would the warrior have it any other way?"

The warrior. I had to give Rooke credit: He knew me, understood me inside out and backwards now. I was bold, and he was about to find out just how much.

I closed the gap between us, splaying my hands against his chest. My hands glided across the hard ridges of his stomach, palms leading the way, fingertips feeling every inch. The soft, cotton fabric of his shirt strained under my grip and blocked my eyes from the same delightful journey of my hands. I pictured him the way I had earlier. Bare skin. Water slipping down. Oh yes, the shower would have been better. Why hadn't I broken into the locker room?

My gaze drifted up to his eyes, expecting to find them overflowing with shock. But they were calm and unwavering like an open lake, as if he'd expected this all along. His breaths were steady. Comfortable. Way too comfortable. That's not how I liked my men.

I weaved my fingers through the drawstring of his training shorts, and pulled. As if the strings were actually attached to his eyebrows, they raised in response. My own marionette. How cute.

"Maybe you should help me," I said softly, leaning into him until our stomachs touched. Even through the fabrics of our shirts, heat from him brushed against my navel. His breaths weren't so calm now. "I'm sure there are a few spots I can't reach on my own."

His eyebrows rose even farther. "Really?"

I pushed up slowly on my tiptoes, sliding my curves up his form. His breath hitched. Better. Then, hot fingers seared against the small of my back and pressed me tighter against him. Now, my breath hitched. Damn him.

Warmth coiled inside, ignited everywhere our bodies touched. The smell of fresh skin from his recent shower and that soft scent of cedar that never left him filled my lungs. Whether it was from all those books of his or his cologne, I didn't know. Or care. I inhaled again and trembled against him. He smirked. A soft chuckle resounded in his chest.

No. I win this fight.

My fingers curled through his hair, pulling the strands taut. Desperate. He brought his head down as I tilted my own. His quickened breaths ghosted against my skin as his stubbled chin swept against mine, ticklish and rough at the same time. Our noses brushed. Our lips grazed. Almost. So close.

Everything else disappeared in that moment. No facility. No tournament. Just us, our bodies pressed together, lips touching but still not kissing. Just the overwhelming scent and taste and feel of Rooke until I was drowning in him.

I closed my eyes and murmured against his mouth. "Just one thing."

"Hmm?"

"Good night."

Reaching around the doorframe, I tapped the control button, and the door slid shut in his face.

# CHAPTER 17

The next day, that's when the shit hit the fan.

All because I went ape-shit crazy.

It started that morning as I scanned through my tablet, reviewing play-by-plays on the VGL's Web site in prep for the night's final matchup. In the top left-hand corner of the screen, a search bar blinked. In fading lettering, it said: Type Team/ Player's Name. Out of curiosity, I typed in Nathan's. What excuse would they have put in as his cause of death? Heart failure, like in the tabloids? Or something even more bullshit-tastic. But the search engine spit back an answer that twisted my stomach, and not in the way I had expected.

Results not found.

No. That wasn't right. I must have spelled his name wrong. I reentered his information, trying various forms of his name, and received the same results. Several times. Finally, I gave up and typed in Team Defiance. Under the Former Members section was . . . nothing.

Nothing.

No former teammates. None.

My chest tightened. My breaths trembled as a rolling, turbulent rage flooded every cell in my body. I punched the screen.

It bowed in with the force and popped back out. Fuck the person who invented flexible LED screens.

I stormed down the hallway, letting my anger carry me to the doc's office. The facility's staff dove out of my path, some suctioning themselves against the walls, others ducking into doorways or closets. Yes, the warrior exists in real life. Luckily for everyone else, I wasn't armed.

At the doc's office, I slammed the door open. It ricocheted off the wall with the crack of thunder. Dr. Renner, who was standing at the window, dropped the tablet in her hands and nearly jumped on her desk.

"Kali?"

"They erased him."

"Who? What are you talking about?"

I slammed the door shut and whirled back. "Nathan. He's gone out of the VGL database. They're trying to wipe him off the record. It's like he never even existed."

Dr. Renner slowly lowered herself into her chair. She maintained eye contact, but an odd look still masked her face, as if a bear had just burst into her office. "I'm sure it's a mistake. Maybe you typed something wrong—"

I smashed my fist on her desk. "I'm not wrong."

She held up her hands, pleading innocence. "Kali, I had nothing to do with any of this. I can assure you."

"I know you didn't."

"Then why are you screaming at me?"

"Because I'm pissed. You're the shrink. Aren't you supposed to handle this?"

She chuckled softly to herself. "That's not really how this works."

I plopped down in the chair across from her, steam still spewing from my pores. "I'm not used to being this angry anymore."

"That's not a bad thing," she pointed out.

"But now I don't know how to deal with it."

"It's best if you just let yourself feel that anger, all of it, in its full force. You know, just get it out," she said. "What is it about the situation that upsets you?"

"Everything," I exploded, jumping up from the chair. "Everything about this fucking industry. Appeasing the sponsors just so they don't drop us the second we're not popular anymore. Owners treating us like used gum. Spitting us out and tossing us away. All while they make more and more money. Meanwhile, we're the ones sacrificing our bodies and minds for ratings. RATINGS."

The doc opened her mouth to speak, but I cut her off.

"And you know what? We're supposed to do it with a fucking smile on our faces. We're supposed to appreciate all this because how many people get to play video games for a living? Yeah, it's real fun when you get hacked to bits every week, or when your teammate dies, and no one cares. Nathan was a person. A FUCKING HUMAN BEING. People don't even remember his name. No, no. As long as there's another match on Saturday, guess who gives a shit? Nobody."

I plunked down in the chair again with a huff. It grunted in protest under my weight. Though my breaths came out in soft pants, the adrenaline pumping through my veins felt refreshing. Life-giving. I'd never felt like this anywhere outside the arena.

I crossed my arms and narrowed my eyes at the doc, waiting for her reply. She tapped a fingernail against her tablet, taking a few extra seconds before trying to talk again.

"Sometimes it takes someone to stand up to what's wrong before people can see what's right," she finally said.

"Oh yeah? What if the sponsors don't like it?"

She shrugged. "That doesn't sound like much of a warrior to me."

My eyebrows went up. "Are you encouraging me to rebel, Dr. Renner? To stick it to the man?"

She held up her hands, signaling innocence again. "I'm just saying it wouldn't surprise me if you did. After all"—she smiled—"it matches your image."

A stunted noise came out from the back of my throat that sounded like "hmmph." It did match my image. And Dr. Renner was just as much a mutineer as I was. Maybe she wasn't like Clarence after all.

"I'll let you mull that over." She tapped her tablet. "I've been meaning to ask about the sleeping pills. Have you needed them?"

A spasm clenched my stomach, and my gaze lowered to the floor. "I, uh, stopped taking them."

"Stopped? So, you did need them?"

I bit my lip as the spasm in my stomach started swirling. Time to own up to the truth. The warrior inside took a step back.

"I abused them, doc," I admitted. I locked my gaze on her face and forced my eyes to stay on target. The doc sat back in her chair, but she remained quiet, allowing me the opportunity to explain. I continued, "I was taking too many. I couldn't sleep without them. Without a lot of them."

She nodded and clicked her tongue, but her features softened. "Kali, I wouldn't have given them to you if I didn't think you could handle it."

"I know. You gave them to me as an aid. As a last resort. I understand that now. I didn't before."

"It's good, though, that you realized all this on your own."

"Yeah, I guess. I mean, Rooke helped, and Nathan's death

made it real for me. Not at first. But eventually, yeah, I realized
I had a problem."

"Speaking of Rooke, how's your relationship with him?"

I clammed up. "What relationship? There's no relationship."

The warrior was back.

A smiled touched her lips. "The training room would say
otherwise."

My jaw set. I crossed my arms. "You spying on me, doc?"

"No, no. But I go down that hall on my way out every night.
How long have you two been going at it?" She cleared her throat
as she realized her choice of words. "Sparring together, I mean."

"About a few weeks now."

"And how has that impacted your relationship?" she asked.
"As *friends*."

*Friends* sounded a little too emphasized for my liking.

"We're better *friends* now, meaning I only want to punch
him in the training room. Most of the time."

Dr. Renner tapped her foot as she thought over my words,
and I swear I saw her suppress another smile.

"Last time we talked, you were motivated to make some
changes in your life. How has that worked out for you?"

"Good. Really good. Fantastic, actually. I mean, I'm not
naïve. I know there's always a chance of slipping down that
path again, but I feel different now. Stronger. I'm in control."

She nodded. "Good. What helped you regain that control?"

"Training. I talked with Rooke over what was wrong with
me. We worked together a lot. I'm also trying to live my life in
balance. It's something I believed in a long time ago, and when
I started practicing it again, it was exactly what I needed to
bring me back from the edge."

She tilted her head. "How so?"

I held up my necklace for her to see. "A yin yang represents balance. One black half and one white half to make a whole. But see how there's a white dot on the black side and a black dot on the white side?" She nodded. "That shows how they're interconnected. You can't appreciate the light without knowing the dark. Otherwise, you'd have no comparison. I realized the same thing about the virtual world and the real one. They're interconnected, and I can only be strongest there when I'm strongest here."

She considered my words for a while. "That's insightful, Kali." She made a few notes on her tablet. "Speaking of the virtual world, the finals are tonight. Are you anxious about that?"

"A little. If it were just me, I'd be hungry for it. But I worry about the team."

"The more you worry about the team, the less focused you are on everything else. You're ready for this. You wouldn't have made it this far if you weren't."

I nodded. "Yeah, you're right. Any other advice?"

"Yes. Get out of here."

"What?"

She smiled. "Kali, you figured out on your own how to handle your gaps in time, and you stopped yourself from taking too many pills. You're stronger than you think, and not just physically. You really don't need to see me anymore. Besides, I think you have some things to consider."

"Like what I should do about Nathan?"

She nodded. "I can't answer that for you. You need to find a way, your own way, to honor him."

I glanced around the office. "But I can still come back if I need it, right?"

It had only been a few weeks since I'd started coming back to reality. While the nightly training sessions and meditation had helped, I'd take anything I could get to stop from slipping back down that slope again.

The doc's smile widened. "Of course. My door is always open if you need me."

As I left the doc's office and headed for the training room, thoughts from the appointment dominated my mind. What could I do about Nathan? Nothing that Clarence and the sponsors would approve of. I couldn't stand up to them, not directly. I couldn't risk getting kicked out of the games, or my team might be forced to forfeit this late in the tournament.

Was there nothing I could do?

In the training room, at the far end, Rooke sat in one of the weight machines. I joined him, climbing into the leg press.

"You're late," he said, glancing at me.

"I went to see Dr. Renner."

He nodded. "How was it?"

"Good. She thinks I'm doing really well. She's impressed with how I'm handling things."

Rooke smiled. "You sound a bit surprised, and you shouldn't be. Most gamers have more trouble pulling themselves back."

"Yeah. She said that, too. She also said I don't need to see her anymore." I started pumping my legs and focused on the burning sensation in my muscles. Never thought I'd appreciate that feeling, but I'd learned to appreciate many things I never thought I would. "But I think I'll still go anyways. I mean, you're supposed to go to your general physician for a physical every year to check that everything is okay, right? So, I mean, why not check in with the shrink once in a while, too. We have enough stresses on our minds to justify it, in my opinion."

Rooke stared at me for a minute as he processed my words, then shook his head.

"What?" I asked. "You don't think so?"

"No, I think you're dead-on." He stood up from his machine and began adjusting the weights.

"Do you ever go to see her?" I asked.

He fumbled, almost dropping the weight in his hands. "Uh, yeah."

"About the drugs?"

He met my eyes. "Mostly."

"Mostly?"

He sat down on the machine, facing toward me. "Look—"

I held up a hand. "If it's personal, you don't have to tell me."

"Yeah, I kinda do."

My brow furrowed. What did that mean?

"Hey."

Lily walked up beside me. She frowned, foreshadowing bad news.

"Clarence is looking for you."

Ugh. The worst news.

I climbed out of the weight machine and started for the exit when Lily called out.

"No. Both of you."

She motioned toward Rooke.

Double ugh.

Together, we headed for Clarence's office. Maybe with two of us, it would buffer the blow of his wrath. The second we passed through the doors, Clarence stood up from his desk. "What do you two think you're doing?"

Or maybe emphasize it.

Rooke and I exchanged glances.

"Lily said—"

"This past week you haven't been out or seen at all. You have an image to uphold." Clarence ground his fists into his desk as his neck turned red. Great. Angrier than usual.

"We're getting toward the end of the tournament," I protested. "I think training and rest is more important than being seen."

Clarence glared at me. "How could you ever think that? You need to be out there promoting the sport and our sponsors."

Oh, yes. The sponsors. How important.

"I'm supposed to do all that on top of leading the team, studying my opponents, and training every daylight hour? I'm one person. Plus, that doesn't include leisure time."

"Leisure time?" he barked. "You think celebrities get leisure time?"

Everyone should. Maybe that's why half of them go crazy, too.

"You want us eating right and exercising every day so we're at our prime," I said. "Don't you think some rest and relaxation should be a part of that?"

"You are the top athletes in the world. You should be able to rise above the circumstances."

"Rise above the circumstances?" My tone matched his, growing louder with each word. "We're gamers, not gods."

"The public doesn't know the difference. You die on-screen, and, like magic, you're fine in real life. You're not a person. You're a character."

Every muscle inside me clenched. We were people, same as anybody. Maybe we had more drive and determination, or maybe we were just obsessed, but we were still human.

"Is that what Nathan was?" I asked through gritted teeth. "Just a character? We're human beings, for fuck's sake."

I motioned at the posters around the room, none of which featured our fallen teammate. Clarence's gaze darted about the room, as if acting against his wishes but too curious not to peek.

Clarence rolled his eyes. "Kali, Nathan's gone. Leave him be."

"No. It takes me longer than two months to forget about somebody."

"Obviously."

My fists balled up, and I made no effort to hide them. "Nathan deserves to be remembered."

"As what? A drug addict?"

"As a person," I spat. "As an athlete and a gamer. Not someone who the sponsors can just wash away because it might affect our ratings or popularity."

"The sponsors run these games. They can do whatever they want. If they don't want the public to know the truth about Nathan, then they never will."

"Why? Are they afraid that people will find out just how dangerous this sport can really be? No, no. It's fake. We promise. No one really dies. No one ever goes crazy." I threw my arms up. "Gamers go crazy all the time. And we do die. Nathan died. And it's all because of this 'sport.'"

"This isn't the reason why I called you in here," Clarence muttered, waving a hand to dismiss the topic. "Half the media think you two have broken up."

He motioned toward the wallscreen behind us. I glanced back as it filled with tabloids featuring the news of our apparent split. Oh, this bullshit again. I'd been inside the facility so much, I'd forgotten about the media and how much it was a part of all this.

"What the hell are we supposed to do?" I asked. "We weren't even together in the first place."

"You need to get out there and convince them otherwise." Clarence pointed a finger out the floor-to-ceiling windows overlooking the city. "I don't care what it takes."

"What do you want us to do? Have sex in the streets?"

He shrugged. "If necessary."

Okay, that's it. I knew he was doing it just to get under my skin and to prove he could throw his weight around, but I'd reached my boiling point. I was being completely rational. He wasn't. Now who was the adult?

I imagined nails bolting my feet to the floor to stop from charging him. "We'll be arrested. Is that the kind of media attention you want?"

Clarence stared back blankly and didn't object.

Rooke weighed in on the situation. "I'm not entirely opposed—"

"Shut up," I snapped, and turned back to Clarence. "You're being ridiculous."

He opened his mouth to reply, but I cut him off.

"No. You can shut up, too."

Silence cut through the room with a heavy dose of tension trailing behind it. Clarence's glare bore into me, and the muscles in his face went tight. At least, tighter than they already appeared. All except for his lips, which had split apart from shock.

Rooke leaned toward me and lowered his voice, though the warning in it was clear. "Kali—"

I held my hand up. "No. I don't care. I don't care if this is what's expected of me. I don't care if I have a contract. Disown me, or fire me. Slander me in the tabloids. I don't care." I marched up to the desk, leveling Clarence with my gaze. "I don't play because of sponsors or media or anything else. I play because I love the game. And if I have to deal with all this bullshit, then maybe I don't want to do it anymore."

I smashed my closed fist on the desk, hard enough that I half expected it to crack. Part of me felt like I was throwing a hissy fit, and the other felt like I was finally beginning to stand up for what I believed in.

Clarence slowly lowered himself into his chair and stared up at me, eyes wide, studying me as if he'd never seen me before. As if this were the first time he'd met the warrior outside of the digital world. The doc had the same look in her eyes when I'd burst into her office. I was beginning to like this.

I took a step back, slowly, purposefully, eyes locked on Clarence. Power curled through me, confidence like I'd never felt before. I was a tiger, and the man behind the desk was a little mouse.

Clarence placed his hands on the desk, but judging by the lack of tension in his muscles and the calm look on his face, I took it as a sign of impartiality, not hostility.

"The sponsors and media will always be a part of this, just like any sport," he said in an even tone. "You can't do away with what you don't like just because you don't like it. How would we fund the tournaments without companies to back it?"

"Companies back themselves," I argued. "We have to lick their feet just so they can drop us the minute we lose or aren't popular anymore. They don't give a shit about us. All they care about is making more money."

"You have your beliefs, and that's fine, but that doesn't amend anything. You can't change the world, Kali."

I didn't know if it was the mood in the air or the confidence still curling through me, but that sounded like one hell of a challenge. And then I knew how. I knew how to throw the sponsors for a loop. I knew how to make them lick my feet instead. How to convince the world Rooke and I were together without leaving the facility. Without the cameras and the red carpet, and all the bullshit. This was my life. My sexuality. I was free to express it how I chose, not the other way around. They'd pushed me too far now, and I was done playing their game.

It was time for them to play mine.

I splayed my hand on Clarence's desk, and leaned toward him. "If the media are so convinced we're breaking up, then maybe they should see just how much we've been fighting together. They want a show? Then let's give them one."

———

By the time Rooke and I had decided on a new plan for the night's matchup, the rest of the team was already in the pod room, suiting up.

"Geez, last minute, huh?" Hannah said, as soon as Rooke and I walked through the doors. "Where have you been? We were getting worried."

Then she winked at me, obviously thinking Rooke and I had been busy doing something in particular.

Internally, I waved her off since I didn't have time to convince her otherwise. "Sorry, guys, but we need to make a few last-minute changes. Lily, you're going on offense."

The room cut to instant silence, except for the soft beeping of the machinery, which only emphasized the awkwardness. My teammates, even the programmers, all stared openmouthed and blinking. Mob mentality of the shocked variety.

Lily sputtered. "But I'm always on defense."

"I know, I know. But the crowd needs to see me and Rooke together. Alone. I want all three of you to take the enemy's tower. No middleman. Don't kill anyone you don't have to. I want every offensive player on their team to make it through to our tower. Understand?"

"Hang on." Derek held up a hand. "You want to purposely go up against as many enemies as possible?"

"That's right."

The trio exchanged glances with each other, then all regarded me with an identical lip-curling, what-the-hell-are-you-thinking expression.

"Trust me," I said, pulling on my own suit. "Oh, and don't take their tower too fast."

"Don't take their tower?" Hannah exclaimed.

"No, no. Take it, but slowly."

"I thought you said a few changes." Derek tossed his arms up. "You're altering our entire gameplay minutes before the match. The final tournament match." He leaned toward me with his last words and crossed his arms.

"Look, I know it's tough to stomach, but you guys can handle it. I'm not going to give you one of those corny 'I believe in you' speeches, but I do. I believe in you guys, and we're not here because winning is what matters most to us. Yes, it's a pretty huge chunk, and it would be fantastic to win the tournament. But bottom line: What we all really love is the game and having fun. We need to fight like we have inside the simulations. This is our chance to prove that training is more important than the media."

Despite what I thought was a great speech, my teammates still didn't falter from their skeptical attitude. I didn't blame them. Derek was right. I was changing our entire plan right before the last match of the tournament, the final before the championship. I could only ask for one thing.

"Please, guys. You need to trust me."

Derek looked at Rooke, who leaned casually against one of the pods.

"You're fine with this?" Derek asked, noting his calm demeanor.

"She's never let us down," he replied. "She's led us to victory ever since she took control of the team, right after Nathan died. Even while she was dealing with all of her own shit. She's stronger than anyone I've ever known, and I don't doubt her."

I had to clench my jaw to keep it from dropping open. Rooke thought I was strong? Even after the pills and everything else? But hell, there was some truth in his words. I'd pushed through the tournament and led the team all while dealing with my own issues. How come I never realized that myself?

Rooke stared at Derek until his gaze flicked to mine, dead-set serious. He wasn't just saying it to convince the team. He meant it. Every word.

Derek shifted his weight and glanced back at the girls. They traded looks with each other before he spoke for them.

"All right, Kali. You got it."

We dispersed from the center of the room, each going to our own pods. I nodded at Elise, sitting at the workstation, before climbing in. When the doors closed, I was immersed in a gray-ish darkness. I took a deep breath and focused, grounding myself in the real. Sterile air filled my nose. Excitement and determination flooded my veins from head to toe, until I felt like dancing inside the pod. The pod's shimmering innards pulsed with iridescent energy as the wires began their slow, ticklish crawl over my skin. I exhaled, lay back, and closed my eyes.

Time to kick ass.

# CHAPTER 18

The virtual world was different now.

Standing inside the tower, with the wind whispering in my ear, I felt both close and distant from this place. The familiar scents of lavender and mountain air brushed against my nose, and the taste of wheatgrass danced across my tongue, sensations I'd long associated with being in my true element, with being home. Now, it was something else. Merely a place to showcase my talents. As glorious as it was, there was something to be had in the real world, too. Behind the towers' stone walls, even the lavender and the wheatgrass and the mountain air, was programming. It was code. Nothing more.

Since I'd started playing these games, I'd always viewed the virtual and the real as two separate entities. The sun-soaked baths of this world against the dreary grays of the real. Organic versus synthetic. But now, they were two parts of a whole. The virtual world couldn't exist without reality, and with virtual programming permeating so many aspects of society, it seemed the real couldn't exist without a little fantasy. What's life without make-believe? But I'd spent too much time in the fantasy. Now, it was time to value the real and everything it had to offer.

The rhythmic beating of my teammates' footsteps echoed down the dirt path and faded into the distance, leaving behind a heavy silence. Streams of sunlight broke through the barred windows high in the tower's walls, cut off by the beams overhead, splicing the sun's rays into fractured spotlights on the floor. The wind danced along my skin and rustled my hair. Despite being inside the game, the voices of the announcers filled my head.

*Losers' bracket finals tonight. The winners go on to the championship round.*

I balanced on the balls of my feet, waiting, muscles tense and relaxed at the same time. The sword gripped in my hand was a part of me now, an extension of my limb. My heart beat soundly in my chest. I was ready. I closed my eyes and took a breath. Everything was still. Peaceful. Inside and out.

A peace broken by Rooke's constant pacing.

His shuffling feet scraped against the tower's stone floor as he crossed over the same invisible line again and again. Why was he so anxious?

Rooke stopped in front of me.

"You nervous?" he asked in a murmur, so the cameras wouldn't pick up the audio.

I drew a deep breath and slowly pushed it out. "No. I'm ready."

Footsteps echoed up the path.

"They're coming," I told him.

The enemy burst through the tower's entrance. Three of them, all men. Not bad, but not as many as I'd hoped.

We went back-to-back in the center of the tower. I breathed, calm and steady. The trio surrounded us, two positioned in front of me while the other baited Rooke. A grin touched my lips.

Let's dance, boys.

They attacked, and not without skill.

Metal clanged against metal as our swords met. Sweat beaded along my hairline as I swirled and ducked against two enemies at once. Rooke and I fought with our backs glued together. The muscles in his back moved in correspondence with mine. Like magnets. I leaned forward, and he bowed back. One warrior with four arms. Three hundred and sixty degrees of death. Zero blind spots. No weaknesses.

A scream cut through the air behind me, and I knew Rooke had nailed his opponent. A body collapsed on the tower's stone floor.

The heat from Rooke's back left mine as he circled around to fight at my side. A few short blasts against his new opponent, and he jabbed his sword straight through his heart.

Our remaining opponent charged straight for me, weapon drawn back. I caught his swing as he brought it down and redirected him to the side.

Rooke rammed into him, full speed. He tumbled back, rolling several feet away. Rooke followed through, taking a few steps ahead. What the hell was he doing? Protecting me? I was going to rip him a new one. If this wasn't the finals match, I would have taken him out myself.

He glanced back at me, winked, and knelt on one knee, back facing me.

My breath caught in my throat. There was ten feet between Rooke and me, and another ten beyond him to our opponent. I'd seen this before.

The simulation in the gladiatorial arena.

Time to fly.

I bolted just as our opponent stumbled to his feet.

My feet swept across the ground and up Rooke's back. As I reached his shoulders, he stood and held his palms up. My feet landed in his hands, and he catapulted me into the air.

I flew.

Time slowed, as if I could actually feel the broadcasting switch to slow motion. Sword reeled back, single knee bent, I was a Valkyrie. An angel of death.

I slammed into my opponent, driving him to the ground and my sword up and into his chest cavity until the very tip broke through his mouth and pierced his tongue. His eyes went wide and never moved again.

That.

Was.

Awesome.

I stood tall. There was no crowd here. No glorious applause. I didn't need it. It pumped in every cell, through every vein.

There was no sudden jolt back to reality. No signal overhead. My teammates really were drawing out the fight, showing off every aspect of their skills. They had followed my command.

We had time.

Rooke turned to me, scowling.

"Nice going, Ling," he spat. "I nearly had to handle that myself. You could at least show up next time."

"What the hell are you talking about?" I immediately snapped back, as if the conversation was planned. "I had two of them on me."

"Oh, please. You only survived because I stepped in and saved you."

I reeled.

"Saved me?" I shouted. "I could've handled both of them blindfolded. You're just pissed I showed you up."

"Showed me up? You're too full of yourself to see—"

"*Me* too full of myself? Try looking in the mirror—"

Our voices started overlapping each other, both shouting at the top of our lungs as the argument spilled into a full-blown fight. All in front of the cameras. Darn. What a shame.

I stepped closer. "—You're such a pompous, haughty jackass, I'd rather have a five-year-old on my team—"

He stepped closer. "—You're so frustratingly independent, I'm surprised you even know how to lead anybody—"

"—What? You acted like you were too good to be on a team the second you showed up—"

Another step.

"—Oh yeah? You act like the virtual world should bow to you—"

Another step.

"—You're so fucking arrogant—"

Closer.

"—You're so damn stubborn—"

Closer.

Then, as the gap between us disappeared, our armor clanked together, and our voices grew until they echoed off the tower walls, he kissed me.

His lips were just as soft as I remembered, when I'd first kissed him in my bunk and he never responded. Now, he held nothing back. His mouth met mine, again and again, every kiss full of wet heat and little nips that sent jolts of adrenaline through every vein.

He pulled away just as quickly.

I stared at him, blinking. His expression mirrored my own, completely stunned, with his mouth slightly agape. The kiss had been planned. The argument had been planned. But that incredible spark of electricity? Soooo not on the checklist.

The kiss left behind a tingling on my lips, and I almost cried out when he stopped. But he stayed close, keeping me wrapped in his arms, as he studied my face. I studied his. The soft curves of his lips. The stubble dotting his jaw. The warmth lingering from his touch, where his hands now rested on my waist. In that moment, I wanted him. I wanted him and nothing else. Judging by the need in his eyes, he felt the same.

I pressed my body against his, and captured his mouth with my own. He tasted like an autumn night. Dark, woody, and sweet. Weapons dropped to the ground, thudding against the dirt. His hands grasped my chin, his skin rough and blistered from wielding swords and staffs. A warrior's hands. They slid into my hair and clamped down, forcing my chin up. I gasped. He chuckled against my mouth, and when he kissed me again, his tongue brushed mine.

Holy camoly. I swear I had knees just a second ago.

Warmth sweltered inside the tower, swirling around us. But nothing compared to the heat pounding inside me. His lips covered mine, again and again. A hand pressed into the small of my back and drove me up against him. Armor plates clanked together. I wrapped my limbs around him, intertwining my body with his. Where skin met skin between the breaks, heat sparked and sizzled until we were melting into each other. In that moment, we were one.

Until a jolt of reality tore us apart.

# CHAPTER 19

Okay. So, yeah. I did that—on national television.

For a reason.

The seven-figure tabloid reward for our first kiss was shot to shit. There would be no grainy photos of a stolen moment outside the clubs, or on the roof of the facility. Sure, the magazines would still be pushing for pictures of us together. But no one—not even Clarence—could tell me how and when to be with Rooke now because I already had. In front of everyone. On my terms. Not theirs.

I opened my eyes to the pod's interior, panting and trembling. My head swam, and my hands shook. Every part of my body tingled, though I doubted it was from plugging in. I closed my eyes and counted my breaths as I negotiated with my hormones to take a step back. Turns out, I'm a bad negotiator. Virtual or reality, they wanted only one thing.

Rooke.

The pod's doors retracted. I pulled myself out and met Rooke's stare. He stood in front of his pod, staring at me, blinking, as if he couldn't fully process what had just happened between us, whatever he had felt, or was still feeling. Hell, I half expected him to touch his lips to make sure they were still there.

Around the room, the programmers stared with wide-eyed,

openmouthed expressions. Guess we weren't the only ones who'd been surprised by the kiss.

My teammates pulled themselves out of their pods, glanced around, then exchanged looks with each other. They might have been unaware of what happened in the arena, but they were picking up on the awkward tension in the room.

Elise rifled out of her chair. "That was a hell of a show!"

Hannah looked around again and took a step toward us. "What did you do?"

On the screen above the door, the footage cut to Marcus Ryan and Howie Fulton, the VGL announcers. They sat behind their booth, blinking for a few seconds, stunned. Then, Marcus shook his head and cleared his throat.

"Defiance wins," he announced, his voice wavering with shock. "Uh . . ."

"They are your losers' bracket finalists," Howie finished for him, coming into his own. "Stay tuned as we go through highlights of the season and prepare for the championship round."

The theme music played, and the camera started to pull away, but not before it caught the tail end of their conversation.

"Well, I guess that's why they've been staying in so much."

"I think we found the climax for tonight's highlight reel."

"Probably won't be the only climax of the night."

Then, an off-camera voice shouted, "We're still on the air!"

I smiled, never thinking that in a world so perfect, I'd be so happy to see a crack in the façade.

A hand came to rest on my shoulder. I turned. Hannah stood directly behind me. "Seriously, what did you do?"

She glanced between me and Rooke a few times. I looked up at him, wondering what to say. He shrugged. "We could demonstrate."

I reeled back to smack him when Elise poked her head around her screen. "Kali, Clarence wants—"

"To see me. Yeah, yeah." I started for the exit.

"No. Both of you." She motioned at Rooke.

"Of course."

I grabbed Rooke by the sleeve and led him out of the pod room. Inside his office, Clarence peered at us over the steepled fingers pressed against his lips. I was beginning to think that was his favorite pose. It made him look both powerful and insightful at the same time, for those who didn't know better.

"You can tell the tabloids I'll take my million dollars in small, unmarked bills," I told him.

"Those don't exist anymore," Clarence replied.

I smiled. "Neither does the reward for our first kiss."

My smile grew even wider. Up yours, tabloids.

"Yes. Now they want more." The cell phone wrapped around Clarence's wrist buzzed. He glanced at it. "The phone hasn't stopped ringing, mostly from sponsors. They all want you, both of you, to be the face of their campaigns. Clothing, however"— he cleared his throat—"won't be part of the shoots."

I swallowed.

Wow, did the air density just triple in here or what? Well, that little plan just turned around and smacked me in the face. Yet my gaze slid to Rooke in the next chair, still dressed in his pod suit. Just what would I find beneath?

Rooke spoke up. "Again, I'm not entirely opposed."

My fist itched for action until the cell phone buzzed again.

"Why aren't you answering it?" I asked Clarence, seizing the chance for distraction.

"Keeps them desperate. Makes them think I'm already busy with others."

My heart fluttered. I'd just found my out. "So I guess it's a good thing then for us to stay inside the facility where no one can see us. You know, leave them desperate."

"Well . . ."

"Think about it. All this came about because no one saw us together for a week. After that matchup, that kiss, people will be knocking down the doors to see us. And if we don't let them, if we stay inside, no sponsors, no photo shoots, nothing, guess what that will do for the popularity of the tournament? If the only place where people can see us together is in the championship match, then everyone will watch."

His eyes glazed over as he considered it.

"Think of the ratings," I added. "The most-viewed championship in history."

More glaze. He rocked in his chair a little, though I doubted he even realized he was doing it.

"Yes, yes," he said, nodding. "That's a good idea. In fact"— he paused—"maybe it's best for everyone on the team to stay in until the championship round. It will add more mystery to all of this."

I pressed my lips together to stop them from spreading into a smile. "Yes, you're right."

"Right, well," he began, eyes still shining like sugar-covered doughnuts. "Good job. You're dismissed."

Rooke and I left the office and walked silently down the hall, no sound other than our feet padding along the corridor. We stepped into the elevator. The doors closed.

I exploded.

I screamed. I jumped up and down. I tackled an unsuspecting Rooke against the elevator's side, still screaming and jumping.

He laughed. "I never thought you'd find a way to convince

Clarence that staying in to prepare for the fights was in the best interest of the team."

"It should be the norm," I said. "For every team. And we should be able to have some free time once in a while."

"Yeah, right." He laughed again. "Why don't you go back in and ask for that? You seem to be on a roll."

"That's all right. I like my head still attached to my body."

The elevator doors pulled open and we walked through the facility's ground floor. A commotion pulled us into the rec room, where my other three teammates sat poised on the couch across from the wallscreen. Lily sat in the middle with a bowl of popcorn in her lap. All three were still dressed in their pod suits, as if they'd run straight from the pod room, and the idea of changing was irrelevant. Rooke and I hadn't changed either. At least we looked like a team.

"It's everywhere," Hannah announced as we entered the room. "Seriously, like every other channel."

Tablet in hand, she used it to flip through the channels on the wallscreen, her fingers moving in a blur. The frenzied look in her eyes made me think her finger was actually on the trigger of a machine gun.

"How can you even see every other channel?" Derek asked, motioning at the choppy blur on the screen.

You could, just barely. Shots of Rooke and me fighting together between commercials, cooking shows, and nature documentaries. It blended into one big blurry mess, as if someone had taken two old movie reels and spliced them together frame by frame. Rooke—a mop—me—spaghetti—swords—a hawk diving for prey.

"Hannah," Derek exclaimed, slapping his hands on his knees. "I'm gonna have a seizure."

She giggled. "I'm hitting the thousands now, and it's still going."

Lily simply held her head with one hand and shook it. She munched on the popcorn in her lap.

Finally, Hannah stopped on the VGL's home channel. When our old friends Marcus and Howie popped up on the screen, Rooke and I retired to the couch. Scratch that. Rooke sprawled himself out so I had to squeeze into the tiny space between him and the armrest, right under the crook of his arm. Had he done that on purpose?

I glanced over his profile, but his eyes were locked on the screen. No cocky grin. No sly glance in my direction. I shrugged it off and turned my own gaze to the television.

The screen flashed through the tournament highlights, showcasing the best moves and kills throughout the last few months of tournament play, including the preseason matches. Spinning, kicking, blades soaring through the air. Gamers became the embodiment of martial arts and short-range weapons. They were gods on the screen.

Then, the footage cut to me in the center of the tower. InvictUS stormed through the entrance. Great. This, again.

I watched as I dodged their blows and delivered some of my own until I ended up on my back, pinned, bleeding out from the neck. I gripped my own throat and shook my head.

The highlights ended, and the footage cut back to the announcers. Howie beamed at the camera. "What a great season so far. We've seen some incredible plays in the RAGE tournament this year. Now that we've finished highlights of the previous matchups this season, let's recap tonight's earlier event: Defiance vs. Rizing Nation."

The scene cut to the sepia fields of the arena. Three lines carved their way through the stalks. The camera angle changed to eye level within the fields. Derek snaked his way through, the girls flanking him on either side. At her size, Lily moved so swiftly through the fields, the stalks barely shook. Stealthy little thing. Maybe she should go on offense more often.

Halfway through the fields, Derek held up a hand. The trio halted and dropped to their knees, crouching low. The stalks trembled only from the wind. Instant camouflage. The rustling fields and their breaths filled the audio.

Then came the distinct sound of the enemy charging through the fields. My teammates crouched even lower, making themselves as small as possible. The rustling grew and grew until the attackers soared past them on either side. One missed Lily by an inch. The axe in her hand trembled, like a magnet jerking toward another, as if the weapon itself desired the kill.

"Nice, guys," I said. "Very smooth."

"Thanks." Derek beamed.

The paths through the stalks rippled away. When silence settled around them, my team picked up and continued toward the enemy tower. Slowly. I smiled. They were following my instructions. My teammates really did trust me. Guess I'd earned it.

The announcers' voices overlaid the footage.

"What was that?" Marcus sputtered, sounding confused. "Did they just let them go past intentionally?"

"Uh, that's a new tactic. Not sure what Defiance is doing here, but this should get interesting."

The camera changed to the trio bursting into the enemy's tower. Two of Rizing Nation stood in the center.

Derek went for one while the girls went for the other. Nation separated.

Big mistake.

Hannah and Lily fought together, blades swirling through the air. Those two were Amazons, warrior women. Hannah took the high ground, seeking out his head and neck, while Lily swiped at his legs and waist. He stumbled back under their wrath.

Lily jumped and spun, blades out. Her axe sliced through his neck, finally landing in the home it had been aching for. Blood speckled her face, but she landed softly on the ground with a menacing grin gracing her lips. A pigtailed psychopath.

"Lily," I began, eyes wide at the screen, "remind me never to piss you off."

She leaned forward on the couch. "Being on offense wasn't that bad, you know."

The smile tugging at her lips told me the axe-wielding blonde enjoyed it more than she was letting on.

The girls joined Derek in his fight, where he was feigning and blocking more than anything. Just holding the remaining enemy at bay. So his sudden strike of pure strength threw his opponent off. When their swords clanged together, the opponent's tumbled out of reach.

Hannah pounced.

Together, Hannah and Derek slammed him against the tower wall and pinned him there, arms spread on either side. His eyes clenched shut as he waited for the kill. No one from my team moved. When death didn't come, he opened his eyes.

"What are you waiting for?"

Derek and Hannah exchanged glances and turned to Lily. She backed up several feet, reeled an axe back, and released. It tomahawked through the air until it struck the tower's wall right beside his head, missing by an inch. If the camera had zoomed in more for the shot, I bet I would have seen bits of his hair falling away from his head.

Lily retrieved her axe, backed up several feet, and repeated the same process, landing her axe a millimeter closer. She shouted at the tower's ceiling.

"Is this all you've got?"

The announcer's voice overlaid the footage. Marcus laughed.

"Wow. They've been training so hard, Rizing Nation isn't even a challenge for them."

"Looks like nothing can stand against Defiance." Howie paused. "Wait a minute. The rest of Nation just reached their tower."

The footage cut to Rooke and me inside our tower just as our enemy broke through the entrance. We went back-to-back. Two soldiers became one as we fought off three enemies at once.

Derek shook his head. "Jesus, look at you two. You move together like one person."

Lily nodded in agreement, and Hannah sat with her mouth hanging open.

When the fight ended, our own began, and I saw the replay of our little display of affection in full. His hands were everywhere, feeling every part of me. Clutching. Grasping. Desperate. The way Rooke looked at me, the heat in his eyes was so thick it radiated off the screen. How much of that was fake?

How much was real?

My heart jumped into my throat and nestled in like it was home. Seriously, it was impossible to swallow or even take a deep breath.

The match ended, and the footage cut out to the VGL announcers and their stunned expressions, staring wide-eyed and openmouthed into the camera.

My teammates burst out laughing.

"Wait, wait." Derek waved at Hannah. "Put it on again."

Hannah complied and pushed the rewind. The stunned

announcers popped up on the screen again, and my teammates erupted in a volcano of giggles. Popcorn rained down instead of ash. A dozen times, Hannah rewound the feed. Each time they slapped their thighs and threw their heads back. One time in slow motion was particularly entertaining—for the people beside me, at least.

I leaned forward and rested my head in my hands, wishing I could use them to cover my eyes without anyone noticing. I risked a glance at Rooke. Luckily, he was watching our teammates-turned-hyenas kill themselves over the announcers' reactions. Wasn't he embarrassed about this? God, I wanted to bury my head in the sand.

Finally, Hannah stopped the repeat and let the feed roll forward. The footage cut back to present time, and Marcus and Howie pretended to laugh at themselves.

"Well, that was unexpected. What will they do next to top this week's performance?"

Our teammates looked at us, heads turning in unison as if all were being controlled by a single puppeteer.

"So, what *is* next?" Derek laughed. "A sex tape?"

Rooke looked down at me, eyebrows raised, a slight grin tugging at his lips. The knot in my throat doubled in size.

I managed to shake my head. "I think not."

"Come on, Kali," Hannah cooed. "Give the people what they want. It's for the show."

The trio erupted with laughter again. Heat burned my cheeks. Until that moment, I thought there was a level cap for embarrassment. Beside me, Rooke chuckled right along with my teammates. At least one of us was enjoying this.

"Be sure to join us next week as Defiance faces off against their longtime rival InvictUS, the team that creamed them in the Death Match."

"I can't wait to see these two together again. This is going to be a hell of a show. Good night, everybody."

The scene cut to snippets of our rivals, the bloodiest of their battles, where their weapons ripped through every opponent the tournament could throw at them.

InvictUS.

The undefeatable team. The ones who now stood between us, the championship, and the rest of our lives.

The channel flipped to a commercial, though none of us really watched. The images from the screen projected odd shapes and images over the motionless room. My stomach swirled, and I doubted mine was the only one. We were so caught up in the moment, we'd all forgotten about the tournament. Reality came crashing down around us even though we'd never really left it. For a few fleeting moments, the game hadn't been anything more than that. A game. Something for fun.

Finally, I exchanged glances with my teammates, all stone-faced with their lips pressed into straight lines. Though no one spoke, a silent declaration rippled through us all.

The championship was set.

# CHAPTER 20

sat in bed studying InvictUS on my tablet. Replays of their fights flashed across the screen. In every single match, they ripped through the stalks like they were weeping-willow branches. Few opponents lasted more than a minute against them, and that was only because InvictUS was toying with them, drawing it out, like how a cat torments a mouse before killing it. These guys were brute force, a runaway train—each of them. Especially Trent, their leader. His weapon ripped through his opponents with ease, like a giant merely swaying an axe side to side, sending men and women alike to the virtual afterlife. Together with his four teammates, they formed the epitome of invincibility. Ever since video games had hit the market, characters had been endowed with temporary indestructibility. Mario had sparkling stars. Ms. Pac-Man had giant pills. But no one had ever thought they'd see it in true form inside gamers themselves.

My eyes glazed over as the action continued across the screen. I let the tablet slump against my knees, and my head against the wall behind me. Screams, blood splats, and other sounds of battle floated in the background even though I wasn't listening anymore. Hours and hours of watching their fights, and I still hadn't found a weakness among their team. Maybe they didn't have one.

For a distraction, I scooped up the tablet and opened the

general eBook and magazine store. Under the sports section, several magazines immediately popped up featuring Rooke and me on the cover, all with the breaking news over the sudden rekindling of our romance. Some captured shots from our little late-night display, others with us spliced together. And that's all they'd ever get.

A buzz came from my door.

I got up from my bed, bringing my tablet with me, and tapped the button beside the door. When it slid open, Rooke stood on the other side.

"Hey. You missed breakfast. I worried you were sick."

I held up my tablet. "Studying. Sorry."

He snatched the tablet from my grip, and kept it out of arm's reach as he looked it over.

"Studying us?"

I swiped for the tablet and missed. "I was looking at our rivals."

He held it up to me, where he'd opened a full-spread shot of us kissing.

"Then what's this?"

I reached again. "A distraction."

He leaned toward me. "Hey, if you need a distraction—"

I squashed his face with my palm and retrieved my tablet. Rooke pulled away, chuckling to himself. As I scanned through the picture on the screen, a knot formed in my stomach. I'd gotten so caught up in shoving the game up the sponsors' asses, I forgot about my true drive behind it all.

Nathan.

I sighed.

"This kinda sucks, though," I said, hearing the heavy, defeated tone in my own voice. "This isn't where I want people's attention."

"What do you mean?"

"The focus should be on Nathan. He died because of this sport, but nobody knows it. All they care about is shit like this." I held up the tablet, now featuring a new angle of our make-out session. Rooke glanced at the picture and shrugged.

"Sure, but what are you going to do about it? I mean, the media will censor you anytime you try to talk about it, if Clarence doesn't kill you first. And then there are the sponsors dropping us in a split second."

"I know." I scoffed. "The media. The sponsors. Sure wish I could censor them."

My breath caught in my throat. Censor them. I should censor them. Just like Dr. Renner had said, I'd need to find my own way to honor Nathan. Here it was, right in front of me. I had everything I'd need right inside this very facility.

I grinned.

"What?" Rooke asked.

I pushed past him and out the door.

"Where are you going?"

I never answered his question. He'd see soon enough.

Down the hall, Hannah and Lily leaned against the wall, talking. Oh, this was easy. Like destiny wanted me to do this. I snagged Lily's arm as I breezed by, dragging the pigtailed blonde along with me.

"Um, Kali?" Hannah called out.

"I'm borrowing your girlfriend."

Hannah made a sound of protest, but I plowed ahead without looking back. Lily hurried along beside me, no complaints, as I led her down the hall. At Derek's door, I buzzed his keypad, repeatedly, once every second, until it became its own techno beat.

The door slid open.

"What?"

Derek stood on the other side dressed in nothing but a sheet clenched at his waist. I offered him my best smile, the one we're taught. "You said you can program anything, right?"

He waggled his eyebrows at me. "I've been a gamer since I was five, but I've been a programmer since I was born."

Behind him, the bedsheets rustled, and the murmured voice of a woman called his name. I had the decency not to snoop at the woman, to crane my neck to see how pretty she was and how many plastic pieces she'd stuck in her body.

Derek glanced back at the woman and turned to me. "Look, now's not a good time, okay?"

He pressed the control button, and the door started sliding shut.

"One favor," I began, raising my voice to get his attention, "and I'll convince Clarence to have our next ad campaign feature you alone."

He caught the door. "I'm listening."

I narrowed my eyes at him. "If you're good at programming, then are you good at hacking, too?"

He just smiled.

I wasn't much for sharing my favorite place, but this was for something bigger than myself.

I stood on the roof of the facility over Clarence's office, looking out at the city with my teammates clustered behind me. Darkness and moonlight had settled on Los Angeles, but it still buzzed with life, a barrage of flashing signs and lights. Puttering vehicles, wailing sirens, and the general ambience of a million voices filtered up to us on the rooftop.

"What's supposed to happen?" Hannah asked, arms crossed as she tapped her foot.

"Just wait," I said, waving a hand to dismiss her impatience. Then I winked at Derek and Lily. My accomplices shared a grin with each other. Hannah noticed.

"Wait, they know what's going on? How come they know, and I don't?"

"Just wait," I stressed. "You'll see."

She sighed but shut her mouth. Rooke waited behind her, patiently, though I saw the wonder in his eyes as they searched the horizon.

Across the skyline, every digital ad, poster, and billboard went dead. Instantaneously. From high above the city's highways to the street-level windows of coffee shops, gyms, and retail stores. Despite the car lights and streetlights, the city's wattage dropped by half, if not more.

Cars automatically screeched to a halt as passengers threw the doors open and stepped out. Heads poked out of buildings and windows, most pointing toward the sky. What was happening? A power outage? A technical glitch? They were about to get the answer.

After thirty seconds of blackout, Team InvictUS's picture flashed across every screen in the city, followed by the words:

THIS IS WHAT THEY'RE FIGHTING FOR.

A pile of money popped up next. Rich, green American moolah in stockpiles. Then it cut to a picture of us, Team Defiance, with the words:

THIS IS WHO WE'RE FIGHTING FOR.

Nathan's picture appeared. Dressed in his typical RAGE gladiatorial armor, he was sure to snag people's attention. Hey, he looks familiar. Haven't I seen him before? For clarity, we'd included his stats.

NATHAN SAUNDERS

2033–2054

TEAMMATE, BROTHER, AND FRIEND.

People gathered in front of stores. Cell phones left their ears, and as if for the first time, they spoke with others on the street, exchanging elbow nudges and nods toward the signs. Remember that guy? Yeah, yeah. I remember him.

Nathan's image blanketed the entire city, across every available digital space, in every direction, on every street. You couldn't look anywhere without seeing him. I took a breath that filled my lungs, and as I exhaled, it left behind a feeling of complete satisfaction. What do they call that? Pride. Lily and Derek shared a fist bump. Their grins told me they felt the same.

"The Internet just exploded," Hannah announced, scrolling madly through her tablet. "It's everywhere. People are posting about it on all the social-media sites. There are already hashtags. Fight-for-Nathan."

She held up the tablet for me to see. The feeds crawled at a blurred pace up the screen. Beyond Hannah, Rooke looked at me over the tablet. I met his eyes and saw the emotion dwelling within them. He wasn't just proud. He was proud of me.

I smiled. So was I.

By the next morning, every tabloid showcased Nathan on the cover. Inside were articles about his life. His real life as a person and not just a gamer. His family. Where he grew up and went to school. His cause of death was still listed as heart failure, but that was to be expected. At least it was heading in the right direction.

On every channel, the television and radio reports went something like this:

"In a bizarre incident, every billboard in L.A. was hacked last night . . ."

"Is this a hoax or a bold media blitz by the sponsors of Team Defiance?"

"Either way, frenzy over the RAGE tournaments has reached an all-time high . . ."

The sponsors all pointed fingers at each other, until one of them lied and claimed responsibility for the debacle. Done purposely, of course, for the show. Handshakes ensued, complemented by pats on the back. *Well done. I'll have to steal that marketing rep from you.*

Everyone on the team knew it was a lie, but we were all too happy to oblige. We were supposed to do this with smiles on our faces, after all.

Later that day, I passed Dr. Renner in the hall. She never looked up from her tablet. "You know, I saw some billboards on my drive home last night . . ."

I held up a hand and shook my head. "I have no idea what you're talking about."

She smiled. "I didn't think so."

Back in my bunk, I scrolled through an online magazine shop. Not one cover featured me or Rooke, apart or together. Nothing on our relationship, breakup, making up, or anything that had happened the night before. In a blink, we were old news. Nathan was the one remembered now. Not forgotten. Not gone. Alive. In the hearts and minds of everyone.

That night, I fell asleep with a smile on my face and Nathan's picture on the tablet gripped in my arms. I'd broken the law, risked backlash from the sponsors, and maybe even jeopardized my career, and never in my entire life was I so sure I'd done the right thing.

Everything was set. We were in the championship, and Nathan was right there with us. I was done going ape-shit crazy. Now, there was only one thing left to do.

Train.

# LEVEL 3:

## THE CHAMPIONSHIP

# CHAPTER 21

Two weeks.

We had two weeks until the championship round. Fourteen days to train, barricade ourselves in the facility, and prepare for the end. Twenty years I'd been waiting for this, my whole life, as if I was born to be here. Right now.

InvictUS had already had a month to rest and practice, as if they even needed it. The final fight would be one round, winner take all. But since InvictUS had never lost a match, and we had, we'd be going in with a handicap.

No fallen players.

If even one of us died, we were done. InvictUS could lose four out of five. We couldn't lose a single player. Against Invict-US. The team that had wiped out everyone they faced and never died. None of them. Not once.

We'd have to fight as a team, now more than ever.

Usually, the matchups took place every Saturday. Not the championship. The Super Bowl got it right. A bigger gap created more tension, more hype. Though the frenzy over Nathan had already hit record levels, crashing the sites for the VGL and Team Defiance every day, the sponsors would milk this for every dollar it was worth. And I'd let them. As long as the general public had their hearts in the right place, and they did. Fight-for-Nathan was everywhere. Painted across windows.

Plastered up skyscrapers. He wouldn't just be in the minds of people for this fight, but for many to come in the future. He would be remembered. Now and always.

"You need to eat sometime, you know."

Rooke sat on the edge of my bed, poking the bottom of my foot as I scrolled through my tablet reviewing news articles and social-media feeds. This had become our new routine, our new standard programming.

"I'm coming."

Flick. Flick.

When I didn't budge, he grabbed the blanket covering my legs and pulled, as if issuing a threat. I fisted my hand in the sheet.

"Don't," I warned.

His eyes went wide, and surveyed my covered lower half. "Why? Aren't you wearing pants?"

"No."

His face lit up. "Really?"

"Yes, I'm wearing pants." I tossed the blanket off to reveal my training gear. "Did you wake up with your testosterone in overdrive today?"

He shrugged and offered no answer. His gaze wandered over the walls of my bunk, and I returned to my tablet. Only the hum of the air-conditioning and the soft clicks of my nails against the screen filled the room. Rooke sighed.

"You can study later. You need breakfast."

"Ten more minutes."

"No."

He grabbed my ankle and pulled. I kicked him off. He swiped for the tablet. I held it out of reach.

"If you don't get up right now," he began, "I'll carry you there myself." To substantiate the seriousness of his threat, he scooped an arm under my knees.

I splayed a hand on his chest and glowered at him. "You wouldn't dare. Not if you like your man parts in one piece."

He dropped my legs and scooted up the bed until his face was parallel with mine. He leaned into me and braced his arms on the wall on either side of my head. With his arms surrounding me and his body in front, I was trapped. I surveyed my Rooke-inspired jail cell and scrunched my nose at him.

"What are you doing?"

He leaned closer and lowered his voice. "Telling you the one thing you've always wanted to hear me say."

Uhhh . . .

My eyes darted around, and my heart beat just a little faster then. I bit my lip and feigned innocence.

"What?"

"Come on, Kali," he said softly. "We've been together every night for weeks now. You don't think I know exactly what you want?"

Somehow, he got even closer until his breaths kissed my lips. The tablet tumbled from my hand and landed somewhere on the bed. The scent of him swirled around me, curling my insides in on themselves. My heart thudded in my ears.

"I know what drives you," he continued, and the timbre of his voice rippled down my spine. I resisted the urge to shudder. "I know what you want more than anything."

His gaze lowered to my mouth. My throat grew thick as every cell inside me pounded with anticipation. He brought his lips to mine and whispered against them.

"There's fresh coffee."

I laughed. I laughed until my insides shook, and soon, he was laughing with me. Knowing I'd no longer protest, Rooke hoisted me from the bed and onto my feet, but not before I swiped the tablet from the sheets. With the tablet pressed to my nose, I walked through the hallways to the cafeteria. Rooke snagged my elbow and redirected me after every wrong turn. At the breakfast table, he sat across from me and watched me read. After a minute, he forced a spoon into my hand.

"Kali. Eat."

I did, munching as I read. I barely registered the oat taste of the cereal or the sweet snap of the yogurt as I swallowed. The gulp of coffee that followed, however, warmed me all the way down.

Rooke waited in silence as I ate, and studied. I flicked through mock-ups of the arena and its sepia wheat fields, surveying the shortest and longest runs between the two towers. No one ever took either. The shortest was through a dirt path that cut directly in the middle of the wheat fields. Too much exposure and not enough coverage. The longest paths ran along the outskirts of the fields. No good either. At least, not against InvictUS. Already blocked from one side by the edge of the map, it was far too easy to get cornered.

In the training room, Rooke snatched the tablet from my hand and immediately replaced it with a bo staff. I flipped the bo around in my hands a few times and rolled my shoulders to loosen up.

I held the staff against my forearm, bowed slightly, and nodded at Rooke. He grinned and came at me. The training room filled with the sounds of clacking staffs and the pattering of our feet against the mats. Neither of us landed a shot. Every thrust was parried, every feint ignored. Even. Equal. A dance, as if we'd been choreographed.

"You know," he said over the clacking staffs, "InvictUS really makes use of Chapter Eleven, 'The Nine Situations.' They concentrate their energy and hoard their strength. I've never even seen those guys winded after a fight."

"Still on *The Art of War*? What is it, your favorite?"

He shrugged, which usually meant yes.

"You could consider Chapter Four as well," I said. "Defending existing positions. InvictUS never lets anyone get through to their tower."

We broke apart, nodding at each other, panting and sweating. Break time. Neither of us had to call it out anymore or let the other get a hit in. We just knew when one of us needed a break, which always seemed to be when the other did, too.

As I caught my breath, I sat cross-legged on the mats and watched my teammates. Rooke took a seat beside me. My vision blurred as thoughts of five indestructible brutes flooded my mind. Rooke nudged me.

"You still don't know what you're going to do about InvictUS, do you?"

Looks like he could read my thoughts now, too. I shook my head. He leaned toward me and lowered his voice.

"A leader is best when people barely knows he exists, so then they believe they did it themselves."

"Okay, you're like the reincarnation of Lao Tzu. I get it."

"No." He nodded toward our teammates. "Ask your people what to do."

I turned to him.

"You don't think that will seem weak?"

He shook his head.

Well, worth a shot.

"Guys," I called out. "No virtual world tonight. We'll study InvictUS together in the rec room, okay? I'd like to know what you think about strategy."

They exchanged glances with each other. Derek took a step forward.

"You're the captain. That's not really our place."

"I know, but I'd like your opinion."

They exchanged glances again. Derek shrugged.

"All right."

One night became every night that week. We'd retire to the rec room to study our opponents on a life-size screen. Debates and strategizing soon became interspersed with popcorn and classic video games. Tonight's game was a remake of Mario Kart 10, a cartoon-style racing game featuring the characters from the Nintendo universe.

"Sometimes I can't help thinking," Hannah said from the couch, taking her turn out, "what if we lose? What if we fought all this way for nothing?"

"This isn't only about winning," I said as I swerved on-screen, cutting off Rooke's kart and dropping a banana peel in his path.

Swearing ensued.

"Kali! Stop targeting just me."

"Yes, it would mean a lot if we did win," I continued, ignoring Rooke. "But think about it: Why do people play professional sports? Sure, they play to win. Is it just for themselves? No. It's to bring pride to their city. When athletes compete in the Olympics, it's not to prove they're number one in the world as an individual. It's to show that their country is the best, and that they're proud to represent their nation."

"But we don't represent a city or a country," Derek pointed out as he tapped his controller. "Who are we supposed to make proud? Our sponsors?"

"Nathan," Lily answered.

I nodded. "And not just Nathan, but our fans." I paused. "And ourselves. Sure, we had fun getting here, but we worked for it, too. Nothing wrong with being proud of that."

On-screen, the characters bumped, collided, and swerved

around and into each other, heading down the final stretch to the finish line. It was neck and neck until the last second, when Luigi slid across the finish line first. Derek jumped up and did a football-inspired victory dance, fingers snapping and hips swaying.

"Oh, yeah. There it is. Eat it, noobs."

We all laughed.

"Try some slang from this decade, maybe," I said.

He pointed at the game on the screen. "And when do you think this is from?"

Before the next race could start up, I powered off the console. My teammates whined.

"One more race," Hannah called out from the couch. "Or three."

"Uh, I think you guys are forgetting what tonight is," I said, flipping the channel. The wallscreen blared with the VGL theme song, and the picture cut to a scene with five twenty-year-old guys in matching training gear and a reporter with a microphone. The reporter held the microphone near his chin.

"Good evening, ladies and gentlemen. Tonight I'm interviewing one of the hottest teams competing in the RAGE tournaments right in their own training facility. These guys just came out of nowhere and quickly became a heavy fan favorite. I know a lot of you have been waiting for this, so I'd like to introduce Team In-victUS. Thanks for having me here."

We booed and threw popcorn at the screen. Team InvictUS traded a few pleasantries with the reporter, general small talk. Yeah, my name's so-and-so, and I'm from the center of a douche bag. This is my teammate blah-blah-blah.

"So," the reporter continued, getting into the real questions, "next Saturday is the championship where you face off against Team Defiance. What are you expecting from them?"

The one closest to the reporter spoke into the microphone. "They're good enough to have made it this far, but if last time we faced off is any indication, we don't have much to worry about."

More booing. More popcorn.

"They're just trying to be hard-asses," Hannah said. "It's probably part of their image."

On-screen, the reporter nodded and spoke into his microphone again. "What do you think of their absence from the media lately?"

Another member of the team answered. "It's expected. Most animals retreat when they're scared."

All five of them laughed. We burst out shouting and waving our arms. While we each had our own remarks, funnily enough, we all used the word *dick* at some point.

On-screen, the reporter posed another question. "What about them dedicating the fight to their fallen teammate?"

A hush fell over InvictUS then. A few of them shifted their weight and glanced at their feet.

"That's noble," one of them finally answered. "We respect them for it. But we hope they realize it doesn't mean we'll take it easy on them."

Well, at least they weren't complete assholes. Maybe it was just for show. Or maybe they realized what had really happened to Nathan. All pro gamers knew about addiction and losing a grip on reality, but none ever think it will be them. Nathan's death had made it real, for more than just me.

"What about their captain, Kali Ling?" the reporter continued. "Do you think she'll give you a good fight?"

The tallest one among them smiled. Their leader. Trent Amos. He spoke into the microphone. "I hope so. I'd love to make her squirm again."

The reporter laughed. "I think she's got a partner now. You'll have to get through him, too."

"That's okay." He looked into the camera, as if he was speaking directly to us. "We'll make him watch."

Huh. They'd resorted to all-out threats now.

Anger flashed inside, just for a second, like a burst of a match that fizzled out just as quickly. A month ago, I would have exploded. Now, the rage I felt was a tiny ball in my chest, engulfed by a cloud of calm. Like all people, I still felt negative emotions. But acting on that anger was a waste of energy. It was fruitless. If someone heaves a boulder into a stream, the current simply goes round and continues on its path, forever pushing onward. It doesn't stop and try to push the boulder out.

"Still think they're just being hard-asses?" Derek asked, peering back at Hannah.

She frowned. "This is getting sadistic."

"Come on, you guys," I said. "You know they're trying to bait us."

"It's working."

Rooke spoke last in a voice I almost didn't recognize as his. I looked over at him and met the stone expression and clenched jaw I hadn't seen in weeks.

I rested a hand on his arm, but my voice was firm. "Don't let it get to you."

"Don't let it get to me?" He stood and started pacing. "He's threatening you because you're a woman playing this game."

I jumped to my feet. "You think I don't know that? I'm the one who's being threatened. But that's my problem, not yours."

"No, it is my problem. It's everyone's problem. If they said something about you being half-Chinese, or Derek's being black, or Hannah and Lily being gay, I'd be pissed at that, too.

Just because I'm none of those things doesn't mean I can't recognize that it's wrong."

I shook my head. "You can't fight fire with fire. When opposing warriors join in battle, he who has pity conquers."

"You're saying I'm not supposed to be angry? I'm just supposed to what, feel sorry for them?"

"Yes."

He deflated then. The tension in his shoulders and face released, and his muscles fell. He stared at me, blinking.

"If you hate, you become exactly like them," I said. "When you face your enemies with compassion, you realize there's still a person behind that hate."

"Oh, so now I'm supposed to like these guys?"

"No. I'm saying be mad at the idea, not at the person conveying it. Fighting people leads to war. Fighting ideas leads to progress."

I blinked and took a step back. What the hell did I just say? Only weeks ago, I'd been teetering on the edge. Every time I'd read one of those damn books, groping for some kind of understanding, I'd questioned if I'd ever really comprehend Taoist philosophy. Now, here I was, doling out Taoist wisdom and principles like they were business cards. Maybe I finally knew what it all meant. At least, I knew what it meant to me, and that's all that mattered.

Facing an opponent head-on wasn't smart. In war, the way is to avoid what is strong and to strike at what is weak. If they had a weakness, I was going to find it. We still had a tournament to win. Not to prove that we were better than InvictUS. To prove that we were better than ourselves.

I turned and marched for the door.

"Where are you going?" Hannah called out.

My other teammates. In the heat of the argument, I'd almost forgotten they were there. I glanced back at them on the couch as I left the room.

"To study."

I sat at a workstation in the pod room, flicking through the Virtual Gaming League's stat pages, specifically the five players who made up InvictUS. Black belts. All of them. Third degree in this, fourth in that. All had MMA training to some extent, years' worth for most of them. I had to chuckle as I recognized the form of martial art used in the UFC—what used to be the most extreme sport on the planet. Virtual reality had upended that like nobody's business. Wrestlers pwned by gamers. Ouch.

When I'd read through all of InvictUS's stats supplied by the VGL, I delved deep into their histories elsewhere. You can find anything online. I went through what medical information wasn't confidential, and secretly wished I could hack the stuff that was. I read everything I could find. Surgeries. Past illnesses. Old injuries. Anything that would make them weak on the battlefield. Anything that would give us an edge. We are our avatars. A broken leg in this world could mean a weak link in the virtual.

Nothing. They'd all had their tonsils out, though I doubted it made the trunks that were their necks any weaker. One had dislocated some fingers on his off-hand. Not much use. Worse still, as I went deeper into the amateur stats and even lower, I discovered that in less than a year they'd climbed from your average gamer to amateur to pro. No one went that fast up the chain unless they had a supreme amount of raw talent. I knew, since I'd done the same.

I sighed and sat back in the chair, feeling the weight of the championship pressing down on my shoulders. The longer I sat, the more it pressed down. That is, until a voice spoke over my head, and I realized the weights on my shoulders were actually hands.

"Kali, it's late."

Rooke's voice. He sat down in the workstation next to me.

"Sorry about earlier. I didn't mean to get so pissed off."

I shrugged. "You feel passionately about protecting your teammates. It's not something to be sorry about."

"I let my temper get the best of me, and that's worth apologizing for." He paused. "But I want you to know that just because I feel like protecting you doesn't mean I think you can't handle yourself."

I grinned. "Little ole me can kick ass? Nooo."

He grinned back as he swiveled the chair from the next workstation over to me and sat. "Try looking at it from my perspective. They're threatening to torture you right in front of me. I think you'd feel the same way if it was someone you cared about."

I gasped and placed a hand over my heart. "Are you saying you care about me? Meaning, more than a friend? Oh, Dear Diary. He said he likes me today."

He frowned and ignored my sarcasm. "There aren't enough rules in this game."

"Maybe if it gets that bad, people won't watch."

He scoffed. "The crowd won't care. They live for this stuff. Ever since they started putting videos on the Internet, people have been watching snuff films like it's nothing. Like it's not a human being who died."

I sighed. "Yeah. True."

It fell silent between us. Together, we stared at the screen, at the impossible force we'd have to face on the coming Saturday.

The weights were back on my shoulders, but this time, it wasn't from Rooke's hands.

"So," he began, eyes still on InvictUS, "you haven't found anything to use against them?"

"Not really." Again, I flicked through all five members of their team. "These guys are freaking mountains."

"Yeah, but you move like the wind. Nothing can stop the wind, even mountains." I peered up at him. He continued. "These guys won't win with technique against you. Not unless they're equally as talented, and they're not. They're just prepared, and stronger than everyone else."

"You think they're using something to boost their strength?"

He considered it. "It's not unheard of, but they'd draw too much suspicion with the way they fight. I think it's their training. Brute force combined with knowing exactly how to take out every team and each person on it."

I looked back at the screen, which still showcased the Hercules-inspired brutes. I fell back against the chair. "With the strength of these guys, it's like David and Goliath."

"Hey. David won, you know."

"Yeah." I clicked my nails against the workstation. "I'm not so sure in this scenario. No matter how I look at these guys, they just don't have a weakness."

"You've only studied them on the screen. Maybe you need to practice fighting someone like them. Hand-to-hand combat against a strong, unarmed opponent. No weapons."

There was some logic to that, wasn't there? Maybe in person, I'd be able to spot a crack in the impenetrable armor of our opponents. And the closest I'd get to fighting one of them in person was sitting right beside me.

I looked him up and down. "Well, you're strong. You have hands. Let's go."

---

We changed into our training gear and met on the mats. This late at night, the hallways were empty of people and life. Only the hum of the building's vital functions echoed around us.

I stepped onto the mat, barefoot, savoring the way it felt, how I sunk in a little with each step. I smiled. This was home. But without the weight of the staff in my hands, I felt naked and a little unsure of myself. I'd spent years in hand-to-hand combat, both real and virtual. I could do this. I took a defensive stance, guarding my body with my open palms. Rooke took the role of InvictUS and moved first.

He swung hard with a clenched fist, holding nothing back. I ducked and came back up to deliver a kick to his ribs. He caught my leg and swept the other out from under me. I hit the mat. Hard. Rooke leaned over me and swiped an imaginary blade across my neck.

"Dead."

I grunted, slapped the mat, and pushed myself up.

Round two went differently—meaning I ended up facedown on the mats instead of faceup. Rooke pressed his knee into my back, weighing me down, and stabbed the back of my skull.

"Dead."

Another round. Thirty seconds, and my back hit the mats again. Rooke took a knee beside me.

"Come on, Kali," he said, sounding frustrated. "You can't let yourself get pinned. It's over."

My stubbornness brimmed at the boiling point. "I'm not pinned, and it's not over."

He straddled me, pinned my legs, and leaned close to my face. "Fine. Now what are you going to do?"

"Stare longingly into your eyes."

He frowned. "I'm serious. If I were on the other team and had you pinned, what would you do to survive?"

I scoffed and let my head roll to the side.

"Oh, I don't know . . ."

I lashed out, hooking my finger right for his eye. He caught my hand just in time.

"Did you just try to gouge out my eye?"

"You asked me what I'd do!"

He grappled with me and locked both my arms against the mat. I struggled beneath his weight, unable to move at all.

Rooke peered down at me. "Now what?"

I stared up at his face, knowing I had only one move left.

"Headbutt."

"So, do it."

I laughed. "I'm not going to headbutt you."

"You'll gouge out my eye, but you draw the line at headbutts because that's too rough?" He lowered his face to mine and cocked an eyebrow. "Think I can't handle it?"

"No. I'm confident you have a very hard head."

He chuckled. "If this were a real match, you'd be dead by now."

I wriggled beneath him again, trying to find an escape route. As I struggled, my hips brushed against his. He glanced between us. "Trying to find my chi again?"

I grunted. "If I could get my knee free, I'd send your chi to high heaven."

"You won't get your knee free. Not with all my weight on you."

He pressed down harder on my lower half, like this whole time he'd been merely holding his weight over me and was now using it to crush my legs. Okay, wow. I exhaled, as if he were pushing all the air out of my lungs through my knees. But I pressed on.

Rooke shook his head and brought his face to mine. "Are you really so stubborn that you won't admit you've lost?"

"No. There's always a way out."

I looked at his face. He studied me with amusement, lips twisted halfway into a grin. Not condescending, though. Like he thought I was cute. Warriors aren't cute. But I found myself studying him in much the same way. His eyes, soft and brown. The stubble lining his jaw. And when my gaze lowered to his lips, I found my escape route.

I kissed him.

His mouth moved against mine, no hesitation. In reality, it was the first kiss we'd had since my bathroom. I found myself focusing without even trying. I felt everything. The softness of his lips. His breaths caressing my cheek. I'd have to remember to thank him later for telling me to focus on the real if my brain was even capable of making mental notes right then.

"I don't think this counts," Rooke said, between kisses, "under VGL regulations."

"Why?" I asked, as his mouth lowered to my neck. "Isn't this putting on a good show?"

He sat up, pulling me into his lap. "Oh, I think we've already proven it is."

I weaved my fingers through his hair and wrapped my legs around his waist.

"Maybe the audience didn't get enough last time," I said, and he chuckled somewhere near my ear, sending little shock waves through my veins.

"But at what point would the cameras pull away?" he asked, murmuring against my neck as his nose grazed the line of my jaw. "When would they stop filming?"

Heat swirled through me. I knew what he was asking, the subtle meaning hidden behind the façade. I pressed my lips against his ear. "They wouldn't stop."

His breath hitched, and he stilled. We stayed like that, woven around each other, not moving. My heart beat everywhere, down to my toes, from the strange mix of tension and desire. Seconds passed. His breaths whispered across my neck, and I fought the urge to shudder, worried if I broke the moment, he'd pull away.

He met my eyes, and I saw the longing within his own. Though there was a sort of pain there, too, like he was unsure of himself and everything happening in that moment. I forced my expression calm, despite the fluttering in my heart and stomach. My fingers itched to feel him. To pull off every stitch of clothing. To graze over every muscle, every inch of skin. But I remained still until I trembled, waiting for him to make the next move.

"Are you sure?" he asked.

"Yes. Are you?"

His answer came in the form of his hands, sliding up my back as they lifted my shirt. I grabbed his wrists.

"Not here."

He surveyed my face a few times, and must have noted how the trembling had spread to my bottom lip, because he captured it with his own. He pressed his lips against mine, again and again, soft and soothing until I moaned against his mouth. That little sound pushed him over the edge.

He took my hand and led me back to my bunk.

# CHAPTER 22

I pressed my back against the mattress and sighed as little aftershocks coursed through me. Rooke leaned over me, nursing the spot between my shoulder and neck. His ragged breaths shuddered through his body and everywhere our skin touched. I placed a hand against his chest, where his heart beat soundly, still racing. He glanced down.

"What are you doing?"

"Feeling your heartbeat." I listened to the steady thumping through my hand. "It's fast."

His lips twitched into a grin. "It should be. You finally found my chi."

I laughed.

He brushed a few strands of hair out of my eyes and trailed his thumb along the outline of my face. Though his eyes were hard as he studied me, like there was pain dwelling behind them. My breath caught in my throat, and I rested a hand against his cheek.

"Are you okay?"

He slid his fingers slowly up my arm, barely touching, and weaved through mine until our hands were one. His eyes watched mine the entire time, and somehow, it was just as intimate as anything. He smiled slightly.

"I'm fine."

He buried his face in the crook of my neck, leaving kisses along my collarbone. I closed my eyes, no longer hiding, and dove into the sensations. His breaths brushed against my shoulder. Sweet shocks of pleasure radiated through me whenever our bodies met. All I felt and knew and understood was him. All of him.

The rest of the world faded into the background. No facility. No virtual world. No media and tabloids and all the bullshit always within a reaching grasp. There was us, and only us. In that moment, only one thing mattered.

This . . . this was real.


The next morning, the bed beside me was cold. Only the imprint his body left behind in the sheets told me Rooke had been there through some point in the night. I swallowed, trying to ignore the thickness in my throat. Friends with benefits. That's all it had been with Nathan. He was a good guy, sure. But what we'd had wasn't much more than satisfaction between two people. A moment of realness. Wasn't that something in itself? Why wasn't it enough with Rooke?

"Hello? Kali?"

I shook my head and looked up at Hannah sitting across from me at the breakfast table. "What?"

"You okay?" she asked, tilting her head to the side. "I've been talking for ten minutes, and you haven't said a word."

I straightened up in my chair and shook my head again. "Sorry. I must have been thinking about something else."

"You mean someone else? Like Rooke?" She grinned. I shot her a look, and her smile faded. "Oh. Is there a problem between you two?"

"We slept together."

Hannah's eyes went wide, then fluttered a few times, as if trying to contain her expression. "You mean, that was the first time?"

I frowned at her.

"Don't look at me like that. You two were the ones always sneaking out of the clubs."

"To practice," I stressed.

"Yeah, I get that *now*." She thought for a moment. "So, what's the problem?"

"He didn't stay the night."

Her eyes narrowed as she thought to herself. She glanced down the table at Rooke's empty seat. "So, where is he now?"

I shrugged. "Don't know."

She turned to Derek, who sat alone in his usual spot. "Hey."

"Hannah!"

Derek looked up from his cereal. "Yeah?"

"Where's your breakfast buddy?"

He shrugged. "In his bunk. Said he wasn't feeling well today."

Hannah turned back to me. "Now you know where he is. Go confront him."

"I'm not going," I told her, and she sighed at me. "If it didn't mean much to him, then that's fine. I just thought I'd read him better than that."

Hannah's gaze trailed across the table, and a distant look filled her eyes. "Speaking of reading, did you ever check out that article?"

"Which?"

"The one in *Pro Gamer Weekly.*"

"What? That industry-owned bullshit?"

Hannah nodded enthusiastically. "Exactly. It's bullshit." She pushed her tablet into my hands. "Read it."

I brought up the article on the screen and scanned through until I spotted Rooke's name. "Defiance recently welcomed new addition James Rooke to the team."

I skimmed. Blah, blah, blah.

"Rooke was best known in the Canadian RAGE tournaments and for dating fellow teammate Katherine Boone." I paused and lowered the tablet to look Hannah in the eyes. "That's it? He dated someone else? So, he's got history. Who doesn't?"

She shook her head. "Keep going."

More skimming. More blah, blah, blah.

"Their relationship ended in August of this year when Boone died in a tragic accident."

My stomach hit the floor.

Shit.

A tragic accident. That was bullshit if I'd ever heard it. Rooke's ex-girlfriend had died, and I had to assume it had something to do with the game. I handed Hannah's tablet back and lowered my forehead to the metal table. I already felt like an idiot. Might as well look like one, too.

Hannah nudged me. "Get up, Kali. He needs you now."

I groaned. "I know, damn it."

After everything he'd done for me, helped me through my addiction, helped cover up what was going on from everyone, now it was my turn to help. I stood from the table and started walking away. As an afterthought, I spun around and returned to retrieve my coffee mug. Hannah was holding it out for me like she'd read my mind. I downed the remaining coffee and slammed the mug down like I'd just done a shot.

"Feeling better?" she asked.

"There isn't enough caffeine in the world."

Hannah chuckled, though the joke didn't make me feel any better. I took a breath and forced myself out of the cafeteria, each step getting heavier than the last as I ventured through the facility's corridors. When I finally arrived at his bunk, I pressed the buzzer on his keypad and waited. Footsteps followed inside. The door slid open. Rooke tensed as soon as he saw me, swallowed thick, and turned his eyes to the floor. His arms folded across his chest, though it looked like his whole body was trying to follow suit and fold in on itself. Shame, embarrassment, and fear had contorted him into one awkward pose.

I spoke before he could say anything or close the door in my face.

"Why didn't you tell me?"

His brow furrowed and he looked up at me. "About what?"

"Your ex. The one that died."

He sighed. No hiding now. He stepped aside and nodded for me to enter. I walked in and sat on his bed.

"You can talk to me," I said. "Nathan OD'd right next to me, and I had no idea he was dying. I understand tragedy. I know what you're going through."

"It's not the same thing." His voice came out dark and gruff, as if he had to force the words out through an ironclad clenched jaw.

"Why not?"

"You didn't push him on, did you? Did you encourage Nathan to get high every night just to enjoy the ride?"

"No. Why?"

"I did. She died because of me. We did so much junk, I don't know how I'm not dead." He began pacing around his bunk, eyes fixed on the floor. "You get wrapped up in this sport, this lifestyle. You live in a virtual world. You die every day and come back to life. You kill other people, and they just keep breathing. You start to think you're invincible. And you know what? We are. Nothing happened to me for what I did. You know why I wasn't convicted of any wrongdoing? Why I wasn't charged with possession or distribution even though I was the one feeding her the drugs? Because I'm a gamer. Because of my status. Can't ruin the chances of a rising star. Just sweep it under the rug. Who will ever know?"

He sat down on the edge of his bed and dropped his head in his hands. The fingers covering his face trembled and clenched, and I half expected him to punch himself in the mouth. I let him have a minute to himself before I spoke.

"Can you tell me what happened? Did she overdose?"

His jaw clenched even harder, and he shook his head. No.

"Then how did she die?"

He was quiet for a long time. Finally, he gave in.

"One night after a match, we were partying in a high-rise with a bunch of other gamers. Everyone was so hopped up on HP we couldn't even tell we were in reality anymore. I remember sitting on a couch next to her when she turned to me and told me she could fly. Then, she went out on the balcony."

My stomach twisted, and my heart dropped down to my toes. She jumped. Holy shit, she jumped off the side of a building. Because of HP. Because of the games.

"I didn't stop her," he continued. "Because I believed it. I didn't even know what was real myself. Then they covered it up, just like Nathan. She died, and no one cared."

He rested his elbows on his knees and stared at the floor.

"After that, I just had to get away from the rest of the team," he continued. "I knew if I came down here, the U.S. was a different league, so I'd never have to see them again."

It was quiet for a minute while I thought about what he said. I placed a hand on his arm.

"You know that wasn't your fault, right?"

"How is it not my fault?"

"You might have been high, and she might have been, too,

because of you, but she would have gone there eventually on her own. If it wasn't already inside her, it wouldn't have come out. Even teenagers recognize peer pressure when they see it. As adults, our decisions are completely our own. You didn't hold a knife to her throat and force her to take the drugs. It was her choice."

He stared at me a long time before he asked, "If it's not my fault, then how come I feel so horrible about it?"

I slid my hand down his arm until my fingers locked with his.

"Because death is something we wish we had power over. Human beings don't like it when something is stronger than them. That's part of the reason why movies about us defeating aliens, or robots, or epidemics are so popular. They represent certain death, and we'd like to think when it comes for us, we can stop it. And as gamers, we cheat death every day. We learned to look it in the face and smile. But death is not something to be cheated. It's simply the end of a journey. The best thing we can do is move on, live the best life we can, and always remember them and everything they taught us." I shifted my weight on the bed and turned sideways, so I was looking at him straight on. "She's not suffering now, and I don't think she'd want you to, either."

Staring right into my eyes, his muscles unclenched, and he sighed, like he'd been holding his breath for minutes. He wrapped me in his arms and held me tight against his chest as he shook. I knew he was finally letting it go.

I circled my arms around him and lightly stroked his back. His heart beat hard against his rib cage. His entire body trembled with each raspy breath. He murmured words to me. Most were inaudible, but I caught *sorry* more than a few times. Sorry for leaving me in the night. Sorry for not saving her. Sorry for every mistake he'd ever made, and even some he hadn't. I said nothing and let him have the moment.

Time hung in suspended animation as we cradled each other. I had no idea how long we sat there together on the edge of his bed, but it didn't seem to matter, either. I could have stayed there for hours. Maybe days. My head fit just so in the crook of his chest. His arms wrapped perfectly around me, strong but comforting. We were equal. Balanced. Like we were each other's halves, and we'd just learned how to become whole.

Finally, he took a deep breath, and when he exhaled, his trembling left with it.

"You're pretty wise, you know," he said. I nodded against his chest.

"Look at me. I know some stuff."

"Yeah," he began with a chuckle, and followed up with a statement that left my knuckles craving to crush his nose.

"Good thing I gave you those books."

# CHAPTER 23

Life was in balance now. Literally.

With less than a week left before the championship match, I thought I'd feel any other way. Nervousness, excitement, anticipation. But inside the training room, as I sat cross-legged on a balance beam, the sounds of punching bags and bodies hitting mats echoing around me, I felt only one thing.

Peace.

The team was strong, stronger than I ever thought we would be. Every day we trained together. Every night we played games and studied. Spending every waking hour at each other's sides, we'd become like family. Life was good.

Footsteps padded along the mats toward me and stopped a few feet away. Eyes closed, I focused, trying to sense who it was. Breaths came from above, signaling height. My admirer took a few steps closer, light steps hinting low weight. Then I caught a whiff of coconut-scented shampoo.

Hannah.

"Kali!" she shouted.

I startled, and my eyes flew open, but I kept my balance.

"What?"

She gripped my arm and rocked my entire body, as if trying to capsize me off the beam. I steadied myself, swaying with her like I was water in a storm. No resistance. I swatted her hand.

"Hannah, what the hell?"

She pulled again, hard, and when I merely bowed with her, she was the one who fell, landing on her butt on the mats.

I peered down at her from my spot on the beam.

"What is with you?"

She huffed and pushed herself up. "How are you doing that?"

"Doing what?"

"That." She motioned at my body resting on the beam. "How are you so balanced?"

I smiled and patted the beam in front of me.

"Sit. I'll show you."

She glanced between me and the beam a few times with a curled lip, as if I'd just told her to jump in ice water. Then she climbed on the beam with the same grace as a puppy trying to climb stairs. After some fumbling and a few choice swearwords, she managed to mirror my position. Legs folded, hands resting on her knees, she met my eyes.

"Now what?"

"You focus on your chi," I told her.

She wobbled, and caught herself with her hand. "What's a chi?"

I frowned. "You took martial arts for years, and you never learned about your chi?"

She shook her head. Inwardly, I groaned.

"It's kind of like your life force," I explained.

She scrunched her nose. "Is this a Chinese thing?"

Wobble, wobble.

"Yes," I answered. "But think of it however you want. Your soul. Your essence. Your energy. Whatever. Just close your eyes and picture it inside you."

She studied me again with that same unsure look, then eventually closed her eyes. Her eyelids fluttered a few times, like when someone dreams. After a minute, she drew a deep breath.

"Okay. I think I've got it."

"You feel it?"

"Yes."

"Where?"

"In the middle of my chest, near my heart."

"Push it down," I instructed. "Below your belly button."

"How?"

"Just picture it sinking slowly, like it's submerging below water."

She adjusted her balance on the beam and took another deep breath. As the seconds passed, her spine straightened, and her wobbles subsided. Her chin tilted slightly up, as if looking toward the heavens. She was a yoga goddess.

For now.

Without a sound, I slipped off the beam and walked up beside her. After a few seconds, I grabbed her arm and pulled lightly. Her eyes flew open as she flailed and gripped the beam. She gasped for air, and I could practically hear her heart thumping against her chest.

She shot me a look. "That wasn't funny."

"You're doing well," I assured her. "Just focus. It takes time."

She did, closing her eyes again. After a minute, I repeated the same action, with the same results.

"This isn't working," she concluded, digging her nails into the sides of the beam.

"Can you still feel your chi?"

"Yes."

"Picture it like a weight, holding you in place. But flexible at the same time."

"That doesn't make any sense."

I sighed. "Like a buoy. Picture it like a buoy."

She scrunched up her nose again and shook her head.

"Think of the wind," I tried. "The wind is one of the strongest forces on Earth. It shapes mountains. It snaps trees in half. But it can also bow around anything, right?"

She thought about it. "Yeah, right."

"So, it's strong, and it's flexible."

". . . I guess."

She considered my words, then sighed and closed her eyes again. I waited a few minutes longer before shoving her. She wobbled, but didn't need to brace herself to find her balance again. A grin touched her lips.

"I wonder if InvictUS trains like this."

I laughed. "Probably not."

I circled the beam and hit her other side a little harder. She had to brace herself but found balance quicker than before.

"Those hard-asses," she began, still referring to InvictUS. "They'd probably only do something like this if they were twenty feet off the ground."

"Twenty? Try thirty, without any tie-offs. No, make it forty."

"Forget it." Hannah waved a hand, wobbled, and steadied herself. "I don't know if it would ever be high enough for them."

I shrugged. "Maybe not, but you never know. I mean, they have to be intimidated by something."

"If they were, it would be one hell of a surprise."

"Yeah," I agreed with a chuckle.

I gasped and went numb as the realization hit. The world around me turned to slow motion as I processed Hannah's words. Dust floated in the air. The sounds of punching bags and the coaches' commands echoed in the background. And none of it mattered to the thoughts racing through my mind.

A surprise. High in the beams.

"That's it," I exclaimed.

Hannah opened her eyes. "What's it?"

I took her head between both hands and kissed her nose. She recoiled from shock.

"Uh, you okay?"

I grinned, not offering an answer. I turned away from her to find Lily standing a few feet away, giving me the raised eyebrow. I kissed her cheek, too, and went flying past.

"Kali, what the hell?" Hannah called out, as I raced across the training room to where Rooke sparred with Derek on the mats. The training coaches lined the sides, pointing out errors and weakness. I shoved them aside, burst onto the mats, grabbed Rooke's arm, and pulled him to the side. He looked down at me, startled.

"Kali, what are you doing?"

I practically bounced up and down. "I know how to do it. I know how to get InvictUS."

He grinned as he surveyed my boisterous attitude.

"How?"

"We surprise them."

"What?"

"*The Art of War.* Chapter Twelve. Using fire to attack your enemy."

Rooke raised an eyebrow. "We can't use fire in the arena. I don't think Chapter Twelve talks about breaking VGL regulations."

I smacked his arm. "I don't mean actual fire. I mean using the element of surprise to throw your enemy into confusion. About using the environment of the battlefield against them."

He shrugged. "Sure, but how does that apply to the virtual battlefield?"

I grinned. "I have an idea."

With only days left before the championship, our training equipment morphed from punching bags to balance beams.

My teammates sat on the beams, one for each, mimicking the pose I'd taught Hannah. Backs straight, hands resting on knees, eyes closed, chins tilted toward the ceiling. I walked between each of them, testing their limits. I teetered up to Lily and waited a minute, before recoiling to punch her side. Eyes still closed, she sensed my movements, blocked my attack, and tangled my arm into a hold. I danced on my tiptoes as pain shot up my limb.

"Okay, Lil. Wow. You're good."

She grinned and released my arm.

Next was Rooke. Of course, he rested perfectly on the beam. Strong but flexible. Focused and flowing. Balanced. As I passed him, he peered at me through one open eye. I held up my hands.

"Forget it. You're perfect."

He chuckled. "About time you realized it."

I punched him anyway. He teetered and stabilized without using his hands. Show-off.

Next was Derek. I gave him a quick jab in the ribs. He grunted but remained steady on the beam.

"Nice," I told him. He nodded but kept his eyes closed.

Last was my toughest student. Hannah. She sat on the beam, balanced, not teetering. I gave her a solid shove. She yelped, tumbled off the beam, and hit the mat with a thud. She sighed and slapped the ground.

"I suck at this."

I knelt beside her. "You're getting there."

"We only have a few days."

I held up a hand. "If that's all you think about, then you won't put your focus where it needs to be."

Didn't the doc tell me that once? Guess psychology wasn't so bad after all.

Hannah pushed herself off the mats and climbed back on

the beam again. After flicking her ponytail away from her shoulder, she rested her hands on her knees. She balanced, wobbled, and braced herself, and repeated the action several times afterwards.

"I keep telling you, Kali. I can't do this."

I climbed up on the beam, mirrored her pose, and pressed my hand against her stomach, just below her navel.

"Focus on my hand."

Hannah took a breath and closed her eyes. Her stomach expanded in and out against my hand as her breathing slowed. Her muscles softened under my touch. I focused with her, as if I were channeling energy through my hand. I breathed in rhythm with her. We were one.

After watching us for a minute, Rooke stepped down from his beam and stood beside Hannah.

"Focus, focus," I reminded her, eyeing Rooke. I nodded at him. He shoved her shoulder. She nearly toppled over before grabbing the beam to save herself.

"No." I pushed my hand harder into her stomach. "Think right here and only here."

"I am," she argued. "One hundred percent."

"Then give it one hundred and ten."

She grumbled something inaudible and nodded. "Aye, aye, captain."

She closed her eyes and inhaled. Her breathing steadied. Her chin tilted up slightly. I held my spare hand up to Rooke, signaling him to wait.

"Think about my hand. Forget about everything else," I told her. "Let yourself go numb, except your core."

She nodded, and her breathing slowed even more. The training room filled with the soft whispers of her breaths. I signaled Rooke. He pushed her shoulder, gentler than before. Hannah bowed with the force and swayed back. I nodded at her, even though her eyes were still closed. "Better. Keep breathing. Slowly."

Rooke hit her again. She swayed but remained on the beam, and didn't need to use her hands to steady herself. I kept my own hand pressed against her stomach. Rooke circled around the beam to hit her from the other side.

Soon Lily and Derek joined us. I stayed with Hannah as the trio began shoving her from all sides.

Hannah frowned as she felt multiple hands attacking her. "I'm not sure if you guys are helping or just using the opportunity to beat me up."

As my teammates continued the shoving fest, I felt Hannah's body change under my touch. Her muscles relaxed. Her shoulders dropped. She melted from rigid to soft to complete jelly.

During the onslaught, Derek snuck a quick jab in Lily's ribs. She grinned and punched him back. He grimaced.

After several minutes, I motioned for my teammates to step away. Then I slammed both palms into Hannah's shoulders. She bent all the way back and bounced back up like a Weeble doll. No wobble. No arm flailing. Balanced. Perfect.

Her eyes popped open, followed by her mouth. Then she screamed. She tackled me off the beam and we landed in a pile on the mats, taking Lily down with us in the process. The three of us rolled onto our backs as the laughter rolled off our tongues. The training room filled with the sounds of our giggles.

The boys appeared over us, peering down at us on the mat, shaking their heads at our shenanigans. Derek nudged Rooke. "This could get interesting."

Rooke said nothing but didn't disagree either. And honestly, I couldn't care less. I felt a sense of peace fill me again. I smiled.

In less than two weeks, we'd racked up over a hundred hours with the staffs and balance beams. In a few days, we'd face off against the invincible InvictUS. My stomach didn't turn. My chest failed to tighten. Win or lose, we'd trained and pushed ourselves as hard as we could. There was nothing more we could do.

We were ready.


That night, the cameras clicked and flashed all around us though we weren't on any red carpet. The five of us sat inside the press-conference room, the only media event we were participating in before the match. It was a frenzy. No one had seen us in the days leading up to the championship match. Reporters jammed the room from wall to wall, some spilling out into the hallways. Everyone shouted and shoved each other. Borderline mayhem.

Perfect.

Security struggled to keep the press back. In fact, they had to call in other staff members of the facility to assist. A few people got punched. Much more, and we'd need to call the cops.

The emcee stood behind his podium, though the terrified expression on his face told me he wished it were a device to teleport him out of the room. He shouted and made a calming motion for everyone to step back and quiet down. After a few futile attempts with some homemade sign language, he gave up and motioned toward one of the reporters, trying to get the conference under way. The reporter shot to his feet.

"In three days, you're heading into the championship match. What have you been doing to prepare?"

The mayhem of the pressroom dulled down to a general rumble as people realized the questioning had begun.

Hannah spoke up, answering a question seriously for once. Our characters were melting away. "We've been training harder than ever and longer every day. We study our opponents, but more importantly, we study ourselves."

The sea of hands waved wildly, like the wheat fields in high wind. Another reporter stood.

"Kali, you've become reclusive in these past few weeks, especially this one leading up to the championship. Is that some part of your strategy?"

In so many ways.

I leaned toward the microphone and unleashed a wicked smile. "You'll have to watch to find out."

Then I winked at the cameras. The room exploded in flashes, and I blinked back stars. The emcee must have motioned toward a reporter, because another question echoed through the room while I blinked away the psychedelic haze of the cameras.

"Rooke, any comment on your relationship with Ms. Ling?"

He paused before leaning into the microphone. "The arena isn't the only place where she's a warrior."

He glanced at me, heat in his eyes. The reporters reacted, chuckling and exchanging bold looks. A few of the men clapped. It's for the show, I told myself, though my foot itched to kick him under the table.

A voice called out from the back of the room.

"Your rivals InvictUS had some incredible things to say about you during their last interview. Some people are calling this the greatest current rivalry in all of sports. Do you have any response?"

Derek looked directly into the camera. "We'll see you in the fields."

A reporter stood in the front row. "Between the millions of dollars in prize money and your reputation as athletes, what's more at stake for you?"

Lily answered.

"Pride."

I smiled to myself, feeling that very emotion swell in my chest. So much that I decided to be bold and pressed my lips against my microphone.

"Win or lose, we'll be dedicating the match to our former teammate Nathan. In case some of you forgot"—I paused to clear my throat of the vindictive tone stuck inside it—"Nathan died earlier this season of a drug overdose. Winning the tournament was his dream. He'll be in our minds and hearts through the matchup, and we ask that you keep him in yours as well."

The reporters stared at me, dumbfounded, throwing sideways glances at each other. I could practically hear their thoughts. A drug overdose? What is she talking about? I thought Nathan died of a heart defect.

Above them all, I could hear Clarence screaming in my head, too, until I pictured him as a little ant that I crushed with my thumb. The emcee shot me a look of sheer shock. He cleared his throat into the microphone.

"Okay, that's enough for tonight."

Like always, he was ending the press conference early while the reporters shouted in protest and hollered more questions as we left, and even after the doors had shut behind us. Clarence called me into his office as soon as the conference ended. I stood in front of his desk as he lectured and stuffed items into his briefcase.

"I know the sponsors were the ones to encourage the memory of Nathan, but I'm not so sure how much they'd like you talking about it."

Ah, yes. The sponsors. Even Clarence was in the dark about that one.

"Gives us something even bigger to fight for, right?" I said, feigning innocence. "The more we stand to lose, the better. The more conflict and tension there is, the more the audience will eat it up."

Clarence halted for half a second, as if someone had temporarily hit the pause button in his life. Then he snapped back to reality and rummaged in his desk again.

"Yes, I suppose you're right," he mumbled. "It doesn't matter anyways. The censors cut out the part about his drug overdose, so no harm done. Good thing there's that ten-second delay to air."

My stomach fell to my knees. I stuttered.

"B-but the reporters—"

"Won't say anything. Hell, half those magazines are owned by the sponsors' parent companies. They won't print anything they shouldn't."

My eyes fell shut, and I let a slow sigh pass through my nose. Defeated. How else was I going to speak the truth? I couldn't hack the advertising database again. No sponsor would claim responsibility for it this time, given the content. And I couldn't get the word out through the cameras or the tabloids. I didn't accept defeat easily, but how was I going to get past the media?

"I have to admit you have a gift for this, Kali," Clarence began, "for manipulating the game in your best interest."

So right, and so wrong. Manipulating the industry for the interest of the game and those who played it, maybe—not the other way around. Though it didn't surprise me that was the way he saw it.

"If I didn't know better," he said with a click of his tongue, "I'd consider you a threat to my job."

Oh, I was a threat, even if I was only a mere blip on his radar. Every day that passed, my desire to rip down the gaming industry grew. Though part of me had to wonder if this was a test. In ancient civilizations, to become top dog, you had to take out the dictator. I was a gladiator, after all. But Clarence wasn't the real problem. He was a puppet.

I was no puppet.

If I owned a team, I'd let them be themselves, not some image created for them. I'd give them regular therapy sessions. Mental checkups would be just as important as the physical ones. I wouldn't falsify their drug tests. Hell, I'd do everything differently because my attention would be on those who really mattered. The gamers and the fans, not the industry and the sponsors.

I watched Clarence jam a few more items into his briefcase and seized the change of subject.

"What are you doing?"

"I have meetings to attend tonight with the sponsors," he said. "We have to finalize any last-minute ads for the championship."

My stomach did flip-flops. He was leaving? Like, really leaving?

"I trust that you can manage the team well enough," he continued, "especially since you won't be stepping outside the facility." He narrowed his eyes at me.

I beamed. "That's the plan."

He nodded. "Excellent. I knew it was a good idea to keep all of you in. The sponsors are chomping at the bit about this. This is the VGL like they've never seen it."

Clarence droned on about the meeting and how brilliant he was. I simply smiled and nodded, though my hands itched to give him a good shove out the door. Funny how only a few years ago I was doing this same thing whenever my parents were leaving for the night.

What? VR Parties? Noooo.

Once Clarence had left for the night, I met my teammates in the rec room and revealed our owner's departure.

"Too bad we can't go out," Hannah said. "We could really party it up tonight without the wrath of god hanging over us."

I stepped forward. "You're right. We can't go out. But you know what we could do?"

We exchanged glances with each other before the screaming started.

"Classic video games."

We raced to the rec room and locked ourselves in for the night. We took turns, one sitting out while the other four played. But all of us laughed, killing ourselves over who won and who lost, no matter what game we played or who was playing.

For that night, we weren't so much a team. We were more than that. We were friends now, and most of all, we were having fun.

The way it should be.

# CHAPTER 24

Friday night. The last night before the championship.

I sat on the roof overlooking the facility, where I'd reclaimed my favorite alone spot as just that—alone. Below me, traffic flowed through the streets in endless streams, like raindrops sliding across glass. Up on the rooftop, high above it all, a soft breeze caressed my hair. I tossed my head back and smiled as I looked out over the city. The atmosphere glowed with the reflection of neon and a thousand blinking lights. I glanced down at one of the countless signs weaving its way across the building blocks. It read:

ESPORTS: RAGE CHAMPIONSHIPS
SATURDAY OCTOBER 31—7:00 PM PST
FIGHT-FOR-NATHAN.

A certain taste hung in the air, but not pollution or smog, or even the coolness of the night. It tasted like triumph.

Tomorrow was the end of it all. The weeks had soared past. High school had always dragged by, endless days, years that went on forever. No one told me how fast time starts to go as you get older. And I realized it was funny how, while I always thought I'd get here, I never figured this would be my path. Fighting for someone other than myself, alongside a team that believed in me as captain and a sort-of boyfriend who believed in me for everything else. Okay, fine. An actual boyfriend. What Rooke and I had was real now. What started out as complete fabrication had evolved into the most interesting and complex relationship I'd ever had.

"I thought I'd find you up here."

So much for alone time, and speaking of the boyfriend . . . Rooke approached from behind and sat beside me.

"Did you see this?" he asked, pushing a tablet into my hand. The screen featured tomorrow's copy of the *L.A. Times*. On the front page was a picture of us during our press conference days earlier. The fine-print caption below the picture read:

Team Defiance focuses their thoughts on their fallen teammate as they head into the championship round of the RAGE tournaments.

I skimmed through the article. There were quotes—real quotes—from all of us regarding Nathan and how we were motivated by his memory. Although his drug overdose failed to grace the morning edition, my lips still spread into a smile. This wasn't just another crack in the façade. This was a rip-off-the-mask and stare-into-the-sun moment.

Below the article was a video feed of the conference. I tapped on it and watched as it scrolled through the interview. I focused in when the cameras landed on me toward the end of the conference, right before the emcee had called it quits. It is weird seeing yourself on a video, at first, but I'd long gotten used to seeing my image plastered over television screens. And digital ads. And T-shirts.

"Win or lose," I began on the screen, "we'll be dedicating the match to our former teammate Nathan. In case some of you forgot, Nathan died earlier this season—"

The feed cut off, still disguising the truth behind Nathan's demise. I rolled my eyes. Clarence wasn't kidding when he said they'd cut my confession out of the press. Marcus and Howie popped up on the screen. They looked pissed. Guess Clarence wasn't the only one I'd upset over my little reveal.

"And that's the report from Team Defiance," Marcus said, pushing his standard-announcer voice through his anger. "In less than twenty-four hours now, they'll be facing off against their rival InvictUS in what is sure to be a fantastic match—"

I paused the video feed, not needing to hear any more. It sucked ass that I couldn't get the word out about Nathan. If we hacked the advertising database again, the sponsors would know it wasn't any of them that committed the act, and we'd be caught. As much as I was willing to give myself up for the right thing, I couldn't ask it of my teammates. Still, at least this was all heading in the right direction. Months ago, this would have never happened in the VGL.

Rooke must have read my mind because he said, "What was it Clarence told you once? You can't change the world, Kali."

I held up the tablet. "It is progress, but I don't think this changes the world."

"All revolutions have to start somewhere."

I pointed a finger at him. "If you start quoting famous revolutions from history, I'll make you swallow this tablet whole." I shook it at him to emphasize my threat.

"Just one?"

"NO."

He chuckled but didn't tempt the seriousness of my warning. Which was good for him because I wasn't kidding. I turned back to the article and scrolled through it some more. I sighed.

"I still wish I could get the truth out, though."

Rooke shook his head. "Kali, you've done enough. Let it go."

I shook my own in response, stubborn as ever. "Not until people know the truth. They don't know why Nathan died or what this sport drives gamers to do."

"Well," he began, not testing the strength of my obstinacy, "you got Clarence to let us stay in to train, and you inspired your teammates to want the same thing. Maybe you'll motivate someone else to follow your lead."

"Is this another one of those 'good leader' things? I don't think everyone practices life through Chinese philosophy."

"Unfortunately."

We shared a grin.

"Where's everyone?" Rooke asked, nodding down at the facility.

"The team? They're sleeping."

He sighed. "Lucky."

"Yeah. I can't sleep either."

"Can't believe the championship is tomorrow. This all went by so fast."

I looked at his profile. "Did you ever think you'd be here?"

"Yeah, but it's like a dream that doesn't seem real even when you're living it."

I nodded. That's exactly what it felt like. A dream.

"Kinda feels like we should do something to mark the occasion," I said.

"How about a round of shots?" he joked.

I laughed. "No."

"Sex?"

I laughed more. "I was hoping for suggestions a little more suited to the occasion."

"Hey, sex works. You could dress up." He waggled his eyebrows at me, and I punched his shoulder.

"Wait." Rooke grabbed my arm. "I know what we can do."

He grinned at me but didn't say anything more. The twinkle in his eye tugged at my curiosity.

"What?"

He didn't answer. Instead, he took my hand, led me to his bunk, and sat me down on the bed.

"Just wait here a second."

"I thought I said no to sex."

He ignored me and went to the side of the room. From a wall compartment, he pulled out a metal briefcase, placed it on the bed, and opened it. I peered inside. My breath caught in my throat at the contents in the case.

Nestled in protective, custom-fit foam was the original Nintendo Entertainment System. The 1985, as-gray-as-the-walls-around-us, it's-a-me-Mario, no-really-it's-a-me-Mario, freaking Nintendo set.

"Are you serious?" I screeched like a twelve-year-old girl. I peered up at Rooke as my stomach did somersaults. "Is it real?"

"You bet."

"Oh my God. Oh my God." I repeated it a dozen times, followed by, "Can I touch it?"

"Where have I heard that before?"

I was too stunned to punch him or even think of a retort.

He nodded at me for encouragement. "Go ahead."

I reached into the case and lifted out the black-and-gray controller, complete with two red buttons and one directional pad.

"Is this the original NES? I mean, the actual original set, not a replica?"

He nodded, still grinning.

Of course it was. Would Rooke have anything else?

"God, this thing is like a hundred years old."

He sat down on the bed beside me. "Not quite, but yeah."

I held up the connection cables to the system. Each had a gray-plastic carton on the end.

"But wait, this is new technology," I said, turning it over in my hand to examine it. "What is it?"

"Adapters. Look."

He pulled a shelf out from the wall, propped his tablet on it, and plugged the cable in. The screen flickered. Then the game's menu popped up, and a pixelated red plumber jumped across it.

My heart rifled into my throat.

"It works?"

Another screech.

Rooke grinned and dropped the remote in my lap. I glanced between it and the screen, openmouthed, not moving, heart still beating in place of my larynx.

"You look tentative," he said, reaching for my lap. "Maybe you should let me—"

I snatched up the remote. "Screw you. I'm going first."

He chuckled to himself but didn't reach for the remote again.

The room filled with the sounds of clicking buttons and 1980s synthesizer music as I plowed my way through the 2D world on the screen. I glanced at Rooke, figuring he'd be bored, but he watched with fascination as I chased coins and broke bricks. Gamers. We never tire of the game.

"Funny how far we've come, huh?" he mused.

Whether he meant the game or us, I wasn't sure. I stuck with the game.

"From stick characters to fully immersive virtual reality in a century. It doesn't seem that fast when you think about it."

"In context it does. The automobile was invented in 1886, but it wasn't until the late 2020s when they became truly automatic and drove themselves. That's 140 years compared to 60, if you consider 2044 as the introduction of the first fully immersive VR system. Hell, it's less than half the time."

Wow. History and math. I'm a lucky girl.

I considered jamming the spare remote in his mouth. "You and history. Two peas in a pod."

Either he missed the sarcasm or ignored it entirely when he started talking again. "You know, the first real video game was invented in the 1950s and ran on an analog comfuterrr—"

His words became a muffled mess as I smothered his lips with my hand.

"Not now, babe. I'm gaming."

As if just to spite me, the screen broke into a pixilated jumble of red lines. I dropped the remote, mimicking the sinking feeling in my stomach.

"Shit. Is it toast?"

"Nah, it's a glitch." Rooke waved a hand at the screen like it was a common occurrence. "Just reset the game."

I pulled the game out of the system and turned it over in my hands, looking for the reset button.

"No," he said with a laugh. "You have to blow on it."

"What? What would that do?"

"I don't know. It's just what everyone does."

I looked between him and the game a few times, and blew on his face instead. When he tried to tickle me as a comeback, I punched him in the ribs, and he doubled over, half coughing, half laughing.

Warriors don't get tickled.

Thirty seconds after I got the game going again, he slipped an arm around my waist, pulled me tight against him, and pressed his lips against my ear. Little shock waves coursed through me. I fumbled, almost dropping the remote, but kept my eyes on the screen. I recovered and resumed pushing buttons.

"That isn't going to get you a turn any faster," I told him. He lowered his mouth to the nape of my neck, pressed his lips against my pulse point, and murmured something that sounded like "I want you."

Good thing even games back then had pause buttons.

We ended up at the foot of his bed, me straddling him. His hands kneaded my hips as I rocked against him in a slow and grinding pace. We clung to each other, every inch touching, mouths brushing. Our eyes locked as our breathing synced. In the moments when our hips met in perfect unison, we'd gasp together. We eased into a rhythm. Soft. Comfortable. Like we'd been together for years.

This is what it was about. Being with another person. Not a release. Not just about pleasure, but what you could give to each other. It was just as much about you as it was about the other person, and all about the connection you created with them. The feel of their body against yours. The taste of their skin. Their vulnerability. Their energy. Their everything.

And to think, I didn't even have to dress up.

The next morning, I woke to his touch. He traced the outline of my hip with his fingers, featherlight touches that sent goose bumps flooding across my skin. I smiled. He'd stayed the night. Sure, it was his bunk, but he'd kept by my side through the moonlight. That was something.

His eyes flicked to mine and back to my hip.

"You know what today is."

My stomach twisted, half from excitement and half from fear.

"Halloween?" I offered. It really was. But the fact that the holiday coincided with the championship was just coincidence. I sighed. "Yeah, I know."

It was Saturday. The last Saturday. Only of the tournament, of course, but it might as well have been a Mayan apocalypse.

For us, there was no tomorrow. There was only tonight. Only the championship.

He pushed out a heavy sigh. "Last one."

"Yeah," I said. "Last one."

Rooke slid under the covers, nestled against my back, and pulled me tight against him.

"We have a few minutes," he murmured against my hair, "before the alarm."

I smiled at the thought and snuggled even more into him. His nose grazed against my neck, his breath tickling the crook of my shoulder. His warmth pressed against my back and curled over me like the blanket. The heat from him rivaled the facility's cool air around us. His steady heartbeat opposed the empty sounds of the facility. This was balance. No. This was pure relaxation.

*Beep. Beep. Beep.*

My chest tightened at the sound of the alarm. This was it. The beginning of the end. Rooke exhaled into my hair, and his grip tensed around me.

"Showtime."


I returned to my own bunk to shower and dress. Showering with Rooke would have been just a little too tempting to end up late to breakfast. After pulling on my training gear, I sat on the edge of my bed to meditate and focused on centering myself on the sensations around me. The soft memory foam of the mattress conforming to my body, the cool hospital smell of the facility around me, and the soft pinging coming from my tablet.

Soft pinging? I opened my eyes.

Incoming call from San Diego.

I scooped up my tablet and tapped the screen. When the image of a middle-aged woman flashed across it, I beamed.

"Hi, Mom."

"Oh, Sweetie. I'm glad I caught you. Are you busy?"

"It's a busy day, but I have a few minutes."

"The championship is tonight, right? What channel is it on?"

I sighed. "You don't have to watch. I know how you feel about this stuff."

"I can watch with one hand over my eyes. You know, between my fingers." She demonstrated, peeking at me through her middle and ring fingers. I laughed.

"Everyone's been talking about it at the office all week," she continued. "They say you're the first girl to lead a team in a championship. Is that true?"

"Yeah, it's true."

"I never realized that."

There was an awkward pause. Our eyes met a few times and looked away again. Finally, she broke the silence.

"I know you really want to win, but your father and I will be proud either way."

"I know." I smiled. "So will I."

A buzz came from my door, and I knew who it was.

"One second," I called out. "And damn it, Rooke, if you say something like you've already been in here before, I will punch you right through that metal door."

I turned back to my tablet to find a coy grin on my mother's face.

"Not your boyfriend, huh?" she said cheekily. "Why has he been in your room?"

I fought a losing battle with the heat rushing to my face. "Well, uh, that's a long story."

"Mmm-hmm. I thought that article in *Pro Gamer Weekly* was . . . What did you call it? Oh yeah, 'crap.'"

Ah, yes. Crap. Poets, my mother and I.

I tried to suppress a smile and failed. "Turns out, not so much."

The door buzzed again. Twice.

Mom grinned. "Persistent little bugger, isn't he?"

I mirrored her expression. "You have no idea."

"He'd have to be to win you over." She narrowed her eyes at me. "You get your stubbornness from your father."

I laughed, knowing it was exactly the opposite. "I appreciate the call, Mom, but I have to get going."

"Okay. I'll let you go. Good luck. We'll be watching."

The screen faded out on my mother's smile until the main menu popped up. I sat on the bed for a moment, trying to process how the call had made me feel. San Diego felt just a little bit closer, now. Maybe once the tournament was over, I'd go home for a visit.

I left the tablet on my bed and walked with Rooke to the cafeteria. I managed to eat breakfast and, more importantly, managed to keep it in my stomach. Even with the table full of my teammates and the facility's staff, every clang of a spoon or thunk of a mug echoed through the unusually quiet room.

We spent the morning training together, all of us in various matchups and attack positions. Time passed too slow and too fast altogether. Awkward silences seeped in between moments of action. Times when we'd meet eyes and just stare at each other, like we were sharing messages mind to mind. *Yeah, it's today. I'm not ready, either.*

The day took on more shape when I met with Dr. Renner in her office for a final check-in before the championship.

"How are you feeling?" she asked.

I sat in the chair, trying not to fidget too much. "Good. Nervous."

"That's understandable. What are you most nervous about?"

"My teammates. This is their future, and it's in my hands."

"They believe in you. Everyone here does."

She stressed the word *everyone*. This woman, educated well beyond what I could ever understand, master of the complexities of the human mind, believed in me?

She leaned toward me and removed her glasses. "Nathan would be proud, you know."

I swallowed thick and blinked back the stinging sensation in my eyes. But I wasn't crying. Warriors don't cry.

"Thanks for your help, Doc," I said, forcing an even tone to my voice.

She smiled and replaced her glasses, sitting back in her chair. "You've changed a lot over these past weeks. I'm glad I got to be a part of it." She leaned toward me once more, as if sharing a secret. "You also impacted the industry. You're about to lead this team to something so much more than victory."

My stomach did a somersault. I held up a hand. "Let's not get that far."

She shook her head and smiled again. "You've been so focused on Nathan and the team, I think you've forgotten about yourself, a little. You're the first woman to lead a team into a championship match. Win or lose, you've already made history."

The somersaults morphed into a high-power mixing machine.

"Okay, stop now."

She raised an eyebrow. "What's wrong? Don't you believe it yourself?"

"It's not that. It's just . . . you're confident I have this in the bag, so to speak. I can't even picture myself winning. Or leading the team to victory. Or anything. And if we don't win, then was everything we did this season for nothing? What if we let Nathan down?"

It was her turn to hold up a hand. "You can't let Nathan down. Not after everything you've done to preserve his honor. And everything you did this season will just prepare you for the next. Does every baseball team only have one shot at the World Series? No. They come back next year and go for it again. There will be other tournaments, Kali. Win or lose, your life isn't over tonight. It's just beginning."

I curled a lip at her words. There was some truth behind them, but that didn't stop my churning gut.

When the doc surveyed my doubtful expression, she leaned toward me again. "It's easier to think about when you envision what comes next. And I don't just mean the celebration afterwards or the press releases, or even the next day. Picture yourself in the next tournament. Picture where you'll be six months from now. No matter what happens tonight, you'll still get there. Then it won't seem like such a big deal."

Right now, it was. It was the biggest deal in the history of the universe. How could losing the tournament not have an impact on where I'd be in six months?

The doc tried again. "Think about it this way: Where is it you'd like to end up, Kali? What matters to you most?"

I faltered. "I . . . don't know."

These tournaments, making it as a pro gamer was all that had mattered to me. But now, living this life, sacrificing parts of myself . . . Was it worth it?

I stood up from the chair and headed for the exit.

"Where are you going?" she called.

"I have some thinking to do."

———

The rest of the day, I considered the doc's words. Even that afternoon, as I looked down at the world below me and smiled at the wind whipping through my hair. The strange thing was I wasn't plugged in.

While most teams plugged in and played from a facility, all the eSports championships took place in an arena. The ten of us, the team and our programmers, were flown in by helicopter to the Riot Games Arena, located in downtown Los Angeles, across the street from the historic Staples Center and the renovated L.A. Convention Center.

Inside the arena, I warmed up with my teammates in the training rooms offstage. Most sports teams had locker rooms. We had dojos. In the center of the room, I practiced my Tai Chi routine for what seemed like the last time. Tomorrow, the season would be over. We'd be champions, or we wouldn't. But we'd still be a team, we'd still be athletic gamers, and there was always next year if things didn't go our way. The doctor was right. It was easier to picture myself through all this. Now, the match seemed like a drop in the bucket.

A big-ass drop in a tiny little bucket, but hey, I was working on it.

Once I brought my routine to a close, I sat on the floor and settled into a meditative position. Minutes passed, maybe hours, as I sat there in silence with my teammates training around me, one with each other and ourselves.

Except I wasn't. I wasn't completely one with myself. Because the question tugged at the back of my mind. The one the doc had posed. What mattered to me most? I wasn't sure. For so long it had been the games. Nothing else mattered. The fame and free drugs were nice perks at first, but those had grown stale.

Worse than old coffee. No, really.

So then, what did matter? Where was I heading? I took a breath and pushed down into my stomach, reminding myself to stay grounded and focused. I was twenty years old and on top of the world. I could go anywhere, do anything I wanted.

So, what was that, exactly?

Not everyone gets these kinds of opportunities. Not everyone has the world as their oyster. I did. I'd been blessed. Now it was time to decide what to do with my gifts.

"Defiance."

I opened my eyes and looked to the doorway, where a woman stood clutching a tablet. She nodded toward the darkened hallway behind her.

"Prepare to get onstage. It's time."

# CHAPTER 25

his was it. Our Super Bowl. Our Stanley Cup.

The time was now.

On the monitors backstage, we had a full view inside the arena. The entire interior gleamed like black lacquer. Embedded floor lights ran in tracks outlining the aisles and seating sections, glowing in an iridescent blue-white. The color scheme and design was a hat tip to the classic movie *Tron*, one of the first to feature a character disappearing into a video game.

In the center of the arena, the stage was the shape of a four-way directional pad, also outlined in a blue-white glow. Enormous, two-hundred-foot screens faced each of the four directions. The east and west stages featured the pod centers for each team, while the north held the announcers' booth, and the south was reserved for interviews and other general announcements.

Sold out at full capacity, the arena was filled with twenty thousand fans. About one in three was dressed as their favorite video game character. It was Halloween, after all. Some paid homage to the more famous characters: Link, Lara Croft, Cloud Strife, and Halo Soldiers. Others were from the most recent games, Queen Ryadoc Serend, ruler of the biggest virtual RPG in history, alongside Nico Reese, star of the latest action game on the PlayStation Platinum console. There were even a few dressed in battle gear that mimicked our own, both Defiance and InvictUS.

The crowd suddenly erupted with applause, screams, and whistles. Marcus Ryan and Howie Fulton walked out onto the south side of the stage, though the larger-than-life screens showed them from all angles so everyone in the audience could see. They smiled and waved, wearing suits and their traditional headsets, which doubled as microphones.

"Good evening," Marcus began, his voice echoing throughout the arena. "I'm Marcus Ryan."

"And I'm Howie Fulton. And this is . . ." He pointed out at the crowd. Twenty thousand voices answered him.

"*Saturday Night Gaming*."

The crowd erupted again with applause and cheers.

Marcus beamed at the cameras. "Ladies and gentlemen, welcome to the Riot Games Arena in Los Angeles, California." Another round of monstrous applause came from the crowd. "Years of prep and training, months of preseason action and tournament matchups have all led to this point. Tonight is the national championship for the RAGE tournaments, what has become the biggest event in the VGL thanks to these two teams. InvictUS vs. Defiance, the hottest rivalry we've ever seen. It all comes down to this final fight. Who will be crowned the 2054 RAGE Champions?"

"That's right, Marcus. This is a groundbreaking moment in league history as we are joined by more viewers than ever before from countries all around the world. We are privileged to watch the top teams compete in what is sure to be history in the making."

Hannah fanned herself in the background. "I think I'm going to be sick."

"Don't listen to it," I said, waving at the screen like it was nothing despite my own churning gut. "They're just amping up the excitement for the crowd."

As if just to spite me, Marcus spoke up in the background.

"Let's check out some of the parties around the world. Locally, in Los Angeles."

The footage changed over to a live feed of downtown L.A. overflowing with a sea of bodies.

"New York City."

The footage changed again to the largest city in the country, and my stomach twisted at the sight. Times Square looked less full on New Year's Eve.

"London, England."

Another sea of people. Union Jacks waved in the background.

"And Seoul, South Korea."

In the country that had always been the biggest for video game tournaments, I watched as the cameras panned across entire stadiums of people who had gathered to watch on screens larger than any I'd ever seen before.

"Okay," Hannah said. "Now I really am going to be sick."

Either the rest of my teammates felt the same, or they were really dedicated to the team—being they were all matching shades of green.

I walked up to Hannah and took her hand. "Hannah, look at me. We trained for this. We're here because we are the best, and we want it the most. We've dedicated our lives to the game." I took a breath and found myself speaking the doctor's words. "Where do you want to be tomorrow?"

"It depends—"

"No, it doesn't. It doesn't depend on tonight. Where do you want to be tomorrow?"

"But, I want to be a champion."

"Then, you try. And if you don't make it, tomorrow you get up and try again. This isn't the only championship. This isn't the only chance you'll ever have. Tomorrow, win or lose, you'll be a gamer who gave it her all to get there. That's what matters."

The clenched muscles in her face and shoulders relaxed as she accepted my words. Eventually, she sighed and nodded. The doctor was right. This was just a moment in time. An important moment, but there would be plenty of those in our futures. How we learned from them was what really mattered.

Onstage, Marcus bellowed.

"In this corner," Marcus joked, as if this were a boxing match. He pointed at the west side of the stage, where five pods sat waiting. "Please welcome to the stage . . . IN-VICT-US."

Deep in the crowd, a set of double doors opened, and the five members of InvictUS walked out and down the aisle between throngs of fans, held back by rails. Music blasted from the speakers, but the crowd's chaotic screams nearly swallowed any other sound. All five stared straight ahead, expressions as ruthless as killers.

Please just be part of their image.

"Shit, they're huge," Derek commented, and we all nodded. It really shouldn't have been a surprise. We are our avatars, so they'd have to be the same size in real life as they were in the virtual world. Still, seeing them in person instead of only inside the game made it all the more real. These guys could have been pro wrestlers.

The stage director shooed us to the doors.

"Get ready."

After InvictUS filed onstage, Howie took over the announcing.

"And in this corner"—he pointed at the east stage featuring our pods—"ladies and gentlemen, we give you DE-FI-ANCE."

The double doors opened, and I led the team into the arena.

Twenty thousand voices enveloped me in a deafening roar that rivaled a jet engine. I smiled my warrior's smile and marched confidently down the aisle to the stage. Inside, my stomach curled. I was melting under the heat of the lights and number of people packed into one open space. My nerves shook until my knees nearly buckled. I felt like I was walking on a tightrope.

We climbed the steps to the stage and faced the audience, leaving a good five-foot gap between ourselves and InvictUS. I purposely turned my gaze away from them and focused on the crowd, thinking the twenty thousand screaming fans would be less intimidating than the brutes standing next to me. I was wrong. Looking out at the fans as they cheered and waved made me realize just how many people were watching us, counting on us to win. My stomach churned. No. I was being stupid. Most professional athletes had to deal with this every single game. I centered myself, calming my nerves.

It was a game. Nothing more. We were here because we were at the top of our form, and we deserved it.

I glanced over at InvictUS, five carbon copies of flesh-colored titans. Taking a deep breath, I calmed my nerves even further. They were people. Gamers like me. Either they would win, or we would. We'd practiced and trained and pushed ourselves as hard as we could, and we had fun through all the blood, sweat, and tears. In the end, that's what really mattered.

Winning, however, would be oh so sweet.

Howie and Marcus walked forward to a stand at the end of the stage. It was covered with a small tarp.

"Tonight, we'll see these two amazing teams face off in what is sure to be an incredible matchup."

"That's right. And they'll be playing for this."

They ripped the tarp off the stand to reveal the VGL Champion Cup, black and sleek like the arena, with blue-white inlays.

It glistened and sparkled in the endless stage lights and camera flashes from the audience. The names of every gamer from every tournament in 2054 were etched in plates around the base. Given the number of tournaments in the VGL and the always-evolving game lineup, there was a new cup issued every year. The cups from previous years sat in the VGL Hall of Fame. Forever.

"Remember," Marcus began, "since Defiance is the team in the losers' bracket, they will need to defeat InvictUS without a single player lost."

My stomach tightened, and I pushed a breath through my lips. We'd trained for this. Studied and planned as much as we could. We were ready.

"Tonight, not only is Team Defiance fighting to win, but also for the memory of their fallen teammate, Nathan Saunders," Howie said. He stepped toward the audience and raised his voice, so he was heard in every corner of the arena. "Despite what you might have heard, Nathan Saunders died of a drug overdose earlier this season. He's not the only one, either. It's a problem that's plagued these tournaments for years."

What the hell did he just say?

Behind Howie's back, out of sight of the cameras, Marcus gave me a thumbs-up.

I stood there, numb and blinking, too stunned to react as the announcers spoke the truth about Nathan's death and the trouble gamers experienced both in and out of the games. They, too, had risked their careers to shoot the middle finger at an industry poised to swallow us whole. Whether the producers had cut it from air or not, it didn't matter. There were twenty thousand people in the audience. With twenty thousand phones.

Rooke lowered his head, and whispered to me, "You've even turned the announcers into rebels."

My open mouth spread into a smile as pride overflowed my veins. Pride for the announcers, for standing up for what they believed in. Pride in my team, for following me this far. Pride in myself, for fighting for what was right.

Like Rooke had said, be a good leader and people will follow.

Oh, God. Blah. He was right.

The crowd went eerily silent, the kind of silence where you hear a single cough, and it echoes throughout the entire room. A phone lit up in the audience, like a beacon from a lighthouse in the dark. Then another. And another. Soon, the entire arena was glowing with the screens of twenty thousand devices. Devices they'd use to get the word out. This was it. There was no stopping the truth now. The Internet would explode. Every social-media site would overflow. There was no hiding, no cover-up that could stop the momentum we'd created.

There you go, industry.

Eat it.

"All right," Howie said, glancing back at us. "We want a good, clean fight. And most of all, we want to be entertained."

The crowd laughed, then cheered.

Marcus turned to the cameras. "As the teams get ready to plug in, here's a quick word from our sponsors."

That was our cue.

I walked with my teammates to the east stage, where our pods sat waiting. Above us on the screen was our team logo, shimmering for the audience to see. Just before I climbed into my pod, Elise nodded at me from her workstation. I smiled back and took a breath. Here we go.

The doors closed around me with a deafening boom. Had they always been that loud? Wires crawled across my skin, triggering goose bumps and chills that only added to the weighted feeling in my stomach. And yet, somehow, I felt numb to it all, as if the lid had just been closed on my own coffin, with me inside it.

I steadied myself, pushing the fear out with a slow, calming breath. After a few more, it evaporated, as if lifting out of my pores. The weight was gone, never to press down again. I focused on the sensations of the real world. The wires tickling as they attached to my skin, the heated air of the arena, and the soft shimmer of the pod's opal core. Last match.

Last time.

I closed my eyes, and when I opened them, I stood inside the tower.

# CHAPTER 26

**B**alance. It had been the key to everything. My salvation. My sanity. Even the game. But I didn't realize just how much until that moment.

Inside the tower, high above everything else, I sat balanced with my teammates on the support beams, completely hidden from view. Several feet below, the tower's stone floor sat cold and empty. Wind curled in from the entrance, sweeping up bits of dust and gravel. The debris kicked and skidded across the stones, then went still. Dead still. I had to wonder. Would the cameras even see us up here? Of course. They could see anywhere inside the virtual world. The audience would know right where we were.

InvictUS wouldn't.

Single file on the beam, we sat the way we'd practiced. First Lily, then Derek, followed by Hannah, Rooke, and myself. Though it had nothing to do with appearances and everything to do with tactics. I looked down the line at my teammates. Hannah had her eyes closed, though whether it was due to the height or concentration, I wasn't sure. Everyone else balanced on the beam, calm and nervous at the same time, deep breaths coupled with fluttering fingertips. That same terrified-but-tranquil combination swirled through my own stomach. I took a breath and released it.

"They're coming," Hannah announced in a hushed whisper, eyes still closed.

Footsteps pounded up the path to our tower, heavy footsteps with the sharp clangs of armor knocking together as they ran. I peered over the edge to watch. In their standard form, four members of InvictUS burst through the tower's entrance and ground to a halt when they were greeted by nothing more than an empty tower. They'd expected to find all of us here since they hadn't crossed anyone in the fields. And we were. They just had no idea where.

Grunts and sounds of confusion echoed off the tower's walls.

"What the hell?" one of them shouted. "Where are they?"

"Did they go for our tower? Maybe they're already there."

"No way. We would have seen them."

"There has to be at least one of them here."

They scurried around the tower, glancing out the entrance-way and in every other direction. One of them ventured outside and circled the perimeter of the tower. They all looked like little ants. Just like when I'd perch on the roof of the facility, InvictUS looked as if they could be crushed by my thumb. Not so undefeatable now.

Still balancing perfectly on the beam, I signaled to Lily at the other end. She caught my eyes. I held up one finger, then made a chopping motion with my arm. She nodded. She pulled an axe from its sheath at her waist, slowly drawing it out into her grasp.

It slipped.

The axe tumbled through the air, descending straight for the ground. InvictUS was about to find out where we were. So much for the element of surprise.

With one leg wrapped around the beam, Lily flipped around the pole and snatched the axe back midair. With the momentum of the flip, she brought herself back up and rested upright, axe gripped in hand, a grin pulling at her lips.

Never underestimate a blonde in pigtails. Never.

A silent breath of relief echoed through us all. I closed my eyes and inhaled deeply, but it failed to calm the heart thudding in my chest.

Lily held the axe up next to her head and made a chopping motion as she aimed. The beam squeaked under her movements, whining in protest. My thudding heart went in my throat. I glanced down at our opponents, but the pattering of their feet and constant swearing covered the sound.

Lily aimed, once, twice, and released.

The whooshing sound of her axe whizzed through the air, like the chopping sound of a helicopter's blades. It tomahawked straight for one of InvictUS. He heard the sound and glanced up.

"What the—"

It nailed him in the head, splitting it open from cranium to nose. He collapsed instantly to the ground.

I signaled to my teammates. Jump.

Three.

Two.

One.

We leapt and landed in perfect unison on the tower floor, a wall of soldiers and death. Short framing the tall. Dark mixing with light. Men between the women. Now we looked like a team.

A real team.

Image isn't everything. But it helps.

The three remaining members of InvictUS stared wide-eyed, then exchanged looks with each other. Their shocked expressions morphed into grimaces, and they charged for us. We held our ground, bringing them to us.

At the last possible second, all three girls, myself included, dropped to the ground, tucked and rolled. Perfect unison. We slid through the gaps between the trio of InvictUS and came up to our knees as they passed, slicing through the air for anything that resembled flesh. Hannah's axe landed home, cutting right through her target's leg. He screamed and dropped to his knees. The three of us pounced on him, ripping into his neck and chest. In half a second, his eyes glazed over with the look of death.

We sprang to our feet as Derek and Rooke wrangled with the remaining two attackers. Five-on-two and surrounded on all sides. They went back-to-back, for what good it would do them. We moved forward and back, sometimes in pairs or threes. Like rippling waves of an ocean, crashing into the enemy with a steady pulse from all angles. Swords clanged together. Metal clanking metal became its own symphony.

I stood between Rooke and Hannah as we battled the duo. Dropping to one knee, I swung for one's calf. He swung down to block me, leaving his upper half unguarded. Rooke landed a solid swipe through his neck. Blood gushed out of the gaping wound. He fell to his knees, clawing at his own neck. We drove our swords into his chest. He seized, then collapsed to the ground.

I stole a glance at Rooke. He grinned back.

One more to go.

The five of us circled him. He spun every way, trying to keep an eye on each of us. Sweat poured down his face, his gaze darting about. Finally, InvictUS knew what it was like to be prey. But unlike them, we wouldn't make him suffer.

Derek retrieved Lily's axe from our first victim's head and hurled it at him. It sunk into the back of his skull. He gasped, dropped to his knees, and fell face forward onto the tower floor, his final breath whooshing out of his lungs. Then it went silent.

Dead. All of them.

That was it. We'd done it. We'd broken through the impenetrable force that was InvictUS. Now, there was a new invincible team on the block.

Defiance.

I could just hear the announcers right now.

*What a show. Underdogs Defiance just owned it like nobody's business. In all the years of virtual gaming, we've never seen anything like this.*

Excitement exploded within until I shook, until I thought I'd go insane from the energy rushing through me. I fought the urge to scream. To jump up and down. The match wasn't over yet. Somehow, on the outside, I remained cool and collected, despite my dancing innards. I nodded at my teammates.

"You guys go. Take out the last member of InvictUS and capture their tower. I'll stay here and hold ours."

They exchanged glances with each other. Hannah stepped forward.

"No way, you have to go." She pointed out the entrance, where InvictUS's tower loomed in the background. "That's your fight."

I shook my head. "Really, it's—"

"Kali, you led us here," she said. "We're about to win, and it's because of you."

She laced her fingers through mine and squeezed.

"Go."

Before she released my hand, she leaned in close and whispered a word that echoed in my mind.

"Champions."

My stomach rippled. No. Not yet.

One kill to go.

Fortitude swelled up inside and solidified. In the moment, I felt strong. But taking on the remaining member of InvictUS by myself? Studying the determined expressions on my team-mates' faces, they believed in me. Maybe it was time I did the same thing myself.

I headed for the tower's exit but paused at the door and looked back at Rooke. Our eyes locked. He nodded for me to go. That wasn't what I wanted. The last fight was mine, and mine alone. But I wanted my partner in crime there to witness the glory.

Victory. I could taste it on my tongue.

Derek clued him in and pushed him forward. "Go with your woman, man. Geez."

Rooke joined me, and together we raced through the fields. Fields that seemed to stretch on forever as they whipped around me, brushing my face and clipping at my heels. A sandpaper whisper filled the air. Like Lily, I seldom went on offense and took the moment to appreciate the sensations of the virtual world, of the mountain air pumping through my lungs, and the scent of lavender caressing my nose. But it dulled in comparison to the rubber smell of the training room or the plastic covering every inch. Even the antibacterial stench of the facility. Because they were real.

I broke through the fields' edge, followed closely by Rooke. Together, we drove up the dirt path, dodging the rocky terrain wrapped around the tower. This was it. The end of the end. Adrenaline pumped in my legs, propelling me toward the enemy's fortress. I'd led my team here. I'd led myself here. The soaring stone walls of the turret that seemed to touch the sky grew a little shorter just then. I could do this. Nothing could stop me now. But when I burst through the entranceway, I skidded to a halt.

Trent Amos stood in the center of the tower.

# CHAPTER 27

The final fight. It all came down to this.

Dressed in minimal armor and wielding a single long-sword, Trent Amos belonged on the cover of a gamer magazine. Somehow, he looked even bigger than the last time we'd fought together. With shoulders nearly three times my width and muscles gleaming in the sunlight, he was a tank, a powerhouse of strength. The perfect gladiator.

And he was all mine.

Funny how life likes to bring things full circle, isn't it?

I should have known it would be him before I even entered the tower. He hadn't been with the four that attacked, so I should have done the math. But the fear, anticipation, and adrenaline had clouded my brain so much, I hadn't realized this would be the final fight until he was standing right in front of me.

His eyes went wide. How could we have possibly made it through his horde of brutes? Then his features softened, and he chuckled, bold and confident. He had no idea he was alone. Because of our handicap as the losing team, it didn't matter either. He could still take the game all by himself. All he had to do was take me out.

He waved me forward. I approached, slowly, sword gripped tight in my hand. Rooke remained behind to block the entrance.

He knew. He knew this was my fight. And he knew to stay the hell out of my way.

We met in the middle and began circling. I stayed out of reach, waiting for him to come to me. He sized me up, still chuckling. I mirrored every step he took. It became a waltz, one where we didn't touch. I counted my breaths. Calm. Even. A breeze snuck in through the tower's entrance. The wind rippled through my hair, and I knew it was there with me.

As we circled, Trent lashed out at me a few times, trying to draw me in. I ignored his feints, perfectly focused, sword gripped in hand. I was a poster child for the Chinese warrior.

No. The Chinese-American warrior. A perfect blend. Both sides as one.

Trent drew back his sword and lunged forward. I moved with him, spinning and ducking. He slashed through the air until our weapons finally met. His strength reverberated down the sword into my hands, somehow even stronger than the last time I'd faced off against him. Guess InvictUS had been practicing, too. I focused, and told myself the same things I'd told Hannah. Be like the wind. Strong but flexible.

He came at me again and again. Every time I parried him to the side, he immediately spun back for another blow. He knew my fighting style now. He knew to move like water and earth whenever he struck. He had no blind spots. No skin exposed.

Reverberations rippled down my arms. A dull ache gripped my muscles. Seconds into the fight, and I was already waning. I couldn't win. I'd never defeat his strength. My throat clenched. My chest tightened. Every muscle seized.

No. Focus. You can do this.

His sword slashed my arm. My weapon-wielding arm. I grimaced, grinding my teeth to stifle a whimper. Blood dribbled out and dripped on the tower floor.

I caught a glimpse of Rooke still in the entranceway. He gripped his swords tight and paced behind me, jaw clenched. Hell, every muscle was clenched. He was primed to jump into the fight, ready to take out Trent before he took me out. But for now, he remained in the tower's doorway, pacing.

Blood bubbled out of my wound as weakness took hold from shoulder to fingertip. Sweat pooled around my neck. My breaths came out in pants. I trembled.

Trent swung hard, and I blocked just in time, my arm feeling both numb and like it weighed a thousand pounds. Our weapons met again, and we locked up. He pushed down into his sword. My feet slid back a foot across the floor. Oh, shit. My knees buckled before I clamped down on them and forced myself to stay on my feet.

Rooke took a step closer.

No. I could do this.

I grunted and strained against Trent, pushing until my arms shook. The edges of my vision blurred. The pain in my arm flared, and only my gritting teeth stifled my yelp. Trent leaned into me, pressing down with his weight. The metal from our swords screeched together under the pressure. Hot pain seared through my arm, and my knees bent again. Then, numbness spread through my arm to my entire body. A sickening sensation curled through my stomach. Something was wrong. How was I both numb and in pain?

Because it wasn't real.

This tower. My opponent. Even the cut in my arm. None of it was real.

The pain wavered then, as if it could hear my thoughts. I pushed into it, like I was pushing out an illness or a virus. In the real world, my arm was fine. I'd wake up and there'd be no cut. This was pretend. This was make-believe. A fairy tale for the masses.

This was meditation on bent knees and knuckles. This was a lesson. To accept the pain, accept the circumstances, and accept myself.

I took a breath, and the pain trickled out with the blood. The cut still slashed through my arm, but it became nothing more than a part of me.

I pushed against Trent with strength that seemed to come from nowhere. He stumbled back several paces, surprise veiling his face. I flipped my sword around, catching it just below the hilt, and tossed it to Rooke. He caught it with a swipe of his hand. I pulled my dagger from my hip and tossed it to the side. It tumbled until it landed around Rooke's feet. I stood tall, unarmed, with renewed energy and self-assurance. I was no longer part of the virtual world. No. Not a part of it.

I owned it. It bowed to me.

I grinned and closed my eyes.

Despite the digital setting, I knew what was happening in the real world. I could picture the crowds screaming. I could hear the announcers going ballistic.

*Open your eyes. What the hell is she doing?*

Behind me, Rooke backed up several steps, though when he stopped, one foot still tapped with excitement.

I stilled inside. Even breaths. No fear. When you fight to the death enough times, the experience dwindles down to mere details. And they'd all be his.

Trent snickered.

The world became nothing but sounds. The pounding of his footsteps. The whoosh of his sword. And the wind whispering in my ear.

The air above me whistled as Trent brought his sword down over my head. I swiveled back, turning side to side, completely avoiding his blows as he sliced through the air again and again.

After dodging several of his downward attacks, he switched tactics and swung the blade sideways, still driving toward me. I ducked and slid under his arm. As he stumbled past, back wide open, I shoved him hard, driving the momentum he'd already created for himself. He ran face-first into the wall.

Behind us, Rooke laughed.

Trent shook his head and looked at me standing in the center of the tower. I smiled and waved. Over here, big guy. The muscles in his neck went tight, and his face turned red.

My smile only widened.

This was just a game, after all. And I was having fun.

Trent grunted, gathered himself, and came at me again.

He thrust his sword at my head. I simply tilted to the side. As the blade slid past my head, I grabbed his wrists, and following his momentum again, slammed him straight into my bent knee. He doubled over, coughing, gripping his stomach.

I took a breath and slowly pushed out the exhale, feeling the air travel through every inch of my body. I was fighting without fighting. Seeing without seeing.

I was one with myself.

When Trent came at me this time, he swung low, anticipating my duck. I dropped down and hooked my knee around his ankle. He fell. His back hit the ground with a heavy thud, and his sword tumbled from his grip. I rolled, snatching the sword for myself, and landed with a knee on his chest. I pressed my weight down. He wheezed as the air rushed out of his lungs.

This was it. In that moment, I never felt more genuine, because I was going home. The simulation would end, I'd wake up, and real life would begin.

I looked down at him as I positioned my sword above his head. His eyes went wide, and he held his hands up, signaling mercy. I smiled.

Sorry, pal.

It's for the show.

I brought my sword down. An inch from his face, he caught it with both hands, skin digging into the blade. Bands of blood slithered down his shaking arms. He strained against me. The blade lifted from his face, pushing the hilt up and toward me. No. I pressed my weight into the sword. We locked. The blade lowered again. More blood slipped out from his hands, speckling his face and chest. He grunted. Sweat dripped off his face in buckets.

The blade rose. And then more. Even with him down and my weight against him, my strength wasn't enough. It never would be. And it didn't have to be.

The wind whispered in my ear.

Let go.

I did.

Not anticipating my sudden release, Trent thrust the sword up until the hilt was parallel with my head. His hands slipped off the blade. I followed the motion through like a pendulum and, with the wind swirling around me, brought the sword back down and slammed it right through his eye.

# CHAPTER 28

Victory.

My entire life had led up to this moment. Not just the past few months of tournament play. Years of training, martial arts lessons, and mastering the virtual world. All of it had coalesced into this life-defining moment.

Twenty. I was twenty years old, and I'd won a national championship. My teammates' futures were set. My future was set.

Shock, joy, and sheer exhilaration swirled together inside in that cool, prickly feeling you get when something amazing happens, as if it were conducted through magic itself. I stood with my teammates, each in front of our respective pods, exchanging glances, afraid to move forward, as if reality would undo what had just happened in the virtual world. They say you'll always remember the moments when your life stood still. This was one of them. I'd remember right now forever.

In the background, the crowd was going ballistic. People cheered, jumped on each other, waved signs and flags. The screens behind us faded into celebrations around the world. Banners depicting Fight-for-Nathan waved in the background as mobs of people paraded through the streets. But it was all background noise, as if we were inside a bubble of peace, and absolute astonishment.

Hannah moved first, pulling me into her arms, followed by

Derek and everyone else, even the programmers, until I was lost in a sea of limbs and bodies. I don't know who shouted first, but soon we were all shouting and screaming and jumping up and down. A mosh pit of hugs and squeals. Derek kissed Rooke's forehead. Hannah and Lily kissed each other. We did it.

We'd won.

Howie and Marcus met us on our side of the stage and led us to the south, where the championship cup sat waiting. As we crossed the stage, InvictUS met us halfway. Trent broke away from his teammates and marched straight up to me. For a second, I thought there would be another fight right here on-stage. Instead, he extended his hand.

"Good game."

My gaze flicked between his face and open palm a few times. Then, I embraced the handshake.

The rest of the team offered their hands to us. We shook and traded compliments and pats on the back. Before he left, Trent leaned toward me and lowered his voice.

"Image is everything," he murmured. "In front of the cameras, we put on a show, but that's not really who we are." He moved even closer. "Off the record, if someone had to beat me, I'm glad it was the warrior."

Then he winked and left with his teammates.

They paraded down the aisle to the exit, the same they'd entered from earlier. They cheered, and high-fived fans, celebrating like they'd won. And really, they had. Runner-up in a championship still meant they'd been picked up as permanent players in the VGL. They were strong gamers and put on a hell of a show. But, for a split second, Trent had shown me the real person under the façade. Though it was difficult to judge such a small moment in time, I had a feeling they were good guys, after all. They deserved this and were going to party as much as they'd earned it.

Howie and Marcus presented us to the crowd.

"There you have it, ladies and gentlemen. Your 2054 RAGE champions. Congratulations, Team Defiance. What a match."

Howie nodded at his counterpart and turned to face the audience. "These guys came from behind at the beginning of the season and fought every inch of the way here. They earned this rematch against InvictUS and proved they deserved to be champions. An amazing team altogether, but an amazing captain as well. Kali Ling, the first female captain to win a championship. You just witnessed history here tonight, folks. It's happening right now."

The crowd applauded and cheered, though the noise had never really died down. Howie and Marcus brought us forward to the stand at the end of the stage, and my teammates motioned for me to take the cup. I placed a hand on either side, and paused. This was another life-defining instant. I took a second to memorize it. The feeling of sheer exhilaration flooded every nerve in my body. The bumps and grooves in the cup from the inscriptions of the names of all the gamers before us. The excitement from the crowd. And lastly, the feel of my teammates' hands on my shoulders. I'd led, and they'd followed me here. They'd follow me anywhere. No matter what happened from here on out, we were more than friends. We were a team, banded together for life. Now, and always.

I raised the cup.

Somehow, the applause and cheers grew even louder until I was drowning in the noise. My teammates surrounded me and gathered me up in their arms. One of those prickly magic waves rushed over me again. Pride swelled within and boiled over until tears spilled down my cheeks. Wrapped in my teammates' arms, I didn't care. The night was full of perfect moments, and I was living every one of them.

Howie and Marcus turned to the cameras. "We're signing off for the night but stay tuned for the press conference with Team Defiance in just a few minutes, and be sure to join us next week for the start of the Dungeon Raids. Good night, everybody."

They waved at the crowd and the cameras, as they zoomed out and panned away.

The stage lights clicked off, and a strong hand gripped my shoulder. Someone plucked the cup from my hands. Security guards pulled us apart and dragged us offstage. Words like "press conference" and "they're waiting" echoed somewhere in the background, like being underwater. The crowd continued their celebration. Their cheers and general jubilation followed us backstage and down the hall.

The doors to the press-conference room opened as the guards led us in. Reporters bombarded us upon entry. Some clapped and cheered. Others pushed their microphones forward and shouted questions out of turn. Cameras snapped and sparkled until the room became nothing but blue fuzz punctuated by white flashes. But it was all a distant jumble, as if the few feet between us and the reporters was really a mile. We were all somewhere else. And somewhere else was wonderful.

Security had to guide us onto the stage as we all walked forward in a daze. At least we managed to sit down by ourselves. The emcee announced himself and scanned through the audience for a question. The first reporter jumped to his feet, asking the obvious.

"How does it feel to be champions?"

We all answered at the same time, which came out as a jumbled mix of synonyms.

"Great."

"Amazing."

"Unbelievable."

The cameras continued to flash, adding to the buzz of the room. The reporters moved in a sea of waves, heads bobbing as they gossiped among each other, grins plastered on all their faces. We weren't the only ones with adrenaline pumping through our veins.

Another reporter stood. "What do you think was the defining factor in your victory?"

My teammates looked down the table to me. The reporters clapped again. One called out my name. I shook my head and pressed my lips against the microphone.

"Everyone contributed. We won because of the team. We trained hard, harder than we had in our whole lives, and gave it our all. Some people never get this kind of opportunity. We didn't want to spit on that."

Spit on that? Well, that almost came out smooth. Thanks, Mom.

"Any words to your opponents, InvictUS?"

Rooke spoke up. "Thanks for making us step up our game. Without them, we wouldn't have gone this far."

How true were those words. We wouldn't have trained and pushed ourselves to go further than we ever thought possible if it hadn't been for our opponents. The fact that we'd kicked their ass was just the cherry on top.

Another reporter shouted a question. "What's the first thing you're going to do tonight?"

Derek waggled his eyebrows at the cameras and unleashed his million-dollar smile.

"Party."

We all laughed. Yes, there would be parties. And probably champagne. At least this time, we'd earned it.

"But before we answer any more questions," Derek continued, "I think we should take a minute to remember our fallen teammate."

The constant buzz of the room cut to silence.

"Nathan was our friend," Derek continued. "We didn't always get along, but he was a good guy, and his skills in the battlefield were incredible. We would like to extend our sympathies to his family. It's long overdue."

Derek bowed his head. We mirrored him.

The room remained silent other than a few soft clicks of the cameras and people shifting in their chairs. The reporters joined us in remembering Nathan. But I knew this wasn't just for him. It was a moment for all those who'd suffered from this sport, off camera and behind the scenes. The forgotten.

When we raised our heads, the audience clapped, a wholehearted sharp applause that conquered the room with its beat. When it finally died down and the room once again descended into an awkward silence, one reporter spoke up.

"Is it true he actually died of an overdose?"

Ah, yes. During the match, I'd forgotten how the VGL's own announcers had joined the rebellion. Bless you, Howie and Marcus. Pick up a sword sometime. We could be the three musketeers.

I leaned forward and spoke clearly and controlled.

"Yes. He overdosed. I was there when he died. I really wish I could have helped him, but there wasn't anything I could do. I'm sorry to his family. He was a good man and a good gamer. He just got caught up in the lifestyle."

With those words, a weight lifted. My stomach rested calmly, not one ripple on an open lake. I no longer blamed myself for not doing more when he died. He was already gone when I woke in the morning, and he was breathing when I fell asleep. How was I to know anything was wrong? The guilt had vanished because I knew we'd done right by him.

"Why was his cause of death listed as heart failure?" someone from the audience called out.

"I think it was just a miscommunication," Hannah answered. "Things get blurred and reversed a lot in print and media. It's like the telephone game. It's no one's fault."

I smiled inwardly. She'd caught on to my hint that I wasn't blaming the industry for what happened. It was an accumulation of events. Team owners, sponsors, hell, even the gamers ourselves were all to blame for the issues in eSports.

Another reporter stood. "Is drug usage really that bad in virtual gaming?"

We exchanged looks with each other. Derek spoke up.

"It's a serious problem in this sport."

"Have any of the rest of you experienced this yourselves?"

"Yes," I said. "I've had my own problems, especially in the beginning of the season. I had enough close calls to admit my life was in danger. I had to crash before I realized I had a problem. But I've been working hard ever since, and I'm stronger now than I ever was before. And not just with a sword."

The crowd laughed.

"What got you through it? How did you recover?"

I smiled. "Through the love of a few good friends."

Beneath the table, Rooke squeezed my hand. I squeezed back. Then he turned to his microphone.

"I did, too," he announced. "I've had problems. So did someone I cared for. And several others."

The emcee stopped calling on people at this point and just let them shout out questions as they liked.

"Why hasn't the industry done something to regulate this?"

Lily found her voice. "I don't think people realized how big of a problem it is. I think now we can count on the VGL to take steps in the right direction."

Yes, now they'd have to. They'd have to address the problems with this sport, and the consequences of spending too many hours inside the virtual world. Drug addiction. Insanity. Death. This was really happening. This was history in the making, and not just because we'd won the tournament.

"Kali," another reporter called out. I lifted my head to a woman standing in the middle of the crowd. "At twenty years old, you've become one of the top fighters in the world and the first female captain to lead your team to a national championship. What's next for you?"

I blinked as I looked out at the sea of reporters and flashing cameras. The doc had asked me the same question that morning, and when I opened my mouth, I surprised even myself at the answer.

"I'm leaving."

A stunned hush fell over the crowd. Gasps came at me from every angle. I felt the eyes of my teammates on me, digging holes into the side of my head. No one knew I was planning to drop that little bombshell. No one. I knew they'd be hurt by it, but for me, another weight had been lifted. It was the right answer. For me.

A flurry of questions followed. I gave them the standard answers, the ones we're taught.

"I don't know yet . . . No comment at this time . . ."

Once we were backstage, my teammates ambushed me. Hannah wrapped me in a tight hug. "Oh, Kali. You're not really leaving us." She pulled back to look at my face. Tears brimmed in her eyes. "You made this team what it is. We can't do this without you."

I shook my head. "I love you guys, but I can't stay here. This isn't me. I'm not going to go along with all the bullshit or sac-rifice who I am to make it in this industry."

"So, you're leaving? Just like that?"

"No, I'm going to show people the right way."

Derek stepped forward. "What are you saying?"

"I'm going to create my own team. A player-owned team. I'm going to change the industry from the inside out."

"You already have a team," Derek said, motioning around him. "We'll go with you."

Lily and Hannah nodded feverishly. I held up a hand. "It'll take some time before I'm ready. I can't ask you to put your careers on hold for that."

Hannah's expression fell. "But—"

"Stay in the tournaments," I emphasized. "Make names for yourselves. When I'm ready, I'll find you."

"We'll be there," Derek said. Hannah and Lily nodded again. Behind them all, Rooke stood with his arms crossed, completely quiet. He was a blank slate. Maybe he was pissed at me, or too shocked to react. But at this point, it didn't matter. I had another stubborn man to deal with first.


Inside his office, Clarence paced over the same line so many times, I thought he'd actually wear a path into that industrial-strength carpet. His blazing red skin and snorting breaths made me think of a bull from an old-fashioned cartoon.

"What the hell was that?" His eyes remained fixed on the floor as he fired the question at me. "You can't just announce that you're leaving."

"Oh, you mean that wasn't cut from broadcast?" I asked, suppressing my grin. I sat in the chair, the same one where I'd been named captain, and watched him pace. "By the way, my contract was only one season."

"Contracts only last for one season in case the player doesn't work out for the owner."

"Well, that goes both ways, doesn't it?"

Clarence stopped dead in his tracks and gaped at me. Then his face returned to the same angered expression it held before. "You don't like me? Fine. That doesn't mean you announce that you're leaving on my time. No one quits these games. Not by choice."

"I seem to be a first for a lot of things."

He scoffed. "Like declaring all that bullshit about drugs in this game?"

"Hey, I wasn't the one to announce it. And it's not bullshit anymore."

"As far as anyone knew, it was."

I narrowed my eyes at him but kept an even and innocent tone to my voice. "You mean you've never had a member of your team lose their mind or dabble in drug usage?"

Clarence shook his head, but if it was from denial or over-flowing rage, I wasn't sure.

"So," I continued, "you're saying you've never falsified drug testing. Are you sure you want me looking into that?" Clarence didn't answer, but he snorted again. I cleared my throat and remained calm. "The world knows about Nathan now, even if you've forgotten him."

Even as the words left my mouth, my brain wouldn't register the impact. The world knew the truth. About Nathan. About gamers. About the virtual world. Finally, things would begin to change. For the better. Not for the owners. Not for the sponsors.

For us. For gamers.

Speaking of the sponsors . . .

"Besides," I continued, "who do you think the sponsors are going to be interested in now? You, or me?"

Clarence sat in his chair as if it would somehow contain his fury. He swiveled a few times, hand over his mouth as he thought to himself. "You won't see a penny of the winnings. I don't have to pay you anything."

"I have a contract that says you do." I stood from the chair. "I expect my share of the winnings or every tabloid in the world will know how you never paid the first female captain in history to win a championship." I leaned toward him across the desk and lowered my voice into a rolling growl that would have made a tiger tremble.

"People will love it."

Clarence's face blanched, and his eyes darted around like cornered pray. His lower lip trembled. Barely, but enough. Then his lips twisted into a scowl, and he stood up from his desk.

"Get the hell out of my facility."

I smiled at him, enjoying how real it felt to smile. Not a condescending smile. Just a genuine, happy smile.

Happy, because I was free.

When I turned to leave his office, I paused at the door and studied the poster of yours truly hanging next to it.

"What are you doing?" Clarence demanded.

I glanced back at him and shrugged.

"Packing."

I pulled the poster off the wall, rolled up the screen in my hands, and walked out.

I walked through the hallways toward my bunk, screen under my arm, with the heavy realization that I was leaving this place just beginning to settle over me. Weeks ago, did I ever think I'd be here? No. I never thought I'd leave. Ever. But now, it felt good.

It felt right.

When I rounded the corner, Rooke stood leaning against my bunk door.

"Are you really leaving?"

"Yes."

I entered the code on my bunk, and Rooke followed me in. He sat on my bed, and I placed the rolled-up poster next to him. He peered down at it with uncertainty but didn't ask.

"When are you going?" he asked.

"Sooner than you'd think," I said, wrestling a pair of metal suitcases out of a compartment. "Clarence just kicked me out."

Rooke stood up off the bed and raised his voice. "He can't do that."

"Yes, he can." I slapped the suitcases down on the bed and flipped them open.

"That's ridiculous."

I agreed but said nothing as I folded up training gear, red-carpet outfits, and everything in between and piled them neatly in the suitcases.

"Where are you going to go?" he asked.

"Home, to visit my parents for a while."

He nodded. "San Diego. Right. Are you leaving right away?"

I motioned at the room. "I can't really stay here."

"We can get a hotel room for the night, and rent you a car tomorrow," he offered. "You can't leave now. We just won a national championship. I think we have some celebrating to do."

I gave him a sly glance. "You mean, with our teammates?"

"Uh, sure, but I'd prefer if they were in another room."

I laughed.

I reached under my bed, retrieved a stack of hardcover books, and held them out to him.

"These are yours."

He glanced down, and pushed them back until they bumped against my stomach.

"Keep them."

My mouth dropped. "But . . . I can't."

He took them from my hands and placed them inside a suitcase. "Yes, you can. I don't know how to say this without sounding weird, but I think you're starting on some sort of path." He nodded down at the books. "Maybe they'll help you along the way." He pushed his hands in his pockets. "So, your own team? What brought that on?"

I thought for a minute and finally gave up. "I don't know. I just decided right then. It felt like the right thing to do. Is that strange?"

He shook his head. "For a lot of people, maybe. But you know who you are now. You know what matters to you and where you want to go in life. So it just came naturally to you."

I considered his words. "A wise man once said, 'When I let go of what I am, I become what I might be.'"

He shook his head. "I don't remember saying that."

We laughed together.

"So," he began, "do you really think you'll do this? Create a team?"

"Yeah. I don't know how yet, but I'll find a way."

I would find a way. Clarence was right about one thing. Gamers never quit. At twenty years old, an entire world of possibilities stood before me. I'd won a national championship. As the first female captain to claim the title, sponsors would be throwing themselves at my feet. Everyone would want me to represent their products. I'd have my choice. Those who'd get me would bow down to my terms, not the other way around. And with their money, along with what I'd won from the championship, I could build my team. Living on our own. Playing whatever games we wanted. Creating our own images, or none at all.

Having fun the entire time.

I already had four other players ready to stand by my side, and I had a vision. Now, I just had to bring them together. Take two halves and make them whole. Luckily, I'd gotten pretty good at doing exactly that.

I finished packing and shut the last suitcase. Together, we lugged my belongings down the hall, toward the door we'd snuck pizzas through.

"I'm just going to visit my folks for a little while," I told him. "I'll be back in L.A. in a few weeks to find a place to live. You aren't getting rid of me that easily."

I playfully nudged his shoulder, and he grinned.

"I'll call," he offered.

"You better."

His grin grew wider. Then, it faltered as he grew serious. He set my suitcases down and turned to me. "With everything and anything you're planning, you know I'll be there, right?"

"I know."

"And . . . I'm kinda proud of you."

"I know that, too."

He took me into his arms and pulled me tight against him. I didn't protest. I melted into him. I closed my eyes and focused on the sensations. His strong arms enveloping me. The perfect way I fit into the crook of his chest. He pulled back and brushed his lips against mine once, then twice. Three times. Like hell, I'm a lady.

He picked up my suitcases, shoved the door open with his

shoulder, and held it for me with his foot. I started to move forward, and paused.

"What's wrong?" he asked.

This wasn't just about creating my own team, or figuring out my path in life. This was about something more.

I could change everything.

They say you have to know the problems, really live them, to understand how to fix them. Good thing I'm so stubborn, because there was a lot in need of repair. Gamers deserved the same rights as any athlete. Respect. Freedom.

Safety.

From the industry, the owners, and themselves. It was time to prove we'd earned it. And if no one else was going to fight for it, I would. I'd fight until the world knew our story. Not one of the glitz and glam of the red carpet. Not one of magazine covers, television interviews, and all-night parties. No. They would know one of hard work and perseverance. Of unfair treatment, sponsorship abandonment, and life inside the games. One day, everyone would know the truth, and apparently, I was the one to speak the word.

My voice would be heard, even if I had to scream louder than anyone else. I'd brought my opponents to their knees in the arena. I was sure I could do the same in any office, boardroom, or conference center, and I wouldn't even have to wait until Saturday night to do it. The thought itself made me smile. I'd done a heck of a lot of smiling lately. Maybe that was my new standard programming.

It would take time to accomplish everything. Years, probably. I glanced down at the break between the facility's exit and the concrete sidewalk. If a journey of a thousand miles begins with a single step, this was mine.

I smiled at Rooke.

"Nothing's wrong. Absolutely nothing."

I stepped forward, crossed the line, and walked outside, into the real.

**THE END**

PERCENTAGE OF GAME COMPLETED: 100%
THANK YOU FOR PLAYING

# ACKNOWLEDGMENTS

First, thanks to Leon Husock for believing in the book, and to Anne Sowards for making the story stronger than I ever thought it could be.

Thanks to my family for your love and support over all these years, especially my mom for teaching me the importance of books, and my dad for teaching me the importance of *Star Trek*.

Thanks to Jessica Parker, Jessica Farwell, Melinda Moore, and Shari Klase for cheering me on and putting up with messages, blog posts, and e-mails that consisted almost entirely of updates about my writing.

Big thanks to Joe Walker and Jason Rush for reviewing and critiquing this novel in its early stages. You're braver souls than most.

Thanks to Michelle Hauck, Michael Anthony, S.C., and the Query Kombat team for all you do in helping writers achieve their dreams. This is in print because of you.

Lastly, thanks to Chris Sedlacek for always knowing I'd be a writer, even when I didn't.

Only the top gamers in the world were invited to the most exclusive spot in all of L.A., and no one knew what was inside.

Not even me.

"The heat coming off the Wall is huge," one reporter crooned, emphasizing the last word until he sounded like a mooing cow. Huuuuuge.

With a name like the Wall, you'd think everyone was talking about a nightclub. But no. It wasn't a boutique or a restaurant, either. Sure, any of those would have made perfect sense. Throughout history, those were the kinds of elite establishments marked INVITATION ONLY for the Hollywood glitterati. It was expected.

A tradition, if you will.

But the year was 2055. Virtual reality had permeated every aspect of society, and pro gamers were the top celebrities in the world. So, let's just say tradition had taken a long-needed vacation and was a little too drunk on coconut margaritas to give a shit about what was to be expected.

I cranked up the volume on the celebrity-gossip channel,

where a drone-camera feed hovered over a single house located in the Pacific Palisades district of Westside Los Angeles. Okay, to call it a house would be an understatement. A compound. Or maybe an estate. Fifty thousand square feet of guarded walls, high-tech security, and absolute mystery. Any gamer who got invited through the armed guards and steely gates never talked about what happened inside. So, after weeks of endless speculation, I'd pulled in a professional on the matter.

"*This* is why you called me in here?"

Dr. Renner sat in a guest chair across from my desk, though it had been turned to face the oversized screen in the far wall. She glanced back at me with a curled lip.

"You're a psychologist—" I began.

"A psychiatrist," she emphasized.

Potato. Po-tat-toe.

"Whatever. You can read between the lines. What do you think is inside?" I nodded at the screen, where the paparazzi camped outside the house in droves, hoping to catch a glimpse of the latest gamer let through the magic gates. Drones hovered above, snapping as many pictures as people did. The Wall had so many of those UAVs buzzing around, it must have looked like a beehive from space.

"Kali, I specialize in virtual psychiatry. I study the effect of virtual stimuli on a person's mind and body. How am I supposed to figure out what's inside some random house?"

I already knew what she specialized in. A few months ago, I was on a pro gaming team under different management, and Dr. Renner was the mental health expert on staff. Since then, I'd bought out the team, and Dr. Renner followed. She believed in me and my dream to erase the corruption in pro gaming. But currently, my concern over problems in eSports had taken a backseat to figuring out what was going on in that damn house.

"Why is everyone calling it the Wall?" she asked. With a high ponytail, buxom lips, and chunky glasses resting on a perfectly straight nose, Dr. Renner looked like someone who paid their way through med school by modeling and then ten years into their career, forgot how beautiful they were.

"It's short for the Invisible Wall," I said.

She glanced at me and blinked. Twice. "I'm afraid I'll need a little more than that."

I sighed. "It's a retro video game term. When you reach the edge of a map in a game, you run smack into an invisible wall. It's a way of keeping the player inside a set area."

"But why bother? Can't a player tell where the end of the map is? Isn't the landscaping just grayed out or something?"

"No. Usually the landscape continues on. It's seamless. The area beyond the wall looks like it's accessible, but it's not."

A wave of understanding washed over her face. "So, everyone's calling that house the Invisible Wall because—"

"You can see it but can't access it. It's off the map. Unless you're invited in." I opened the television remote app on my tablet. "Here, watch this." I brought up an old video of a pro gaming team entering the house. It didn't matter which one I chose. The rundown was always the same.

It starts at the airport.

The television screen went black for a second as the video loaded up. LAX appeared on the screen with the video's title superimposed over the image.

ANOTHER GAMING TEAM VISITS THE WALL.

Paparazzi and fans were camped out around the airport's pickup/drop-off zone. More were inside, and a few had even bought tickets to the cheapest flights to get past security. From baggage claim to the getaway vehicle was one long line of cameras, flailing arms, and screaming admirers.

The team exited the terminal, and the crowds erupted in cheers. They wore hoods, pulled low over their faces, so no one knew who they were. It didn't stop anyone from losing their mind. Airport security and private guards cleared a path for them through the airport as they clung to their sunglasses and filed into an SUV with tinted windows.

Sunglasses. Tinted windows. As if pro gamers could conceal their identities nowadays. But they tried. Some of them even succeeded.

The video cut and the same vehicle from the airport (verified by license plate) appeared at the house. More fans and paparazzi assaulted the car, pounding on the windows. The gates opened and the SUV slid through. Armed security at the gates kept the riffraff out. Once the SUV rounded the driveway and stopped near the door, the team piled out, hoods still pulled low over their eyes until they disappeared inside.

Dr. Renner crossed her arms and leaned forward in the chair. Her brow furrowed. "Why are they hiding their faces?"

Even she sounded interested now.

"Exactly."

Dr. Renner pressed her lips together and adjusted her glasses. "How do we even know these are gaming teams?"

"A few have been revealed. Either a fan pulled their hood off or the paparazzi got close enough to snap a picture of their faces."

Dr. Renner considered it and sighed.

"What do *you* think is inside?"

Ah, flipping the question around on me. Psychology 101. Oh, excuse me. Psychiatry 101.

"Drugs," I said. "That's why no one's talking about it, and

why everyone is hiding their identity. I think they've cooked up something more addictive than HP."

HP was the ecstasy of the gamer world. It makes you feel invincible, just like a game. And just like a game, you'll hit it. Again, and again, and again.

"Kali," she began. "If you had relapsed, you'd tell me, right?"

"I'd whiz into a cup for you and put a bow on it."

Her lip curled again. "Please don't relapse. And not just for your own sake." She eyed my mug. "How many cups of coffee did you drink today?"

"This, plus one."

In a Big Gulp.

"Really?" She raised an eyebrow. "You seem a little jittery."

Raise the threat level to Defcon Four. She's onto me.

"Look," I said, holding up my tablet to distract her, secretly hoping my hands weren't shaking as badly as I thought they were. "It's in all the tabloids. Read through them. I'm sure you can wade through the bullshit."

Dr. Renner took the tablet in her hands, flipped through it a few times, and peered over the edge at me.

"You hate these magazines."

I only hated them when they screwed around with my love life—when I had one. Funny how actors, rock stars, and heiresses used to compile the fodder that fed the tabloid cows. Now they came second, behind gamers. Since the mystery of the Wall, nearly every article centered on the virtual elite.

And yes, I used to sneer at these magazines. Now I had a subscription to every one of them. The mighty fall sometimes, okay?

Dr. Renner eyed me again.

"Kali," she began. "I know this must be fascinating to you,

but I'm not completely comfortable encouraging you to indulge in this compulsion—"

"Interest," I emphasized. "It's a healthy interest."

"I'm not so sure."

"Oh, come on." I pointed at the television screen. "If there was something this interesting going on in the world of psychology—"

"Psychiatry."

"—wouldn't you be intrigued?"

Something interesting in the world of psychiatry. Pffft.

She considered it, shrugged, and flipped through the magazines on my tablet a few more times.

"Any idea who owns this place?"

"Tamachi Industries. A Japanese company that specializes in artificial intelligence."

"So, it's about technology."

"No."

"Why not?"

"What does artificial intelligence have to do with pro gaming?"

"There are chilling towers." She pointed to a picture of the house, holding up the tablet for me to see. "Are you sure it's not tech related?"

"Nah." I dismissed the suggestion with a wave of my hand. "That's just to throw people off."

"Why are you so sure it's a drug house?"

"Everyone knows it's something I stand against."

She studied my expression for a minute with narrowed eyes and slightly pursed lips. I hated when she looked at me like that. It felt like she was reading my mind.

"Oh," she began with a smile. "That's what this is about.

You don't care what's in the house. You just want to know why you haven't been invited."

Well, her psychic powers hadn't failed her. Actually, I did care about what was in the house. If it was drugs, I wasn't interested. Not anymore. But I did have a bit of a reputation in the gaming world. I was Kali Ling, the warrior. Holder of three Virtual Gaming League records, and the undisputed queen of the RAGE tournaments, the VGL's most brutal fighting game. Didn't that at least merit an invitation? You know, delivered on a platter. Maybe silver.

"Can you give me any other clues?" Dr. Renner asked, eyeing the television screen, which had gone dark at the end of the airport video.

Hook, line, and sinker. From doctor to detective in less than five minutes.

I flipped the television back to the celebrity-gossip channel. "They're always debating it on *Hypnotized*."

*Hypnotized* was the biggest gamer-celebrity news channel in the country. Lately, debates over the Wall took up nearly all of their programming. When the channel popped up, a group of reporter-journalists sat on a couch, talking about . . . guess what?

"Okay, let's talk about who hasn't been seen at the house."

"What about Kali Ling?"

Well, look at that.

The volume went up.

"I mean, she won a championship last season, and was the first female captain in the VGL. You'd think she'd be at the Wall."

See? Invitation.

"You're out of your mind. What's she done since then? Nothing."

Nothing?

"Hey, three words. Youngest team owner in history."

"That's five words."

The cell phone wrapped around my wrist buzzed. I tore my gaze away from the television screen long enough to glance at the caller identification. Speaking of my love life . . .

JAMES ROOKE

My heart clenched, and I forced my eyes to read the name several times. No, that couldn't be right. He hadn't talked to me in weeks. So, what was with the sudden phone call?

**Holly Jennings** is a lifelong gamer who has spent innumerable hours playing *World of Warcraft* and *Call of Duty*. *Arena* is her first novel. She lives in Canada, where she is working on the sequel. Visit her online at authorhollyjennings.com, twitter.com/HollyN_Jennings, and facebook.com/authorhollyjennings.